"Want a scathing social and political satire? Look no further than Norman Kelley's second effort featuring 'bad girl' African-American PI and part-time intellectual **NINA HALLIGAN**—it's X-rated, but a romp of a read . . . Nina's acid takes on recognizable public figures and institutions both amuse and offend . . . Kelley spares no one, blacks and whites alike, and this provocative novel is sure to attract attention . . ."

—*PUBLISHERS WEEKLY,* starred review of *The Big Mango,* the second installment in the Nina Halligan mystery series

ALSO BY NORMAN KELLEY

Black Heat (A Nina Halligan Mystery)
The Big Mango (A Nina Halligan Mystery)
R&B (Rhythm and Business): The Political Economy of Black Music (editor)

A PHAT DEATH

(OR, THE LAST DAYS OF NOIR SOUL)

AKASHIC BOOKS
New York

This is a work of fiction. All names, characters, places, and incidents are the product of the author's imagination. Any resemblance to real events or persons, living or dead, is entirely coincidental.

Published by Akashic Books

First printing

Design by Sohrab Habibion
ISBN: 1-888451-48-3
Library of Congress Control Number: 2003106945

Printed in Canada

Akashic Books
PO Box 1456
New York, NY 10009
Akashic7@aol.com
www.akashicbooks.com

IN MEMORIAM

Andrew Marc Dellon
September 3, 1955–June 4, 2001

Son, husband, father, friend, musician,
music lover, and the last of a vanishing breed:
an all-around nice guy and decent human being.

PLAYLIST

TRACK 01 STANDING ON THE VERGE OF GETTING IT ON [NASTY VERSION] (00:09)
TRACK 02 THE NOISE (00:21)
TRACK 03 THE NEW WORLD PLANTATION (00:31)
TRACK 04 TO BE REAL (00:43)
TRACK 05 SIESTA SEX (00:49)
TRACK 06 MAGGOT OVERLORD OF INFONEW$ (00:57)
TRACK 07 MEETING THE COMPETITION (00:65)
TRACK 08 BABY CAKES (00:74)
TRACK 09 A SMART GAL (00:83)
TRACK 10 CODE Z (00:86)
TRACK 11 SIESTA SEX II (00:93)
TRACK 12 BABY CAKES'S GREATEST HIT (00:99)
TRACK 13 THE LESSER OF TWO EVILS (01:07)
TRACK 14 NIGGACOOL™, OR THE END OF BLACK CIVILIZATION (01:15)
TRACK 15 WINSTON CHAO (01:28)
TRACK 16 A SNARKY AFFAIR (01:36)
TRACK 17 THE MERCHANT OF DESIRE (01:42)
TRACK 18 WHAT'S THE BUZZ? (01:50)
TRACK 19 A GRRRL PARTY (01:60)
TRACK 20 IL DUCE (01:68)
TRACK 21 THE TEN PERCENT SOLUTION (01:74)
TRACK 22 SOLID CITIZEN BUT WANTED BY THE HAGUE (01:84)
TRACK 23 TELL ME SOMETHING GOOD (01:92)
TRACK 24 A WALK BY THE RIVER (02:00)
TRACK 25 LOVECHILD (02:07)
TRACK 26 RADEEM [DYIN' FOR DA RIDDIM] (02:13)
TRACK 27 THE LAST DAYS OF NOIR SOUL [NINA'S THEME] (02:18)

“Everyone needs at least three things in life:
something to do, someone to love, and
something to look forward to.”

—Attributed to Cantinflas,
Mexican actor and comedian

TRACK 01

STANDING ON THE VERGE OF GETTING IT ON [NASTY VERSION]

When he slowly pulled down the zipper of my dress I knew I was ready for the okey-doke. I could feel his warm breath on the back of my neck; it was in sync with my breathing and that meant we were about to enjoy the rhythm of the one. Or, as the vulgarians would say, the Big Nasty.

He peeled away the shoulder straps of the garment and it slid down to my waist. Delectably, I was being peeled like a grape. Moments before I had asked him what he wanted to hear, some Sassy or Betty Compton? I was looking through his music collection, my back turned to him, and when I said "*Hmmm?*" he slowly rose from the couch and stood behind me in his CD-infused and record-laden lair. The man had more records than Imelda Marcos had shoes—boxes and cartons of them.

I could smell his natural odor mixed with cologne; it was a volatile scent that made me, uh, moist. Some men have a way of doing that to me. I call them "moist specialists."

Slowly and lovingly, he turned me around and I gazed into his beautiful gray eyes. The man was gorgeous: dark-skinned; a very pleasant smile surrounded by a rich black, neatly trimmed beard. He had a full head of glorious dreadlocks that gave him a sort of mischievous, leonine countenance. He was dressed in a wheat-colored linen suit, confirming my universal opinion that there was nothing finer—Nothing!—than a good-looking nigga in a light-colored or white suit. Olódùmarè's choice selection. In his right earlobe he wore a gold stud.

Uh-huh. Dat t'ing. Dat t'iiiing.

When my cousin Maxine introduced us he took my hand and kissed it. My reputation had preceded me, and he knew how to work his magic. Now, he was slowly unfastening the front of my brassiere. My girls tumbled out as he slipped the bra straps from my shoulders. I moved away from the wall unit that housed the stereo component and let the bra and the dress slide to the wooden floor. At that moment I had on nothing but my thong, my last line of defense before surrender. I was willing to let him take command.

Willingly, without a hint of hesitation, he began around my neck with kisses and just as I thought he was moving down to my shoulders and the girls, his tongue glided back up and into my ear. Then the okey-doke went into full force. Zamzow!

He inserted a leg between my thighs and he was holding on to my waist as his lips began their slow descent to my breasts. He licked one then the other and took a nipple into his mouth. Things were beginning to heat up in my southern valley as he continued sucking and licking. I worked a hand over to his crotch and felt his malethang throbbing through his linen trousers. He was a hungry fellow. I also knew how to work a zipper. It's one of those basic skills your parents teach you, though not necessarily intended for the present situation.

My red-tipped fingernails went into his trousers and grasped his lion of Judah. The brother moaned and now it was questionable as to who was in control of the negotiations. I could tell that he liked the hand job, for his hand went over to my arms and began stroking and kneading my muscles. Our gazes locked in a fit of passion.

Boing.

"Nina—" he breathed. I was about to make him pop, but he did something with his abdomen and checked his flow. Ever the gentleman, a rare thing with men these days, black or white, he gently lifted my hand from his erogenous center and began kissing my fingers. Soon I found his other fingers working the cloth that covered my hot spot and I was becoming more than hot and bothered. I was beginning to tingle. I did the James Brown thing—I broke out in a cold sweat—and inquired about a condom.

"Unnnhh," I breathed, and wrapped my arms around his neck as he began furiously working his hands through the mound and between my legs. I was holding onto him as if he were the Father, the Son, and the Holy Ghost. At some point it all became a blur of sensations. I was clutching onto him, lasciviously bucking my hips, my tush rocking back and forth, biting his ear and telling him that he could do all sorts of things to other parts of my body, my soul, my heart, and my mind. That got him humming as I hoped it would. After all, this was about sex, and it's a mutual endeavor in my scheme of things.

The man lifted me up by my waist and guided me onto the lion. I came down on his upstroke. To keep his balance he widened his stance and I deliriously rode him, biting his lips and pulling on his beard with my teeth. It was all too much. He held onto my waist, my legs locked around his. I let go of him and slowly arched myself downward, bending over backward, my braids sweeping the floor. I was viewing his living room from upside down as he was tearing into me with such majestic force.

Oh, yeeaaahh . . . Uh-huh . . .

I must've peaked about three times in less than a minute. I was confused, lost but also sure of one thing: I wanted more. Give it to me. The man wasn't going to let me leave that night, and I was sure of that when he came inside me. Sex, like the law, is nine-tenths possession. After my pleasure trip I rose into a normal position, my legs still wrapped around his waist, my valley's muscle clenching him into place. I would have continued showering his face with kisses, feverishly licking it, but he gently lifted me onto his shoulder and carried me over to his bed in his musically cramped quarters. Talk about door-to-door service.

As he pulled off his clothes—now he was "nigga buffed," gorgeously cut and muscularly accented—I pulled the phone's cord from the socket and then guided him down onto the bed. I immediately wanted him between my lips, and knowing where his malethang had been only excited me more.

"And then what happened?" asked Zee. She pulled the towel up around her breasts as the sweat poured down her neck and onto her shoulders, her black skin glistening.

"What do you mean, 'What happened?'" asked Anna, leaning back into Esperanza, who had her hair tied up in a bun to keep it out of her face. "Zee, does she have to spell out the whole thing?"

"It's graphic enough." Esperanza smiled. She held onto Anna.

"She knows," said Magdalena, who had entered the sauna with another tray of glasses filled with champagne. Magdalena placed the tray down and stuck her finger in her mouth and pulled at her cheek, making a loud popping sound. "Nina popped him! Right, doña?" Her towel almost slid off.

I only winked as she handed me another glass of champagne. I held up my finger and looked at the wedding band.

We—Zee, Magdalena, Anna, Esperanza, and myself—were having a Bad Girls International celebration of my marriage to Glen Sierra in the sauna of the hotel where Magdalena VillaRosa, the ambassador of the Republic of Dechoukaj, formerly Misericordia, stayed. It was a shower of sorts.

These were the women I had bonded with over the past few years. They have become my best friends and my sisters, my family, and they wanted to have a big to-do about my marriage to Glen. We, Glen and I, didn't have a real marriage ceremony, the church stuff. After seeing each other for two months we were married at the city's municipal hall by my godfather, Judge Phillip March.

Things happened so quickly. I met Glen at a party that was given by Groove World Music and the CEO of the firm, my cousin Maxine Devereaux. Max invited me to the party because I was responsible for introducing her to Veronica Thorn Martin, who had taken over Paul Tower's Black Christian Network (BCN) after he had been exposed and deposed by yours truly.

Veronica had come a long way in the last few years since she assumed the reins of BCN and the Malik Martin Foundation. At first she didn't know what to do with BCN, but then she caught the downsize fever of corporate America and decided on a whole lotta headrollin'. Boom! She fired the entire executive staff and then sold BCN's television and radio stations to another concern, Groove City Records, the only black independent record company standing, meaning it distributed its own records. That turned "the Groove," as it was called by the public, into Groove World Music (GWM), a competitive world-class media organization that was going to compete with the big five record firms that controlled the world's manufacturing, marketing, and distribution of music recording, a.k.a., the "Five Fingers of Music." And the Devereaux, owners of GWM (relatives on my mother's side), never forgot who allowed them to make the leap—Veronica Thorn Martin and me. She was asked to serve on the board of the new and improved Groove.

I'd handled the legal work for the foundation and Leon Devereaux, the chairman of the board and former ambassador to Nigeria, also my uncle, was grateful for an opportunity that would make the Groove the leading black multimedia company. With Maxine at the helm and a set of ambitious ideas in her head and underneath her arms, she had announced that the Groove was back and it was going to be in Harlem. She and her father were determined to return Harlem to its glory days. They had constructed a postmodern "Afrotextured" building to house the GWM office and the Devereaux Museum of African-American Music. That was Uncle Leon's pet project. Anyway, I was invited to the gala celebration along with many others, one of whom was this delicious-looking man.

I had known of Glen Sierra from my uncle Phil, whom I sometimes refer to as Teo. Teo was part of the troika of civil rights and labor activists that included my father and my late husband's adopted father, the great West Indian activist and theoretician Raymond Belmont. Teo regularly played bass downtown in a jazz band and Glen, a saxophonist, sat in. But there was another Glen Sierra that I had also heard about on the music grapevine: the troublemaker. Glen was a maverick in the music business: he hated the record companies' exploitation of musicians and black music; he detested how some musicians were trying to create a jazz canon, trying to block off musicians in so-called genres, trying to stop hip-hoppers from experimenting with jazz and jazz musicians from experimenting with hip-hop. He didn't like how hip-hop had degenerated into a morass of gangsta-ism and how everyone was just concerned about "getting paid," but praising God on every demented record about "bitches and ho's." No one was laying down a foundation for decolonizing black music. Except maybe the Groove.

The man had a brain and could do the do as well: a heady attraction for any intelligent woman. His views more or less put him into conflict and opposition with the music powers-that-be: the clubs, record companies, jazz purists, some hip-hoppers, and the jazzerati, headed by music critic Clemon Grouse and the overrated trumpeter Hugo Baron. But Glen was as ambitious as Maxine; he could write. So he started an underground music magazine that floundered but got him noticed by some of the more established magazines because he had a good critical eye. He had carved out a niche for himself, garnering a reputation for being an aggressive investigative journalist in black culture and politics, particularly in the realm of how the music business operated.

He uncovered the dirty deals and examined how even some black record executives at both black- and white-owned firms were complicit in exploiting African-American artists. Glen named names and that got him, uh, *white*listed.

So he was independent—a trait I admire in any man or woman—and had established his own record label, KS&P StudioWorks, and that was now being considered for a deal by GWM. He was still writing articles about how black culture had become a cash cow for predatory marketers and how certain blacks were doing nothing for those being colonized by the five fingers that effectively controlled music. At the gala we had gotten into a conversation about an article of his on how the music industry got Congress to pass legislation prohibiting musicians from using the bankruptcy laws to get out of onerous record contracts—citing TLC and Toni Braxton. Of course, Congress wasn't going to scrutinize how the record industry had been ripping off black artists. After all, blacks are "special interest" and don't deserve special treatment.

"Nobody wanted to publish it," he said as we stood in a cozy corner, with drinks in our hands. Colorfully dressed people of color—red, black, green, and gold—were swirling before us as the various bands on the Groove's labels mounted the stage and did minisets.

"Why not?"

"I named names." He smiled, a twinkle in his gray eyes. "Did you know there's a suit going on that's accusing the big five and others of racketeering?"

I arched an eyebrow. "Under the RICO statutes?" I asked as my body moved closer to his.

"Yes." He then looked at me more closely. "You know about RICO?"

I nodded and rattled off an explanation of the racketeering and corruption act that the feds used to bust the Mafia and that civilians could use against individuals and organizations if they could prove a pattern of criminal activity. I had used it in Brooklyn against some drug gangs and upscale white-collar criminals.

"Are you a lawyer?"

"I have been known to practice the profession," I confessed.

"Anyway, I had to get the article published in a socialist magazine, because my usual venues were afraid of losing advertising support," he said somewhat bitterly. "Even the newspapers and magazines are being eaten up by large corporations."

As a joke I said, "Then you must have tried some of our courageous and cutting-edge black magazines such as *Black Finance* and *Converge*."

He chortled. We both agreed that black publications primarily *weren't* telling any thinking person what he or she didn't already know. They were so pro-black that they weren't really critical or investigatory about anything of substance. Most of them were so chock-full of killer liquor and tobacco ads that they were compromised beyond redemption.

Glen sighed and looked around. "This is the last chance."

"For what?" I inquired.

"If the Groove doesn't get up and battle the big boys, it doesn't look too good for black music," he said, peering around the huge and spacious atrium of the museum where the gala was being held. "If black folks can't control our music, which comes from our own labor, then we will never get it together."

I knew I liked him at that very moment. His statement reminded me of my late husband's view of the convergence of politics, economics, and culture. This guy was *thinking* and that is something that, in my opinion, black folks just don't put much stock in. Nowadays it's all about getting paid. You say anything that's critical and you're accused of "tearing things down." It was the exact reason that Lee, my late husband, was so unpopular when he was alive. Now that he's gone people can't stop buying his books. It must be the smell of blood.

"Ever read an article called 'Rhythm Is Our Business' by Dr. Lee Halligan?"

"Sister, that's my bible." He smiled through his dark beard. "There are some of us who form an informal Lee Halligan school. Have you?"

"I was married to the brain who wrote it." I had pleasantly set my sights for the evening. "Care to dance?"

"Wow," he said. As he led the way he asked, "Are you still . . . ?"

"Married? No. Widowed." I smiled faintly. We assumed the position and grooved to Sade's "No Ordinary Love."

The girls laughed.

"What's so funny?" I asked.

"That's just like you," said Anna, leaning over and kissing me on the cheek. "You like those intellectual types, especially reporters."

"Rugged intellectuals," said Zee. "The last of the independent operators."

"Look, a good mental fuck is a vital precoital stimulus," I offered. "At least for me."

That got a lot of cackles and hoots from the bitches in attendance.

"No, Nina is right," said Esperanza, the voodoo *madrina* of Misericordia. "Let's face it. We all want either a good marriage or a relationship with love, affection, and some good sex. *No es verdad*?"

Sí. We all nodded our heads in agreement.

"And if you don't have any other sort of stimulation after the act in regard to a partner and/or mate, it won't last long," she continued. She then raised her glass. "To Doña Nina and her new husband!"

"To Doña Nina and her new husband!" repeated the rest, and we sipped from our glasses.

"So how old is this guy?" asked Anna.

I smiled. "He's not even thirty."

"Cradle robber!"

"Go, girl! Get 'em while they are young and hot and don't want to stop!" said Zee.

We all turned and looked at her. "That was something I heard from the streets—years ago," she demurely explained.

Uh-huh . . . Too much bubbly for her.

"I thought he was our age, Anna," I answered, looking at Zee out of the corner of my eye, "but it's the beard. It makes him look older and he is very mature for his age."

La Bomba—Magdalena—balled her fist and stretched out her arm. "And he knows how to, uh, go for . . . the . . . what did you call it . . . the okey-doke?"

"It's just a nonsensical word." I shrugged. "I really needed him in my life. After Luc I was a disaster."

Since the loss of my family, I've felt that killing the man who had ordered their deaths would bring me some sense of closure, but all it did was bring me more death. While looking for Nate Ford down in Misericordia I'd lost my former lover, Luc Malmundo, and had discovered my feelings of guilt about being disloyal to my husband, Lee—a man whom I did truly love but not in the same way I'd loved Luc, who was lurking in the back room of my mind.

Traditionally, when one marries one forswears those sorts of feelings for another. Although I seldom acted on them, they were in a secret compartment of my heart. I had to confront the unpleasant truth that my rage at Nate Ford, although legitimate in one sense, was a cover-up for the fact that I was still in love with another man, even while loving the man I was married to, the father of my children. Both men, Luc and Lee, were now dead.

What made things even worse was that Anna had decided to remain in Misericordia after Luc's death. She had fallen in love with Esperanza Pomona, the innkeeper whose establishment we had stayed at in Misericordia. They were just beginning a hot romance when Nate Ford kidnapped them. Esperanza was my closure, for she killed the man who sanctioned my family's death before I could get my hot hands around his throat.

Despite that harrowing adventure, Anna was a lucky woman. She had found her true love, Esperanza, and didn't want to leave Misericordia. I couldn't believe it when she told me. But she had found the woman she loved. I mean, she had found what most of us wanted, as Esperanza had said: a strong marriage (or relationship) based on love and affection, with good sex. Talk about the gods showering you with good fortune. Especially when I learned that Esperanza was a hermaphrodite, a natural she-male, so to speak.

"Look, Nina, this is the best of both worlds," Anna said when she told me of her decision to stay. "I got a beautiful woman with a dick and no male attitude. She ain't gonna fuck me and run. And I can indulge my illicit desire for some dick without feeling like I'm being a politically incorrect dyke. In reality, I'm probably more bisexual than monosexual, gay or straight. Double fun!"

Well, girlfriend had worked out the angles that were important to her.

In some ways she was torn between remaining there and coming back to the States with me, but she had found the woman she loved—and then some. I still couldn't believe that Esperanza was a hermaphrodite. But even that crazy bitch, Magdalena, confirmed it and I didn't even have to ask how she knew. She had a ferocious sexual appetite and was a known shlong specialist as well as an expert muff diver. La Bomba just smiled, licked her lips, and spread her two index fingers to indicate how large Esperanza's unique appendage was.

"To suck a *madrina's* cock would be an honor for a true Maerican," Magdalena had said back then. "Especially Doña Esperanza's. That would be drinking the nectar of the gods!"

I had flown back to the United States in bad shape. It took me almost a year to recover from Luc's death. I began wearing black again, as I had when Lee and the children were killed. But it wasn't until I quit my law practice and began slowing down my investigation work that I realized I was tired of being alone and unhappy: I wanted to connect with someone, but I knew I couldn't until my private war over Lee and the children had ended. *Finito*. Burying Luc Malmundo was the final straw. I was getting out of the business. My closest friends, Anna and Zee, had gotten married or had found someone special. I was the last woman standing, and it isn't any fun when you are standing alone in the cold wind and the rain.

Then Mister Magic came into my life. I started hearing the music again and started feeling the funk. It felt good to cuddle up in a man's arms and sense that he would protect me from my worst demons. I wasn't afraid to say I needed him. I was tired of being a so-called strong black woman. I wasn't looking for a strong black man but found a guy who liked and cared about me, and wanted to share the same space with me. He liked holding my hands and kissing me on my forehead. He made me feel like a young girl again. And he definitely made me feel like a woman. He made me want to run and talk about it all over town. His concern about black music reminded me of Lee's work on the subject.

Then he pulled a fast one on me. Marriage. He proposed to me over dinner one evening. Glen told me that he couldn't start the day without speaking to me over the phone and he needed to end it with his arms wrapped around me.

"I want to marry you," he said passionately. "Tell me I'm the only one in your life that's special."

I was seven years his senior and I knew I wasn't going to get anyone better than Glen. We were both what the other person wanted. Crazy. Sexy. Cool.

"Yes," I said without the slightest hesitation.

"Oh, God," he said, relieved. "I was sweating big bullets." His hands went through his dreadlocks. "I thought you'd say no."

"I'm yours, Mr. Sierra," I replied loudly. "You own me, gorgeous!"

"Nina," he said, looking around at the other diners who surrounded us. "Chilleth, my dear."

I was getting loud and didn't care. It was a time for a shout-out. Crank up a joyous noise. People were looking around in the Soho bistro, but I was hot and bothered—and getting married. I got up from the table and walked over to him, pointing my magic finger.

"I'm going to make you the happiest man on the planet." I plopped myself onto his lap and began kissing him. I scorched him. "You still want to marry this crazy woman? I burn for you, Glen. I really do, darling."

"You could have fooled me." He laughed embarrassingly. That's what he liked about me, my unpredictability. He was a nice combination of funky and formal. Glen was raised right: He knew how to act in public and around different people, depending on the circumstances and the contexts of reality. He looked at me with both awe and appreciation for my feminine mystique.

I stood up and let the world know: "This man wants me to be his WIFE!"

"Nina, don't invite the whole place! We can't afford it!"

The rest of the diners whistled and clapped. The waitrons congratulated us, pouring more wine into our glasses.

"And the mother of my children!" Glen added, getting into the act also.

"*Chico*, you didn't say anything about that," I feigned.

"*What*? I thought that came with the traditional package."

"Well, *mi chico*, we'll have to negotiate that, won't we?" I stated as I returned to my seat.

He thought for a moment. "I know a very secluded alley," he offered.

I raised my eyebrows. "You dog. You know I'll bite."

He asked for the check and moments later we were gone.

"In the alley?" asked Zee. "You couldn't wait to get home?"

"It was the call of nature, Zee. The man drives me mad. He's a good rockin' daddy, as they used to say in the old days," I replied. "Besides, it was a nice summer night . . ."

"Zee, you have to understand something about Nina," said Anna.

"What's that?"

"She has always had a powerful soft drive," Anna reported. "That's what got her exiled to a parochial boarding school. Am I right, Nina?"

I sighed and raised my arms over my head, the towel slipping down and exposing my nipple-hardened breasts. "Yeah . . . I was much more physically mature than most of the girls my age and I had developed a keen interest in sex—via Daddy's *Playboy* magazines."

"Ah!" exclaimed La Bomba. "Then you knew about the okey-doke."

"You got it, girl," I laughed. "My mother caught on to the sudden surge of boys calling me at home and stories about me making out with guys. Granted, I hadn't gone all the way 'cause I was reading other things as well and had discovered that most boys weren't on my intellectual level. But that didn't stop me from heavy petting and anatomical inspections. Besides, being a chaste middle-class Negro, I didn't want to give in to the image of the promiscuous black woman who was a slave master's rape specialty."

"That's what got her sent away to school," said Anna.

"All that did was get me locked up with a bunch of fucking girls who were also thinking about sex and some doing it with each other," I responded, "like Candace Winthrop."

"And what's wrong with that?" asked Anna, arching an eyebrow.

I then remembered that of the five of us, Anna, Esperanza, and Magdalena were switch-hitters. That is, either gay or bisexual. Zee and I were the only zealots for male plumbing.

"Nothing," Zee stepped in. "It's just that some of us are, uh, more traditional."

I thanked Zee for her diplomatic intervention and continued with my story about the school I had been exiled to. "Of course, they were white and weren't scrutinized like me. I was under constant surveillance, and all *that* ever did was instill a burning resentment in me toward my mother."

"She was looking out for your own best interest, dear," said Anna, who was getting her head massaged by Esperanza as she leaned against her.

"What she *thought* was my best interest," I corrected. "I was researching methods of birth control. I wasn't going to get knocked up like her!"

"But were you . . . uh . . . ?" began Zee, before a telephone rang.

Everybody stopped and looked at me. "It's not me. I told you I left the business," I said. "Which one of you is packing?"

"That could be me," confessed Magdalena. "As an ambassador at the UN, I have to be in contact with . . ." She turned over a folded corner of a towel lying next to her and picked up a C-phone.

"I hope the heat wilted its wiring," I said. "The rule was no phones, just us girls."

"Nina, you know I never play by the rules." She smirked. "That's what makes me La Bomba!" She flipped open her phone like Kirk contacting the *Enterprise*. "*¡Hola! Sí* . . . Nina? . . . Yes." She then handed it to me.

"Who's that?" I asked, reluctant to take the phone.

"Mr. Okey-doke," she smiled. "Your husband."

I narrowed my eyes at her. I was beginning to regret her learning that bit of slang. I reached over and took the phone. "Hi, baby . . . You know . . . with the girls, steaming and dreaming . . . What? Oh! . . . When? I'm sorry to hear that . . . At the police station? Are you all right, Glen? . . . Yes! Right now, baby. Right now! I'll be there!"

I sat stunned, knowing that I had to get a move on. It was a full thirty seconds before I realized that my friends had been peppering me with questions: *What? Is Glen all right? What's going on*?

"I'm sorry," I said, collecting myself. "I've got to go. My husband's been taken in by the police."

"For what, Nina?" asked Zee.

I drained the last of the champagne glass. "Murder. SugarDick is dead!"

TRACK 02
THE NOISE

Things were now up in the air. I'd expected to see them later at my—our—apartment for a post-wedding party that Glen and I were throwing for our families and friends. That would be at seven P.M.—unless this downtown situation was really serious, and murder always is. Glen didn't say he had been arrested for murder, but he had been taken in for questioning regarding the death of SugarDick, a controversial hip-hop artist. His death was the third one in a year. First Headmoe and then Big Time.

It had happened too many times for anyone to have shed a tear, certainly not over the talented but notorious SugarDick. SugarDick went beyond gangsta to being certifiable. In fact, he reveled in the nastiness he conjured up: the violent, sex-crazed nigga who could not be tamed; a sex machine "fuckin' white bitches"—and letting their fathers know about it, a really bright idea.

He had been a member of Mbooma Shaka's crew as one of the background rappers, but had none of Mbooma's political consciousness, such as it were. When Mbooma left the scene due to his involvement with the late Roy Hakim in the conflagration at Eve Shandlin's estate in Pennsylvania a few years back, the mantle of rap was passed to SugarDick. The word was that he was a serious player who scored a "100 percent nigga rating" in the *Black Street News* when he popped five hundred thousand units—*without* radio play. He broke out of the pack with "Must Be the Nigga in Me," making his CD *TestiLying* a smash hit. He'd signed no deal with any major labels and was picked up by Nigga Lovin' Records, Mbooma's former label, one that was commercially astute at *appearing* politically and socially conscious.

But Big Poppa Insane, the CEO of Nigga Lovin' Records, understood the market; when the rap trio Sanctify Nation started slipping, and with Mbooma off the map, he switched gears and began looking for knuckleheads who could deliver the nasty.

Big Poppa Insane wanted to be a player, and that meant acts that could move units beyond the 'hood and get the white mainstream's green dead presidents. The nasty little secret about gangsta rap was that seventy percent of it was purchased by white kids who wanted to rebel against their suburban lives and scare the hell out of their soccer moms and Republican dads.

You couldn't bring one of them home, but you could invite them over *aurally* and assault your parental units with the disturbing, raucous ravings of the imbecilic urban Bantustans.

Thank God for the 'burbs and the police. Il Duce knew what he was doing after all. If it took police brutality to keep the black bastards back, so be it. It was the black noise that bothered a lot of people, black and white.

The second dirty little secret was the record companies. When rap began kicking up in the late seventies, the record companies ignored it, but after several years they saw it making money and they went for it. Glen had written about how the big boys wanted to have it both ways, disdaining rap but profiting from it. Things had been getting out of hand and SugarDick's death, without me knowing all the facts, was the end result of a hip-hopper who had been too impressed by the size of his own malethang. The cheese flashing and the reckless gunplay had led to others being wasted over stupid male ego trips. I couldn't say that I would miss him, either. He had made dogging women a perverted art form for confused males—black, white, and brown.

But I wondered how Glen had gotten involved. I had a weird feeling about this. I had gotten out of the business because I wanted to have a normal life, a husband and a family again, but this made me feel once again as if I were cursed, truly a black widow that inadvertently destroyed everything that she cared about. That thought made me sick to my stomach as I stepped on the gas, zooming to the station in record time.

By the time I parked the car and walked up to the sergeant's desk I was almost fit to be tied. I told the sergeant, a new guy, who I was: Mr. Sierra's attorney. I was given a visitor's badge and escorted to Captain Matucci's office by one of those overbuilt Long Island bruisers who pretends to be a police officer. Before the cop knocked on the door I heard laughter coming from the captain's office.

"Enter."

I opened the door and saw Glen sitting in the chair and Matucci perched on the end of his desk, arms crossed. He was smiling, and Glen didn't look too put out, either.

"Counselor, congratulations," said Matucci, whom I had a decent and cordial relationship with. I always thought that he was much too elegant and nice a man for this kind of work. "Mr. Sierra told me of your recent marriage."

The captain extended his hand and I shook it. I wasn't prepared for this. In a city where any young black male might wind up mauled, humiliated, or dead before he's arrested, I had fantasized the worst outcome.

"Uh, thank you, captain," I said. I quickly looked at Glen, who smiled at me but wore a bandage on his left eyebrow. "What happened?"

"Nothing. Just a little something I picked up."

"Did one of *your* people do this to *my* husband?" I hotly demanded of the police captain, pointing a finger at the evidence I presumed to be police misconduct.

"Certainly not," Matucci responded. "You know I run a tight ship, counselor."

"Well, what happened to him? He wasn't wearing that this morning when he left home. If one of *your* officers—"

Matucci stood up, moved from the edge of desk, and was about to assume his authority, when that man of mine cut in.

"Honey, it's okay," said Glen, standing up and coming over to me, calming me down. "Nothing happened."

"But you're wearing a bandage, Glen. I know this score. I've prosecuted police brutality cases!" I was trying to contain myself. After all, I was down here as his attorney as well as his wife, but I knew too well of police "techniques" when it came to the people they hauled in. Suspects just happened to bump into this or that.

The captain started to clear his throat. I had hit a nerve in the NYPD. The police had garnered a terrible reputation for the deaths of black and Latino males while under arrest. I knew that the NYPD was one of the best departments in the country and their officers had more rules and regulations controlling them than any other police force, but the department also had a legacy of brutality and corruption, a historical record. Granted, they had done an excellent job in bringing down crime under the administration of Mayor Kevin J. Carlucci, but there were two thousand officers out of a force of thirty-eight thousand, roughly the equivalent of two army divisions, that behaved as an occupation force.

"Nina, it's not like that," Glen said to me reassuringly, touching my face. He looked over his shoulder. "Are you through with your questions, captain?"

"Yes, Mr. Sierra, we have a statement from you."

The two of them shook hands and Captain Matucci congratulated us again on our recent marriage. He was such a gentleman. Matucci understood a newlywed's anxiety.

"You two seem pretty chummy," I said to Glen as we walked down the hall.

"We were talking about jazz and how we both thought that a certain trumpeter was the most overrated jazz musician of the age," he replied. "I thought I was going to need your assistance. That's why I called you down here as my attorney. They kept telling me that I wasn't under suspicion, but I wanted you at least on your way."

"Good move," I said. "Next time, don't say anything until I or another mouthpiece arrive."

It wasn't until we got outside the station that I threw my arms around him, putting my mouthpiece to his. He kept telling me that he was okay, that the cops did nothing to him, but he had been cut when he had received a blow.

"From whom?" I asked as we drove to our place.

"From the person who killed SugarDick," he replied. "I went to an apartment building in the Village, where Sugar said he wanted to meet me. A friend of his, Baby Cakes, called and said that he had to see me and talk about some things. I got to his place and when I stepped off the elevator I heard a *pop-pop-pop*. I'd been around enough hip-hop madness to recognize the sound of gunfire, so I quickly headed into a stairwell, and someone else had the same idea, a brother with a gun. I went for him and the gun and I knocked it out of his hand, but he went upside my head with a fist that had an enormous ring or something. I fell back into the wall and he bolted down the stairs, but without the gun."

"What did he look like? What was he wearing?"

Glen shrugged his shoulders. "Average guy. Black. Nothing distinctive, Nina. Clothes? Just black denim shirt and pants and baseball cap. Had a scar on the side of his face. It happened so quick. I left the gun where it fell and went to SugarDick's apartment and saw—" He sighed. "I've never seen freshly murdered bodies before."

"Bodies?"

"Yeah, SugarDick was, uh, 'entertaining' some white thighs . . . some skinhead babe."

I shook my head. "Poor child."

"Yeah . . . Now I can see why you are out of this business. You had to deal with stuff like this all the time?"

I kept my eyes on the street and my vehicular competitors and nodded my head, thinking about all the dead bodies I'd seen, beginning with my family. "All the time, darling. And then some."

We stopped at a traffic light. I told him that I would fix him up when we got back to our ranch.

"Fix something else for me." He winked.

"You're bad," I told him, and tugged a strand of his dreaded hair.

"I know, but that's why you like me."

I stepped on the accelerator. He was right about that.

When we arrived back at our apartment, I changed his dressing and got him to lie down for a nap. I reminded him that we were expecting this evening and I wanted him fresh. Our folks were coming over, and it would be the first time that our families and friends would meet us as husband and wife.

I went into the living room and called Anna and told her that everything was okay. I asked her to call the rest of the girls for me and let them know. I then called the caterers and made sure that they would get here at six-thirty and that the liquor store would make its delivery an hour or so before the food. With all that done, I decided that I also needed a nap.

When I reentered the bedroom Glen was standing by the bedroom window looking out; he was wearing a brightly striped Japanese-style robe. I slipped out of my clothes and put on an oversized T-shirt and padded over to him. I snuggled up to him and he readily received me.

"Want to talk about it?" I asked, leading him to the bed and placing my head on his chest, where his heart pounded rapidly.

He sighed. "I know I should be coldhearted about the thing, but . . ."

"Baby, seeing dead people isn't pleasant or intellectually invigorating," I told him. "I'm sorry that you had to see that."

"First Headmoe, then Big Time, and now SugarDick. I can see the covers of the hip-hop magazines: 'When Will It End?' Most of them have been egging on the great East/West rivalry. It's like niggas are programmed to kill each other and then the killers are never caught. Isn't it interesting how neither Headmoe's nor Big Time's killers were caught?"

I explained to Glen that their deaths were considered CBH—community-beneficial homicides—and such crimes are usually a low priority with the police.

"But if it had been police officers?"

"Glen, you answered your own question," I said. "In the eyes of a lot of people, Sugar had it coming to him. He had flirted with the so-called thug life and the image of the bad nigga for too long—"

"But Nina," he interrupted, "it was all an act." He lifted himself up and that made me rise from his chest. We sat upright on the bed, against the pillows.

"That rape shit wasn't an act, sweetheart," I countered. "He and those other knuckleheads held that woman down."

"I know," replied Glen. "But she was enjoying it."

"Up until the point she said 'no,'" I reminded him. "What part of *no* didn't SugarDick and his boys understand? Hmmm? Unfortunately, as you and I have discussed, this is just another black eye for hip-hop, the music that has so much potential but causes so much trouble."

"Clemon Grouse is going to have a field day with this," said Glen, shaking his head.

Grouse was the black conservative of choice who said the things that whites wouldn't dare say nowadays. When Glen had taken issue with Grouse's blanket attacks on all hip-hop without making any distinctions, Grouse had accused Glen of being "intellectually and morally deficient" by performing on one of SugarDick's earlier albums, *ZDO*. *ZDO—Zones of Diminishing Options*—was an updated version of "Inner City Blues," an aural and sonic examination of the decline and tenacity of the black working class: black men and women laboring and striving, putting food on the table and knowledge in their children's minds. It started off with jazz and soul, and hip-hopped its way into a new interpretation of Marvin Gaye's classic single from his *What's Going On* album.

The supreme irony was that it wasn't about "getting paid"—that is, being commercially cynical and offering listeners lurid stories about sex, gunplay, fine bitches, and skeezing whores—but about trying to define some new type of politics and viewpoints. However, it hadn't sold well with the wiggas—white suburban kids who dressed "black" and purchased most of the hardcore gangsta madness—and that "caused" SugarDick to go G101, gangsta mean. Since most rappers have a short "shelf life," it was explained to him that he better come up with something that could move some units. *ZDO*, nonetheless, was the record that Glen had performed on, and while he had cemented a friendship with Sugar, he was denounced by Grouse and his muse the trumpeter, Hugo Baron, merely for playing on the album.

No matter what I thought about SugarDick—and I didn't think much of him after *ZDO*—he was Glen's friend. My new husband was mourning his death, and one of the most important duties of a wife or husband is to comfort one's spouse.

"I'm sorry about SugarDick," I told him as I gently pulled him toward me and laid his head on my chest. I ran my fingers through his dreadlocks and kissed his musk-scented hair. Although he was in pain, I had the curious sensation of feeling whole, complete, and needed. My baby needed me.

"Ella?" I asked, looking through the collection, wondering what music to put on, remembering what happened the last time I asked that question.

"Yes," said Glen, who had brought out another tray of pâté from the kitchen and placed it on the table. "That will set the mood nicely. Then we can work our way up to Celia and La Lupé, and then save Nusrat Fateh Ali Khan for us late-nighters."

The buzzer rang. "Okay, honey," said Glen. "Get ready for our debut as husband and wife." Glen had on a turquoise banded-collar shirt and pair of black twill trousers and looked comfortably neo-Afrique.

I went over to buzz the door open downstairs.

"Oh, Nina," he started, as I crossed the room, blowing him a kiss. "There's just one thing I forgot to tell you about my mom."

I reached the intercom unit and pressed it.

"GLENITO!—"

That snapped my eardrums and Glen raised his eyebrows. I pressed the buzzer.

"My mother," he said with a deep sigh.

"Okay, she's loud. I can handle that."

Glen smiled. "She's a racist, too."

"Huh? What do you mean?"

Before boyfriend could answer, there was a knock at the door. I opened it and a strawberry blonde waltzed in flamboyantly and thrust a bottle of champagne into my abdomen. No hello or even *hola*.

"Glenito," she crooned, and walked over to her son and put her arms around him more like an old lover than a mother.

"Hi, Mom," said Glen, trying to duck his mother's panoply of kisses and escape from her diamond ring–encrusted grip.

"Where's this woman? This Nina?" she demanded. Her tone implied a front-and-center inspection.

"You walked right past her," said Glen.

"*¿Como?*" Mother turned from her son, who mischievously raised his eyes, and looked at me.

I have manners. I was raised by civilized people—Negroes, but still civilized. I went over to her and offered my hand. After all, we were, uh, family. She was my new mother, theoretically replacing the one who had passed away a few years ago.

The woman, whom I placed as a gorgeous forty-five-year-old, was of mixed heritage: Euro, Indo, and vaguely Africano. She looked at me with a short range of facial expressions: surprise, disgust, and resignation. Of course, with such an attitude the Euro was clearly dominant.

"Mother, this is Nina," began Glen. "Nina, this is my mother, Delores Sierra-Vargas Estaban."

"It's a pleasure to meet you . . . Delores."

Delores struggled for words. I got the distinct impression that I'd seen her on a Spanish-language *telenovela*, *Azúcar de Cana*. I couldn't figure out what her problem was until I remembered what her son had said moments before she walked in. Did that mean she would have an issue with me? Glen was as dark as me, but then that's her son. I was the "alien bitch" he'd married.

"Glen?" she said. She kept looking at me and then at him. I wasn't getting her Mother's Seal of Approval.

I told them I would put *her* bottle of champagne in the refrigerator and left mother and child a respite of privacy. They began speaking in Spanish, and I couldn't translate any of it except for the word "*negra*," which meant *black woman*. Well, she got that straight. Fuckin' bitch, uh, *puta*.

Glen then switched to English. "Well, what the hell do you think I am? *Norwegian*?"

"We're Dominicans!" she informed her Glenito.

"Excuse me," corrected her son, "I think my father was Puerto Rican. A Boricua!"

I smiled. Now I understood her problem. The buzzer rang again and I went to answer it as Glen took his mother over to the table, trying to keep her mouth occupied with food. I didn't care: The man belonged to *me* and I was having a good time!

The gang was soon there: Zee and her husband, Ibrahim; Zee's parents, Mustapha and Amal Kincaid; Anna and Esperanza; my NYPD buddy, Captain Chuck Murchison, and his wife, Erika; my godfather, Judge Phillip March; Charles Warren, my brother's boss; Veronica Thorn Martin and her daughter, Malika; my brother Gary and his wife, Miriam (whom I had to forgive for the sake of the family, despite past betrayals), with my nephew and nieces, Kareem, Monique (a.k.a., "Neeky"), and Yolanda; Her Excellency Magdalena "La Bomba" VillaRosa of the Republic of Dechoukaj; my cousin Maxine Devereaux and uncle Leon Devereaux of GWM; a small detail of musicians and writers who were friends of Glen's; WFUNK's Kenny Sterling and his squeeze, Malorita Ortega y Dias; Robin Zott, Flaco Colt, Ishmael Montoya, Toshiro Fleming, Maya Chang, and Mimi Goddard.

The place was thick with the people I loved and who cared about me, and a whole new posse of friends. The room crackled with laughter and toasts. People sat in my rocker, on the couch, and on the edge of the oak coffee table, or stood in corners. It reminded me of my old home in Brooklyn when Lee and I used to entertain friends and hold political receptions. When Glen's Dominican friends rolled in I told him that I would put up with his mother for the evening, but not with his friends' attitudes if they were like his mother's.

"Don't worry, *azúcar*," he said, pinching a cheek. "They've been thoroughly indoctrinated: They know they're niggas in America."

"I didn't mean that," I responded, slapping his hand away.

"Yes, you did," he said, kissing me as he carried some bottles of sparkling apple cider into the living room. "You *Norte Africanos* can sometimes be as culturally chauvinistic as *los blancos*."

"Hey! What do you mean by that?"

"We'll talk about it later." He winked. "And I do mean *later*."

Then the big guy came in, the most influential man in my life: Big Earl Butler, my father. He walked in with his brickwall-sized self and filled the room, picking me up as he always does, to let me know that I am still his little babygirl even though I had once been the mother of his grandchildren.

"Careful, Daddy, you'll strain your back," I said, laughing.

"Not lifting my babygirl," he huffed and slowly placed me down. "You thinkin' you be gettin' too big for the old man, huh? Okay, where is this new dude in your life? Boy got any family here?"

I jerked my head over to a corner where Glen's mamou sat in the armchair, bobbing her foot, a shoe dangling off of it. Esperanza and Magdalena were conversing with her in Spanish. My mother-in-law felt safe surrounded by quasi-white people.

"The one sitting down. *La Dominicana*."

He peered over his eyeglasses. "Funny, she looks Puerto Rican to me. When did you go over?"

"Hey!" I playfully slapped him on his arm. "Stopping being a cheap nationalist."

"You still didn't answer me," he said in his raspy voice that echoed a cousin of his, Howlin' Wolf.

My hands went to my hips and I looked at him.

"You know, you do a pretty good imitation of your mother."

I caught a whiff of *his* scent and felt someone squeezing my tush. I turned and saw Glen. I grabbed him and brought him up to meet the new man in *his* life.

"Daddy," I said in my most important voice, "this is my husband, Glen Sierra. Glen, this is my father, Earl Butler."

"Welcome to the family, son," he greeted, shaking Glen's hand. "I hope you and Nina have many happy years together, and I hope you can help her make up for some of the lost time in her life."

"I intend to do just that, sir." Glen pulled me closer to him and I placed my head on his shoulder.

"Call me Earl. Now, you can be a good son and do me a favor."

"What's that?"

"Introduce me to your mother." He winked at me.

"Don't even think about it," I told him.

"My mother is a racist," said Glen. "You'll never catch her reading *Race Traitor*."

"That can be cured if properly cultivated, son," Daddy replied. He smoothed back what little hair he had left and tugged on his bolo tie.

Resigned, Glen led him over to his mother. I was about to trail off to the kitchen because someone mentioned a lack of ice, but I felt a hand clamp onto my shoulder and turned. Anna. I was glad to see her, but she had a very funny look on her face.

"What's wrong?" I looked back at where Daddy had gone and saw that Esperanza was still hanging out with Glen's sexy mom. "Don't worry, Big Earl's on the scene."

"And so is Mbooma," added Anna. "He's in the hallway."

A very closed-in feeling was settling on me. I thought I was getting there, back to that moment in time where I could relax and not think about the bad things in my life, but now—

I touched Anna's face and told her to go and fix us both a stiff drink, and if I didn't come back, pour a drop on the floor for me. I started for the door and turned. Anna hadn't moved.

"Go, girl. I'll handle this."

Breathing deeply, I placed my hand on the door and asked God not to do this to me. I opened the door and saw a bluish flash of metal with a singular hole directed at me.

Back in the saddle again.

TRACK 03
THE NEW WORLD PLANTATION

With the assistance of Dexter Pierson, a news reporter and a chilled love of mine, I had discovered that Paul Tower, the former CEO of the Black Christian Network, had conspired years ago to kill Veronica Thorn Martin's late husband, Dr. Malik Martin. Tower had embezzled funds from the Nation movement. The FBI suppressed an audit report that would have implicated Tower as an embezzler and instead blackmailed Tower into spying on the last great black man. Subsequently, Tower assisted a shadowy ad hoc group in murdering Dr. Martin.

Not only had Pierson and I discovered the audit report written years earlier, but Dexter had acquired a film of Tower conspiring with a member of the ad hoc group, Harold Kirby, a young NYPD officer (and a member of that department's Bureau of Special Services), to kill Dr. Martin. At the plush Wall Street office of Warren and Grimke, in my brother's inner sanctum, with the documents and the film in hand, I confronted De Lawd (as Tower was then called) with his treachery, and he took a mighty big but merciful fall. He was the last of the Big Ticket civil rights leaders, the First Negroes Club.

I, my brother Gary, and Mr. Warren decided that if we released the information regarding Tower's backstabbing, it would be the death knell of an already moribund civil rights movement. Instead,

Tower was forced into signing over all of BCN's assets to Veronica Martin and her daughter, Malika. He was saved from criminal prosecution. Of course, this made us liable for criminal prosecution as well: We knew of a capital offense, murder, and conspiracy, but didn't report it. As a former prosecutor, I knew we could be held accountable for obstruction of justice. Yet since the state and its agencies were "behind it"—namely, the FBI and the NYPD and some quasi-governmental group—we decided to say, well, "Fuck you," and handle it internally. We kept it a "family affair."

A year or so later Tower committed suicide. I believe what really led Tower to hari-kari was that he had become an anonymous Negro again. Like the Juice, Tower had darkened beyond white recognition and they had no use for him.

I closed the door behind me and looked at Mbooma. He had resurfaced after the carnage at the Republic of Malik in Pennsylvania where he and Roy Hakim sought to establish some sort of black fantasy based on what they thought was the philosophy of Dr. Malik Martin. The whole thing went to blazes when federal agents attacked the place. This was pre-Waco, before the Branch Davidians. My assistant, Donna, had fallen in love with Mbooma and perished in the inferno. Mbooma was the last man standing. And when he returned he wanted to kill De Lawd, the man who had betrayed the last great black man. We hatched a plan to bring down De Lawd that started with the recording of Mbooma's last song, "Deal of the Century," which exposed De Lawd's treachery. It was a successful guerrilla action that had prepared Tower for the coup de grâce in my brother's office.

For the last two years Mbooma had been underground, so to speak. Zee, Mustapha, Anna, and I had gone out of our way to establish a new life for him, with ID, past history, and present. But now he was standing before me in a dark blue suit, pointing a gun at me. Such gratitude, I thought.

"What are you doing here?" I hissed, trying to keep my voice down. I stood with my back to the door and stared at him. "And what are you doing with that?" I pointed at his gun.

"I saw that Five-O mothafuckah enter," he said, referring to my friend and guest, Captain Murchison. "I was coming up to see you . . ."

"About *what*?"

"You heard about what happened to my boy?" he asked. "SugarDick?"

I sighed. "And?"

"I want you to investigate what's going on, Nina." He slid the pistol into his right coat pocket. "First Headmoe, then Big Time, and now SugarDick. Something funny is going on."

"Yeah, your boys have been acting out their big-dick fantasies for too long and now they've come back to bite and kill," I informed him.

"No, it's not like that!" he shot back, agitated. "You gotta help me do something about this, Nina!"

I shook my head. I could hear people calling for me back in the apartment and I felt my heart pounding. Somebody was bound to come out, sooner or later . . . Glen . . . Murch. Somebody at the wrong moment.

"I'm out of the business, Walter," I said calmly, using his pseudonym. He still had his burly build but had grown a full beard and an even fuller head of hair. He also wore a pair of phony eyeglasses. All in all, it neatly masked his signature scowl that had titillated the white hip-hop buying crowd a few years ago. Back in the early nineties he took pride in being "da nigga ya daddy wants to kill," an image that his "boy" ran with and died under.

"What do you mean, you're out of the business?" he wolfed at me.

That ticked me off. His tone of voice signified a lack of responsibility on my part, as if I were in the wrong. I'd buried *his* woman in a piece of earth that belongs to *my* family and he had the temerity to come to *my* home, waving a goddamn gun and bassing at me! I held up my left hand and showed him the ring on my finger. "I'm married, Walter! I want a normal life, and that doesn't include cleaning up after dead hip-hoppers!"

Mbooma inched closer to me. "Look, Nina, I know you really have done a lot for me . . ."

"If you really believe that," I said, "you'd get out of here and leave me that gun! The war is over, Walter! Hakim is dead! Donna! And now SugarDick, the bitchbeater who wore Bobby Whyte shirts and promoted forty Oh-zees!"

"And hip-hop, too?" he asked. "We're going to let Poppa Insane pervert it?"

"Yes! They own it and control it! Insane works for them! The same plantation, my friend! It's called the New World Plantation!"

"NINA?" cried a voice from inside the apartment.

The voice belonged to Glen. I was beginning to panic. I felt a big wet spot of perspiration forming on my back, seeping through the fabric of the jacket that was part of the off-white ensemble.

"SugarDick was trying to move beyond that . . ."

"It's too late now, Walter, they own the world. Rap is nothing but another billion-dollar chit for them."

The door handle began twisting in my hand. I heard Glen's voice again. He was trying to open the door, but I was holding it in place. Soon I heard Anna intercepting Glen with some bogus story that distracted him.

"And you don't care, do you, huh?"

"*La guerre est finie*," I said. "The war is over. I'm a civilian. Go home, Walter—"

"MY NAME IS MBOOMA SHAKA!" he roared. "NOT SOME FAGGOT NAMED WALTER! I'M A SON OF AFRICA AND I SHALL AVENGE MY BROTH—*Oofff!*"

I had had about enough of his Afrocentric histrionics. My knee went into his groin. My young, agitated friend doubled over and I grabbed him by his gun arm, twisted it behind his back, pulled out his pistol, and reacquainted him with the rules of the lioness. I pointed the gun at his temple. The door opened and Neeky, my niece, poked her head out. I snatched away the weapon from her sight, but she saw me strong-arming Mbooma.

"Close the door, girl!"

Neeky looked at the scene in awe and fright, seeing me gripping a strange man. "Do as I tell you! And keep your mouth shut!"

She quickly closed the door. I shoved Mbooma down the hall, away from my door, and cocked the pistol beneath his chin as I jacked him up against a wall.

"If you ever come to my home and threaten me, my husband, my family, or my friends, I will kill you, Mbooma. Do you understand me?"

He croaked out a yes.

"I did all I could to help you, but you're hell-bent on destroying everything," I continued. "I once told you that you're a death freak, and you still have that scent on you! You stink! Now get the *fuck* out of my life!"

I shoved him away and watched him almost tumble downstairs. I walked back to my apartment, stripping off the jacket I was wearing so I could wrap the gun in it. When I entered the apartment I was struck by the room's cacophony: peals of laughter, bodies shifting and sashaying, cigarette smoke, the clink of glasses, the smell of food. Home. The window had been opened and a spring breeze was streaming in. The room was pulsating with life and it was where I wanted to be. The music was louder than I remembered it. Somebody had slipped on a collection of Afro-Peruvian music I'd discovered a few years back. I saw Anna holding onto Esperanza and walked over to her. I gave her the package.

"Be a sport and place this in my bedroom," I said. "On the upper shelf in my closet."

"Contraband?"

"Uh-huh."

"Is everything all right?" A worried look appeared on her face.

"As far as I'm concerned it is." I placed a hand on her shoulder and squeezed it. "I love you."

"Wow, you never said that before. It must have been deep out there. As your attorney, is there anything I need to know?"

I shook my head, but Anna pulled my skirt to something else. "Look, I like Glen, but he seems a little *too* preoccupied with this stuff about music ownership," she said. "I don't want you becoming a music widow."

I shrugged my shoulders. "He's still young, Anna. He hasn't even busted thirty. Guys tend to be into lists and get thing-oriented: guns, cars, sports, women. He'll grow out of it."

"Or *in*to it." She walked away before I could tell her that one night Glen and I had slept with his saxophone between us, cradled like a child.

Anna headed into my bedroom with the wrapped gun. I felt that I had to be around in plain sight. Esperanza looked at me. I knew she sensed danger even if Anna hadn't told her anything.

"*Madrina*, I need you to read my future."

Esperanza took both of my hands and we closed our eyes. I could feel her energy mixing with mine, surging through my hands and the rest of my body. When I opened my eyes she was smiling.

"You are going to have a very good life, doña."

"Are you sure?" I asked.

"What about Glen and me?"

"He has another love in his life," she said. "Music."

I sighed and embraced her. That I could handle. "Thank you, *madrina*." I kissed her hands, as is the custom in Misericordia.

"You two will be very happy together," she said. "Happier than most of us."

She thanked me for being such a good friend to Anna and bringing her into her life. When I turned I found Neeky staring at me from across the room. I excused myself from Esperanza and walked over to Neeky and took her by the hand to a corner of the room.

"Look, I'm sorry I snapped at you, but you saw me at a very tense moment."

"God, Aunt Nina, you are awesome!" she beamed. "I want to be like you."

I pulled her over to me and hugged her. "No, you don't. I forbid it. Please don't tell anyone what you saw, okay? This is a family night."

She agreed but kept saying that I was superbad. An Amazon.

Then I went looking for my husband, whom I found in the kitchen with Murch, Erika, the judge, and a few people I didn't know.

Glen looked at me. "Where have you been?"

"Dealing with an irate neighbor," I lied. Glen opened the refrigerator and handed me the drink, a gin and tonic that I had asked Anna to prepare for me.

"Anna said you needed this."

I thanked him and sipped it.

"Are you okay?" he asked.

"Yeah? Why do you ask?"

"Well, your hand is shaking."

I looked at the drink in my hand and saw that the ice cubes were clinking against the glass, the liquid swirling about. "Family jitters," I lied again.

"Your girl Anna is cute, but the *madrina* is beautiful," he stated between his sweet lips.

"Don't even think about it," I told him. "Anna is my best friend and Esperanza is packing."

"What do you mean?"

I surreptitiously turned my back to the others in the kitchen and cupped his balls and winked at him. "She's a hermaphrodite," I purred.

"You're joking," he said, sounding like Sean Connery portraying 007, being informed by Q of some outlandish gizmo-weapon.

"There's only one way to find out, but don't even think about it, mister."

"Well, actually, I was thinking about something else, my good woman."

"Oh, really now."

"Oh, stop it, judge!" protested Murchison from behind us. "I can't believe you really think that garbage has any redeeming qualities."

"I've heard some of it that's quite good," said the judge, "that's akin to poetry. It's just a sad state of affairs that things have gotten to this point with the killings."

Glen and I looked over at them. "What are you two talking about?" I butted in.

"Rap," said Erika in a bored tone of voice. "If I have to listen to this . . ."

"You don't have to listen to this," said Murch. "You can go and get drunk. Your preferred state of being."

Glen looked eager to join in, but I pulled him by his hand out of the kitchen. "This is beginning to degenerate," I said.

Hours later, after the guests had left, Anna, Esperanza, Glen, and I quickly policed the kitchen and the living room and tried to get the place in some order so we wouldn't have to clean it the next morning. Anna and Esperanza were staying with us. Glen finally put on his favorite singer, Nusrat Fateh Ali Khan, the late Pakistani qawali singer, and fired up a joint. As I kicked off my shoes, we sat on the couch while Anna parked herself on the arm of the chair that Esperanza sat in.

We passed the joint around and got happy. This was the wind down with the inner family. It was a good party, and the highlight of the evening had been my father taking Glen's mother back to her hotel.

"I don't want to hear about it," said Glen. "The shit borders on incest or something to that effect."

"Don't worry," I said. "If she's half the racist you claim her to be—"

Glen blew out a lungful of smoke. "When did that ever stop people from—"

"Doing the okey-doke," giggled Anna and Esperanza, whom I had never smoked with before.

Glen glanced at them and then at me.

"New word of the day," I explained.

Anna handed the joint back to me; she and Esperanza were speaking softly to each other. Glen was watching them. His interest was piqued by the *madrina*. We smoked and talked and then each couple began making out, and soon we all reached that point where it was time for more explicit things in a more intimate surrounding. The girls got up and we exchanged good-night kisses. They left first.

Glen turned to me. "The woman had a bone, Nina. A bone, *chica*. I saw the impression of it against her dress."

"I told you she was packing, my brother."

He then leaned over and kissed me. "Nina, we are going to have an interesting life. You have such unique friends. Let's go to bed."

I don't know what happened to Glen, but he had his own bone that knew no end that night. I think it might have been the transgressive implication of Esperanza that inflamed him. He took me seven ways past Sunday and still it wouldn't go down. I remember holding onto it as I drifted off to sleep, his head cradled on my shoulder.

"Glen?"

"Hmmm?"

"This stuff about music?" I said, playing with one of his locks. "It seems a little obsessive to some people. I mean, I understand where you're coming from, but other people may get the wrong idea."

"What idea?"

"That you're a nut. A one-trick pony."

"But I'm a special kind of nut: a musician," he said. "And I have a special trick for you." He began waving his fingers over his crotch. "Seemseemsalabean." His malethang began rising and hardening . . .

The next morning he got up before me. Coffee was brewing in the kitchen and the aroma was pleasant to wake up to. I stumbled out of bed, put on my robe, went to the bathroom, and answered nature's calling. I quickly brushed my teeth and then jumped into the shower.

When I entered the kitchen I caught Anna and Esperanza seriously smooching while the bacon was sizzling. These women were as bad as Glen and me; they couldn't keep their hands off each other. I cleared my throat and said, "Good morning, ladies."

Esperanza jumped off Anna's lap. She was slightly embarrassed. Anna, like me, was of the American hussy school. She was shameless; a sensible slut.

"Good morning," said Anna. She got up and patted my face. "Somebody had a good night, eh?"

Anna continued over to the stove and checked the home fries that were cooking. Esperanza plopped down where Anna had been seated.

"Not as good as the morning you two lovebirds were having." I smirked. "Seen the man of the house?"

"Glen . . ." said Esperanza, who suddenly crossed over to the cupboards and began pulling down plates, "went out to pick up some milk and the newspapers."

I thanked them for cooking breakfast and told them that I'd be back in a few seconds, after I dressed. I slipped into a pair of slacks and a long-sleeve cotton pullover. I heard the apartment door open and close.

I called out to Glen, but he didn't respond. I was going to put on a pair of shoes but then felt no need to. When I entered the kitchen Glen was seated at the table looking at the newspaper, and Anna had stopped cooking. Esperanza was watching the two of them. Something was up.

"What's wrong?"

Anna carefully looked at me. "Mbooma was killed last night by the police."

Before I could react Glen spoke. "According to the *Daily News* he firebombed a hip-hop club that was owned by Icy D. The press is trying to play it as a continuation of an East Coast/West Coast thing."

Anna glanced at me, and I gave her a look that could only be read as *Keep your mouth shut*.

"'Mbooma Shaka, wanted by the FBI for questioning in regard to a shoot-out in Astonia, Pennsylvania with federal authorities,'" read Glen, "'was heard crying out before he tossed his firebombs at the empty building, 'She said it was the New World Plantation! The New World Plantation!'"

"Is that what you said to him?" Anna blurted out.

That was the first time I ever wanted to slap her, because the comment led Glen to look up from the newspaper and say, "Him? Was Mbooma here last night?"

I didn't say anything. I could only hear myself breathing. I sat down at the table. "Yes, Glen. He was the irate neighbor."

"Damn, that really could have been an interesting interview had I known about it." Glen lowered the newspaper and looked solemn. "Damn, the end of an era. Two of the Five Points, damn. SugarDick, Mbooma."

"The five what?" I asked.

"The Five Points," said Glen. "A somewhat obscure but very influential rap group. It consisted of SugarDick, Mbooma, Big Poppa Insane, Radeem, and Icy D." Glen looked wistful for a moment and sighed. "Some people have to die for the rhythm, I guess."

"What?"

Glen looked up at me. "Huh?"

"You said something about dying for the rhythm?"

"Oh, that was something people used to say back in the day about rap and hip-hop. It was just a saying about the love for the music. The Five Points originally coined it in a song."

I looked at Anna and Esperanza. We were all perplexed by Glen's last statement.

"He wanted me to investigate SugarDick's death and I told him no. I told him that I had just gotten married and I was no longer working as an investigator."

Glen held the newspaper open and stared at me. "Then what happened?"

I explained to him and the others that Mbooma had been persistent, almost demanding that I help him, and I refused and had to clock him in his balls to keep him from disturbing the party. I told them about my remark, the New World Plantation.

"You didn't want me hearing it, huh?" asked Glen. He shook his head to get a lock out of his face.

"No, dear, I didn't. I also didn't want Murch stepping out in the hallway and engaging Mbooma in a ballistic exchange—with me in the middle. Mbooma was packing a heater. I had to take that away from him. It's up in the closet."

Glen slowly shook his head. "Well," he said, "it's interesting that he asked you to find Sugar's killer. The police have already figured out who killed him."

"Who's the suspect?" asked Anna.

"Mbooma," said Glen. He read from the newspaper how the police suspected that Mbooma was the perpetrator of SugarDick's death. Mbooma had been seen leaving the building where SugarDick was killed. The police were drawing on the fact that SugarDick had come from the West Coast and had strong ties to the West Coast hip-hoppers, and that a series of shoot-outs had occurred between East and West factions. Icy D was a hip-hopper who had bad-mouthed some of the New York crowd.

"But wait a minute," I said. "SugarDick was in Mbooma's crew."

"Yeah," replied Glen. "Funny how things like that are overlooked, that and a few other aspects."

"Like what?" asked Esperanza.

"Well, for one thing," continued my husband, "all the witnesses who described seeing him at the club said that he was bearded . . ."

"And?"

"I saw the man who ran from Sugar's apartment. He had a cap on and I couldn't remember exactly what he looked like, but he wasn't as dark as Mbooma and he definitely wasn't wearing a beard. He was clean shaven with a scar on the right side of his face."

Anna nodded knowingly. "A community-beneficial homicide," she said. As a former assistant district attorney she also knew the score. "This is a two-fer. The cops can say they closed the case on SugarD's death with Mbooma."

"What?" replied Glen. "Are they going to say that the case is solved? That there's no need for an investigation? He wasn't even armed when they shot him."

"No, dear, they don't work that way," I explained. "They—the police and the prosecutors—have no real evidence to link them, the two deaths, other than guilt by melanin. So they'll use words like 'suspect' . . ."

" . . . 'Believe,' 'think,'" added Anna as she dished out the eggs and home fries onto the plates that Esperanza was holding.

I collected glasses and mugs from the cupboard and placed them on the table. "Those words will be used over and over again as the police explain to the public via the media why they *think* Mbooma murdered SugarDick . . . that they *suspect* Mbooma murdered SugarDick . . . that they *believe*, but nothing *conclusive* will ever happened. It'll slowly fade away from the press because the media in this country no longer informs the public, but entertains them, and we all know how pussy-whipped the New York press is, courtesy of Il Duce. The public, then, will associate Mbooma with SugarDick's death. They'll say, 'Hey, didn't he kill that other rapper back in—?'"

"Certainly no grand jury will be called," said Anna. "Why call a grand jury to be empaneled if the person who is suspected of the act is dead?"

"The media isn't going to dig too deep because they are mostly white and they got a two-dead-nigga story to peg it on," I added. "The black press will run with a knee-jerk if-these-people-had-been-white-then-the-police-would angle. You know how worthless the black press is today. We're into 'positive' images."

Esperanza placed our breakfast down before us and we ate slowly. Glen still wanted to know the answer to the big question.

"What's going to happen?"

"Nothing, dear." I sipped my coffee and looked at him and sighed. I thought about the outcome of the night before, but it was out of my hands. If I started pushing this I might wind up in jail. Anna, too. My brother and Mr. Warren could end up in prison. All of this hinged on the fact that we decided not to expose Tower, and Mustapha, Zee, Anna, and I had created a new life for Mbooma as an upstate electronics salesman in one of Mustapha's stores. By Mbooma returning, he had exposed the rest of us. He was wanted by the feds and we could be prosecuted for aiding and abetting. His death was truly a community-beneficial homicide. Cold but true.

"Well," sighed Glen, digging into his eggs, "at least Reggie is on the case."

"Baxter?" I said. "What do you mean?"

Glen snapped open the paper, folded it, and handed it to me. I quickly searched for and found the article, a small paragraph that was headlined:

BAXTER CALLS FOR A MUSIC SUMMIT/QUESTIONS ROLE OF EAST COAST–WEST COAST DISPUTE/PLANS TO LOOK AT THE ACTIVITIES OF THE MUSIC INDUSTRY

The Reverend Reggie Baxter, the putative president of Black America USA, was calling for a summit and that meant he was looking for cash. Baxter was basically doing a Tower without the latter's economic base, and at its rankest form it was a shakedown operation. Baxter's *modus operandi* was to spot a problem between a group of blacks and a white institution and then to strut in proclaiming the defense of the race to advance the cause of Malik Martin's social capitalism and integration. He would then offer the good offices of his enterprise, Mandate for Progressive Action, a.k.a., Money in My Pocket, Inc. He would move behind closed doors to elicit money from both parties and then move on to the next camera.

With Reggie on the case, the fate of the race was in good hands—and in his wallet.

TRACK 04
TO BE REAL

"Ouch!" I cried, rubbing my ass that was stinging from where Glen swatted it. "What was that for?"

"For not telling me, your husband, about last night. What other secrets are you hiding?" he asked as we changed our clothes. I had a class to teach and he was going to interview a subject for one of the magazines he wrote for. He had waited for me to step out of my pants to ambush me. Sneaky bastard.

"Glen, it's not that I'm hiding things, it's just that my work as an attorney and investigator required me to be confidential," I explained, pulling off my top and reaching for a peach shirt that hung in the closet. "There are just some things I can't tell you. Not that I don't want to, but I have to protect clients. Confidentiality. Believe me, sweetheart, I'm not trying to play games. I want us to be able to trust and confide in each other. Those things that I can't speak about are in the past."

"What about last night?"

I raised my right hand. "I won't ever do that again. If a dragon comes to our door, you can kick its ass."

That calmed him down.

But it wasn't only he who needed to be calmed down. I walked into my Late-Twentieth-Century African-American Politics and Culture class at Borough of Manhattan Community College and, once again, faced the impact that hip-hoppers like Mbooma and SugarDick have on young blacks, particularly when they die. My class was made up of young men and women who were barely out of their teens, and it was a battle to get them to even read. To think beyond the superficiality of blackness was out of the question.

I didn't believe they were stupid or uneducable, but they did have a different sensibility and reference points that made them creatures of their age and a world they didn't create but they, to some degree, affected. On the street, they would be signifying and engaging in all sorts of verbal gymnastics. However, place them in a classroom and ask them to express a coherent thought that wasn't media-driven, and you had a better chance of receiving rain in the desert without the assistance of Jesus.

I noticed the mood as soon as I walked in. Some of the girls were sullen or crying; the boys were standing in knots and clusters of twos, threes, and fours, their hands in their oversized, almost-down-to-their-knees trousers. I was beginning to see a change in their accoutrements: Instead of the ubiquitous baseball caps, some were sporting boonie hats or boonielike hats that were popular during the Vietnam War era.

Pulling out my texts of the trade, *The Crisis of the Negro Intellectual, Funk*, and *New Day in Babylon*, and getting ready to rock, I noticed that no one had responded to my greeting of "Good afternoon." I looked up and saw the wet-eyed wounds of the sisters and the silent rage of the young brothers.

"What's wrong?"

One of the girls, Myra, looked up and said, "They killed another one of us."

"Who?" I was concerned because there had been some altercation at the school, which was unusual since it was a college and not a high school. When they mentioned Mbooma, I inwardly rolled my eyes. I had to check myself. I remembered how when I had gotten Mbooma to reappear to make the "Deal of the Century" attack on Paul Tower, some of his crew had gathered to help, and they treated him as if Malcolm X had returned. I shouldn't have been surprised, but I was.

"Mbooma Shaka, the warrior prince," announced Maulana Rangoon. He strode down to his chair and looked at me. "The rollers took him out because he was spreading the word."

"He firebombed a building that was frequented by black folks," I threw in. "Luckily, no one was there at the time."

"That's what the cops say," asserted Tyrone, a student who had drawn a rush of notoriety a few years back when Erykah Badu used his name for a character in one of her songs.

"SugarDick, then Mbooma," said Myra, a tear rolling down her cheek. "Why?"

"They had to take out the black man . . ." Maulana began.

I didn't think much was going to get done classwise, but the deaths of these two rappers meant something. I figured I could roll with it and perhaps make my points about the subject matter . . . But instead I just sat down and listened:

SugarDick was keepin' it real. Mbooma was the keeper of the true black knowledge. SugarDick was all about gettin' paid. Mbooma was trying to elevate true black consciousness. SugarDick was a student of the Honorable Saddiq Farouk. Mbooma represented the black revolutionary tradition. SugarDick was killed because he was too strong, too black.

While all this was unraveling—the fantasies of a stressed-out race constantly besieged by forces internally as well as externally—I noticed that every student making a revolutionary or pseudo-intellectual argument was slaving for major clothing manufacturers. They were all wearing something by the likes of Tommy Hilfiger, Ralph Lauren, DKNY, Nautica, Nike, Reebok, Versace, Bally, Calvin Klein, Bobby Whyte, etc. They were all "branded," so to speak. I'm surprised that someone hasn't started an Amistad line of clothing.

They, to some degree, represented what one writer had called "the conquest of the cool." They, like their heroes Mbooma and SugarDick, talked black but bought *white*. They couldn't think of rebelling because for blacks that meant sudden death. Instead they consumed and gave all their money to white manufacturers, rather than investing in black concerns that might—*might*—benefit their communities. And those who were the most vociferous in talking about it—racism—usually wore the most expensive or the most popular brand-name items.

All the girls had relaxed their hair—a high-tech, chemical version of frying it—by purchasing Congo Sheen products that were highlighted by television ads developed by the celebrity filmmaker Spunk, who had allied himself with a global advertising firm. Black culture was for sale and black advertisers were denying it while walking to the bank. It made sense that the culture was up for sale—it was nothing more than a commodity, just the way our ancestors had been.

A wave of depression washed over me. I realized that what I was doing didn't matter because I wasn't with the noise that's called hip-hop, and I certainly wasn't on television the way SugarDick or Mbooma had been, or would be, like Baby Cakes, SugarDick's protégé. I was old knowledge and gals like Baby Cakes were down with champagne, fur coats, flashy niggas, rocks on their fingers, and sex on demand. Okay, I could roll with the mouth sparkle and the sex, but I got down to business and took care of my work.

Perhaps what troubled me so much was that everything was out in the open—the greed, the sheer stupidity of some people—and that it was masked as "irony" or as a condition of postmodernity. Granted, I talk lustfully out of both sides of my neck, but only in private, among friends and loved ones. If New York was the naked city where everything was out in the open, then the whole country had become one huge nudist colony.

"That's right!" said Tyrone. He slapped Maulana's hand and snapped me out of the private world of Nina Halligan.

"What is?" They were grinning as if somebody had scored with a magnificent slam dunk.

Maulana gave me a very smug look. "The New World Plantation, teach! That's what Mbooma was delivering to the new black man. Yo, teach, you have to git wid it if you want to hit it!"

I had decided to quit practicing law and had hung up my guns as far as being a private investigator. Now teaching was also beginning to seem stale to me . . . They weren't going to listen: I wasn't young. I wasn't hip. And I wasn't dead.

I didn't want to admit it, but after I left class I felt old and useless. Maybe I was trying to hide from the fact that I did feel bad, if not guilty, about Mbooma; but another part of me screamed *NO*! I had done all that a person could do. I had even lost my family trying to rid crime-plagued black neighborhoods of the scourge of drugs, a scourge that even the mighty United States government could not seem to stop. The best it could do was to lock up every black on crack charges and stop and frisk you to death.

That was the state of my funky mood. I was sitting in the upstairs lounge of Byron's, waiting for Mr. Magic to appear for a late lunch at three P.M. I had two Jack Daniel's and they weren't bettering my outlook. I was thinking that perhaps Glen and I had made a move too soon. Maybe I had married under the illusion that being with someone would make me happy, and we all know what an illusion happiness is in this postmodern era. The only way to be happy is to buy things, consume them, wear them, desire them. Was my desire for Glen, my voracious sexual appetite, a form of consumption, a salve for my unvarnished idiosyncratic tendencies that couldn't be dealt with in a mad world of incessant product-hyping and self-promotion?

I sat in my favorite semi-secluded corner in an old, carved wooden love seat with red velvet upholstery, and dug my toes in the plush carpet. I watched the waitrons at the bar attend to suits who appeared to be cyberexecutives. The punks had set up their powerbooks and pulled out their cellulars. They were wired and fired, cutting deals, moving cash around, condemning millions to peonage. They were hip, cool, and multicultural. Not a racist bone in their body, provided that the other party dressed as well as they did. No, they were on the cutting edge and I was a black blunt one.

When Glen appeared I was deep into my own thoughts and didn't see him. He had a bouquet of flowers.

"So, how is my little sex machine?" he asked as he floated down beside me. "Oh, you started early," he added, smelling the liquor on my breath after kissing me.

I sniffed the mixed array of flowers. It was so good to see him. I'd stopped thinking about us being a mistake.

"Are you all right—or are you drunk?"

I told him that I wasn't drunk, but happy to see him. I asked him how his interview went and he said fine, though something funny had happened.

"What's that, dear?"

"Well, I went to see Captain Matucci," said Glen. "And he wasn't in."

"Nothing funny about that, baby." I had tucked my legs underneath me and was nestling up to him. He was so beautiful, his eyes, his beard . . .

"Well, he's no longer with the police force," said Glen.

"What do you mean?"

"He resigned."

I swung my legs back to the floor and folded my arms. "Huh?" Retiring is one thing, resigning is another. "How did you find this out?"

"Nina . . . c'mon, I'm somewhat of a journalist. I didn't go to J-school, but I know how to cultivate sources. I asked around. Since Matucci was a jazz man . . ."

"But the blue wall is stronger than jazz."

"But the blues is the foundation of jazz."

"Okay, beautiful, we're getting off point," I said. "What else?"

"Two things. I remember who told me that SugarDick wanted to see me."

"Who was that?" I was unbuttoning his shirt and slipping my fingers inside, tickling his nipples and chest hairs.

"Stop it, *chica*," he said, trying to suppress a smile. "Baby Cakes."

"That slut?"

"Da Slut moved six hundred thousand units *without* airplay," he duly informed me. "She made the call and I want to know why."

I bit his ear. "What else do you want to know?"

Glen reached into his jacket and pulled out a notebook and flipped through it. "Valerie Gordon."

"Who the hell is that? The next slut of the month? Speaking of which . . ." I began fumbling with the zipper on his fly. He pulled my hand away.

"Nina, I need your help."

"Well, you're going to get that, sweetie, one way or the other." I went for the zipper again.

"I mean help in finding about this Gordon woman . . . or the 411 on Matucci."

I grabbed the notebook out of his hands and climbed on top of him. I've seen more outrageous things at Byron's this time of day, and we were in the back. I wasn't going to do anything *too* risqué. I began kissing him, and he knew better than to put up any resistance. Granted, Glen could throw me clear across the room at the snap of a finger. I was hot and just wanted to be on top, his arms around me. We made out for fifteen minutes, shooting deep tongue, until a waitron calmly asked us if we needed any drinks. She smiled.

"Yes," said Glen. "I have to catch up with my wife." Glen downed the drink when it arrived, paid the check, picked up his notebook, and got us a cab back to our place for some big-time sensuality.

When we got home he used one of my silk scarves to restrain me, and strategically arranged my posterior. It was lucky that the girls were out of the apartment. While still under the influence, I was assigned the task of finding out about Matucci while Glen checked out Valerie Gordon, the dead skinhead who had been found with SugarDick at his denouement.

TRACK 05
SIESTA SEX

"Mmmm, my man, that was good to the last bone," I murmured, feeling like a wanton and wicked hussy.

Glen untied the scarf and I reached for him. We tussled on the bed and fumbled onto the floor. The lioness within had been aroused.

"*Chica*!" he gasped, sprawled on the floor with me on top of him. The sheets had come with us. "Nina, you're too much."

"I know, but isn't that why you married me?"

"No doubt 'bout it," he said, trying to get me off of him. Glen slowly rose and I sat on the edge of the bed, watching his tight, round buttocks as he walked over to the door and slipped into a pair of jeans and a T-shirt that had been hooked up on the door. He was hungry and was going to prepare a snack for us.

"Why don't you put on a robe, baby?"

"Because, my sweet, if Yin and Yang should appear," he explained, "and see me in a robe, they will know what we've been up to—in the lonely afternoon."

"Good thinking, detective." I smiled. He cooks, too.

Glen went into the kitchen and I got to work, thinking. If John Matucci had resigned, that was indeed odd. Matucci still had time on the clock and he would only resign if he'd been made a better offer. But I felt that something else was going on and, if so, there was only one person who would know, my own deep throat: Chuck Murchison. They, Murchison and Matucci, had started off as patrolmen together and had a friendly competition going, clocking their advancement by each other's rise through the ranks.

I reached over to the nightstand and dialed Murchison's direct number at his precinct command.

When I reached him I first thanked him for coming to our party the night before. He thought that Glen and I would make a nice couple and wished us luck.

"Thanks, Murch. So, what's this about your boy, Matucci?"

"What about him?"

"It's my understanding that he resigned from the department."

"John? No way, sister. That guy wouldn't make a move like that without telling me."

"It's like that, huh?"

"Look, sister, the only thing deeper than the black is the blue."

Just as I thought. "So, check it out for me, will ya? I'll put you in a dream of mine."

"I thought you had retired, Señora Sierra."

"Dabbling, my brother, dabbling. So check out this rumor about your partner, Matucci, and if it's true, why?"

Murch smugly told me he would do so and then call me to correct my erroneous information.

Loverman returned with some food on a tray.

"Such treatment, my kind sir," I responded.

Glen placed the tray over my legs. It held some pâté, fruits, bread. Enough to sustain us until dinner. Yin and Yang—Anna and Esperanza, and we knew who had the "yang"—were going to take us out to eat that night.

I told him that I'd made contact with my source at the police department and he was on the case.

Glen looked shocked. "That quick?"

"Baby, I'm the professional in the family," I explained. "You're the artist."

"And what is that supposed to mean? An artist?"

Uh-oh. "I merely mean, my dear, that this is second nature to me. I know how to pick up the phone and who to call. I've been doing this for a while."

"And I'm just a musician, right, Nina? A horn player?"

The "Nina" did it and I had to think fast. "Look, I was just joking. I'm only assisting you on this. It's entirely your call, but I have a problem that you could help me with." He smiled. "Not that, gorgeous . . . Well, yes and no. I mean, look, I'm beginning to reevaluate my relevancy as a teacher and I think I want out."

"And do what?"

"Have a baby?" I squeaked.

"Children, huh?"

I nodded. "At least one."

"I would love to do that, but—"

"But what?"

"I think we need more time under our belts as a couple and some money . . ."

I told him that I had some funds, but he still thought it was important that we first have a year or two together as man and woman, as husband and wife, as Nina and Glen. He was concerned about the future and had some things in the works that could bring income into our household. I was concerned about my age: I was thirty-five and that would mean having a child when I was thirty-seven. Glen would just be breaking thirty in two years. I wanted to get it on, a family, mind you. Was he ready for the responsibilities of being a father? Was he willing to give up his other love—music—for that of a child?

But something big was brewing for him. He had been asked by China Mercury, the funk diva, to produce her next album for Groove Records; she had decided not to re-sign with Nigga Lovin' Records, the label of her last five CDs.

"Baby, that's wonderful!" I exclaimed. China Mercury was the best, a very creative musician-singer. In my opinion, she could really sing, and she had lyrics that were sexy, funky, and socially provocative. She was an Afro-Asian hybrid, very beautiful and controversial in her biracial gender-bending; she was as frank about pleasure as I was, but with a big difference. She was bisexual. "When did this happen?"

"It's been in the works. China and I are old friends."

Old friends? For some reason that took the bloom off the rose. She was considered one of the most beautiful women in the world. She had also been a friend of my late husband and together they had intended to produce a controversial cable show called *¡Niggerama!*

"Were you two . . . uh . . . ?" I began.

"Well, honey, if there are some things about your past that you can't speak of . . ." He trailed off.

I was about to smack his smart black ass, but he raised the tray from over my lap, preventing a clear shot. The telephone rang and I picked up the receiver. "HALLIGAN!" I shouted. It was Murchison. Glen was leaving the room, smirking, and I began gesturing for him to stay there and talk to me about China Mercury. Glen puckered his lips and moved into the kitchen.

"Damn," said Murchison, reacting to my shouting.

"Sorry, Murch."

The brother in blue delivered the verdict: Matucci had resigned. Why? Something had come down the chain of command from One Police Plaza in regard to SugarDick's death. Murchison didn't know exactly what, but Matucci decided that he was in disagreement with it and left. Murch had spoken to Matucci, who wasn't saying much. Then Murch had picked up other things from his sources at police headquarters.

After we hung up, I told boyfriend what Murchison had relayed to me. "What do you think?" My arms were crossed and I was still in bed.

Glen, standing at the door to our room, thoughtfully stroked his beard. "We don't know what came down."

"We can speculate, gorgeous."

"Well, the only thing I can figure out is that reports were altered to make Mbooma look like SugarDick's killer."

"And that could have happened. Evidence is suppressed. Reports misfiled. Witnesses intimidated . . . But who and why? Why in the case of SugarDick?" I know about suppressing evidence. Anna caught me doing it a few years ago, before I left the prosecutor's office to become a private investigator. "That's what you're going to find out," I told him. As far as I was concerned, my part in this was over. I wanted to know about something else. "Okay, what about you and China?"

Glen shrugged his shoulders. "Woman couldn't make up her mind."

"Showdown between you and another man?"

"More complicated," said Glen, with a touch of melancholy. "My competitor was a woman."

Yipee! I jumped for joy—internally. That definitely made things simpler for me. Nothing deflates the male ego more than his female object of desire wanting another woman. Oh, they like the two-fer concept, all that lezzie sex fantasy, but when she wants her as well as him? They can't go for that.

"Come here, baby," I cooed. I held my outstretched arms to him and he was about to walk over when we heard Yin and Yang unlocking the apartment door. "Close the door," I said quickly.

"Children, we're home. *Las hermanas* have returned."

Too late. Anna walked into the room and took off her sunglasses. She looked at me still in bed and then glanced at her watch.

"Siesta sex, huh?" She winked.

"I have food to put away," said Glen, and he excused himself.

"Does he dislike me?" asked Anna, out of his earshot. "You didn't tell him what I said about him and music, did you?"

"No, he probably isn't used to close quarters with a bevy of hot babes like us. Also, he's a little more formal. Where's Ranza?"

"She's putting some food in the kitchen." Anna sat down on the end of the bed. "Well, for a guy, your husband is gorgeous. I'd think about jumping over the wall again." After I had figured things out about Glen and China, Miss China Dyke USA now throws me a curve.

The door was open and we could hear Glen and Esperanza conversing in Spanish in the kitchen.

I whispered, "Get this—loverman had a thang with China Mercury."

Anna gripped my leg. "Glen was stroking her?" She floated down on the bed. "Oh, man, to paraphrase Richard Pryor, I would blow him if his thang had been—"

I threw the covers over her just as Esperanza walked into the room. Her hair was uncharacteristically down to her shoulders. She stopped when she saw that I was naked, with Anna lying perpendicular to me beneath the sheet.

"Oh!" She blushed and retreated to her room.

Anna threw off the sheets, which I used to cover myself, and sat up. "Was that Ranza?"

I nodded. "She saw me bare-chested."

A gleam appeared in Anna's eyes. She got up and kissed me full on the lips. "Thanks, sweetie, for prepping her."

She charged out of the room and told me that we had dinner reservations at eight and that she was looking forward to hearing some music tonight.

The girls had picked an old Italian restaurant in Chelsea that had the ambience of a mother's kitchen. The food was first-rate. We then got into a cab and headed over to Greenwich Village where

Glen was playing with the Phillip March Quartet at The Place. My godfather, the judge, had retired from the bench to become one of the best-kept secrets in jazz. Three nights out of the week, Wednesday, Thursday, and Friday, he held court and featured Glen. The club had not been doing too well before Teo—Uncle Phil—began playing there. On bass, he led the band and began cultivating a reputation for the show as one of the premier "postgraduate" sessions for aspiring musicians. Soon he began attracting other high-quality name artists for jam sessions.

Teo ascended the stage and played for a half an hour that night with the drummer, the pianist, and the percussionist, before Glen came on. You could tell that Glen had star quality, as the audience was familiar with his work and clapped ecstatically. It was a mixed crowd, blacks, whites, Latinos, predominantly young, but with a fair section of middle-aged aficionados in their forties and fifties, people who had money and knew something about jazz.

Glen thanked the audience and told them about his recent marriage, then dedicated a song to me that he had composed, "Nina." Anna, Esperanza, and I sat near the back, not wanting to interfere with his concentration. I was focusing on the music until I saw a certain man enter the club.

He was dressed very casually: khaki slacks and button-down shirt. I watched him take a seat at the bar then start listening intensely and drinking. I was trying to figure out what he was doing there while simultaneously digesting the news that Anna and Esperanza were thinking about opening a restaurant in the city, in partnership with Magdalena. They were going to call it "La Bomba" since Magdalena had an international reputation. Esperanza thought that the city could use a dose of Misericordian cuisine. I was half-listening to them and the music, while keeping an eye on the man at the bar. After the tune ended, the band began another. I excused myself and went over to the bar.

"Good evening," I said. John Matucci turned to me and smiled.

"Counselor," he replied, "may I buy you a drink in celebration of your marriage?"

I answered affirmatively and took a seat next to him. The bartender poured my drink and I turned to the captain, who toasted me and my husband. He sipped on his Cutty Sark, and he appeared jovial, but things were clearly on his mind. His handsome face had seemed bright and youthful the day before yesterday, but it now appeared tinged with frustration, concern, and bitterness.

"Captain?" I broached.

"Call me John," he quickly responded, as if trying to consign the recent past to another realm. "May I call you Nina?"

"Certainly." I smiled. "I, uh, understand that you resigned from the department."

Matucci nodded. "Word travels far and fast. Yes, I did. It was time to go."

"But your time wasn't up."

"Oh, yes it was, Nina." He lit a cigarette and blew the smoke away from me. Another gentleman, I thought. "You know, Nina, when a man or woman joins the police force, he or she is concerned about helping others, about justice, bringing in bad guys. I *was* an officer of the law, as you are an officer of the court. Justice, Nina . . . It's supposed to be about justice. Now, I know, as you must know outside of your role as an attorney, that justice isn't always perfect, but our society is based on the concept of law—and the law as an instrument of human beings is not infallible—but when you . . . when you . . ."

Matucci turned away from me as if he was recoiling from his own moral repugnance. Something had gotten to him, something foul and decrepit.

"When you *what*, John?"

"It's all politics, greed, and corruption," continued Matucci, "but it's mainly politics." He gulped his drink and motioned to the bartender for another. "It's fucking politics, and the politicians work for the boss, the *big* bosses, Nina."

Matucci was stewing over the big picture, but I wanted to know about two pieces, SugarDick and Mbooma. "John, is this about those two dead rappers?"

The lines around his eyes tightened. Matucci squinted at me and then away. "I shouldn't be talking about this, Nina."

Bingo. I looked around and kept my voice low. "You can trust me, John."

He peered at me again and let out a short laugh. "You may be the last honest woman on the planet I could tell, but I have members of my family who are on the force. I don't want them going down an alley and not having backup because their old man is considered a rat."

For a moment our attention was riveted to the sound of a crashing cymbal and rimshot. We both turned and watched Glen blowing hard and melodiously, ripping through chorus after chorus of a Bobby Watson tune, "In Case You Missed It." It was meant for two or more horns, and he obliged the composer by picking up an alto and playing it with his tenor at the same time. The audience went wild at such showmanship and virtuosity. Behind my back I heard Matucci saying something.

"What?" I turned and asked.

"Life is a beast." He had been talking to himself and realized that something had slipped. Matucci threw some money on the bar and stubbed out his cigarette, said good night, and left.

The audience was clapping enthusiastically and I looked back to the stage to where the girls had been sitting. Anna glanced at me, and I went after Matucci, chasing him into the street.

"John! Wait!" I quickly walked up to him, dodging people on Sullivan Street, a narrow street in the heart of the Village. Matucci turned around and stared at me.

"I can't talk, counselor. There are other people's lives and careers at stake." He moved on.

Giving chase, I kept walking and held onto his arm. "John, so is justice. If there's no justice, will you be at peace with yourself?"

"Justice," he said ruefully. "Well, you know how easily that can be plea-bargained, counselor . . . Right? As for peace . . ."

The policeman let out a long sigh and surveyed the immediate area. It was a beautiful spring night in May and the city was humming. According to Il Duce, the mayor of New York, the city was back from its long decline and he was taking credit for it, along with the work of the New York police, of course. But there was one man who had experienced the seamy side of that rejuvenation.

"Nina," Matucci finally said, "that's something I'm just going to have to learn to live with. You have a very talented young man in there. Take care of him. He deserves your attention. Good night."

"Good night, John."

Matucci started walking and crossed the street. Moving fast in the opposite direction, down the one-way street, shot a black motorcycle that had appeared out of nowhere like a coal-colored bullet. The driver sped up as he approached Matucci and a person on the backseat fired rounds from what appeared to be an Uzi. Matucci was hit in the front and back as he spun around, and the killer turned and kept firing at him. I stood there and couldn't do anything; it was so fast.

Quickly, I ran over to him and knelt down. I yelled for someone to call for an ambulance and the police. The man had fallen against a car, his mouth gaping with blood and his eyes looking up obscenely with the sudden shock of death. Matucci's shirt was soaked with blood and I could see a wound in his neck. People were screaming and running away from the sight of momentary mayhem. I held his wrist and felt his pulse disappear. Before I rose I closed the eyes of the last of New York's finest.

TRACK 06
MAGGOT OVERLORD OF INFONEW$

The police wanted to know what happened and I told them everything that had occurred—except the essence of my conversation with the late Captain John Matucci. I lied about that: We spoke about jazz, my marriage, and I had followed him out because he left so abruptly, before I had the chance to invite him and his wife over for dinner. If John Matucci no longer trusted his colleagues, why should I? They would not have put a hit on him, but his death had to be linked to SugarDick and Mbooma. The simple questions were how and why? That kept me tossing and turning in bed for days. I didn't teach at school. I didn't answer the phone or take calls. Seeing Matucci murdered before my eyes rendered me helpless in a way that I hadn't been since I'd lost Lee and the children. It was the cruelty of humans, how we take each other's lives not for defense or for food, but for other reasons: power and money.

Anna and Esperanza moved back into Anna's old apartment that had been turned into a gallery prior to her coming with me to Misericordia. The two of them had entered a new life, with plans for a restaurant, yet I was still dealing with something I thought I had left behind, the business of death. But now there was a difference: Glen.

He was very sweet. He just let Nina be Nina and held onto me, told me that everything would be all right. That we could drop this thing, the investigation, and get on with the golden business of living our lives. I didn't have to pretend and be some fucking super black woman.

"I keep forgetting how much you've been through, Nina," Glen said one afternoon as we listened to the sky crackle, the rain splashing against the window in uneven strokes. That just made me feel . . . hmmm . . . nice. Somebody recognized what I'd been through. The only close girlfriends I had were Anna and Zee, and I'd known Miss Chinatown for ten years. Gale Simmons had been a friend since junior high school, but we were now on the outs because of the way she had resolved her widowhood: immediately marrying Pierre-Pierre Bernard, the president of the Republic of Dechoukaj, formerly Misericordia, before her late husband's body was even cold. That offended me, especially after she'd hired me to track down her husband's killers.

Toward the end of the week, while it was raining once again, I slowly woke up one morning to find Glen gone. On his side of the bed was a book, *Media Globalization: The Agenda of the New World Order*. It had a bluish cover with the "o" of the word "global" as a large letter made to look like the Cyclopean eye of a television set. I turned the book over and read the back blurb.

> *Media Globalization* details the rapidly increasing domination of a small number of transnational corporations at the forefront of transforming the various aspects of media: publishing, telecommunications, filmmaking, and the Internet. Controlled by a handful of international conglomerates, the convergence of global media and telecommunications systems are fueled by the rapacious ideology of the marketplace and the weakening of the public sphere. The authors believe that an important feature of this trend is advertising, which tries to reduce all human activity to the mere purchasing of products. Increasingly, media globalization undermines public broadcasting systems that have taken on more public and controversial issues necessary for an informed public to govern itself.

Thumbing through the book I saw several marked chapters. Glen had underscored passages regarding InfoNews Corporation, a transnational company owned by Rolf Fergus, a South African who had recently become an American citizen when he realized that ownership of multiple media outlets was reserved for only the richest Americans. Some people called Fergus "the Saint" because of his large charitable contributions, but he was also known as "the Beast" for his cutthroat business practices.

From the next room I heard the sound of furious keyboard clacking.

"Glen?" I shouted. When he answered, I got up from the bed and went into the room that had been transformed into a command and control center. Boxes of newspapers, books, and magazines about music cramped the room that once belonged to my assistant, the late Donna Taylor. On one wall was an organizational flow chart of the InfoNews Corporation. On another was a photo of the devil himself, Rolf Fergus, and pictures of his three children, who worked for him: Heather, Willem, and Peter.

"Glen," I said, looking at the photos and the chart on the wall, "isn't this a bit extreme? Are you planning on going to war or something?"

"Death isn't final enough for a rapist like him," he commented.

"Whoa. Whoa," I replied. "Rapist?"

"I meant defiler of black music," he corrected. "To him, black music is just another commodity. It's the same way the white man has always treated our people here. We're just things to them. They raped our culture. They killed our men. They raped our women. Fergus is in the tradition."

"What's that?" I asked.

"White predator."

Glen was seated at a desk that housed two computers and his musical keyboard, an extra phone, and a fax. He was trying to access something on the Web. Spread out on his desk were copies of articles by my first husband, and others on InfoNews, Nigga Lovin' Records, Black Death Records, and Valerie Gordon. I picked up the Xeroxes and noticed that Valerie was a dead ringer for Sinéad O'Connor, a pretty woman with very expressive blue eyes.

"Baby, isn't this the woman who was found . . . ?"

"With SugarDick?" he answered without turning around. "Yeah. Valerie Gordon. Former lead guitarist for the Violent Vaginas."

Rolling my eyes at that one, I sat on the edge of the desk while he tried to make his way through the maze of the Internet. I put the article down and looked at the others. "What are you looking for?"

"I'm not sure, but I remember seeing something on Nigga Lovin' Records and Black Death, about them being either purchased or having taken in investments from—"

"InfoNews?" I held up the book.

Glen glanced over his shoulder at me. "Yeah. Fergus is known to have immense global ambition and he said that one of the places he is weak is in music."

"That's one of the reasons that the Groove decided to expand," I added.

"Yeah, look out: The Beast is coming," said Glen. Fergus was known to be a ruthless businessman and it had even been suggested that he wasn't beyond murder and mayhem. In his younger days, a partner of his had disappeared and it was rumored that Fergus had him murdered, and then blamed it on the African National Congress. After all, the ANC was affiliated with the Communist Party in the struggle against apartheid, so why not blame it on them? The man was never found.

"What does this have to do with SugarDick?"

He shrugged his shoulders. "I don't know if it does. I'm just trying to get into a site that has some information about those record companies. I think Fergus was on a shopping spree and—*Coño*! I got it, *mamasita*."

Glen opened a website sponsored by some collective called Mu$icWatch. Its mission was to "empower individual artists to make collective changes in the music industry." Glen clicked on "Today's News" and a photo of Valerie Gordon came up on the monitor. Mu$icWatch mourned her death and reported the circumstances of Valerie's demise and her activities as a union organizer. It seemed that Ms. Gordon had been a writer as well as a performer and a member of the American Writers Union (AWU), which was affiliated with the Communications Workers of America.

AWU had been in existence for about twenty years. Valerie had been spearheading a special project that was investigating or making preliminary inquiries into the lives of rappers and other musicians, making connections between their plight and that of writers.

What made this even more interesting was that Glen was also a member of this union but didn't know anything about this project.

"Shows you how many meetings I've gone to," he said, "or how many of the union's newsletters I've read. I'd been talking about it, though, to other people."

"Talking about what, baby?" I asked, pulling up a stool and placing myself on his left side.

"Organizing hip-hoppers . . ."

"Into a union?" I looked at him skeptically. "You have a better chance of getting your mother to blow my father."

Glen cocked me a disapproving look. "I can see that you're up from your nap. Feeling better, are we?"

"I'm sorry," I apologized, and then spotted something. "Is that what you're looking for, honey?"

Glen was in a section called "Money & Music" that basically reported on big moneymakers and how they—mostly record companies—were cleaning up. It also detailed how individual artists were being taken advantage of, mostly through bad contracts. There was a link to an article called "Contractual Slow Death." It was a history of the record industry's exploitative practices in contract negotiations with artists.

"Hey, that's my piece," said Glen. "Oh . . . now I remember her. She called me up and identified herself as being with the union and asked if I would help her some by either organizing artists or writing something for this site. I gave her this article."

"And that was the last you heard from her?"

Glen nodded and proceeded to the archives, where he found what he was looking for. Nigga Lovin' Records and Black Death had each been purchased by InfoNews for about $100 million, and Big Poppa Insane and Icy D were kept as heads of the firms.

"Now what?" I said. "What have you got?"

Glen thoughtfully stroked his beard. He let out a low sigh and rose from his chair. "I don't know," he replied as he began pacing. There was a picture of Donna, myself, and Anna on the wall. Still sleepy, I rose from the stool to return to my bed and continue reading. Cloudy days make me tired and moody.

"Where are you going?" he asked.

"Back to bed." I yawned.

"I thought you were going to help me figure this out."

"You'll get there." I winked. "I have complete confidence if you. If you want me, you know where I am." I left with the book and some of the articles he had downloaded from the 'Net.

I slipped back into bed and continued reading the passages that Glen had marked about InfoNews; it seemed that Fergus had his tentacles into just about everything. His firm ranked sixth in the world in annual revenues (over $11 billion), and his family controlled forty percent of the firm's stock. Fergus was the role model for the global mogul; his plan was to have—own—every form of programming—news, sports, film, music, kids' shows—and beam it via satellite into every corner of the globe.

Fergus fell heavily into debt during the 1980s in order to start a fourth television network out of an old film studio. Ten years later he had climbed out of debt snatching audience shares from the other networks. He achieved this with a slew of shows centered around narcissistic young Cali babes and studs living in upscale nabes, or nignorant comedy shows that featured buffoonish young blacks, once again wearing brand-name clothes. When HØT TV was securely established, Fergus had dropped the black shows, and developed even more upscale programming to attract advertisers who were looking for that special demographic—whites with disposal incomes.

InfoNews now owned: 150 newspapers in the United States, Britain, South Africa, Canada, and Australia; HØT Films, a major film and television production apparatus with a library of over five thousand movies; HØT TV, the broadcasting network; twenty-four U.S. television stations, making it the largest group of stations in the country and reaching into almost fifty percent of American homes; twenty radio stations in the top two American radio markets; a major book publishing company; a fifty-percent share of another media firm that had stakes in several cable networks in the United States; Eastern Sun Television, a satellite service and television network aimed at the Asian market; controlling interest in various digital satellite services in Latin America, Asia, Europe, and the Middle East (Africa evidently wasn't even considered because it had no significant middle class with disposable incomes); and the recently established HØT MUZIK, a conglomerate of record labels which, once again, appeared to be black-based. And he was looking into the purchasing of sports teams.

The ownership was immense, spread out, and deep, and it was frightening. Fergus had pioneered the model for integrative global media domination, and InfoNews was now one of five media corporations that "controlled" what most people read or viewed and, in effect, thought. The other four were AOL Time Warner, Disney, Bertelsmann, and Viacom. Did I read anything about violations of antitrust laws? No. The pace of mega-mergers had gotten even more out of hand after the passage of the Telecommunications Act of 1996.

The government had deregulated the control of the telecommunications industries and allowed the big boys to gobble up and own multiple media outlets in individual cities, creating a small cabal of firms that controlled the communications apparati of the nation and the world. The power of the government was feared, but no one said anything about these private ministries of infotainment.

The Beast was politically connected as well: Elected officials were willing to do his bidding because he called the shots at media outlets that could easily affect their political fortunes. Even Il Duce, the mayor of New York, interceded on his behalf when Fergus wanted to elbow his way into one of the television cables that had already been franchised to another; somebody else was going to get bumped for Fergus's HØT Cable.

Yet lurking in the background was something that scared even the Beast: MP3, a new technology that could digitally compress music and distribute it over the 'Net without the need for giant record labels. The record industry was trying to figure out how to get it under their control. Some musicians, however, were seeking an alliance with Erik Arendt, the CEO of ÜberMusik, a German concern that was developing its own form of digital music in association with MacroWorld.

Slowly, very slowly, another thought occurred to me: Matucci's words, "Life is a beast." The *Beast*, not the *bitch*. Fergus? What would Fergus have to do with the deaths of SugarDick and Mbooma? Matucci was upset that he had been asked to countenance something that went against his personal integrity as an officer, yet he felt he could not expose it to the public, for that would jeopardize his loved ones who still served in the department. But I couldn't make the connection with SugarDick. If Matucci had said "Beast," meaning Fergus, what was it that Fergus wanted, if indeed it was him? I couldn't make the mental leap from a lowlife SugarDick to a world player like Rolf Fergus. Yet—

I got out of my bed and began snapping my fingers. I was looking for something in the back roads of my mind, trying to make a connection. I pulled a large volume called *The Secret History of the CIA* from my bookshelf and found Fergus's name in the index. When I entered Donna's old room, Glen was standing at the window, looking out.

"Baby," I said, moving over to him, "who was SugarDick under contract to?"

"Big Poppa Insane," Glen replied. "Nigga Lovin' Records. Why?"

I thought for a second. "Was he having contractual problems?"

"*Was* he?" said Glen. "He was leaving Big Poppa. Poppa was ripping SugarDick off and SugarDick wanted out. He was shopping for another label. The Groove was interested and he was sick of that gangsta shit, sick of the life."

"Baby, I got a wild card, a wild fatherfucking card."

Glen's brows furrowed. "What are you talking about, Nina?"

"Matucci was referring to Fergus."

"Fergus?" Glen looked at me carefully. "Are you sure? What triggered this?"

"Reading the book, the book about those media corporations. It dawned on me that's what Matucci said."

"But what's the—?" Glen seemed as confused as I had been moments before. "I don't understand. What's the connection?"

"It has something to do with SugarDick's death—I think. Matucci was upset and I think he had been told to do something in regard to SugarDick and Mbooma. Perhaps fudge the records of witnesses who reported what the suspect looked like."

"But what makes you think it was Fergus?"

"Because the stakes are so high. Look, the prime minister of England went to him on his hands and knees before he was elected. The man owns the world, or at least part of it. He wants it all. And when it comes to dead niggas, you can always get away with that. I think it came down from Il Duce; he tried to intervene once before, as you know. The whole city knows Il Duce is the real police commissioner and not Ronald Blinkon. And besides, do you know how Fergus got his nickname?"

My baby shrugged his shoulders. "His business practices?"

"I thought so too, but not quite, honey," I began. "Rolf Fergus once served in the South African security forces. He got his name because of his specialty."

"What was that?"

"Torturing blacks," I said. "Hey! Didn't Terry Teasdale relent and lose interest in his cable feud with Fergus after Teasdale's son was murdered?"

Glenito thought for a moment and began shaking his head. "Nina, Teasdale's son was killed in a holdup."

"What we *think* was a holdup," I replied. "Some of the witnesses only described the suspect as being black and . . ."

". . . having a scar." Glen snapped his fingers.

"The Beast hooked up with two record owners who are known to have criminal backgrounds, Big Poppa Insane and Icy," I continued, "record executives who are known to make offers people can't refuse. And we do have two dead hip-hoppers who've made millions for them. Their new overlord may be willing to punish those who *don't* want to continue that relationship."

"But Teasdale?" asked a skeptical Glen. "I could buy Headmoe and SugarDick getting whacked by Insane and Icy, because black folks are now programmed to kill each other, but Teasdale's son? He's white, Nina."

"And business is war, my sweet," I replied as I left the room. "Business is war."

TRACK 07

MEETING THE COMPETITION

When we went through the records we found that before Headmoe was murdered, he too was having contractual problems and had been in contact with Valerie Gordon, the AWU organizer. Headmoe was on Icy D's label and wasn't interested in re-signing with Black Death Records. As a matter of fact, he had been taking classes about how the music industry worked and had been counseled by an attorney provided by AWU. He was getting some real knowledge and was beginning to ask questions and talk about it in public.

The criminality of the music industry is perhaps one of the great untold stories of American history, and the whole enterprise has been essentially founded on either the theft of black music forms or the outright stealing or cheating of musicians'—usually black—publishing rights. But this isn't totally out of the view of the public. Books like *Hit Men, Stiffed, Payola in the Music Industry, Mansion on a Hill*, and *The Operator* all, to varying degrees, outlined what a racket the industry is. The supreme irony is that black intellectuals have never studied the music industry, an interesting twist given that blacks have developed various genres of music over the last two centuries but don't control any significant portion or aspect of it. Funny how things work out that way.

Headmoe had been talking about rappers getting organized, stopping the internecine hip-hop war that had been characterized as an East Coast/West Coast thang. But he had been taken out by people alleged to have been associates of SugarDick, and SugarDick, prior to his murder, had been advocating that rappers become more organized and end the incessant feuding. But one was East Coast and the other was West Coast. That was more important to the press than what they had in common, namely, exploitation by the black side of a white-dominated music industry. This was a form of black-on-black crime that was never scrutinized.

But that was Glen's department. I had gone uptown to speak to Murchison, and Glen went out to take care of some business. We agreed to rendezvous later on. Murch and I met at the Metropolitan Museum of Art in the Michael Rockefeller Wing. He was in a somber mood as we walked through the exhibit amid artifacts of the so-called Third World.

"Headquarters is viewing John's murder as a retaliation by hip-hop gangs. Ever heard of something called the Five Points?" asked Murchison. "It's led by a rapper named Radeem."

"What? That's a cover-up, Chuck," I replied. "Ever since Mbooma died, some of your colleagues have been smoking the department's contraband and have been quite interested in tying up neat little packages and delivering them to the press and the public."

"Ever since some of *your* people have lost their ability to control themselves in public places, the department has been watching them."

"What? Now you're profiling rappers?"

"Headquarters thinks that this Radeem has been advocating the killing of police officers. A payback for Amadou Diallo and others who have been shot by the police. There's an underground song called 'Dyin' for da Riddim' and it advocates killing cops just like that other song, 'Fuck tha Police.'"

Matucci's precinct, explained Murch, had been enforcing the mayor's crackdown on hip-hop clubs and breaking up of youthful gatherings with a vengeance.

"Whoever killed Matucci was probably the same person or persons who whacked SugarDick, not some off-the-pigs stuff."

"You have any candidates, Nina?" he asked.

I wasn't ready to drop on him what I had dropped on Glen. I was speculating with Glen and I wasn't ready to share that with Murchison. "I have my suspicions, but it's too far afield—at the moment. What do you know from your end?"

Murchison stopped in his tracks and glanced ahead. Two people were looking at an exhibit of a shrunken head. He jerked his head over toward the large wall of glass that allowed people to look out on the park side of the museum.

"Something wrong?"

Murchison said nothing and led the way over to the glass. As we stood near the huge window, with Murch's back turned to the tourists, he looked at me.

"Are those people still there?"

"Who? Those people?"

Murch nodded his head. I moved slightly and looked beyond his shoulder. "Ah, yeah."

"Keep an eye on them."

"Why?" He gave me a withering look and I said: "Okay . . . okay."

"I spoke to some people," began Murchison. "Matucci had a visitor from headquarters, an inspector."

"Who?"

"That's not as important as who visited the inspector: Babe Volaré."

I puckered up like a buttercup and whistled. "Now, that's interesting," I said.

Bathsheba "Babe" Volaré was the mayor's "special assistant." She had joined the mayor's team, proved herself indispensable, always at his side, and was known to deliver messages that needed a special thrust. Called the *Stiletto Cunt* by those members of the press she had humiliated, she was a former newspaperwoman who had worked at one of Fergus's tabloid newspapers, *The New York Forum*. A pulchritudinous red-haired woman, she was suitably partisan for that newspaper when it came to demolishing Democrats, attacking blacks, and smacking around her "sisters." She had covered a few cases that I'd prosecuted and always thought it was a pity that I wasn't a Republican.

It was rumored that she was Fergus's direct link to the mayor, and that the mayor partly owed his job to the Beast. And there was an even more vicious story: The two, Il Duce and the Beast, shared her favors. That was the sort of story the boys in the pressroom comforted themselves with. They resented how both she and the mayor emasculated and ridiculed them. The fact of the matter was that the New York press corps at City Hall, room 9, was pussy-whipped—and dick-beaten—and they all knew it: the mayor, the babe, and the press.

"So . . . what was the command?" I asked.

"Fuck if I know," said Murch.

"Well, something funny happened. Matucci gets a visit. He quits and is then shot in the streets. Sounds like something to me."

"Then what?" snapped Murchison, his voice on edge. He was giving me a cold, hard look, as if he had come to a nasty conclusion that he didn't want to face.

"Murch, think about this: Why would the mayor send Volaré to an inspector's office, and an inspector who I assume has a political connection to the administration?"

I told him that I suspected something funny was going down with regard to Fergus, and I finally decided I'd relay it to him: the connections between Fergus's InfoNews and certain hip-hop acts; between Fergus's past and the labels Nigga Lovin' and Black Death, with their thuggish behavior toward their artists.

"That ain't worth shit, Nina," said Murch, as if he'd opened a bag and looked in it. "You don't have anything conclusive. Just fucking speculation."

"I'm working off of motive, captain," I replied. "Something that your department doesn't have, while trying to pin these murders on a bunch of brand-crazy hip-hoppers!"

"You're slipping, Nina," he retorted. "Damn, girl, I remember when you used to make a solid case out of less than that. Your boy's lovin' is making you—"

"Look, if you think I'm walking down the wrong alley, here's something to check," I interrupted him. I didn't like that cheap crack about Glen and me. "You go to Matucci's command and see if the witness statements have been altered. My husband didn't positively identify SugarDick's killer, but he did see a scar on his clean-shaven face. He mentioned it to your colleagues. Mbooma didn't have a scar and had a full beard! You go and check it out, brother!" I turned on my heels and began walking, swishing my hips and letting him know who was putting the bounce in them.

"Nina! Where are you going?" trailed Murch.

"Home to get something that you aren't getting from your sweet thang, captain!" I replied over my shoulder.

"Oh, God, girl," sighed Glen. He was breathing heavily. His arms were stretched out at the northwest and northeast corners of the bed, his hands restrained, as mine had been. I was incessantly devouring him. At that very special moment when a man truly and willingly submits to a woman as his lord and mistress, I could feel his muscles contracting in his abdomen and throbbing in my mouth. Baby let out a deep and guttural sigh, a low ferocious growl of satisfaction.

"God," he said, "what are you trying to do to me?" Glen lay back on the bed, glowing in the sweat I produced from him.

"Trying to make you forget about her," I said. I crawled toward him, slowly licking his abs, swirling my tongue in his navel. I wasn't through with him yet. This was a man who could be aroused three or four times in an erotic session when lovingly inspired. I had discovered his erogenous zones and went to work on his nipples, teething them, sucking on them, licking them. Within seconds he was up and running again and I mounted him, my hands braced against his chest. Slowly and deliriously I rode him.

When the phone rang we were enjoying some postmarital bliss, nestling together. Normally we would have let the machine get it, but he heard *her* voice and answered the phone.

"What's wrong?" he said into the mouthpiece.

"Tell her you're married," I said, annoyed.

"*Shhh*," he whispered to me and continued speaking.

I was about to snatch the phone away from Glen when I heard him say, "Don't let anyone in until we get there." He hung up the phone and I angrily sat up.

"What *le* fuck is going on?" I asked, trying to add a touch of elegance to an emerging bad feeling.

Glen heard me but was still processing something. "That was China."

"No shit, Sherlock," I said faux-cheerily. "Tell her this isn't Rent-a-Dick."

"She's having contract problems," said Glen.

"I don't do legal work, Glen. I retired, remember?"

"The way Headmoe and SugarDick had," he continued. "When she arrived at her house, there was someone in her home . . . waiting for her . . ."

"And what?"

"He didn't do anything to her, but he suggested that she 'stay with the program.'"

"Big Poppa's?"

He nodded his head. "I told her that we'd come by."

"What's her problem?"

"She's frightened, Nina, and she needs our help. Besides, a certain someone has been hovering around her."

"Who's that?"

"Baby Cakes. I want to find out what she has to do with this." Glen slid out of bed and began dressing.

I picked up my copy of Brontë's *Wuthering Heights* and started reading. I have my limits. I wasn't going to go down there and defend one of his exes. He stopped dressing when he saw that I wasn't moving.

"Nina, look, the sister's in trouble."

"Well, with a strong brother like you in command . . ." I said, my eyes still on the page.

He snatched away the covers and told me to get my posterior out of bed, that he needed my help and if I didn't get out of bed he was going turn me over on his knees—

I stared at him. This buster didn't know to whom he was speaking. "You wouldn't dare."

She was even more beautiful than I had imagined. China Mercury was gorgeous, but she wasn't acting like some rock bimbo. She had offered me a seat, but my bottom was still a bit sore. Hubby had proven himself a man of his word.

China sat in an armchair and told us how she had come home and found a man sitting in the front room of her West Village town house.

"What did he say?" I asked, looking around the room. It was nicely furnished, nothing ostentatious. Upscale Ikea.

"He said that I ought to stay with the program," she said, running her fingers through her hair, looking distraught. Her almond-shaped eyes reflected how much she had been unnerved by the visit. "He kept saying that blacks had to stay with the program. That we always started off with a black thing and then wanted to go white when we got a little bit of money."

"What did he look like?"

China shrugged her shoulders. "Like any other brother."

"That's not good enough, Miss Mercury," I said.

"Call me China." She smiled faintly. She thought some more and added, "He wore a cap and dark glasses."

"What else was he wearing?"

"Dark clothes. Jacket and pants."

"A suit?" asked Glen, who sat on the couch.

"No, Glenny," she said. "Denim jacket, I think. Jeans also."

"What else?"

China bit her lips and sat back on the L-shaped couch that ran the length of the room. "He had an accent."

"What kind of accent?"

"He sounded African."

"African?"

"Yes, and he had a scar that ran down his right cheek."

My husband flashed me a knowing look, but I still remembered her calling him "Glenny."

"What about this Baby Cakes?" I asked.

"Well, she's been acting like some emissary."

"From who?" asked Glen.

China rolled her eyes and sighed. "From Big Poppa. He wants me to stay with NLR. I said I wasn't interested. I told him it wasn't just about the points."

"Points?" I asked.

"Yeah," said Glen. "It's music biz lingo for percentage of your royalties. Thirteen points is thirteen percent."

"So what was girlfriend doing?" I asked. I was watching their body language, trying to discern if there were any lingering vestiges of desire. I easily saw how they could have been a couple, both so beautiful.

"Baby Cakes was trying to get me back with the program," said China, "telling me that we could help build a strong black record company, and I told her that was my intention in signing up with Groove and not with NLR. Let's face it. The label is practically a criminal organization. I didn't know it at the time, but there are stories about Big Poppa Insane being in the crack business. The way he handles disputes with people . . ."

"And how does he do that?"

"With a baseball bat," said China. "The way he treats some of his female artists . . ."

I watched her closely. "And how does he do that?"

China looked at me and then at Glen and then back at me. "He tries to strong-arm women. Baby wanted me to meet her tomorrow."

"Where at?" I asked.

"At Casbah's," she said. "I . . . don't know what to do."

"Well, are you going to sign with the Groove?" I asked.

"Yeah. I'm just worried about the time between now and then. I sign next week."

"Well, get somebody to stay with you," said Glen.

"What about tonight?"

Glen glanced at me. I was the former security queen, so I got on the horn and called Mustapha. He said that he would have someone over in thirty minutes and that he would make a security assessment of her home the next morning. China looked relieved, but I couldn't help thinking that she would have liked to have "Glenny" as her sentinel of desire.

"Bathsheba Volaré?" said Glen. "Hmmm. Miss Stiletto, huh? Now, that's interesting. What else did Murch say?"

We were sitting at a café on Sixth Avenue, having a bit of dinner before we returned home, watching the denizens of Greenwich Village.

"He thinks that your lovemaking is having a deleterious effect on my forensic capabilities," I answered. I sipped on my hard cider and looked at him. "I think this woman still has a fever for you, Glen."

"China?" He sighed, put down his fork, and wiped his mouth with a napkin. "Nina, I find your jealousy charming, but a bit off-putting. It's not a quality that I admire in women."

"Glen, uh, let me remind you that we were in our home, in our bed, and your friend called."

"My God, Nina, the woman was in trouble," protested Glen. "Don't you help out your friends? Besides, she's helping *us* find out about what's going on. We got a lead on da slut. Honestly, my dear, if this stuff is going to get you bent all out of shape, then I'll just figure it out on my own."

Everything had been nice and easy until Mbooma showed up. I couldn't get away from the past. No matter how hard I tried or how much I wanted to have a normal life, there was always this hand coming through, pulling away what I perceived to be the veil of my happiness. I sat and said nothing, watching a stream of people flow by.

"Well?" said Glen expectantly.

As I was about to speak, my cellular phone began vibrating in a 6/8 pattern. I reached into my trousers' pocket and pulled it out. It was Murchison. I watched the people around me and just listened to what he had to say. I flipped the cover down.

"Okay, my friend, *you're* in business," I said. "That was Murchison."

"And?"

"He went to Matucci's command to check out the witnesses' statements and to look at yours. They are gone."

"Surprise, surprise," he said.

My beautiful one was learning quick. But if we were going to go through with this, I wanted only one thing: I wanted to be the first one to die, because I just couldn't go through another monumental loss. I raised one of his hands to my lips and kissed it.

TRACK 08
BABY CAKES

Glen had gotten up the next morning and gone downtown to cover a demonstration—being held in protest of Mbooma's death—for the *New York Drum*. Mbooma was being positioned as another victim of police brutality despite the fact that he had been seen running from the scene of a crime, a firebombing. He had been shot several times by the police, but he made the list because he had been unarmed. He was a questionable "martyr" in my book and thus tainted the cases of those killed or brutalized by some of the knuckleheads in the police department.

There were people who really had been victimized, for instance a Latino man choked to death by a cop in the Bronx, and another unarmed guy shot on Christmas day by an officer who had discharged his gun eight or nine times on other occasions. And before that there was a Dechoukajian immigrant who had been anally brutalized with a mop handle in the bathroom of a Manhattan precinct. These people were truly victims. Mbooma? I didn't think so.

Of course, I didn't go to the march. I also didn't attend Matucci's funeral. I was still persona non grata in certain police circles due to the circumstances of the late Captain Harold Kirby's death. He had been trying to kill both me and Dexter Pierson, now the editor of the paper that Glen was writing for, in Washington, D.C. Kirby was part and parcel of an old conspiracy and was trying to "tie up loose ends" by eliminating both of us. The suspicion had been so deep that Murch almost didn't get Kirby's job because some of his colleagues thought he had something to do with Kirby's death.

Given that I had been present at John Matucci's death, I thought that it would be better not to attend his funeral. Raised properly and somewhat of a lady, I sent Mrs. Matucci a letter of condolence and offered my services if ever needed.

Glen was getting hyped in a way that I hadn't seen in a while. He was really excited about the smell of blood. When I had told him about Babe Volaré, he saw that as an interesting angle, which, in fact, it was. It was also the kind of thing that couldn't be proven because the principals would deny it. But that didn't stop him. One could conclude that Carlucci, the mayor, the man who always lets you know that he's in control, would not be letting his special assistant deliver messages to the police department without his sanctioning it.

Glen was going to use this, though. He was loving this aspect of journalism, working on a real story, something with legs. I was hoping he'd get back to music. As a matter of fact, given the sort of mayhem that had thus far surrounded the case, uh, *story*—four people dead—I wouldn't have minded if he was working with China, and shtupping her. That would have meant he was safe, at least.

But when we got home that night he was immediately click-clacking on his laptop, prior to lights out and love in.

"Are you really going to write that?" I asked.

Glen took a long drag on some killer Cali rolled into a phat blunt and blew it into my mouth. As I forced the smoke down into my lungs, he kept typing the story I had relayed to him from Murchison about Volaré. We were sitting up in bed, with me continuing on with Heathcliff and Catherine.

"Damn right, *mi azúcar*," he said. "Of course, I can't mention the mayor's *puta* by name, but I can do enough by insinuating and situating to give readers the flavah. Also, I'll let people know that I saw the suspect and that I had reported that he didn't look like Mbooma."

That was when my dear husband began to make me nervous. He could be making himself—us—targets. Il Duce was running an authoritarian regime in NYC; he was getting the crime figures down by any means necessary, and that meant an increase in police criminality. (Even outside monitors like Amnesty International and Human Rights Watch had issued reports on the NYPD's conduct.) The mayor was also holding back reports that ought to go to duly constituted branches of the city government as part of their oversight responsibilities, and he threatened the press corps even while sucking up to one of the press lords (Fergus). He fired low-level employees who unofficially disagreed with his policies. Carlucci had perfected the art of municipal intimidation.

Glen, however, was on the hunt. He could smell blood and was after the big story. It had everything. Dead niggas. Big-time money. A greedy corporatist mogul. Possible collusion between the mayor and the mogul. The mayor's main squeeze acting as a go-between. A murdered police officer who opposed a cover-up.

Years ago, I would have been on top of this if it had come my way as a prosecutor or an investigator, but that was then and this was now. I had been scorched. I had been hot on the trail of a major drug dealer and killer and all it had gotten me was the death of my family. I was supposed to be out of the business, but Glen was pulling me back in and I didn't like the way things were going. I got the distinct impression that it was going to be a mess. And by that I meant blood, dead bodies, and ruined lives. The stuff that nightmares are made of.

Over some damn music? People had to die for the rhythm? That sounded like the kind of death wish that had been cropping up in some outposts of black music. I didn't think Glen was of that ilk, but he could be like so many other reporters and writers, people who get a thrill being around violence and the violent ones.

Anna wanted me to come up and see her at her old apartment, but I called to tell her that I had another errand to run and that I would be there a little later. That was cool with her so I caught a cab uptown—having loaned Glen the keys to my car for greater mobility—to visit the *New York Drum*. I was going to pay a wifely visit to my husband's employer, who happened to be a former lover of mine.

The *Drum* was located in what appeared to be a rejuvenating Harlem. Dexter Pierson had moved back uptown, purchased a brownstone, and was determined to wage a battle for a Harlem being eaten up by "outsiders," but not developed by its residents. The problem was always the ancient one for African-Americans: lack of primitive accumulation. As my late husband Lee once told me, capitalism abhors a vacuum, and there's no reason to expect Harlem to stay black since it hadn't always been black.

I wasn't expected, but Dexter didn't balk at seeing me. He had become a little grayer and had pudged out. He looked happy sitting behind his desk at a newspaper that was making waves and asking tough questions. Like many news offices, his was strewn with newspapers and magazines. It had been about three years since we had last seen each other. We had broken up over the fact that I was a little too close to the kind of action that took away his wife, meaning mayhem.

After exchanging pleasantries, I came out with the reason for my visit: I wanted him to either spike the story that Glen was working on or fire him. Do something.

"My God, Nina," he said. "Why?"

"Because I have a bad feeling about this, Dexter, and I don't want to wind up a widow again," I explained. "Glen isn't going to accede to my wishes on this."

Dexter began swiveling in his chair. "Have you spoken to him about this?"

"Not so much . . ." I responded.

"So why are you asking me?"

"Because I don't think he would listen to me. He might think I was impugning his manhood."

"Oh, I see." Dexter looked at me thoughtfully. "Well, Nina, you *are* a womanful."

"Meaning what?"

"Well, you may give any man reason to think that he doesn't have anything to offer you."

"Look, I'm like any other woman out here."

"Oh no you're not, sister." He chuckled. "Nina, you're an—"

"I know, I know . . . I'm an army of me," I interrupted. "Look, Dexter, Glen and I just got married. SugarDick gets killed and he feels duty bound to try and do something about it . . ."

"And what's wrong with that?" he defended, cheerfully swaying back and forth in his wooden chair. "People should feel some passion."

I sighed. "Look, this thing could get really out of hand."

"How?"

"By getting deeper than anything that he or I could imagine."

"But with you helping him—"

"That's just it, Dexter," I said testily. "The more I help him, the deeper he goes. I really don't want to get involved. I don't want him involved, either."

Ex-boyfriend shrugged his shoulders. "Then don't. You're coming up here to ask me to be a marriage counselor and not an editor. Glen has the makings of a good reporter."

"Look, Pierson, don't start putting on some tough journalism act for me! I remember when you were quite willing to drop the ball!"

My voice grew louder and the two men in the front part of the shotgunned room looked back to where Dexter and I were seated. I wanted to keep this in a civil tone. After all, I was up here to ask a favor.

I noticed that Dexter was wearing a wedding band on his finger. I leaned over on his desk from my chair and saw a photo of him and a woman. This wasn't a photo of his first wife. The first one had been black and the woman in the photo was white. I decided on a new tack.

"Look, Dexter," I began, "I just married this wonderful guy. Why can't you understand that I want the same kind of happiness and chances that you have? You and I have both lost loved ones to violence and all I'm asking is that you at the very least honor a request of mine." I lowered my voice: "I kept your confidence. No one has ever known otherwise about your giving me the Tower film."

Suddenly Dexter stopped swiveling and peered at me. Any sort of mirth he had momentarily displayed now disappeared.

"I've resigned from being an investigator. I'm no longer in my legal practice. I have grave doubts about being effective as a teacher," I confessed. "The only thing that gets me up in the morning is this crazy, sexy, cool musician I married. We're even talking about having children. I don't want him dead, Dexter. Can't you understand that? Is that such a foreign concept?"

"No, Nina, it isn't," he said sympathetically. "I understand how you feel . . ."

Praise the Lord. I was going to start going back to church.

". . . But I'm running a newspaper and I can't allow personal feelings to interfere—"

I flipped. I screamed something—I don't know what—and reached across the desk and found my fingers around his neck.

"Get off of me!" he yelled. The two men in the front room pulled me away from Dexter as papers slid from his desk and his computer crashed to the floor. I knocked over a lamp as they dragged me out screaming and kicking. It was my finest moment.

"And then what happened?" Anna poured a shot of strong bourbon into my tea.

"They just deposited me on Convent Avenue," I said wearily, leaning back on her couch, wiping my eyes. "They could have tried to have me arrested, but then Pierson would have to tell the courts the whole damn story of how he punked out on the Tower thing."

"Nina," said Anna, "you really think this stuff is going to blow up?"

"I don't know, Anna. I just don't want to take the chance." I sniffed and wiped my eyes. I had been crying all the way down to Anna's place. Her spacious apartment had gone from being a nice comfy abode to a small gallery—with the furniture moved out—to being an apartment again. She had been in the middle of unpacking her stored items when I arrived.

"Look, it's one thing to have a passion about your art," she began, "but Glen and this music thing? Having you sleep with him *and* his saxophone? That's beyond kinky, girl. That's fucking weird. And you know what comes after weird in my book?"

"What's that?"

"Sick."

"Don't say that!" I protested. "He's a good man."

"A good man can be sick, Nina. Perhaps it would have been better if you hadn't talked to Dexter. Suppose Dexter tells Glen what happened?"

"I doubt that," I said. "He thinks that Glen is on a big story that might put the *Drum* on the map."

"Is it that big?" she asked, moving from the coffee table that she was sitting on to beside me on the couch.

I told her about what Murchison had discovered, about Glen's statement missing at the police station, and about Babe Volaré telling an inspector to visit Matucci. Matucci walked and was then murdered. Anna let out a low whistle.

"Oh, shit."

"Yeah, I'm not saddling up and leading a cavalry charge, Anna. I just want to sit back and relax with my man. I'm having a good time." I began crying again. "What's wrong with me, Anna? I just want to have a family and a nice life. After what I've been through I wouldn't mind a *reasonable* amount of trouble."

Anna pulled out leaves of tissues and handed them to me. I wiped my eyes.

"So, what's doing with you? How's Ranza?"

An embarrassed look came over Anna's face, the sort of look which could mean an embarrassment of good fortune. "I'm pregnant."

"Who the *fuck* by?" I asked, not wasting any time in being delicate.

Anna said nothing.

My hand went over my mouth. "Esperanza?"

Anna smiled and nodded. "Usually it doesn't happen with people in her condition, but . . . uh . . ."

"Anna, that's wonderful! Oh, girl, I'm so happy for you!" I hugged her. "That's the best news I've heard all day! What about Esperanza? We'll go out and celebrate—"

"*That* was the good news."

"What's the bad news?" I asked.

"She doesn't want it," said Anna. "She wants me to have an abortion."

The A-word. That, along with affirmative action, Israel and the Arabs, and a small host of other subjects, bores me to tears. I looked at her. "You're kidding?"

Anna slowly shook her head. She rose from the couch and walked barefoot into the kitchen to retrieve the bottle of Tea That Burns. When she returned, she poured us each two more fingers of bourbon. Anna sighed and kicked it down. "Well?"

That was a cue for me to do the same, and I did.

Anna explained to me that Esperanza, the *madrina*, a hermaphrodite, was a traditionalist after all.

"Meaning what?"

"She thinks that a child should have a mommy and a daddy, not two mommies. Ain't that a kick in the head?" Anna poured herself another one and drank it. "She told me that she loves me but she could not be the mother of a child that she hadn't given birth to, and she doesn't feel masculine enough to be its father. When I told her that I wanted the child *and* her, she left. Hot, hot passion cools down to smoke and ash."

I was flabbergasted. "Esperanza walked out?" I snapped my fingers. "Like that?" What could I say? "I'm sorry, Anna."

Anna shrugged her shoulders. "I'll have some crummy nights, but I'll get over it . . . I think."

I nodded my head slowly. "What about the . . . ?"

"The baby?" She held up the glass. "Well, I'm kind of a traditionalist, too. Children should at least have two parents. I'm not ready for that by myself. I don't think any woman should go through that by herself. I know it's the thing to do, but I'm just not the sort of person to do it by myself."

"Amen."

Anna's fist went up to her mouth and she slowly shook her head. A tear streamed down her face. I put my arm around her and she laid her head on my shoulder and we held hands. "Annie, I'm sorry."

"The supreme irony," sighed Anna, "is that with Esperanza being as she is, I was getting used to being stroked without a dildo. I was beginning to enjoy the real thing again and I thought I had it all worked out, Nina. Didn't I say the best of both worlds? A woman with a dick and no male attitude? And then she does the ultimate, she leaves me because she doesn't want to be a father and a mother. It's just a little too deep for me, girlfriend."

"You know what's wrong with us?" I asked.

"No, what?"
"We're just a couple of fucked-up babes."

I would have stayed uptown all day and spent the night with Anna. She was my pal, my sister, and we had gone through wars together. I felt that she had been very much alone ever since she came out. Her family had distanced itself from her because she was gay. She was building up a coterie of new friends, but they hadn't gone the distance with her as I had. Anna was an integral part of my life. She was family. Anna had come down to Misercordia with me and I felt responsible for the way things had turned out. I was shocked that Esperanza would walk out on her over something like that; I guess I didn't know her very well.

But Anna wanted me to go home and work things out with two people: Nina *and* Nina. She felt that I was trying to control things too much and that I had to "go east," which meant do nothing and let things sort themselves out. There was no use in both of us acting as if we were widows or abandoned women. I did make her promise not to drink any more liquor even if she was going to abort. The fetus deserved not to be pickled. She agreed to that.

I trudged out of the subway and walked home and tried to notice it was spring. The sun was out and I should have been happy about that. The pungent smell of male urine hadn't assaulted me yet. Some guy was selling abandoned novels and I discovered a relatively good copy of Gore Vidal's memoir, *Palimpsest*. I gave the grizzly bookseller a couple of dollars and went about my business.

As I was about to enter my apartment building, I heard a car stopping and turned to see a taxicab. A woman was paying the cabbie and when she got out she looked at the building's address and then at me. She was petite and walnut-complexioned, and she wore her hair straight, as so many young black women are wont to do these days. A pair of sunglasses masked her face and she wore an obscenely bright red plastic raincoat. I proceeded into the building as she rushed up the stairs.

"Excuse me," she said in a slightly Brooklyn accent. "Do you know if Glen Sierra lives in this building?"

She was quick. I had entered the building but still held onto the door. The woman was also holding the door, and at that point I noticed she had on lipstick as bright as her coat and displayed a pair of earrings made out of dollar signs. They looked as if they were gold, and that certified her as a tacky denizen of the People's Republic of Brooklyn.

I peered at her and said that he did, that he wasn't home, and that I was married to him.

"I need to speak to him."

"He'll be playing at The Place tonight."

"Yo, I need to speak to him *now*." The young woman, whom I took to be no more than twenty-five, looked over her shoulder and seemed nervous when cars passed by.

"You didn't hear me, my sister," I said firmly. "He's not in and will be at The Place tonight. Nine P.M."

She smiled. "Do you who know I am?"

I wasn't interested in speaking to a refugee from an old American Express commercial. I shook my head and said no. I was about to close the door, but girlfriend got real huffy.

"Bitch! Don't close that motherfuckin' door on me!" she snarled.

With being addressed like that, I was steadily on my course and definitely trying to close the chapter on her. However, girlfriend had this quaint conversation piece: a 9mm pistol that she pulled out of her plastic raincoat. She pushed the door open and forced her way in, with me backstepping, holding onto my literary purchase of a few moments ago.

"I don't want to hurt you," she said. "I need to speak to Sierra. It's important. Motherfuckin' important!"

I tried to calculate the precise moment to snatch the gun away from her but remembered that Anna and I had been drinking and that meant my reflexes were slowed. I decided that I would go upstairs, make some coffee, and then throw her out of my window if I had to.

With the gun in her coat pocket, she followed me upstairs at a good distance, not getting in the way of my foot. I opened up the fort and Glen wasn't in. When he was on assignment he usually wouldn't come home until hours before a gig, and that was to pick up his horn and, uh, get "re-acquainted" with me and our needs. I walked in and tossed my purse on the sofa and turned to face her.

"Okay, I have a rule," I said, my hands on my hips. "If you're in my house and have a gun, you at least have to identify yourself."

She whipped off her sunglasses and shook her head in a white-girl fashion, getting her locks flowing and flying. She cocked her head in b-girl fashion and announced, "I'm Baby Cakes!"

"Baby Cakes!" I gushed. "Girl, you lay down some wicked rhymes. Glen be saying your shit is . . ." I snapped my fingers twice. She smiled. We bonded.

I held out my right hand to shake hers. She took it and I yanked her toward me and clocked her with a tight left cross. She fell on the floor, her coat flying open, exposing a sheer black body-stocking suit with a gold floral pattern.

TRACK 09
A SMART GAL

After depositing the flattened Cakes on the couch to let her get her beauty sleep, I pulled the gun out of her coat pocket, popped the bullet out of the chamber, and yanked the clip from the handgrip. I added it to my collection with Mbooma's heater. I placed it in an enveloped marked "*To the police for destruction*" and locked it in a strongbox. Back in the living room, I checked on my guest. She was curled up on the couch in a fetal position and had placed her thumb in her mouth while still unconscious. I shook my head: She was someone else's daughter.

In the kitchen I turned the flame on under the kettle and made some coffee for myself. When Glen walked in I was leaning against the wall unit that housed books and the music component, sipping a cup of French roast and staring at the woman-child who had been packing a nasty little piece of metal. Glen had a serious look on his face and told me that he had spoken to Pierson from the street and that Pierson had told him what happened. Before I could respond our guest started to moan. Glen turned and saw Baby Cakes laid out, sucking her thumb.

"What is she doing here?"

"Looking for you, sweetie," I answered between sips of coffee. "How was the demo?"

"The usual suspects," he commented as he turned toward me. "How long has she been here? Why is she out on the couch?"

"She had a gun and demanded to see you," I told him. "I have a no-gun policy for strangers in my home and I proceeded to, uh, *disarm* her. I might add that by the way that she's dressed you may be in trouble." I raised an accusatory eyebrow.

"What does that mean?" Glen frowned. He pulled out his notebook and a tape recorder from his coat pocket and set them on a shelf behind my head.

I told him that she was wearing only a body stocking beneath her coat. "Only," I repeated.

Glen rolled his eyes. "Is that all? She's known to walk around in a bikini and a fur coat during winter while she's on a shopping and sucking spree. I want to talk about your little uptown escapade. What's getting you bent out of shape, Nina? You're beginning to worry me."

Sighing, I told Glen that I'd seen too much in the last few years and that I wasn't wrapped too tight. "You're the best thing that has happened to me in a long time and I'm afraid of losing you."

"And you don't like me on this story, is that it?"

"Darling, I know trouble and this thing has trouble written all over it." I nodded in the direction of the snooze queen on our couch. "Look at her. She came busting in here with a gun."

"Maybe she's in trouble, Nina."

"Exactly, Glen. I don't want it in my home or in my life."

Glen took the coffee cup from me and held both of my hands, looking deeply into my eyes. "Nina, I'm slowly beginning to realize that you're a very . . . complex person . . . and . . ."

He glanced over his shoulder at Baby Cakes; she was still unconscious. Glen then led me by the hand over to the kitchen. We didn't go too far into it; he wanted to keep an eye on her. "It distresses me that my work bothers you. If it's not this story, then it's something about China Mercury."

"I'm sorry, Glen, but I'm crazy," I admitted. "That's why I wanted out of this business."

"And I'm taking you back to where you don't want to go . . ."

I nodded. "I love you very much and I'm just scared. Once upon a time it wasn't a question of fear. I did what I had to do, but now . . ."

Glen peeked out and looked at the girl on the couch. "But what?" he asked when he returned his attention to me.

I knew what I wanted to say, but my lips failed me. "Just hold me, darling."

Glen wrapped his arms around me and I felt so small and safe and secure. "Sometimes, Nina, you seem like such a child."

I smiled. "Some men do that to me."

He caressed my face and kissed both my hands and palms. I swooned. I wanted him to take me right there, against the kitchen wall, but I decided to save that for dessert. He asked me if we had any amyl nitrite; he wanted to wake her up. I told him that I had a first-aid kit in the closet and I would get it for him, but first I wanted a kiss, and it was a sweet and soulful one that was interrupted by the sound of glass breaking and something bouncing on the floor of the living room.

Glen stepped out of the kitchen and I was behind him. Frantically, he jumped back, pushed me into a corner of the kitchen, and covered me with his body. The explosion ripped through the entire living room. Various items in the kitchen tumbled off the shelves and flew every which way. An old family heirloom, a waffle iron, slammed into my head before it crashed onto the floor. The force from the explosion also knocked out the kitchen window and showered the floor with a thousand shards of glass.

The living room was heavy with smoke and upturned, destroyed furniture. I could hear voices outside the apartment as Glen and I made our way through the smoky, burning room. We were coughing, the crooks of our arms over our mouths. The windows had been blown out and the wall unit was lying across the floor, blocking our path. The couch had been thrown across the room and we found her, pieces of her, near the door and in another corner of the room. It was her severed head that did it for me. Her flayed skin and singed hair made her head look like a grotesque basketball with blackened eyes.

I kept it together until we made our way outside the apartment and onto the landing. My neighbors were standing in the hallway, wondering what had happened. All I remember was seeing Lee, Andy, and Ayesha's bloody bodies again. I passed out in Glen's arms. I knew it was coming. I'm a real smart girl and I knew it was coming.

TRACK 10
CODE Z

Needless to say, it was too late to stop now. Someone had bombed my home, and that was an act of war. Oddly, I felt strangely serene. I had expected the worst and it had come—and we had both survived it. I couldn't say that for Yvette Watson, the late Baby Cakes. But if there was any consolation, she, too, like SugarDick and Headmoe, would enjoy a phat death. Her fans would pick up her latest CD, coincidentally titled *Nasty to Death,* and she would be heralded, once again, as one of the heroines of hip-hop, regardless of the fact that all she ever talked about was getting shtupped and sucked, sipping champagne, and wearing fur coats and diamonds. Undoubtedly, a real heroine. I had no doubt that her album would become a big hit and make Big Poppa Insane a richer man, and that would make his new overlord, Fergus, even wealthier.

She had always claimed that she was putting on an act, being a "slut bomb" as opposed to a sex bomb, and was about receiving pleasure as well as giving it. I doubt if she had bargained on her demise this way. I didn't think my family would get wiped out when I was prosecuting Nate Ford, either. And I definitely didn't think someone would fire a grenade into my little happy home in Chelsea. But all that had changed.

When I finally gained consciousness, I realized that I had been hoisted onto Glen's shoulder and

I could see the apartment building receding in the near distance. Smoke was billowing out of the windows. He was heading to my car, my black four-wheel-drive. When we made it to the vehicle he slowly let me down and leaned me against it. I mumbled something about going to my office.

"What?" He was holding onto me, opening the door to the passenger's side and noticing a cacophony of sirens. Police cars and emergency vehicles were turning the corner onto our street.

I coughed and told him that I needed to go to the office and pick up a special attaché case. "I need to get my protocol files, Glen."

Glen helped me into the car. I was still groggy, but I noticed that he was holding his horn and something in a blue pillowcase. He just wanted to get away from the scene. I was insistent about us going to the office.

"Not now, Nina!" He turned the key in the ignition and I gripped his arm as he was about to handle the stickshift.

"Goddamn it, Glen! When are you going to listen to me?" I snapped. "I told you to get me to the office! Now do it before the cops haul us in for questioning! Do it now! NOW!"

Realizing that he had married a madwoman who happened to know what she was talking about, Glen did as he was told. We drove down Seventh Avenue and made a turn at Fourteenth Street to get to my office. I told him to reach underneath his seat where he would find a small, magnetized box. He pulled it out and handed it to me. I told him to keep the engine running and that I wouldn't be long. I got out of the car, ran up the stairs, and removed the keys to the office from the little box.

I ran into my smaller office, into a closet, and used another key to open up a safe that was embedded in the floor. I pulled out a black leather case and a black aluminum case, closed the safe, locked the doors, and bounded down the stairs. I opened the back passenger door and placed the aluminum case on the floor behind my seat and brought the leather one up front with me.

"Where to?" he asked.

"Connecticut. We're ditching the car there and then doubling back to New Jersey—maybe."

"Okay, you're the boss." He sighed and pulled away from the curb.

"I wish you had that attitude a couple of days ago, my *pet*," I said tersely. I placed my elbows on the case and rested my face in my hands.

"Are you blaming me for what happened back there?" he asked.

"No, honey, I'm not, but . . ."

"But what?" Glen was agitated. I had to remember that he was probably reacting to the sudden introduction of a dead body into our happy home, and the reality that we were almost killed, and would have been killed had we stayed in the living room. Although you would have thought that he had gotten used to it by now. After all, he did see SugarDick and Valerie Gordon dead. But no two people handle death the same way. Granted, I passed out and he had soldiered me through, hoisting me up like a marine in 'Nam or Iraq. The tone of his voice was slightly accusatory, but I had been trying to tell him . . .

I breathed slowly. "No, but I knew this was coming and you wouldn't listen to me. I don't blame you, honey. I just wish you had dropped this thing so we could have gone on with our lives in a more pleasant way. Now . . ."

"Now *what*?" Glen kept his eyes on the street traffic as we drove east to the FDR Drive. We were going to head north to the Bronx—the only part of the city that is actually attached to the mainland—and then make a connection there to Interstate 95 and on to my brother's place in Connecticut.

"I don't know, Glen. I have to figure this out. I know I passed out. But did you check the rest of the apartment?"

"Kind of, sort of," he said. "While you were out I laid you to the side and had a neighbor watch after you. I went in to get my horn and a few other things. The other rooms were okay. Some things knocked on the floor, but no general damage."

"That's good." I thought for a second. We were leaving the scene of a crime and we could get tagged by the police for that. On the other hand, we didn't commit the crime and could make an argument that we feared for our safety. I was concerned about Glen's work. The cops may try to seize or destroy it, just as things had been missing at Matucci's command. I had no illusions about the police. I understood them as a paramilitary force that had its own political agenda and competing power centers.

The fact that an inspector had come down and delivered the word to an honest cop like Matucci, who then wound up dead, made me reluctant to deal with them further until I knew what was going on. I was the last of the independent operators and that meant I had to put my plan into action to save my own black ass and the black ass of my handsome but naïve husband.

After about an hour on the road, I opened the case with a key and pulled out a small, thick book the size of a Filofax. It was a book of protocols and procedures that Mustapha Kincaid made us develop—Anna and me—in case of a situation like this. It was very tedious work to put it together, but it made us think through and plan for an emergency or a very radical change in circumstances—and that bombing rated a *Code Z*. And that's what I told Anna when I called her.

Given that we resided on the third floor of a four-story walk-up, I assumed that the grenade or missile, whichever it was, had been fired from the building across the street, either from the third or fourth floor, or possibly from the roof.

"Are you two all right?" she asked. "Where are you guys?"

"We're fine, but somebody else didn't make it." I told her about the young woman. I also said that we had left town.

"Why, Nina?"

"Anna, I don't trust the police," I replied. "Surprise, surprise."

"You think they did it?"

"No. The cops aren't that stupid. I suspect the same people who are taking out the other hip-hoppers, but I don't know for sure. Listen. I'll call you from where I'm at. Take your phone and get in touch with people on the Z list and tell them to stand by."

"Gotcha," she said. "Take care of yourself and Glen."

"What's a Code Z?" Glen wanted to know after I ended my call.

"That's when an attack occurs and you either have to retreat to a safe house or go underground."

"Are we going underground?"

"I'm not walking around in the broad daylight with this shit going on!"

He glanced at the attaché case. "Who's on the list?"

I shook my head. "I can't really tell you. You don't need to know."

"What, you don't trust me? I'm your husband."

"It's not that, love of my life. Security. There are other people who are involved and they hold high-profile positions, and they may need to be protected from retaliation."

We had gotten on the FDR before the beginning of rush hour. Other than the bombing and the death of Baby Cakes, it was a nice day. As we drove I paged through the protocols, looking at who was available for what and thinking through what to do. I have a place in upstate New York that we could head to, but didn't think it was wise to go there. The safer place was Connecticut. Ditch the car and pick up a new one. I might have to have new IDs made for us.

"What else is in there?" asked Glen, pointing with his chin.

"Cellular phone. Listening monitor. Handcuffs. Protocols. Two 9mm pistols," I rattled off. "In the other case are a laptop and an electronic surveillance monitor."

"Pistols?"

"Yes, dear. His-and-her matching set."

"It's that serious, huh?"

"Glen, didn't you see that girl's severed head?"

He grimly nodded as I placed a clip in one of the guns. "The one on the right is yours—"

"Mine?"

I stared at him. "You do know how to use a gun, don't you?"

"Yeah, but, uh . . ."

"But what?" I put a clip into the other and placed it back in the molding that held it in place. I closed the case after putting the protocols back in. As the car headed north, Glen kept stealing glances at me while I tried to figure out the moves and countermoves of adversaries I had yet to recognize. "Don't worry, I only use them if I have to."

"You folks are really organized, huh?" he finally said, perspiration forming on his forehead.

"Yep. Some of us aren't sitting around and waiting for affirmative action programs to continue," I replied. "We've *read* and *know* our history."

Something was beginning to whir in Glen. He had the sort of look that a man gets when he truly realizes the kind of woman he's been sleeping with. A querulous expression sprouted forth. "Nina, have you . . . uh . . . have you ever . . . shot . . . ?"

"Baby, your devoted wife has gone beyond just shooting people."

"You mean you've *killed* people?" Glen kept his eyes on the traffic.

I merely nodded, and refrained from explaining the circumstances: I had when I rescued Veronica Thorn Martin in a hospital, and down in Misericordia when Anna and Esperanza had been kidnapped. Things went bang-bang. "All in the line of duty—and survival."

He said nothing for a few seconds. "We're in this shit deep, aren't we?"

I slammed the dashboard with my hand. "Yes, Glen! We're in it up to our motherfucking necks! And I'm tired of it! You may like playing Nick and Nora, but I'm not wild about the idea of having to leave my home once again because of a dead body! I've gone up in the world, though. Now it's strangers and not family members. God is shining on me!"

"I'm sorry, Nina. You're right. I wasn't listening and I thought that this would be just another story . . ." He stopped. "I don't know what I thought . . . Whatever, I should have just dropped it, but . . ."

I crossed my arms and tried to think about what I had to do, and about us. "Well, I accepted you for better or for worse, and I suspect that this is about the worst it is going to get."

"I'll make it up to you," he said, his hair flecked with dust and debris. "After this . . . whatever you say . . . but you have to understand something . . ."

Hmmm, I thought. I began calculating the date nine months from now. He cleared his throat. "About to tell me something?" I asked.

"SugarDick was on a mission."

"Honey, I don't think this is the time for you to explain Sugar's motivation to me," I replied.

"No, Nina, I'm not talking that shit," he continued. "SugarDick was trying to *save* black music."

"*What*??!!" reverberated and echoed throughout the car. "I think we ought to concentrate on saving our own asses! Do you remember what we just came from? Somebody blew up my apartment!"

Glen looked at me with a serious expression. "That may explain how we're onto something."

"Yeah, we're onto getting our asses wiped out!" I countered. "Look, I'm not into this cavalry cowboy shit!"

"Now he's dead. Once again, some people have to die for the rhythm. We ought to carry on the fight in his name, in the name of the rhythm!"

"What are you talking about?" I broke in. "*Dying for the rhythm*? It's a musical form, Glen! Not a religion! All for some stupid music?"

"The music isn't stupid!"

"In *my* book, when it costs people their lives and any sense of proportion, it is!" I argued. "Besides, it's too late to save black music. The major labels have already gobbled it up. You've read the *Harvard Report*! That happened thirty years ago!"

"No! You're wrong. Rap and hip-hop represent, to some degree, the emergence of an autonomous black youth nation," he reasoned. "It has the power to transform! If the Jews once had a media empire of their own, Hollywood, why can't we have one based on our people's talents!"

"Perhaps, in a perfect world . . ." As far as I was concerned, it was too late and a dead issue. Baby Cakes was but the latest example of a music that ate its young.

"You just don't understand, Nina," he said, shaking his head. "You just don't."

"Keep your eyes on the road." I thought about what he'd said. I listened to the music but never considered myself part of the hip-hop nation. I'd always thought that black people were one nation under a groove, but Glen was now telling me something different. There was an autonomous youth component. Maybe he was right: I just didn't get it.

When I finally turned my attention to the passing countryside, I realized that we had arrived in Connecticut, with its prim and neat Norman Rockwellesque little towns, miles away from the neon squalor of Nuevo York, the Big Mango. I wondered what deep, dark secrets these people were keeping from each other behind the walls of the large-frame and expensive houses. My own dark "secret" was sitting next to me and I was in love with him. But I realized there was a part of me that was alien to him. I just didn't get it.

TRACK 11

SIESTA SEX II

We drove around to the back and parked the car behind the old nineteenth-century Connecticut mansion that was the home of my brother Gary and his family. Glen followed me through the back door that I opened up with a spare set of keys. It was spring break and Gary and Miriam had taken the children to Europe while he conducted some business on the Continent. We had the place to ourselves and that meant we didn't have to explain our sudden appearance to anyone. I nodded my head in the direction of the front of the house and Glen followed me with one of the two cases I had taken from my office, along with the blue pillowcase he had brought from the apartment.

We passed through the large dining room and then entered the living room. I placed the attaché case on the couch and Glen unloaded himself, placing his items on the carpet near one of the two easy chairs that flanked the couch.

"Now what?" he asked as he stood in the center of the room, looking around.

I told him that I was ready for a drink and where he could find the liquor in the kitchen. Glen left and I wearily sat down on the couch. I opened the case and pulled out the cellular and dialed Anna. I picked up the remote and turned on the television for the news. Anna was also watching the news when I reached her.

Everything was more or less okay—if you discounted the late Baby Cakes. The police wanted to speak to us. No surprise about that. The police suspected that a person or persons fired a grenade into my third-floor window by way of a grenade launcher or some kind of small bazooka from the building across the street. Then the news report produced an interesting twist: Glen Sierra was suspected of being aligned with a group of outsiders—the union project?—who had been instigating the feud between the East Coast and the West Coast rappers. Also, the police had found a cache of guns—the two guns I had taken away from Mbooma and Baby Cakes—and both of us might be part of an anti-gangsta fundamentalist group called Black Jihad.

"What in the world are they talking about?" asked Anna. "This is Character Assassination 101! Who's spreading this sort of stuff?"

"Now you know why I don't trust the police department," I replied. "Okay, girl, this is what you have to do."

Anna took down her instructions. The game plan was to have her represent Glen and me to the media and the public. If the police were leaking this kind of stuff about us, we would have to fight them on *our* terms. As our attorney, she was to hold a press conference in my office and lay out our story and the reasons why we would not appear before the police. We had questions about the way they had handled the investigation of SugarDick's death by blaming it on Mbooma.

"I don't know," said Anna. "That's not going to wash with the press. You need Murch to back you up on this."

"Murch isn't ready to quit the police force," I said. "But if you make the link or imply that Carlucci's administration has a history of suppressing information to the press . . . to the public . . ."

"Hmm. That might work," she responded, savoring the possibility.

I told her that I'd call later and that I would draft a press release and e-mail it to her at my office. I turned off the television and leaned back into the couch's pillow. "Hey, Black Jihad!" I called out.

I waited for Glen to reappear and then thought I heard something. It sounded as if it came from upstairs. I listened again and was about to head to the foot of the stairway.

"What did you call me?" asked Glen, who brought in the drinks.

"Black Jihad, honey," I replied in my native D.C. accent. Glen sat on the couch and I took my drink from his hand. "To Black Jihad."

"What the hell is that?"

"That, my dear, is the deep black conspiracy that we—urban Bonnie and Clyde—are said to be members of. Rumored."

Glen turned himself around and stared at me. "What are you talking about, *azúcar*?"

"There's a rumor going around, supplied by the cops, that we belong to a fundamentalist group called Black Jihad." I sipped my drink. Glen crossed his legs and folded his arms against his chest after setting his drink on the coffee table. I placed my drink down as well and pulled off my shoes.

"So what happens now? They shoot us on sight?"

"No, baby, it doesn't work like that," I explained. "They will shoot you, the black male, on sight."

"And what about you?" He poked me in the side.

"They'll gang-bang me." I laughed. "Bang the bitch." Glen kept poking me and the next thing I knew we were wrestling on the couch. I was giving him his money's worth and we tumbled onto the carpeted floor, tickling and wrestling, until I heard that sound again.

"Wait a minute, baby," I said, trying to calm down from laughing. "Did you hear that?"

"I know your tricks, Nina." He grinned, pinning me to the floor.

"I'm not kidding, Glen. I heard something."

"Like what?"

Before I could reply, we both heard the sound of footsteps above us. Glen looked at me and let me go. I placed my finger to my lips and told him to take off his shoes.

The house had two more floors upstairs. Glen and I, both armed, slowly made our way up the stairs and checked the rooms on the second floor. There was one more room at the far end of the hallway, and as we approached it, we could hear movement. We stopped and listened. The door to the room was cracked open. Cautiously, we proceeded. Glen stood behind me as I quietly began opening the door.

I carefully listened and my ears soon adjusted to what sounded like heavy breathing. Slowly, I pushed the door open wide and saw a woman, a white woman, going down over a large black man who looked remarkably like my father in the throes of ecstasy. When the blower pulled her hair from her face I immediately recognized Delores Sierra, administering the specialty. I quickly backpedaled, but Delores caught a glint of me out of the corner of her eye and screamed. I quickly shut the door and pushed Glen away.

"What's going on?" asked Glen.

Before I could answer, Big Earl had fired two rounds through the door. I pushed Glen back against the wall.

"What the fuck?" gasped Glen.

"It's our parents!" I said, holding onto him.

"What?"

"It's Daddy and your mom," I said. "Daddy!" I cried out. "It's me, Nina!" I waited a few seconds. "Daddy, it's me and Glen!"

The door slowly opened and Big Earl filled the doorway. He had on a robe and held a gun leveled at us and was glowering.

I smiled sheepishly. "Care to join us for drinks?"

Understandably, Daddy was slightly annoyed. First, the two of them had been caught in *flagrante delicto,* and then he had fired on us. But what had really shocked *me* was seeing Glen's mother with him, and judging by the way that she was sitting next to him on the couch—and by the way I had seen her moving on him—she truly seemed to like him. Well, why shouldn't she? Daddy was a handsome, robust man in his seventies. The fact that he had only a white swatch of hair surrounding the back and sides of his head didn't detract from his rugged good looks. With his white cookie-duster mustache, he looked like the photographer Gordon Parks.

While they had been dressing upstairs in preparation for coming down, I tried to talk to Glen about this situation, but he didn't appear to be interested in the implications. I remembered him calling her a racist, but now I wondered about that.

"Nina, don't be naïve," he said, inserting a corkscrew into a bottle. "A person can fuck another of a different race and still be a racist. I don't know about the vulva, but a stiff dick has no conscience." Glen twisted the corkscrew and slowly pulled it out with a loud pop. "Delores fucks black but usually marries white. Maybe she's getting one of her routine infusions of blackness. Anyway, your father seems to be the kind of man who may be familiar with her type: white slut. Shall we join our esteemed predecessors?"

When we arrived in the living room they were sitting on the couch. We placed the wine, cheese, apples, and crackers on the table. It was kind of awkward. Glen and I were married but Daddy and Glen's mom were having some sort of hot romance. Big-time sensuality. It is always surreal when you realize that your parents had to engage in sex to bring you here. And then there was the interracial dimension. I also couldn't get over the fact that Delores was white and Glen was very dark. He has a sort of just-stepped-off-the-slave-ship complexion. Well, so much for genetics and the dispensation of one's DNA.

It seems that Daddy had driven Gary and the others to the airport and had met Delores in the city, and they had decided to drive up to Connecticut to spend a quiet weekend in the country. Daddy had parked his car in the barn that doubled as a garage.

"What are you two doing out here?" asked my father when he tore himself away from his overripe sex kitten.

"We're on the run from the law," I said, with an ironic undertone.

Taking that as smarty talk, Daddy looked at me and turned to Delores. "Nina has led a very complicated life."

He didn't get the point and I was glad.

"Is that so?" said Delores. "Well, we professional women are always torn between home, career, and children."

Delores, as I'd suspected, was a former actress on *telenovelas*, but had parlayed her fortune gathered from her TV years into a series of television and radio stations in the Caribbean and Latin America. She was one of the very few Latina executives in the telecommunications industry and she was up here, from Miami, for a special event: InfoGlobal.

"What's that?" I asked, sitting across from them in one of the armchairs, sipping my Merlot. I had poured the scotch Glen served me earlier down the sink.

"Oh," she said, "Rolf Fergus wants to meet those of us in the minority markets."

Glen and I exchanged looks. We were vibing on the same received information. Oh, the power of male-female bonding.

"At first, I was interested in attending, but . . ." Delores lovingly looked at my father and ran a well-manicured finger along his jaw-line. Daddy smiled.

"Well, Earl made me an offer I couldn't refuse . . . A weekend in Connecticut—"

"Alone," emphasized my father. He looked at me closely and made sure I got the idea. Out of *la casa, amigos*.

"So you're not going, huh?" I asked. "Won't be attending InfoGlobal?"

"No, no." She pouted and shook her head. She appeared leisurely stunning in a red jumpsuit that accented her shape and displayed a wicked cleavage. She had that thick sort of frame that some black men like, particularly of my father's generation. Men of his time called it "healthy."

"I might have one of my people fly up from Miami. Mr. Fergus has a hotel suite waiting for me."

Suddenly, the man in my life saw an opening and took it. "You know, Mother, if you like, I could go and represent you."

A wide smile appeared on Delores's face. "Would you, Glenito?"

"Why, certainly, Mother. You deserve a break and I can see that you would much rather spend the time with Señor Earl."

"I've been trying to get this young man to take an interest in this business for years!" she said to Earl and me. A happy mother, Delores rose from the couch and went over to Glen and plopped herself down on his lap and began showering him with kisses, talking to him in Spanish. This was Glen's punishment for taking a filial interest in his mother's business.

I was slightly taken aback (and aroused) by her overt expression of parental affection, but then Big Earl opened up the humidor on the table and took a cigar from it.

"Nothing like family life," he said, as he lit up the smoker and perhaps began thinking of what he was going to resume with Glen's mother when we left. I knew where his head would be.

TRACK 12

BABY CAKES'S GREATEST HIT

A change of plans occurred under the cover of night. Hours later we had returned to the Big Mango in a different car and parked in a garage on the west side. I wanted to head down to the office via taxicab, but the explosion had been big news and was a repeated theme throughout the evening's newscasts. I began to rethink going to my office. It was only a matter of time before the cops would come in, if they hadn't already pitched a lookout on us. Delores had called the hotel where her room had been reserved and told them that her assistant, her son, was coming in her stead, with his wife. Normally that would have been a problem, but when the conference was being organized by Rolf Fergus for *his* guests, nothing was out of the question.

I figured that we had to pick up some things to authenticate that we were coming from out of town. I didn't want to be seen at Anna's, and that would have been my first stop. I also thought about the Situation Room at Mustapha's store, but didn't want to risk exposing it. We needed a place to retreat to, and Glen came up with the perfect suggestion.

China Mercury's town house.

Considering what had happened in the last four or five hours, I wasn't going to worry about her. Glen placed a call to her and it was a done deal. We took a subway downtown, got off at Christopher

Street, and moved westward until we came to her house. We pressed the buzzer and Bass, my cousin from D.C., opened the door.

"China told me that you were coming," he said, rooting a toothpick around in his mouth. Bass was another one of those "big guys" on my father's side of the family. "Never a dull moment when you're around, cuz."

I introduced Bass to Glen, his new cousin-in-law. My "competitor," China, came into the living room and warmly greeted us. She embraced Glen and then me. She was wearing an overflowing, ecru-colored, Arabic-looking robe—with some hefty cleavage. (All the girls must know about this aspect of loungewear, I made a mental note.) I suddenly felt shabby. I had good reason to be, but it unnerved me that she was looking so fresh and vibrant while I felt hounded.

"I want you two to feel at home here," she said. "As you know, Glen, *mi casa es tu casa*."

"*Gracias*," said Glen. "We need to clean up."

"Of course," replied China. She then led us upstairs to a guest room in the back.

Glen went first into the shower and I called Anna to let her know that there was a change of plans, and that Glen and I both needed a change of clothes for a conference at the Universal Hotel. We had picked up some jeans and shirts while in Connecticut, but we both needed luggage and more businesslike attire. Anna knew what to do and whom to get the items from. She already knew my clothes sizes, but I had to step into the bathroom while Glen showered and get his specifications. By the next morning we would have all that we needed.

After the phone call, I stripped off my clothes and stepped into the shower with my husband.

"What's with the clothes size?" he asked, offering me a squeeze tube of soap.

"We can't show up without the proper accoutrements of the status quo, honey," I told him, as I squirted some liquid soap onto my hands and then lathered up my face, neck, and shoulders. Glen was finished, but he remained in the shower for a few seconds and scrubbed my back. He then left and I continued alone, thinking about our next moves and vigorously rubbing off the dirt that I felt was etched into my soul as well.

Moments after I stepped out of the shower I was looking at myself in the mirror, wondering if this current situation warranted a radical change in hairstyle. My face had been blasted over the newspapers once before, when Lee and the children were murdered. I'd been photographed on my knees, imploring God over the death of my family. Now, as seen in the windows of some electronics stores, my face and Glen's were being bandied about on television. In those images, my face had been darkened and my braided hair hung like tentacles. I was a black Medusa wanted for questioning by the NYPD.

"Honey," I called from the bathroom, "I think we may have to go deep undercover on this." I thought about cutting off my braids. I was lifting them and trying to figure out my line of attack when it occurred to me that Glen had not responded. I stepped out of the bathroom. Glen wasn't in the bedroom. I grabbed a towel and wrapped it around my torso and stepped back into the room. Wondering about Glen, I was about to leave the room but heard two voices from the hallway, Glen's and China's. I couldn't make out what they were saying, but they were speaking in hushed tones. Quickly, I skipped back into the bathroom and took my position in front of the mirror. In a matter of seconds Glen returned to the room.

Glen had on a white terry cloth robe that I hadn't noticed before, but he also had something else, a cassette tape.

"What's that?" I asked as he closed the door.

"China told me that this was given to her by Baby Cakes."

I arched an eyebrow.

"Yeah," said Glen. "That's what I'm thinking." On the nightstand there was a tape player–clock unit. He opened the deck and placed the tape in. "China said that she had been hanging out at some club in the Village when Baby Cakes came up to her asking for me. Cakes knew that China and I are friends so she slipped her this and left." Glen activated the tape player and we listened:

> *Yo, Sierra, this is Baby Cakes. You know me. I'm the fly chick who said she'd blow you for a good review and you said, "You certainly don't think too well of yourself."*
>
> *Anyway, listen up. I'm sending you this tape just in case I don't see you. I've been up here in Bronxville—not the Bronx—at Bobby Whyte's house. He threw a huge party for some of the players in the record industry and all the big-time niggas were there. Not just in hip-hop but in R&B. Carl Judson, Tommy Thomas, Greg Watini, as well as Big Poppa Insane and Icy D. Anyway, Bobby Whyte, who by the way is a fucking faggot even if he do design some fly shit, hosted a party for them. Guess who was there? I was introduced to this friend of Bobby Whyte. People say he be one of the most powerful men in the world. Rolf Fergus.*
>
> *Now listen, I know some people in hip-hop be getting killed and I ain't got nothing to*

do with that shit. Poppa asked me to talk to them about coming back. I told you that SugarDick wanted to speak to you about something. That was a lie. Big Poppa knew he was meeting some people from a union and the union was starting trouble and he knows that you had talked about that also and accused him of ripping off hip-hoppers. Anyway, I think he knew something was going to go down and he wanted to get you all together. You know what I mean?

China called me after you and your wife came to visit her and told me that some dude was in her house and he wanted her to get with the program, but, look, I'm not into this killing shit. I don't want people to think that I'm setting people up and they get whacked. That be bad for my reputation. You know what I mean? Baby Cakes is about good times and feeling good and all that. I ain't into that violence shit. That's Headmoe and SugarDick's stuff. Look what happened to them!

So anyway, Poppa wanted me to come and put on a show for the people at Bobby Whyte's. Telling people that I'm the future of R&B and hip-hop. I came there and hung out and there was all these people there. Guys going into rooms with some of the gals and some of the guys going into rooms with other guys! Yo! Tori Sluddge would love this shit! I think this Fergie is also a big freak. People call him the Beast. Poppa said he has certain needs that only black women can supply. But I ain't sucking no white motherfucker's dick—even for points!

So anyway, I found this real cute dude and we started foolin' around in one of the rooms and then the door opens up. Big Poppa steps in with this Fergie dude. This Fergie dude has this strange accent and he tells Big Poppa that he couldn't go along with some of the recent eliminations that had taken place. Fergus said that things were getting too risky and that he didn't want Babe involved.

I was really scared. I left the room with the dude I'd been with and then I heard Poppa behind me. He was with some African dude, a guy with a scar. He wanted to know where I'd been, and when he saw me near the room I just left, this African dude pulled out a pistol with a silencer and shot the guy I'd been with and then told me that he would kill me if I said anything. I was screaming. Poppa told me to shut up and I did. He and this Africa dude took me to a room and I stayed there for a while. I got out when I enticed the nigga who was guarding me to come in and give me a smoke. We got to talking and

I told him that he was cute and I zipped down his fly. I started rubbing his dick and acted like I wanted to shoot some tongue, but I grabbed a lamp and whacked him and took his piece.

I got down to the street and caught a cab to a friend's crib in the Bronx. I had to tell this story. They been looking for me. They called my mom's place and have been talking to my friends. Word. You been writing about this shit, so I'm telling you. In case I don't see you, you know something about the sick shit that's been going on.

I tried to get Andre to help me, but he said I was on my own! Do you believe that shit? I had that nigga's baby and he acting like he don't even know me! If I don't make it, I'm saying that Big Poppa Insane put his dogs on this bitch!

I looked at Glen. "Who's this Andre?"

"Andre Taliferro," said Glen.

He switched off the tape player and sat on the bed, digesting what Baby Cakes had left him. I started snipping off my braids one by one in the bathroom, thinking of this new variable. What made this even more interesting was that Delores had with her a list of participants at InfoGlobal and Andre Taliferro was one of them. Ta-dah.

Andre Taliferro was the slickest of the slick. Positive proof that all one needed was the will and a scheme. When small black firms began selling "urban couture" to wannabe ghetto heads, A.T. figured out that there was a market for those items in white, middle-class kids who loved to dress black and buy black things, particularly music. Through market research he had also discovered that certain classes of blacks would pay more for brand-name items, and he was able to take this information to white firms that wanted a larger market share for their products. The trick was to market their products to the black consumer class. Once established, they could then concentrate on the real money: whites.

It was Taliferro who put Bobby Whyte's Anglo-Saxon, prep-school motif in the mind of every gang-banga in the 'hoods of America's urban Bantustans. He got Bobby Whyte to give away his clothes to people like SugarDick and Headmoe, who were then seen wearing oversize shirts with the ubiquitous *B/W* logo. Bobby Whyte apparel shot up from being a minor $4 million company to a $38 million firm in three years.

That made Taliferro a conceptual guru and he refined it until he came up with a masterstroke: niggacool™. What was niggacool™? No one was quite sure. It was Taliferro's concept and company, but what did it produce? What service did it offer? Pure attitude. Or it was, as one person put it, "strategic vapor marketing."

When major firms wanted a black theme or wanted to signify blackness, Taliferro was called in; he and only he could tell if an ad was . . . niggacool™.

Taliferro was credited with infusing the 'hood with ghetto glamour: Bald-headed brothers in Armani and Versace suits were ready to do business, dripping with diamond and gold rings. Sistahs with chemically refried hair and DKNY outfits were acting out their Terry McMillan fantasies. Nigga gang-banging was out and the return to the Godfather aesthetic was in; it was a total-empowerment fantasy trip that some blacks could relate to, especially those who had nothing but their dreams to sustain them. Those already in power were using various mechanisms to maintain it.

The emergence of niggacool™ underscored a reality that very few blacks were ready to deal with: Black culture had been hollowed out. It was no longer about a people's way of expressing themselves through language, folkways, and customs. The artifacts of everyday existence had become cultural products. That was dead, the culture; it was now a product. The nostalgia over the civil rights movement had become a product; some blacks had taken to reading insipid spiritual inspiration books—more product. Black America, as a whole, had become merely a product.

It was now a spectacle that was constantly resold to blacks (and to whites), but they didn't own the means that were producing the show. Black folks had become either glorified employees of those who owned the show or passive consumers of it. And you didn't need a Ph.D. to figure out who owned the show. The same people who owned us, or those who had more or less usurped the previous owners.

Andre Taliferro was a very successful New Age Negro at the age of twenty-five. Short, corn bread–colored, he had a perfect, haughty laugh. He was seen at all the "in" places, escorting and shtupping all the hottest, blackest babes. "I got a thing for black women," he told a multiculti magazine when asked why he *didn't* date white women. "And I now have my choices. Besides, I already have that white shit in my blood."

It was rumored that he was hot for China, but she would not give him the time of day. He was into having beautiful things but didn't appear to appreciate beauty in and of itself. China was an aesthete and he was one of the new vulgarians.

"What are you thinking about, Glen?" I asked. I was still busy snipping off my locks. I had sent Bass out to find me portable electric hair shears. I was going incognito.

"This thing is getting deeper than I thought," he said, somewhat perplexed.

I stepped out of the bathroom and looked at him. "You wouldn't listen to Mama. We could have had a nice life making love all over the planet, but you wanted to play cop-a-rama, be Wally Re-write of the *Nigga News Beat*. Now we have SugarDick, Headmoe, that girl from your union, and Baby Cakes, all dead."

"You left out Mbooma," he said.

"The cops killed Mbooma, sweetheart," I reminded him. "Oh yeah, John Matucci."

"Oh, yeah . . . Who do you think killed *him*?"

"The same fatherfuckers who rearranged our home, gorgeous. And they could be frontin' for the police or other parties." I stepped back into the bathroom and resumed my laborious task, singing "Mama Didn't Lie." Snip-snip, here . . . a snip-snip there. I hadn't realized how thick my locks had grown since I let them go natural. Unexpectedly, I discovered a streak of gray that began at my hair-line and continued to the back of my skull. The thickness of my locks had kept it hidden, but it was now in plain sight. Then a thought occurred to me and I stuck my head out of the bathroom. "Didn't you go to school with the high priest of niggacool™?"

"Yeah. Crown University," Glen replied. "We graduated from the same class but didn't run together or hang out. What about it?"

Standing in the doorway of the bathroom I thought for a moment. "That's your mission. You get this guy in a corner . . . and find out what he knows. He knew enough about something to wash his hands of Baby Cakes. He'll be at this InfoGlobal thing and I bet he's signed on with the program, like Insane and Icy."

"You think everybody has signed on with Fergus?"

"Baby, you know as well as I do that *your* people believe that white folks are the eighth wonder of the world, and they won't do anything to establish their own economic base without asking whites for permission first. Even Mr. Civil Rights, Reggie Baxter, is giving the invocation. The mayor is going to be there telling everybody what a great place New York is now that he's locked everyone up. Well, at least if they are black . . . Baxter will be begging for money."

"You mean lining his pockets," he corrected.

When I came into the room, Glen almost screamed. I had finally lopped off all my braids and had about two inches of a choppy, modified hairdo. I snapped my fingers. "Oh, this would be perfect for China," I thought out loud as I ran my fingers over my hair.

"What?"

"Sic her on Taliferro. Isn't he crazy about her?"

"Yeah. But she can't stand his corn bread–colored self."

"Honey, the girl loves you and she'll do it for—"

"Nina, I'm flattered that you think that I'm the still the object of Miss Mercury's affections, but there's only so much a woman will do for a man. And there are some things that I wouldn't even ask a friend."

I crossed the room, found another terry cloth robe hanging in the closet, and put it on after returning the towel to the bathroom. I marched over to and up on the bed, stood above Glen, placed my foot on his chest, and lovingly *and* menacingly looked down at my truly beloved.

"Look, when we got married I retired!" I exclaimed. "Now you have gotten us—me!—knee-deep into this! You get that *puta caliente* to talk to him! She doesn't have to blow him, but she better use what she has to get what we need! *¿Tu comprendes*?"

Ever alert to my low threshold and taking advantage of his inferior position beneath me, Glen began caressing my thigh, pulling away the robe and revealing the taut muscle of my leg, showering it with hot, needling kisses.

"And what's that, *mi azúcar negra*?"

"Information," I gasped, before I floated down to him. Whatever operational authority I was trying to establish was deliciously shattered.

TRACK 13

THE LESSER OF TWO EVILS

It's amazing, the twists and turns of this jagged thing called life. Forty-eight hours ago I was eluding the police because my apartment had been bombed and I was thus forced to run to my brother's house in Connecticut, only to discover my father boffing Glen's mother (actually it was *she* who was actively engaging him). Then I had to take refuge at China Mercury's in order to prepare to infiltrate a party that was being hosted by Rolf Fergus that Delores Sierra was going to attend but had decided instead to stay with my father at my brother's place. And having my toes wondrously sucked . . . Talk about sexual blitzkrieg. Plus, I had discovered my very own doppelgänger.

Now I was seated in the private jet of one of the legends of American music, Mohammad Ibn, known as "the Pasha," the president of Fez Records, en route to France. It was then that I realized that I was finally being afforded the kind of solitude and peace of mind that I'd wanted, the very reason I was trying to get out of the business. I listened to the humming engine of the Learjet and gazed out the window, intermittently seeing the Atlantic below me as we soared above the clouds.

The Pasha excused himself and went over to his workstation to attend to some matters. He was still slightly shaken from the assault I had just rescued him from. It only underscored what he had said earlier at the Universal Hotel: The music industry was being taken over by a vicious class of criminals employed by Fergus. Blacks had sold themselves out just as surely as Africans had sold other Africans into slavery. That, of course, made him no friends among black executives who were waiting to bend over for the Beast.

I couldn't help but be amazed at how one set of circumstances melded into another. Glen and I were trying to figure out what was going on with Fergus's InfoGlobal, and by my stepping in and getting a couple of hoodlums off the Pasha, he was now leading me to what could be a prime source of information. The trick was that I had to come to France with him to get it. I'd told Glen that I was going to seize the opportunity and take the Pasha up on his offer.

It was a queer feeling not having Glen around, and it made me realize that we had been together practically 24/7 since we had first made love and been married weeks ago. I sat back and closed my eyes. I wanted to get some sleep, but my mind kept wandering over the previous days' work, and the shenanigans . . .

At China's town house, Bass had brought me some electric shears, and I trimmed my hair down to a half-inch after my initial rough cut. In all my years, I'd never worn my hair so short. Usually, I kept it either long naturally, relaxed for the mainstream look, or locked into braids. Now I had a somewhat petite Afro, and I liked it. It did make me look different. It was one less thing I had to worry about in the morning.

Glen zipped his mane down to the same length as mine and took off most of his beard except for a goatee. As a decoy, we both donned bogus eyeglasses: I wore a pair of gold-wired ones and he took up a pair made of tortoiseshell. Nouveau buppies. Glen looked much younger without his locks and his full beard. As a matter of fact, he looked like a boy with a young beard. I tried to get him to sit on my lap, but he got a big attitude about that.

"I'm just teasing, sweetheart," I said. "You're so cute." I tried to pinch him, but he not-too-playfully slapped my hand away.

"Look, I don't need to hear that kind of shit from you," he snapped. "That's Delores's department."

"Huh? What do you mean?"

"Nothing," he said hurriedly. "So what's the game plan?"

"We're waiting for Zee's arrival with a car to pick us up and get new IDs, clothes, and luggage." It was ten o'clock and we had eaten our breakfast with China, after she got over the initial shock of seeing both of us radically altered. I guess it was a particular shock for her seeing Glen. I could easily imagine her gripping his headful of locks the way I had when he went down on me, pressing his face deeper into my moist crevice of desire.

Glen was pacing the floor of the living room while I read the newspapers. Before we came down for breakfast we had drafted and e-mailed Anna our statement of events concerning the explosion at our apartment. We felt, our statement said, that the police were incapable of doing an impartial investigation due to Glen's missing statements at Matucci's command, statements that had clearly identified SugarDick's killer as someone other than Mbooma.

Glen was going through one of his primordial male moods. Pacing and preoccupied, he was trying to figure things out. I wanted to know what was going on in his mind, but he wasn't making me privy. Oh well, living together is largely a matter of getting used to the other's ways and not taking things *too* personally.

I suggested that he go upstairs and practice on his horn. China returned to her ground-level office. With them gone, I pulled out the C-phone and dialed Anna at my office. She had our statement and was getting ready to receive the men and women of the press. I told her that Glen and I were going to hole up at the Universal Hotel and that some particular threads were there for the plucking.

"Such as?"

"Well, for one, Baby Cakes mentioned Andre Taliffero cold-shouldering her, so he must know something about what's going on."

"Who's going to talk to him?" she wanted to know.

I told her that Glen had a secret weapon that no man could resist: China Mercury. Taliffero was hot for China and she might be able to get him to loosen his tongue.

"Okay," said Anna, not too convinced. "Uh, Murch called me this morning."

"And?"

"He wants you to come in for questioning."

"He's got to be kidding."

"I think he's under a lot of pressure," said Anna. "The police know you two are friends and . . ."

"And they want him to deliver the goods. I'll call him—"

"Don't you fucking dare!" said Anna forcefully. "Are you out of your mind? The cops are probably waiting for you to call him. Murch is the last person you should be speaking to."

"You think Murch would set me up?"

"Nina, the guy's a police officer and they may be breathing down his neck. The hell with maybe. They *are*."

Something must have gone down. "What do you know?"

After Murch called her, Anna had contacted Sergeant Michael Segundo, a police officer and president of Cops of Color, Inc. (COCI), called "Cocky," a fraternal organization of minority police officers that challenged the police department on many issues. Anna handled some of COCI's complaints in court regarding discrimination and departmental forms of harassment when certain black and Latino officers spoke out.

The word was out that the department was looking to see if Murchison was a team player and that he was under pressure—minor infractions that would normally be overlooked were now being considered detrimental to his career advancement—to bring in yours truly, at least for questioning.

"Murch was checking out some things about Matucci's death," I said. "He did verify that Glen's description of SugarDick's killer is missing at Matucci's command."

"Good. He can make that statement on your behalf in front of the press." Anna wasn't going to have any residual sentimentality. When she was in her lawyerly mode she could be as tough as nails.

"Look, Anna, Murch may be feeling isolated."

"Then let him go see a fucking departmental shrink! Nina, this is no time to be harking back to our old Brooklyn days when Murch used to swagger into our office. You're the one who doesn't want to talk to the police, and I say forget about talking to Murch because he's trying to save his own goddamn neck! Don't even think about it. As your attorney, I say stay away from him, Nina. You and Glen have enough stuff to contend with. Let me take care of things from my end."

"Anything else, pal?" I asked.

"Nothing, really—oh, this is the latest news in the sordid affairs of the late great SugarDick," she said. "He had been deemed one of us."

"What do you mean?"

"SugarDick is—was, excuse me—gay. It's all over the media."

"Glen is going to love this," I replied, pinching the space between my eyes.

Anna went on for a few seconds about what a sick puppy SugarDick was until I told her that he and Glen had been friends.

The story, according to Anna, was cruising around the 'Net and was first circulated by "Toxic" Tori

Sluddge, "Negro Rumor Mistress Extraordinaire," as she bills herself on her website, [The Sluddge Sheet], and her hit cable show, *In Your Face!* Sluddge could definitely give a libel lawyer a hard-on, for she was always discussing the reputations of HNICs, making insinuations about their peccadilloes and goings-on. It wasn't that she was critical of them but that she, too, had seen something that Taliferro understood: a market. But this was one for scurrilous black gossip.

Now that any meaningful black politics or movement had been hollowed out, the new black middle class was drowning in a sea of commodities. They wanted something to meditate on and [The Sluddge Sheet] and *In Your Face!* were perfect vehicles. They were slick, nasty, stupid, and vicious, perfect for today's aspiring Negro class. She had gone after rappers who "talked street but sucked dick" and exposed several of them with a glee that would have pleased Torquemada, Spain's grand inquisitor. SugarDick was now a posthumous target.

There was nothing more to say. I had to tell Glen that SugarDick had finally been outed. I told Anna to keep me informed about any other developments in regard to the bombing or Matucci's killing.

"Will do," said Anna. "By the way, what handles are you going under at the hotel?"

"Eduardo and Alexis Sierra-Vargas," I replied, using my middle name and Glen using his middle name. "Okay—I'll . . . Oh, I'm forgetting my manners." I suddenly remembered that only yesterday Anna had told me about her being pregnant and breaking up with Esperanza. "What about your world, my dear?"

"I'm reconsidering my situation," said Anna.

"Yeah . . . Meaning what, dear?"

Anna was silent. "Well, someone offered me their hand, so to speak . . ."

"Who?"

"La Bomba."

"Magdalena VillaRosa?" I said loudly. "Wait a minute, girl. Wait a minute, Anna."

"She can't conceive, Nina, and she wants to have a child and a family."

"Tell her to rent one," I said, not too sympathetically. "Anna, don't do anything . . ."

"Well, since I have *you* and your stud husband for clients, I can't readily make it to Planned Parenthood, girlfriend. Listen, I have to run. Your phone is ringing and the show is about to start. Good luck and I'll talk to you in a while, right?"

I said yes and signed off. Magdalena VillaRosa and Anna Gong? Something didn't click about that. Luckily, I didn't have to think about Anna too long because Zee arrived with a car to chauffeur us to InfoGlobal. She entered the living room with a suit of clothes for me and Glen, but stopped in her tracks when she saw the newly shorn Nina.

"Now I know why you asked for that extra something," said Zee, handing me a garment bag. "Merciful Allah, you look regal, Nina. A nice job. Very Africano. The haircut accentuates your high cheekbones."

"Thanks," I replied.

I gave Glen's garments to Bass and he took them upstairs to him. I went into a bathroom down the hall and slipped into my standard black suit and red blouse. When I came out, Zee handed me a pair of black pumps. She then gave me a yard of Ashanti striped-weave fabric and I placed it on my head and folded and twisted it into a gelai, a headdress that some West African women wear.

Zee bowed her head. "Your Royal Highness."

"And ooga-booga to you, sister." I then picked up the wire-framed glasses and put them on. And attached some ivory earrings that represented some vague Yoruba icon.

The former army officer nodded approvingly. "No one will know it's you, Nina, and God knows they been blasting yours and Glen's faces on the news."

"That's the point, my sister," I concurred. "So after you drop us off at the hotel, who's our back-up? An executive like Señor Vargas needs an assistant."

Zee pointed to herself. "Me."

I shook my head. "I can't ask you to do this, Zee. You now have a husband. Besides, you've already resigned from the military. You don't need another operation like this."

"I wouldn't think of having it any other way," she protested. "Ibrahim argued with me. I told him that it would be my last time, but you were attacked in your home and it is my duty to accompany my sister and friend. This is the last one for me, too. *Inshallah*." At this point I finally noticed that Zee was dressed in a woman's navy-blue blazer, a white blouse, and black watch-plaid trousers. She had assumed the part.

"God willing," I said. "Thank you, Zee." I walked over and hugged her. I thanked God that I had such friends, even crazy ones, who cared about me. While embracing Zee I realized that she was wearing a holster. She was ready to rock 'n' roll.

"Father has prepared the Situation Room," she said, "and it's on standby."

"Good," I replied. "So, how is he, your father?"

Zee broke into a full smile, her dark features glowing. "He's very happy, and proud. I'm with child, Nina."

I was momentarily speechless. Babies were popping up all over. "That's wonderful, Zee. Congratulations. I'm sure Ibrahim is elated."

"Supremely so. And that's part of the reason why he protested so vigorously." She smiled. "If it's a girl, we're naming her after you."

A multitude of different emotions swirled and surged through me. I felt honored, but also sad. And I'm quite sure some of this appeared on my face, prompting Zee to ask: "What's wrong, Nina?"

"I'm just shocked . . . kind of." I turned my attention to the attaché case Zee was holding. "What about IDs?"

Zee searched my face for a few seconds and then lifted the case from the floor, set it on the coffee table, and opened it. She had prepared a whole roster of bogus credit cards and false IDs. Two passports were placed inside leather passport holders. She handed me two envelopes of mad money, a thousand dollars each. She also gave me a file on Rolf Fergus.

"Anything interesting?" I asked, skimming through the dossier.

"He has CIA contacts," Zee informed me. "Has been and may still be an asset."

"Now why doesn't that surprise me?" I replied ruefully.

I closed the file and placed it back in the case. This was going to be interesting, but not as interesting as the news that my two closest friends were carrying children, while here I was ready to saddle up and be about something I really didn't want to do. It didn't seem fair. This is what I get for not going to church, I thought.

"Let's get this show on the road," I announced. I put two fingers in my mouth and whistled loudly. I patted Zee on her shoulders. "Excited about being a mother, hmmm?"

"Yes." She smiled, but then the smile quickly disappeared. "But I can see that it is troubling you."

"Me? Oh, no, Zee, I'm very happy for you and Ibrahim . . ."

"But?" queried Zee, eyeing me carefully.

"I just heard from Anna and—"

"She's pregnant."

"Oh, so you know," I began, "and she's been—"

"Thinking about aborting it," said Zee, shaking her head. "She called last night and we talked about you and Glen, what has to happen, and then I told her that I was pregnant and she said she was as well."

"Do you know by whom?"

Zee nervously shifted and began tugging one of her dreadlocks. "Yes. I didn't think that such a thing was possible, but Esperanza was—is—a hermaphrodite. I was flabbergasted. She looks like one of us. In the sauna, she looked like a . . ."

"She *is* one of us, Zee, but with a little extra," I reflected. "Yes, an interesting combination of father and mother. But she doesn't want the child. Anna just told me that Magdalena wants her to keep the child . . ."

"I told her it was the lesser of two evils," said Zee, "so to speak."

"The lesser of two evils?" I echoed.

Zee didn't approve of Anna's alternative lifestyle—that is, being gay—but she had accepted it early on because Anna was my friend and, other than that, she wasn't any different from us, except for being of Chinese heritage. Also, the two of them had then become friends, and people tend to make allowances for things when it pertains to their friends. It seems that Zee told Anna that it would be better for all—Anna, Magdalena, and the unborn child—if Anna accepted Magdalena's offer of partnership and domesticity, particularly since Magdalena couldn't produce a child and wanted one.

"Zee," I said, "do you know what you're countenacing? This isn't the sort of thing that one could find a teaching or a law about in the Koran. Am I right?"

"I know, Nina. If this had been presented to me weeks ago I would have shook my head and said nothing, but this is about a child and the possibility of some sort of family." Zee shrugged her shoulders. "I don't know, Nina. Suddenly the world looks different when you start taking certain things into consideration. Sometimes one does have to be flexible. The demand for consistency is often the hallmark of an unimaginative mind."

"Who said that?" I wanted to know.

"Oscar Wilde," remarked Zee, as she closed the attaché case.

TRACK 14
NIGGACOOL™, OR THE END OF BLACK CIVILIZATION

I felt a jolt and instinctively gripped the armrests. "Whaa . . . ?!" I cried, waking up from a semiconscious nap, remembering my conversation with Zee before we left China Mercury's town house. It took me a few seconds to remember that I was traveling fifty thousand feet over the Atlantic Ocean on my way to France.

The Pasha put down his *Financial Times* and calmly looked at me. "Slight turbulence, my dear. There's no need to worry."

Rubbing my eyes, I looked out the window. It was dark. "How much longer before we land in Paris?"

"We're halfway there, Señora Vargas," said the old man, who continued watching me rather than going back to his newspaper. The Pasha was an owlish-looking man in his sixties who sported a white Vandyke that gave him an interesting appearance, a combination of roguishness and sagacity. Behind rose-tinted eyeglasses, he peered out from a set of hooded eyes.

"How did you get into this business, Señora Vargas?" he asked, with a slight Egyptian accent.

I half smiled. "That's a long story, Mr. Ibn. A very long story—"

He shrugged his shoulders and ruffled the newspaper loudly as he folded it. "I've read enough about making money today. Let's talk about you, young lady. We have lots of time, my dear. Would you care for some tea?"

I accepted the offer, but my thoughts turned back to the preceding hours that led up to this unscheduled flight.

"This is going to kill SugarDick's father," said Glen as he paced around our imperial suite on the twentieth floor of the Universal Hotel. The spectacular view of the city's southern vista was somewhat consoling. I'd told Glen the news of SugarDick's outing before we left China's. He knew that it was only a matter of time before it became public knowledge, but it was *who* had reported it and *how* that incensed him. The fact that Toxic Tori Sluddge had done it infuriated Glen.

"She's pissed because she blew him in a club and everybody knew about it," sneered Glen, as we watched her deliver her darts on the TV screen. "Tori's a frustrated starfucker. She had a sex panic when she learned that he was gay."

"Yes," explained the woman with big hair and garishly long nails on the screen, "the Sugar was sweet in more ways than one." Relaxing in a bathtub of bubbles, pampered by negroid beefcake studs who poured her champagne and handed her faxes, Sluddge delivered her report from her opulently large bathroom. "Yes, boys and girls, SugarDick, a.k.a., Darryl Mont, was another homo hip-hopper who thought that by bashing bitches he could cover up the inner bitch within. In short, he was frontin'. Frontin' big-time. Yes. He was keepin' it real—in the closet. Yours truly had been hearing about this for years and had even been threatened by the late big-dick wonder, but now one of his former lovers, who'll testify to his—hand me my towel, dawg—"

I couldn't stomach any more of it and turned off the television. Glen took his cellular phone out to the terrace and phoned his mother to get some further business instruction. Zee and I watched him; his head hung low as he spoke to her.

The two us turned our attention to InfoGlobal. We had just finished checking out the rooms and phone lines for electronic surveillance devices and were sure that the room was clean for the time being; we would check it again when we got back later. I assumed that a man like Fergus would like to know the thoughts of his business guests.

"Primarily, we're here to check out Fergus and see what's going on with his global thing," I informed Zee. "But Andre Taliferro is also here."

"Yeah," said Zee, "I saw his name listed in the brochure they gave out—niggacool™?"

"The wave of the future, my friend," I responded. "He was mentioned by the late Yvette Watson, Baby Cakes, and may lead us to piecing together what's going on."

"What do *you* think is going on, Nina?" she asked.

I leaned back on the elegant couch. My eyes did a fast sweep of the crème-colored room with gold trimming. The suite was imperiously large and it fit the ego and image of the global titans who commanded the new world order. The living quarters of the suite had another set of rooms that included a bedroom with a king-size bed, a master bathroom that any woman would kill for (with a large oval bathtub for decadent and sinful luxuriating), plus a physical-fitness room complete with Nautilus equipment and a treadmill. The suite also had an office that included the latest computer and telecommunications equipment that no cybertitan could exist without. Plainly, these gods didn't have to come down from the clouds to sweat and strain with mortals.

"Fergus, it appears to me, is after the world and is consolidating his empire via music, especially black music," I finally said. "From what I've been able to learn, by way of Glen's research, he's been buying up black labels that want to get paid in full. Some of these firms, particularly the hardcore gangsta labels, were already involved in drugs and violence. They are at the point where they want to go legit, especially thugs like Poppa. They can funnel their illegal money through a legitimate corporation."

"And Fergus doesn't care?"

"Who's going to stop *him*," I asked. "The United States government? I read a list of his contributions to Congress from the Center for Public Politics, and in my opinion, he basically *owns* portions of the government!"

"How does SugarDick's killing fit in?" she asked.

"I'm coming to that, Zee." For a second I gathered my thoughts and then tried to explain another part of what I'd been piecing together. "It seems that SugarDick and others were resisting coming back to their old labels under the same conditions as before. Headmoe, Big Time, and SugarDick were all advocating new technologies called MP3 and Napster. They allow you to digitally compress music to files that you can send over the Internet and directly to a listener, cutting out the record labels. SugarDick, Headmoe, Big Time, and others were big moneymakers for their labels, but were slowly figuring out that they were getting ripped off instead of getting paid. SugarDick was murdered at the same time that he was seeking help from the American Writers Union, which had a special project that was trying to organize rappers. The woman who was found with SugarDick—"

"Valerie Gordon?"

I nodded. "She was a union organizer."

Zee gave me the same look that I'd given Glen when he told me about the union drive. "Nina . . ." she said skeptically.

"I know, I know. But think about it this way, my dear: Rap takes in at least a billion dollars a year."

Zee's eyes widened. "I didn't know it was raking in that much money!"

"Black music is a significant engine of the multibillion-dollar music industry, but black folks don't control it and people like Fergus don't want hip-hoppers to even consider organizing outside of it. Think about the ripple effect that would have in the music industry. If rappers, young blacks, started organizing and pressing for changes in the industry, might that also have an effect on white rock and rollers who are also getting shafted by the music companies? And rock still pulls in more money than rap."

"You mean the threat of a good example," added Zee. "But what about John Matucci?"

"Okay, this is what I think happened. The word came down that when Mbooma was murdered, he was the perfect patsy. You know, a dead nigga. The cops are saying this and that. The press is picking it up. According to Murch, an inspector came over to Matucci's command and told him to fix or squelch the report that had Glen's identification of SugarDick's killer. Glen had described a man who clearly was not Mbooma."

"Who ordered the change?" Zee wanted to know.

"Gonna find me a phat joint if it knocks your socks off?"

Zee crossed her arms. "Try me."

"According to Murch, Bathsheba Volaré," I informed her.

"Il Duce's secret squeeze?" Zee shook her head. "You are staying stone-cold sober, Nina. The mayor would not allow that to happen—not because he's righteous but because he's an absolute authoritarian control freak! He's not going to let anyone fuck with *his* police force."

"Look, somebody killed Matucci and I think they're the same people who killed SugarDick. They went to work on Matucci because he could name the inspector, and that inspector would have been forced to save his own skin by giving up Volaré."

"But the mayor? Look, we all know what a racist SOB Carlucci is, but he's a former federal judge and wouldn't allow somebody to mess with his precious cops. Why would Il Duce allow that to happen?"

"I think that Fergus has something on *him*," I answered. "What, I don't know. That's why we are here. I think Fergus has something on Hizzoner and uses it when he has to. Volaré used to work for the *New York Forum* and I think she covered the federal courts when the mayor was on the bench."

"I don't know, Nina."

"I don't know that for a fact, either, Zee, but there are things going on and connections to be made. Everyone is making his move and getting into position—and killing people in the process. I'm going to throw in a monkey wrench and bring it to a grinding halt."

"If you can figure it out," countered Zee.

"I'll figure it out. Believe me, I'll figure it out." And that would be far easier than having to confront what Glen was saddled with at the moment, dealing with his mother.

Dressed in a dark blue suit with subtle gray windowpanes, Glen entered the room, slowly shaking his head. "Your father and my mother," he said as he handed me the phone. "But I'm glad I'm not the one who has to explain to Sugar's parents this new facet of his life after his death . . . Okay, ladies, I'm tired of being a punching bag. Let's go downstairs and start some trouble."

We left our suite and caught an elevator to the mezzanine, which floored a series of conference rooms and meeting suites. We walked into a hospitality suite that was welcoming the InfoGlobal participants. A woman at the door greeted us and we introduced ourselves and entered the brave new world of InfoGlobal. It was filled with smart cyberexecutives, mostly white and mostly male, who were gabbing and drinking, talking about either sports, business, or clocking babes. There were various tables laid out with food and drinks and corporate propaganda.

The three of us walked around and decided that there wasn't much happening after tomorrow's big presentation, only some workshops and panels about culture and marketing. I couldn't help but notice that all the gold-plated black intellectuals from Harvard, Yale, Columbia, and the other citadels of intellectual corruption—the same crowd that had rationalized the "ironic" temperament of niggacool™—were moderating these panels. It didn't take much to figure out who was getting paid by whom.

I looked at a brochure and saw that Andre Taliferro was presently giving points on "How to Use Black Culture to Reach White Markets to Get Green Dollars." The guy was on the road to becoming a post-dot-com zillionaire.

"Now, children, this is where we're supposed to be," I said. "That is the new nationalism. Black, white, and *green*."

Moments later we squeezed our way into a room where the oxygen had to be rented. The place was jam-packed with eager participants listening to the master marketer of the illusive niggacool™, and he dispensed his knowledge munificently. The Cool One was dressed in a yellow sports jacket, rust-colored slacks, and a black T-shirt. Tali had on dark glasses, and was energetically moving back and forth between charts that displayed the dynamic of black culture and its marketing potential as a hook for white consumers, the ur-consumers in the American mainstream. The man had an unctuousness that would even chill slime's viscosity.

"The point is that blacks have been defining popular culture ever since they arrived here," explained Taliferro, "and it's the popular culture that makes money, and that is what America is all about. Even girls in Japan want to become 'soul sisters' because that's what they see on television and hear in the music. They know that blacks are the prime example of niggacool™. Can I get a witness?"

The crowd let out a tepid "amen." It was then that I noticed that most of the audience was black and about a quarter were people of pallor.

"So any company that wants to remain competitive will have to up its"—he stopped and leered—"excuse the expression, *nigga content*," he said dramatically. "It won't be enough to have the fastest modem and the illest website. You're going to have to have content—nigga content, that is."

The three of us stood in the back, pressed against the wall, with me in the middle. I gave Glen and Zee each a look and muttered something about the end of black civilization as we have known it. The audience was paying attention, though. I noticed people were busily jotting down notes; this was a professional crowd, every man suited up in blue and gray. The womenfolk, of course, departed from the duo-chromism of male couture.

Jazz. Dope. Sex. Rock 'n' roll. Elvis Presley. Ray Charles. James Brown. Tina Turner. Interracial sex. Black Power. Rap. Hip-hop. Malcolm X. Afro. Michael Jordan. These were all vestiges, to varying degrees, of niggacool™.

Taliferro had launched a glossy magazine called *Da Niggarati*, subtitled: *For Dem Who Know Who Dey Be*. It was chock-full of shop-and-fuck items. Whyte Boy and Whyte Girl cologne. Lexus. Rolex watches. Armani clothes. Versace stylings. Gucci timepieces. Items from the GUESS? collection. Liquor ads. If it was expensive and could be afforded by the average chowderheaded Negro, then it went into the magazine.

Of course, the NAACP and the so-called responsible black leadership squawked about the devaluation of black culture. But when Taliferro pointed out they, too, were getting paid by shilling for the federal government or "blackwashing" the exploitative practices of U.S. manufacturing companies paying "virtual" slave wages to other people of color, or when Taliferro mentioned how a certain minister had been caught in a time-share abode with a woman who was a former embezzler, they backed off. When the real niggarati, black intellectuals, started chiding traditional black leaders' inability to appreciate Mr. Taliferro's "ironic project," he knew he had gotten over. Soon, he was able to fill the pages of *Da Niggarati* with intellectual content—that is, if you take anything the black intelligentsia has to say as having any intellectual worth. Content?

Listening to Mr. T. convinced me that I had no future in teaching, for people like Taliferro and the others in the room would have greater influence over my students. And if our research was on target, people like Taliferro were lining up suckers for Fergus, who had the apparatus and the money to put ideas like niggacool™ on the map. Taliferro ended his presentation and asked for questions. That's when we squeezed our way through and entered a smaller room that had a bar and was filled with clusters of other people.

We stood in a corner and watched the participants. Glen pointed out some of the major players in the music industry, mostly black executives at white-owned record firms. Greg Watini. Carl Judson. Tommy Thomas. A thought occurred to me and I turned to Glen.

"Weren't some of those guys mentioned by Baby Cakes?" I whispered.

Before Glen could answer, Big Poppa Insane and Icy D walked in, "loud and wrong," as my mother used to say, with their entourage. The volume went up in the room and you knew that some of *us* had landed. They were dressed like refugees from a bad gangster movie, with homburgs and derbys and cigars—and pinky rings, diamond cuff links, cravats, stickpins, and boss double-breasted suits. Big Poppa was letting his overaggressive pit bull cut them a wide path. All eyes were on them because they were, supposedly, locked in a bloody East/West feud.

Then the flow of humanity entered the room, and that indicated that Taliferro's presentation was officially over. There was an excited buzz, the kind that surfaces when people have been given the word, the knowledge of how to get over.

"Brilliant! Just brilliant," waxed one executive-looking gentleman.

"I have seen the future and it is niggacool™," nervously laughed another man, a pallid professional.

"Tonight I'm writing to my home office to make sure it increases its, uh, NC content," announced one woman, a black professional who probably wouldn't be caught dead saying the dreaded N-word but would surely issue a report advocating its strategic use.

"Well, kids?" I said as I sipped my drink. "In the wilds of Babylon . . ."

"This is sick," concurred Zee. "That is the most twisted, perverted justification of ripping off our culture . . ."

"But Zee," I said mockingly, "it's all about getting paid. Dollar bills, y'all."

"That's what people like King and Malcolm and Martin died for?" she asked, muttering into her white wine.

"No," said Glen, "but that's what we're left with in the new world odor. The big stink is in, and everybody wants a whiff. This is what I mean by trying to save black music. These people are coming into our culture by the back door of our music."

"Glen," I reminded him, "they already did that from day one, when they once owned our ancestors."

"What do you mean *once*?" remarked Zee ruefully. "They still do. We've always been commodities. Even our culture has now been thoroughly commodified."

I thought this show was going to get better before we left. I scanned the room and noticed a line of people waiting to approach a small bearded man who wore tinted eyeglasses, seated on a small couch. He seemed really out of place, given that it was mostly a young crowd. He wore a fez and had a black cane between his knees and he either curtly nodded to the men or kissed the hands of the women. I watched him and he seemed like he was in his element, able to swim with the sharks and tear out a shank of flesh if need be.

"Who's that?" I nudged Glen, nodding in the direction of the elfin figure to whom homage was being paid.

"That, ironically, is one of the men who put black culture on the map. That's the Pasha."

Immediately, I knew who he was talking about. While Taliferro had a scheme to market black culture through his twisted concept, there, quietly, without great fanfare, sat Mohammad "the Pasha" Ibn, the president of Fez Records. While Motown was selling records to whites, Fez and the Groove were selling music, *black* music, to black people and people of pallor, then called whites, who wanted the unadulterated sound of black folks having not just fun but *Big Fun*.

Mohammad Ibn, the scion of a wealthy Egyptian family, fell in love with black music as a student in the United States. A polymath, he parlayed his inheritance into the creation of one of the major rhythm-and-blues record firms in the country and pocketed a sizable fortune. Motown was now just a catalog of music publishing rights, but the Fez and the Groove lived on.

When you wanted soul music you bought Fez, the Groove, or Stax—not Motown. Don't get me wrong: I love Marvin Gaye and Martha Reeves and the Vandellas, but those other labels gave you the real sound of black people making black music. They had that unmistakable energy and immediacy and weren't slick and assembly-lined like Motown. It was funky—no one would ever accuse Motown of being too funky. The Groove and Fez had the unmistakable scent of the people, while Motown deodorized them. But that music, as Émile Zola had once said of the French lower class, had "the authentic odor of the people." That's why it was funky.

People approached the elderly gentleman and greeted him, and he smiled beatifically and nodded.

"He's the last of the great R&B makers," said Glen, "Of course, he moved beyond just R&B, but he still has great respect for black music. The man also gives decent contracts to black artists and he doesn't talk all that nationalist shit while still ripping off—"

"*The black man*," we all said in unison. We all had gotten fed up with cheap, gender-centric nationalism.

"I wonder why he's here," I said.

Glen shrugged his shoulders. "The Pasha is a player and Fergus may have asked His Excellency to join him. Also, word is that Fergus is interested in acquiring Fez." Glen explained that Fez Records hadn't aligned itself with any of the major record or media companies and was still distributing its own records, albeit with some difficulty nowadays. "If Fergus and the others continue gobbling up the other record companies, the Fez and the Groove may soon have their distribution blocked."

"Oh," I said, nodding and watching the cute little man with the fez and the cane, the tassle on his conical "beanie" swaying back and forth. He reminded me of an Arab nobleman granting his subjects a request on a special day, like a wedding ceremony or an Islamic holiday.

The host of InfoGlobal, Mr. Fergus, was having a dinner for some of the prime players, to be followed by a major party, and tomorrow would be the unveiling of the InfoGlobal concept.

We left and went back upstairs to prepare for the evening. Zee was going to hold down the fort, getting on the wire to track down some information for us. When we arrived at the suite there was a message for me slipped underneath the door in an envelope.

Why don't you come down and see me sometime, big girl.

It was signed: *Room 1820.*

I showed the message to the others.

"Who do you think sent that?" asked Zee.

"We'll soon find out." I dialed the front desk and asked for the occupant of the room and then hung up. I slowly shook my head.

"Well?" said Glen, loosening his tie.

"Our lady from the Caribbean. La Bomba."

I kissed Glen good-bye, told him to keep the bed warm, and reminded him to work on his friend China in regard to Taliferro. He grunted something that I couldn't make out. Zee said that she was going to call her husband and check in with him and her father. If La Bomba was around, then the show was going to get interesting.

"What the fuck are you doing here?" I said as I entered her suite.

"Going Afrocentric, Señora Vargas?" she asked. She was snickering, but I shut her up when I unwrapped the gelai.

"*Muy linda!*" she exclaimed. "Now, doña, you are gorgeous with that haircut. Take off the glasses."

I did so.

"You have such an exquisite face, doña," she continued, still not answering my question but waiting for a traditional Misericordian greeting, the kind of continental kiss that Anna and I give each other. "You know, you could have a career as a dominatrix. You look royally butch with that haircut. I know many powerful white men who would love to sniff and grovel at your exquisite black feet."

I kissed her on each cheek and then grabbed her little café au lait nose and tweaked it. She patted the couch with her hand for me to sit down.

"I still want to know what you are doing here," I demanded.

She offered me a drink and I accepted, provided that it wasn't alcoholic. La Bomba got up and poured me a ginger ale and began fixing herself something more potent.

"Rolf Fergus invited me," she answered. "He's been offering me a label."

"You know him?"

"Doña, I not only know him, but . . ." Magdalena looked over her shoulder and winked as she worked on her drink at the bar. She handed me my ginger ale.

"You shtupped him? And I thought *I* was horny beyond repair."

"I like your expression 'okey-doke' better. There's something marvelously American about it," she said.

"Who *haven't* you fucked?"

"Well, I haven't gotten you *yet* . . ."

"And you won't ever. I'm married," I reminded her, "and not into women."

"Oh, that's not what Anna told me." She smiled.

"That was a slip-up, a momentary bout of emotional weakness. Look, let's talk about *you* and her." I wanted to know about her offer to Anna.

"No, let's talk about Babe Volaré."

That stopped me. "Okay." I slowly exhaled. I still wanted to know about her and Anna, but this crazy woman, who I admit is a friend, knew how to entice. "What about Babe Volaré?"

Magdalena stretched out her arms and settled more comfortably into the couch. As an envoy to the United Nations, representing the Republic of Dechoukaj, formerly Misericordia, Magdalena VillaRosa was coming into her own. She had let her hair grow out and was amplifying her reputation as a singer and sex diva. "She's coming here. Tonight."

"And what?"

La Bomba stared at me. "Don't be naïve, Nina."

"You two are having an affair?" I was shocked.

The ambassador nodded her head. "The woman is hot for me, Nina. Want a smoke?"

I shook my head no. "I don't smoke, La Bomba; only the illegal brands, Schedule I."

"That's what I got, darling. Sealed in my diplomatic pouch."

This was already getting interesting. She pulled out a joint from her purse and told me how she had met Bathsheba Volaré at a lezzie joint called Elizabeth III, an expensive club/restaurant for professional Sapphoes here in the Big Mango. The two of them got into a conversation and Magdalena mentioned that she would be at the Universal Hotel, as a guest of Fergus's, and Volaré said that she would be delivering the welcoming address for the mayor.

"This sounds fascinating, Bomba," I said between puffs, "but what was she doing at a Geegee joint?"

"Geegee joint?"

"Girl-on-girl bar," I explained. "She is supposed to be getting banged by the man at City Hall."

"Well, that's why she's cruising," said La Bomba. "The woman's a retro-power freak. I think she likes men *or* women who are domineering and aggressive. She's a succulent bottom. *Grrrr*."

"She would enjoy your down-on-your-knees style," I said. Since Volaré worked for our power-hungry mayor, I wasn't surprised at my friend's summation. Anyone who had a normal ego would have told Il Duce to take a flying leap.

"So, since I'm going to have her to myself, what do you want to know?" She smiled. "I might have her in an advantageous position for questioning."

This was going to be tricky, I thought. She couldn't ask Volaré the kind of direct questions that I needed to know without her becoming suspicious. Instead, I told her to get a sense of the mayor and Fergus's relationship. That would be enough for me until I knew what was going on.

"I gather Anna told you about all this, huh?"

Magdalena nodded. "Of course. I offered my services. After all, you are remembered as a sister of the revolution. There is no way I can turn my back on a sister of our struggle. Besides, we had that special man in common."

"Don't remind me." Thinking about Luc's violent death in Misericordia only depressed me. I had too many dead men in my life: Lee, my son Andrew, and Luc.

As we got to the door, I thought about Anna. "What's the deal with you and Annie? Don't yo-yo her, Bomba. She's already been jilted by Esperanza, who totally surprised me."

"Esperanza is a complicated woman," explained Magdalena. "In some ways she hasn't gotten over the loss of her husband." She paused for a second. "When he was murdered, she had a miscarriage."

"Oh . . . God," I said. "I didn't know that Esperanza had been pregnant." I wondered if Anna knew.

La Bomba plaintively shook her head. "It's like that, doña. She does care for Anna very much, loves her, but . . . As for me . . . I'm infertile and believe me, I've tried, the natural way and the new-fangled techniques. If Anna wants the child, I would love to be a second mother."

"But you're not in love with Anna?"

La Bomba shrugged her shoulders. "Look, I'm practical. I have an old worldview about marriages. They are about partnership and alliances. They are about families coming together building an empire, thwarting enemies. The individual is insignificant in certain cases."

I then remembered how she had been preparing to marry my Luc as an act of statecraft, while still offering me visitation rights. Talk about collectivism. Of course, being an American I was shocked, but then . . .

"Besides," added Magdalena, "I could never compete with the woman Anna truly loves."

"Esperanza," I said knowingly.

La Bomba shook her head negatively. "Anna is in love with you, Nina, but knows she can never have you."

"That's ridiculous," I said. "Anna and I are best friends."

"That's why she knows she can never have you in that way. I noticed the way she looks at you, her eyes fluttering over your dark, majestic skin."

I stood there and La Bomba faintly touched my face.

"You know, for a woman who is so worldly and forthright," she said, "there is something touchingly naïve about your imperviousness to matters of the heart."

TRACK 15

WINSTON CHAO

When I returned to the suite, Zee was stretched out on the couch, her head propped up on a pillow, giggling into the phone, her eyes on the door. As I moved into the master bedroom I saw her pistol resting on her stomach. I want a daughter like that, I thought. She knows how to have fun and still take care of business. I went into the bedroom, half the size of the room I just left and equally as imperious, and didn't see Glen. The bathroom door was open. I stepped in and gorgeous was relaxing in the oval tub.

"What kept you?" he said, eyeing me seductively. "I thought we'd get ready for the evening's events." There was a bottle of champagne and caviar, compliments of the house. Glen's muscular arms were resting on the rim of the tub, a cigar stuck in his mouth. "I've been thinking. Why don't we kidnap Fergus and torture him? He used to do that to the brothers in South Africa, right? I heard he even raped some of the sisters in jail. He should get a taste of his own medicine. A dog like that—"

"Glen, I don't do torture," I said as I slowly peeled off my clothes. Glen approvingly scanned every inch of skin that was exposed. "It's for sick amateurs who are power freaks."

Naked, I walked up the small set of stairs that led to the tub and held onto the rail as I lowered myself into the—

"OUCH!" I recoiled. "That water is—"

"*¿Caliente?*" he said, swirling the sudsy water.

"*Muy*," I affirmed. "Would you mind, darling. I need something cooler."

Singing that old western song about cool, clear water, Glen turned the ivory handle and water poured forth. I placed a toe in the tub and it still felt hot, but not as bad as before. I lowered myself in and settled down at the end of the tub.

"So what's up, buttercup?" he asked, as he poured a glass of champagne and handed it to me.

I relayed to Glen the deal that was going to go down between La Bomba and Volaré.

"She's going to put her mouth where Il Duce has been sticking his . . . ? Oh, God," he moaned. "La Bomba must really love you to do that."

"What makes you say that?" I thought his comment was kind of strange, given the tenor of the conversation that I just had with her concerning Anna's alleged love for me. I didn't need to be hearing that from my husband. My inner doubts were beginning to annoy me.

"Nothing," he sighed, sinking deeper into the tub. "*Sisters are doing it to each other*," he sang, subverting a tune by Aretha Franklin and Annie Lennox.

"That's not funny!" I said, grabbing a toe beneath the water, twisting it. Glen pulled his foot away and splashed water in my face with his hand.

"This is a demilitarized zone, *azúcar,*" he announced. "What is your problem, my *bad* woman?"

Instead of answering him, I stood up, my body covered with suds, waded over to where he was, and lowered myself next to him.

"Glen, do you think I'm sexy? I mean, you don't think of me as being, uh, butch, do you?" Okay, I was being solicitous, groveling for male approval, but I needed some affirmation. For years, people have called me tough. I've always considered myself intrepid but feminine. But with La Bomba calling me "butch" and then telling me about Anna's undying love, I needed something that only a man could offer.

"Is this a trick question?" he asked incredulously. "We're going from war to peace in thirty seconds, are we?" He reached down and pulled my hand up from beneath the water and kissed my palm. I shuddered and placed my hand on his shoulder and caressed it, moving down to his chest. I enjoyed seeing the water glisten on his dark skin. Glen had a nicely proportioned physique that gave evidence of him working out. He was buff but not bulging to the point of obscenity like a lot of bodybuilders. The man was tasty.

"Is there something on your mind, Nina?" he asked, touching my face with a wet hand.

Instead of answering him, I placed his wet finger in my mouth and began sucking on it. I went fishing for his submerged item and found it, when Zee knocked on the door and whispered, "Nina?"

"We're *busy*, Zee," I said, my fingers around my man's thang. Glen's breathing began to modulate; I began to purr. We were entering that zone where man and woman synchronize their existence.

There was no noise from outside the door for a few minutes, only the sound of water splashing about and heavy breathing from both of us. We were, uh, concentrating, cultivating that special vibe.

"Nina?" called my second-in-command.

"*What?*" I snapped. Man and woman were about to engage in some serious quality time.

"Winston Chao is here to see you." That slowed my motor.

I said I'd be out in a minute and then told my husband, "Hold that erection, gorgeous." I kissed him and slowly stepped out of the tub, grabbed a towel, and dried myself.

"Are you going to tell me about this schmuck who is interrupting our little interlude?" he asked. Suddenly Glen reminded me of my father when we had stumbled upon him and Delores.

"Anna's old boyfriend," I replied. "If he knows I'm here, I think I better find out why." I opened the door and then looked back over my shoulder, the towel wrapped around me. "I won't be long and I'll have a warm spot for you between my—" I blew him a kiss, went off into the bedroom, and quickly put on some clothes.

When I entered the living room, Winston Chao was standing there nervously, looking out a large window. At first he stared, not quite sure if it was me, but then broke into his very charming smile when he recognized the genuine article.

"Boy, what a razor job," he said as he hugged me.

I hadn't spoken to or seen Winston since he and Anna had broken up—she dumped him when she decided to jump the fence, so to speak. I was fond of Winston and had found him to be nice but somewhat stolid. Anna thought he was boring but a good fuck—for a guy. He was a very attractive man and reminded me of Chow Yun-Fat, the Hong Kong-turned-Hollywood actor. He had an athletic build with boyish good looks and smiling eyes.

I'd known him for years and didn't feel awkward embracing him as an old friend. I also felt bad for him: Anna's rejection had devastated him. It was a total shock, and he felt that he had failed her as well as himself. He couldn't satisfy his woman. He had lost face. People snickered behind his back, and he even punched one or two who dared to say something in front of his face. Three years later he hadn't gotten over her. The man was still in love with Anna.

"What are you doing here?" I'd motioned for him to sit. Zee had made herself scarce by going into one of the other rooms. Glen, I was sure, would park himself on the bed and take a nap.

"InfoGlobal," he said. "Representing my firm."

"The bank?" I asked.

"No, Black Dragon Multiworks. I left the bank a couple of years ago. I got bored with it. No juice. BDM is on the cutting edge of cyberproductions and communications. We're producing a reality-based comedy show called *The Bobby Mao Show*."

No juice, I thought. That was a curious use of words. That had been Anna's complaint about him: no juice. As a banker, of course, Winston was somewhat conservative, but successful. Anna's mother thought that he was the perfect new China boy for her daughter, Miss Chinatown.

"How'd you find me, Win?" I asked, as I took a seat on the couch, spinning a black ocean globe, an art deco centerpiece on the coffee table.

Winston explained that he saw me at the hospitality room where Glen, Zee, and I had retreated after listening to that niggacool™ marketing propaganda. He was standing at the bar when Glen had come up to get our drinks, and he recognized Glen's name when he read it on his lapel badge. Win also remembered Zee from a visit to my office two years ago. My getup, the African headdress and the wire-rimmed glasses, had thrown him off at first, but then he recognized my smile as the three us stood laughing about some new jack bullshit.

"Oh, you are still such a flirt, Win."

"I'm not lying, Nina," he said. "You've always had a very nice smile."

"You've just got a black gal fixation," I teased. "Everybody wants one. As the Italians say, 'Ba-da boom, ba-da *bing*!'

"Anyway, I knew it was you," he continued, "and then I went to the registry and asked for Vargas. I heard you'd gotten married. Is that your name now?"

"Yeah," I lied. "So tell me about Black Dragon," I added, feeling not too impressed with my disguise attempt and wanting to get off the subject of me. Winston, looking relaxed in a black-and-blue checked sport coat over a black shirt and dark gray trousers, shrugged. "Nothing much, you know. Just a more fun way of making money."

"The great American pastime, making money. Great therapy, I'm told."

Winston nodded in agreement. "So when did you marry this Vargas guy?"

It was at that point that I had to make a decision. This was someone who knew me as Nina, but I had registered as Alexis Vargas. He could possibly blow our cover. "Look, Win, you know I'm an investigator, right?"

"Yeah."

"Okay. I'm here on an assignment working with Anna." I threw that out, hoping it would assure his silence. He had come to my office a few years back trying to get me to explain where he had messed up, where he went wrong when Miss A decided to go gay-gal hunting.

Now Winston nodded; he got the point. "Hope I didn't blow anything."

"Not at all, darling," I said. "I'm glad it happened the way it has and not in a crowd of people who know me as a different person. Just call me Alexis or don't call me anything at all."

"So, uh, how's Anna?" The man hadn't wanted to ask—I could tell by the concern in his voice, the kind a man or woman gets when he or she still cares for someone. It's torture, a form of emotional masochism. It's like a child perversely taking pleasure in picking scabs.

I thought for a second. Anna, bless her loose lips, blabbed about our little tryst to everyone she was shtupping—or about to. "She's doing all right for someone who's pregnant."

I noticed a change slowly coming over Winston's charmingly placid face. I could see a series of questions coursing through his mind by the way his skin was becoming flushed, his brow knotted, his nostrils flared. Finally, the corners of his mouth tightened. "I thought she was . . . uh . . ."

"Gay?" I sighed leisurely. "Yeah . . . but you know some of us gals . . . Some of us still want to go through the pain and pleasure of motherhood." I shrugged my shoulders.

"Without the dude," he said flatly, picking at his scab. He had been rejected and it had seared him.

"Something like that," I confirmed. "Can I fix you a drink, Win?"

He protested at first but I insisted, for old times' sake. I went over to the bar and poured him a scotch and some orange juice for myself.

Winston sipped his drink and I watched his Adam's apple bob up and down. "Is she happy?"

I shrugged again. "Not really. She may have to abort."

A look of grave concern appeared on his face. "Why? What's wrong?"

I explained to him that the woman she was involved with didn't want the child. He wanted to know why they—Anna and Esperanza—didn't know that before the insemination.

"It wasn't done by that method, Win."

"Oh, some guy was the surrogate, huh?" he snorted. His eyes narrowed and he drained the last of his drink.

"Uh, no," I said coolly. "Esperanza is, uh, uniquely endowed . . ." I drifted. "You want another?" I stood up, took his glass, went over to the bar, and poured him another. One . . . two . . . three . . .

"You mean a *fucking* she-male? A goddamn freak?" he said, taking the second drink from me.

"*Au contraire, mon ami*." I shook my head. "*Authentique*. No she-male. The real McCoy. A real woman with a real—"

"I don't want to hear any more!" His complexion changed drastically. Suddenly, he stood up and walked over to the window, to the spot where he had been standing when I entered the room. He placed his hands in his pockets. I felt like a bad girl but I thought that this had promise. I was going to do Anna a big favor.

"Is she going to go through with . . . this?"

"Well," I started, rising from the couch, slowly walking over to him, my arms folded, "she has been propositioned by another woman . . . to keep the child. The other party is infertile."

"This is insane, Nina!" he said, enraged. This was the sort of thing that turned a man into a stark-raving Republican. Winston was going through a bit of a sex panic, trying to figure out the sexual configurations and contortions that Anna was involved in.

Sighing somewhat dramatically, I patted him on his back. "It's the way of the world, my friend. Modern women and their modern ways."

"Is she going to go through with this?" he asked again, turning to me.

"Going to make her a better offer?" I challenged.

"What did he say to that?" asked the Pasha, who was stroking his beard, taking a delight in the tale I was spinning. "Ah, sex was so much simpler in my day, young lady. We didn't have all these options: Boy on boy. Girl on girl. Boy plus girl plus boy plus girl . . ."

"No, Pasha, you just had unlimited access to different women based on your wealth," I reminded him.

The plane was beginning its descent and we would be landing at Charles de Gaulle airport within thirty minutes.

He bowed his head and looked at me over the top of his eyeglasses. "You have heard things, my dear?"

"From what I've seen in newspapers and magazines, you escort women who aren't your wife to various functions, kind sir. And there are stories about your, uh, generosity as a lover," I said, fastening my seat belt. "I'm assuming that Mrs. Ibn is a very understanding woman—with the emphasis on *understanding*."

The Pasha also fastened his belt, and sighed. "What can I say? Women are my weakness." He remained silent for a few minutes. "I like sex, Ms. Sierra. I worship women as the goddesses they are."

"You won't be convicted in my court, bey," I said, using an Islamic honorific in addressing him.

"Did I tell you that my wet nurse was a Nubian?" he asked. "God, such a gorgeous black woman with deep dark skin and a glowing smile."

This conversation was getting a little too intimate for my comfort. I felt a sudden need for that gorgeous guy I'd left behind.

When I had reentered the bedroom, Glen was seated on the small love seat in a robe, brooding over his earlier conversation with SugarDick's father, I surmised. Deciding not to invade his space, I went over to the bed and began dialing my good friend and partner, Anna.

I had left Winston Chao in a state of piquancy. He was bewitched, bothered, and bewildered—a state of being that some men use to seduce women, to confuse and distract them. I told him that Anna was expected at the hotel this evening and I could arrange for a tête-à-tête, but he wasn't interested. If I told Anna to appear at the hotel in a fuck-me dress with some cock-sucking red lipstick on, however, he, as Grace Jones once commanded, would get down on his knees.

When Anna answered the phone, I questioned her about the press conference "Oh, it was a piece of cake until I added your and Glen's misgiving about the impartiality of the police investigation."

"I bet Il Duce's flying truth-squad zeroed in on that." I smirked.

"You two were quickly denounced by Hizzoner and the commish when I announced Glen's missing report at Matucci's precinct and how that might be tied up with Matucci's death. Then the press started asking them questions, and faxes started flying. When I alluded to a possible police-on-police hit, of course, I was criticized as irresponsible, but I reminded them, the media, that this mayor had a history of holding back public information. I think the press tasted blood."

"Ready for some extracurricular activities, *chère*?"

"What's up?"

"A party like 1999," I said. "You should come up and check out the digs."

Anna begged off. I told her about Magdalena's date with Babe Volaré. She yawned. In Anna's mind, Magdalena was doing this for me and she didn't seem bothered. Their relationship was solely one of convenience. The day's events had tired her out and she was still slightly depressed and confused over her choices. Running interference for me and Glen kept her from dealing with her problem, and she was happy about that. Understandably, she missed Esperanza.

"I thought you were going to go with La Bomba's offer."

"Yeah, I thought so, too," she confessed. "She's just a little too . . ."

"Wild?" I offered.

Anna was slow to admit it. She had always felt that she was on the cutting edge of experimentation.

"Yeah, Nina, I guess I'm getting old and looking for something more stable. I get the impression that she'd be good at being Aunt Mommy but wouldn't be around when it comes to changing a diaper or giving me emotional support. Let's face it, she now has a double career. She hasn't stopped performing and she has assumed diplomatic duties for her country at the United Nations. I imagine I would be the career-wife appendage—while she's out having fun, sucking and fucking and doing non-mommy-type things."

"Annie, are you thinking about keeping the child?"

She sucked in her breath. "Yeah, kinda, sorta . . . I don't know, Nina. I really don't want to abort but I don't want to have one by myself."

I thought for a second. "Look, why don't you come up here. I'll make some girl time and we'll talk about it. Hmmm?"

"I thought you and Glen were hot on the trail of what is and what ain't."

"Yeah, but I always have time for you and your problems."

She had been planning to stay home and read a book about the Japanese army's rape of Nanking. I don't have any issue with someone knowing about her history, but I thought this was a bit morbid. Instead, I told her that she should come up and witness the destruction of the old order and view the creation of a new civilization in the making. I told her it would be NC.

"What's that?"

"niggacool™," I informed her.

TRACK 16

A SNARKY AFFAIR

At our hotel suite Glen and I decided to host a little party for ourselves and our band of brothers and sisters: Zee and her husband Ibrahim, along with Anna and Winston. As Eduardo and Álexis Sierra-Vargas, we were scheduled to attend a reception and dinner hosted by the new millennium maggot overlord himself, Rolf Fergus. Zee had taken the opportunity to float around the hotel and meeting rooms and had learned that there were some serious players conducting deals. In one suite of rooms, Big Poppa Insane was having aspiring hip-hoppers present themselves and their tapes or CDs for on-site inspections.

". . . And if they are women, private A&R sessions are arranged," I told Glen as he looked over the room's liquor cabinet.

"I'm shocked," he said mockingly. "Shocked that a notorious gangsta label executive would engage in such less-than-gentlemanly behavior. Imagine that, taking advantage of hip-hop floozies. What do you think they do in closed sessions, Nina? Discuss Toni Morrison? These are the big moneymakers and that means if you be a fly-looking sistah with some phat beats, then you best have some juicy lips."

Glen continued looking at the various bottles.

"Speaking of juicy lips, is your girl coming up here to assist us, my pet?"

"China?" he asked. "Yes. As repellent as she finds Taliferro, she's willing to help out, provided that we're nearby." He began pouring gin into a shaker.

"But of course," I answered, sitting back on the couch and waiting for our guests and the evening festivities to begin. "We don't want the angel of funk left alone. Although I'm quite sure she knows how to handle a man under the right set of circumstances."

Glen ignored my comment and walked over with a martini. "It's high octane. Perfect for you."

"What does that mean?" I took the drink and arched an eyebrow. "Hmmm, *Negrito*?"

Glen stood over me as I sipped. He was looking me across, his eyes trailing my body cloaked in evening wear: a black silk, sleeveless, collared mandarin dress with some very revealing slits on each side. I liked the way his gaze washed over my body; I could feel my nipples hardening.

"I don't know if I'm going to let you out of the room dressed like *that*," he informed me. "That's very provocative. And . . ." He stopped and stared at my thigh. "What in the devil's name are you wearing, *azúcar*?"

Glen pointed to a band of Chinese kung-fu stars that I was wearing around my right thigh. I shifted and pulled the fabric over the exposed items. I placed my drink on the table.

"The same thing I'm wearing on my left arm, sweetie." On my upper arm I revealed a bracelet made out of four matte-black metal stars. "I thought a gun would be a bit gauche, don't you?"

"What are you going to—?"

Before my skeptical husband could finish his question, I had quickly pulled off two stars and embedded them in the wall behind him.

"Be a dear . . . get them for me," I said.

While he complied, I replaced the ones I'd thrown with two from my thigh arsenal. The bell to our suite chimed. I stood as Glen handed me the stars. When I went to answer the door, he gave the same look he had worn earlier when he realized the sort of woman he'd married. *Danger! Danger!*

Zee walked in with Ibrahim, her fair-skinned, sandy-haired Egyptian husband. They seemed to be in a tizzy over something. Zee remarked that I looked dangerous and sexy. I reintroduced Ibrahim to my husband, and Glen offered to make them drinks. Ibrahim, ever the cosmopolitan Muslim, accepted the offer of a martini. Zee took a ginger ale; she considered herself on duty, security-wise and maternally. Ibrahim and Glen began a conversation. I looked at Zee and jerked my head to the bedroom; she followed me in, but not before hubby coyly remarked: "Oh, I guess you two are going in there for a bad-girl security session, huh?"

Graciously, I bowed my head to my lord and master, letting him know that it was the lioness who brought home to the king of the jungle his more than rightful share.

I closed the door, hiked up my dress slightly, and placed the stars on the band. "What's with Ibrahim?"

Zee sighed. "I embarrassed him."

"What did you do?"

Husband and wife were on the elevator when two apparently drunk "brothers" got on and made a comment about "all these white devils taking our women." Zee and Ibrahim didn't say anything but decided to get off on another floor and wait for a different car. Zee had smelled liquor on their breath and didn't want to chance anything in close quarters. She was wearing a pistol. While they waited, the same car returned and the two men got off and—

"One of then lunged at Ibrahim and . . ." Zee searched for words. "I just went into action, Nina. And took care of them quickly, but . . ."

She didn't have to say any more. Zee saved them from an assault but may have impugned her husband's sense of masculinity. "You see why I want to get out this shit?" I said, placing my hand on her shoulder. "The only guys who can really deal with us are cops and soldiers."

"And we're not interested in them," said Zee.

"Right. So let Ibrahim deal with it. He's lucky to have you. Now let me tell you what's about to go down."

"Check," she said. I told her about the impending tryst between La Bomba and Babe Volaré. Zee let out a low whistle. "You were right."

I wasn't yet triumphant. "I just don't know about what. What Fergus has over Il Duce. Hopefully, Magdalena will use her charms to find out." I then told her that Anna was coming up here.

A concerned expression appeared on Zee's face. "Do you think that's wise?"

"It's a big hotel," I reminded her.

"Not when it comes to sex, my dear sister."

"Don't worry." I smiled. "Anna's old boyfriend, Win, seems to be interested in her."

"But Anna's gay!" exclaimed Zee. I knowingly shook my head. "Girlfriend is reconsidering her options. I think she'll invoke her bi clause. If Win is smart and acts like he can't live without her, she may decide that he can offer something that La Bomba can't—tolerable predictability."

Zee was skeptical but she didn't know Anna as well as I did. We decided that all we could do was create the conditions and let the actors respond. We came back into the main room and our husbands turned their heads and looked at us, the lethal femmes fatale.

"Zimbabwe, I think our men have been discussing us," I said cheerily as we went over to them. "So what have the good men of our hearts been conversing about? Wife swapping?"

Shocked, everyone stared at me. "You see, Ibrahim, I bet Zee doesn't talk out both sides of her neck like that!" responded Glen.

"No, she doesn't," he said good-naturedly. "She just breaks down doors."

Zee blushed in a girlish way that belied the fact that she's an adept weaponist and martial arts bone-crusher. Shyly, she glanced at Ibrahim, who placed his arms around her. Playfully, she tapped him on his cheek and said something in Arabic.

"It was an icebreaker," said I. "Okay, let's do something traditional. Let's toast Zee and Ibrahim's forthcoming child."

"I'm down with that," said Glen. "Get your drink, woman."

I went over to the table and picked up my martini and the door chimed again. I looked at my watch. Anna, I thought.

She screamed when I opened the door. I hadn't prepared her for Alexis Sierra-Vargas's look.

"What the fuck happened to you?" she asked, as she circled me, inspecting my new coif.

"You like?"

She ran her hand over my old-school modified 'fro, then sighed. "I'll get used to it." She was about to continue across the room but stopped. "Nice streak of gray, ancient one."

"Well, thanks a lot, pal," I said snarkily. Anna kissed me on both sides of my face and I heard a signifying cackle coming from Zee. Glen must have said something smart. "What was that?" I demanded. Anna and I went over to the bar where the posse was gathered and Glen poured her some ginger ale.

"Nothing," said Glen. "Look, let's get back to the festivities."

I ambled over to the stereo, turned it on, and found the jazz station in Newark. "Okay," I said, snapping my fingers.

We raised our glasses and toasted Zee and Ibrahim and wished them good fortune as an expectant couple. Then I asked Anna if it was all right if I made an announcement about her.

"Uh, I don't know. It all depends on the subject," she said hesitantly.

"I'm going to make one anyway," I began. "Anna is also with child."

The men began clapping. It was cool with them as long as they weren't the father.

"But she hasn't decided to keep the child," I continued, "and I want her to know that whatever you decide to do, Anna, I will support you. You're my friend and I care about you very, very, very much, girl."

Anna's eyes began to water and shift about. She wasn't quite ready for this. I wasn't ready for it, either. Anna quietly said thank you and announced that she was going to the bathroom. She turned and left the room. Everything became very quiet until the third chime of the evening sounded.

"Now who's that?" asked Glen. "The coke dealer?"

"The cavalry." I decided to save time by stepping on and over the couch instead of walking around it.

"Nina!" exclaimed everyone simultaneously as I moved across the furniture.

With a flourish, I opened the door and in stepped Winston Chao, wearing a dark green-black houndstooth suit with a black turtleneck. He didn't look like he was headed to a reception, but since he was in new media he wasn't beholden to the same evening-wear decorum as we old media types. Win, a traditionalist, had a large bouquet of roses. He looked around for his "It" girl.

"Where is she?"

"In the bathroom," I said sweetly. "I softened her up for you."

Win said hello to the others and proceeded into the bedroom and we all heard quite clearly, "WHAT ARE YOU DOING HERE?" It didn't sound hostile as much as surprised. As I was trying to close the door, Anna was doing just the opposite, trying to get out.

"What is he doing here?" she asked me.

"He has something to say to you and I think you should consider it."

"You set me up, Nina!" she accused. "Telling me all that girlfriend babble! You are so *fucking* dead, girl!"

"No, Anna," I replied, "I'm quite sincere about what I said. I love you and will support your decision, but you ought not turn your back on a good man. At least hear him out."

"Please, Anna, let's talk," pleaded Win.

"You stay out of this!" she shot back.

Instead, Win walked behind her and yanked her away from the door and closed it, winking. For the next few minutes the rest of us were exposed to some high-voltage Mandarin. I turned up the volume of the stereo and looked at my watch.

"Well, kids," I said to Glen, Zee, and Ibrahim, "we have this reception and dinner to go to, and at eight P.M . . . there's a slew of parties ripe for intelligence gathering. Why don't we meet back here at, say, nine-thirty?"

Everyone looked at me when we heard something like a lamp crashing behind the bedroom door.

"That means he's making sense, but she doesn't want to listen to her heart," I told them as Glen and I left the suite. "She's still in denial."

TRACK 17
THE MERCHANT OF DESIRE

Zee and Ibrahim decided to go to dinner at a nearby restaurant. Glen and I made our way to the Monticello reception/dining room and were met by a hospitality assistant who asked for our invitation to the inner sanctum of the select. The Monticello, named after Thomas Jefferson's home, had the decor of an old-fashioned men's club with blond- and natural oak–paneled walls and squeaky leather furniture.

The room was partitioned into two sections, with the "club" offering several overstuffed leather and cloth chairs and tables, and a bar with leather-upholstered stools. A set of shallow stairs led down into the dining area, which had several medium-size round tables for dinner guests. As we descended the stairs, the sound of falling water became prominent. At one end of the room was an interior decorator's sign of madness: A huge waterfall had been constructed inside the room. People gathered at the waterfall's end, separated by a small ledge, and gazed upward at the colossal structure that ushered water.

We had arrived. As we stepped into the reception room we were presented champagne and trays of hors d'oeuvres. The place was filling up and the room had the sort of buzz of the select few. Many of the people I assumed to be major players in the infotainment and communications industries.

Glen and I stood to the side, sipping our drinks and watching them, after we had come back from gazing at the waterfall. Taliferro was in attendance, giving neophytes the nod. There was also a cluster of black record executives about, and some of the main players seemed to be in a heated discussion with Mohammad Ibn, the president of Fez Records. And then there were the new jacks, the Icy Ds and the Big Poppa Insanes, smoking fat cigars and making lewd remarks about some of the women in attendance. Class A gentlemen.

I noticed one woman making her way through the crowd, greeting individuals and small knots of people. I took her to be in her late twenties or early thirties. She was about my height, a few inches short of six feet. The woman was a better-looking version of the late Diana Spencer, with friendly blue eyes, longer hair of the same sort of coloring, and slightly sharper features. When she approached us, she pleasantly and quite unpretentiously announced herself.

"Hello," she said in slightly melodious voice. "I'm Heather Fergus."

"Hello, I'm Alexis and this is my husband, Eduardo."

We shook hands and I immediately liked her, knowing full well that she was the daughter of someone I considered "the enemy," the incarnate of the new world order. She asked us about our trip and the hotel accommodations, and she listened, fastening her eyes on me, "the housewife," as well as the "junior executive" who represented his mother's firm. Heather began speaking to Glen in Spanish and that left me out for a few seconds. Her eyes shifted about and latched onto an average-size man with a large forehead and thinning hair who wore eyeglasses. He was talking to another person.

"Nice tan," I said.

"Why, thank you," she said, rather proudly. She then turned to the man with the glasses. "Oh, Father."

Glen and I exchanged *major* glances and got ready to meet the Big Kahuna himself. Rolf Fergus nodded his head to the person he was speaking to and turned his attention to us. Fergus gave Glen a vigorous handshake and then bowed and kissed my hand. I wanted to say, "I bet you do this to all the kaffir kuties," but I stifled myself. As one of the most powerful men in the world, Mr. Fergus did not have the bombastic swagger of the nouveau riches. Instead, he had the calm serenity of a man who knew he owned the world, or at least part of it.

Dressed like an English banker in one of those elegantly pinched and constricted suits that bordered on S&M couture, Mr. Fergus addressed some questions to Eduardo. The Beast tilted his prodigious forehead toward my husband, his arms behind his back. He had thinning gray-blond hair and a skin tone that reflected a generous use of Perma-Tan. With his leathery skin and swollen eyes he looked like a cross between Humphrey Bogart and Albert Camus. Mr. Fergus, I assume, was too manly to engage in face-lifts (and since he had money he did not need to look youthful); his cheeks were deeply creased, as well as his forehead. I gathered that when he focused his blue eyes laserlike on someone he could read bar codes forming in his or her brain.

"Well," he concluded, in a croaking voice that belched up his South African accent, "I'm sorry that your mother was unable to attend. I hope you and Mrs. Vargas find InfoGlobal interesting. Please enjoy your stay. I will speak to you later." He nodded toward me. "Madam."

"Mr. Fergus," I replied, gesturing likewise.

With that said, he shook our hands and was off. Heather followed her father. I learned from Glen that she was apprenticing under him, ready to take over the firm.

"And she's in competition with her brother, Willem," said Glen, as we watched father and daughter fade into the dark-suited crowd of players.

"What do you think?" I asked.

"He has the smell of—"

"Money?"

"No. Power," said Glen. "The smell of power. And I could see him fucking with Il Duce. Carlucci likes to flex his muscles. Fergus is the kind of guy who'll let you know that he knows how to twist a dagger, Boer dog motherfucker. The word is that while Heather is the most competent of his three children, Fergus is going to pass one of his sons the mantle. I think this has something to do with his wanting a cock behind the wheel."

I nodded in agreement and then spotted something. I nudged Glen and glanced over at the bar. Magdalena was talking to a coppery-headed woman who could only be the babe—Babe Volaré. The whole interaction appeared very professional; the subtext, though, was quite sexual. Seated next to Volaré was a blond woman with a buzz cut, dressed in a black cocktail dress. She was smoking a cigarette and trying to fend off some not-too-attractive black guy in search of a physical negotiation. Maybe she was making herself available for the same thing. The whole reception room had the faint odor of sex that Glen had identified that accompanies power and money. People were lining up their after-hours activities.

"The marines have landed," said Glen, his eyes on the doorway of the reception room. I turned and saw China Mercury entering; half of the suited-up brothers and male pallids registered her arrival as well. She smiled when she saw us and sashayed over. The woman had every male's eyes trailing her afterimage. I couldn't compete with her.

"Eduardo," she said throatily, pecking Glen on both sides of his face. "Alexis," she said to me, and gave the same greeting. After taking a glass of champagne, she mumbled, "Okay, where's the rolling piece of human excrement?"

Glen looked around and casually nodded in the excrement's direction. China wore a crème-colored two-piece dress suit with a lace-up, rich brocade bustier. The suit accented her golden brown complexion, and with her raven black hair falling to her shoulders, China looked hot, Hot, HOT, and it appeared that almost all the men agreed. Even La Bomba was taking notice.

"China," I began, for I felt I should say something about her "assignation," "look, you're just getting a sense of what Taliferro knows about Baby Cakes."

"If indeed he does knows anything," doubted Glen.

"He knows something," I argued. "You don't have to go all the way. Men are stupid and . . ."

"Hey!" shot Glen, taking umbrage.

I thought about Zee's faux pas with her husband. "Excluding present company," I hastened to add. "He'll just be happy that you're talking to him and may deliver the goods."

"Yeah, some guys are that stupid," said Glen testily. "*Coño.*"

"Don't interrupt your wife, Eduardo," said China playfully, turning her attention back to me.

"I see I'm going to have to bring some of those hardco' niggas over here to back me up," he replied archly. Glen started to move away and we both instinctively grabbed him. A delicious sensation swirled through me. I had a fleeting image of me and China double-teaming Glen.

"Now, baby, you be the man of my heart," I said soothingly. "Look, two of your biggest fans are here."

"That's right," said China. She reached over and straightened Glen's tie. "You the man."

The two of us nestled Glen between us. "Okay, girls, we have to remember that we are supposed to be upper-middle-class, professional Negroes and don't display sexuality in public. We're the neutered class."

"Are you serious?" said China, knowing she had the power. "Most of these guys already have raging hard-ons."

"I wonder who put them in that state of preparedness," said Glen.

"Look, Glenny, uh, Eduardo, you asked me to do this," she replied. "Normally, I'd be home taking matters into my own hands, doing needlepoint."

"Kids," I interrupted, trying to get them to focus on China's mission of mercy. "All you need to find out, China, is what party he'll be at, and one of us will back you up. You won't be alone."

Relieved, the funky diva nodded. She understood that she wouldn't be sacrificed on the altar of niggacool™. China sipped her champagne and relaxed.

"You look beautiful," I told her, and she did . . . the bitch.

"Thank you," she said. Her eyes fluttered and she returned a compliment. "So do you. Nice dress."

"Thanks. It comes with the husband."

People started leaving the reception and heading for the dining area. We descended the stairs and found a table where Pasha Ibn was seated, and prepared ourselves for a meal that was being cooked by the White House chef. Fergus was a heavy contributor to the party that presently controlled the White House and thus could even rent an employee of the chief magistrate of the land, the president of the United States. Reverend Reggie Baxter, who had reconciled himself to the necessity of market forces, blessed the dinner. I'm sure the good reverend was pressing Mr. Fergus to attend the Economic Reconciliation Summit that he was planning as part of his new empowerment agenda—since his other schemes of perpetual self-promotion had petered out.

After the meal, Mayor Kevin J. Carlucci's special assistant, Bathsheba Volaré, began her after-dinner remarks that were accompanied by cognacs, aperitifs, and stinking cigars. Although it wasn't mentioned, it was understood that Volaré was a stand-in for the mayor, who was attending an affair on Staten Island (read: snub). Volaré addressed the diners and welcomed them to the "capital of the world." The speech could only have been written by Carlucci himself—it basically highlighted his accomplishments as mayor of the *new* New York and listed the faults of his (black) predecessor, the kind, courtly, but ineffectual James J. Jenkins.

Volaré then touched on the basic premise of InfoGlobal, that the new technology was offering a way of superior communication, making the world smaller and more of a community, all thanks to a free market and, of course, less government regulations of business (and more government regulation of people, I might add). This allowed her to introduce the man of the hour, the person who had summoned them all. Rolf Fergus rose, went to the podium, thanked Ms. Volaré, and welcomed the audience to InfoGlobal. He adjusted the microphone, looked at the select, and delivered his wisdom.

"There has been some consternation about the decline of politics in the United States," croaked Mr. Fergus, "and much has been made of the fact that citizens are voting less but are shopping more and more. Some would see this as a pernicious result of consumerism, but I would say that in a democracy, people do have the right to choose what they want to be concerned about. Perhaps we have reached an era where we can turn *away* from politics. Perhaps the turn from politics to art, in the broadest and most democratic sense of the word, will allow a golden age to flourish in the greatest nation in human history. With the defeat of communism, the rapid advance of technology and communication, and the unfettered development of the market, we have reached an era of *postpolitics* and an era that can best be epitomized by a philosophy called 'the art of living.' The public desires more than the noise of politics and we, the telecommunications and media industries, the merchants of desire, are the conduits to their dreams.

"We needn't concern ourselves with the state because the state can no longer regulate human conduct. Only the market can provide for—"

A shard of audio feedback interrupted. Fergus stopped to adjust the microphone. He was about to resume but was interrupted once again, this time by a loud and indelicate voice coming over the public address system:

"*COCKSUCKER*!"

That sent a bolt of attention through the audience. Here was one of the most powerful men in the world, offering an important policy/philosophical presentation, interrupted by a vulgarity. Fergus wanly smiled and continued on.

"We needn't concern ourselves with the state—or the ignorant rabble—" reiterated the master of the universe, and that got him a laugh, "because the state can no longer regulate human conduct. Only the market can provide for—"

The feedback returned and so did the voice, but this time it was smooth, velvety, but indicting:

> *You like fucking over the world, don't you, Rolf? The world is nothing more than a bitch for you to fuck over. You have all the power in the world but you still can't get enough. Here you stand before a crowd, not of respected peers but of frightened lemmings. How big is it now, Rolf? Take it out and show us. In reality, that's what this gathering is all about.*

"I no longer find this a funny joke!" snapped Mr. Fergus. "Will somebody inform the hotel of this perversion!"

And the tragedy is the bootlicking Negroes assembled here before you, ready to bend over and get fucked by your great white phallus. We know who they are . . . Carl Judson . . . Tommy Thomas . . . Greg Watini.

All eyes zeroed in on the selected: Carl Judson, Tommy Thomas, and Greg Watini—the nicely attired black-music division chiefs of the major record labels. The assembled were too polite to say anything, not even snicker. But the accused had the mark of Job on them and people didn't have to wonder about their transgressions. Most already knew the story about the great rip-off of black music, aided and abetted by blacks themselves. No one was going to utter a word except the new jacks. Big Poppa Insane, however, who had always experienced scorn from the black-music establishment, was delighted.

"YO," Big Poppa barked in his loud and decibel-piercing voice, "THAT BITCH GOT THAT SHIT RIGHT! YOU MOTHERFUCKERS SOLD OUT BLACK MUSIC! DIDN'T STAY TRUE TO THE GAME!"

And we need not forget the so-called new jack style of today's black sound, a sick form of mental masturbation that dares to call itself music, and is marketed as gangsta rap. Put out by sick and twisted bastards like Big Poppa Insane . . .

"NOW WAIT A MINUTE, BITCH!" countered the newly accused, rising from the table and addressing the P.A. speakers that stood on opposite sides of the main table where Fergus, Heather, and a few others sat.

And we know that Big Poppa loves himself some white dick and that's why he's willing to suck yours, Fergus, the master cocksucker.

That pushed *his* button. The two-hundred-pound whopper marched over to one of the speakers, yanked it from its stand, and energetically smashed it against a wall. Needless to say, this embarrassing display of raw Negro emotionalism ended what should have been Fergus's triumphant vision at InfoGlobal. Fergus and his party left immediately and the buzz turned into a sour fizzle.

"What was that all about?" asked China. She, like most in attendance, wasn't sure what she had witnessed.

I was about to answer, but the Pasha had, as an old song went, beaten me to the punch: "Guerrilla warfare, Ms. Mercury. Guerrilla warfare."

TRACK 18

WHAT'S THE BUZZ?

The general sentiment, shared by Glen and China, was that a party mood had been ruined by the assault that occurred at dinner. There wasn't going to be any party after that. To a point, they were right. The assembled crowd would probably not be partying, particularly the big money-makers, the guys who were called out and embarrassed, not unless they had dicks of steel. Icy D hadn't been cited, but that was only because Insane had destroyed both speakers before the voice had spoken any further.

The whole affair had been permeated with suspicion and hostility. Nobody knew who the voice belonged to and how it had been able to breach the hotel's public address system. It had undermined the bogus multicultural façade of InfoGlobal, for now a rumor was going about that the whole thing was a premeditated attack on black music. Some of the blacks were convinced that it had been a *white* voice and that the attack was racially motivated. The question was, by whom? The assumption was that a black would not have attacked others in such a public way.

Fergus would not leave for two reasons: (1) it was his hotel and he was going to take delight in executing—a figure of speech, mind you—the management; (2) being of British and Boer stock, he wasn't going to quit. He would stay and politic through the night to let the others know that this was some aberrant and sick joke. But it wasn't. The Pasha was right. It was a guerrilla tactic, and the voice did sound "white"—whatever that meant.

That's what I was musing over, seated at the bar in the Monticello. Glen and China had heard about a party being given by Taliferro in his hotel suite and had gone up. I was going to retreat to our room at about nine-thirty and hook up with Zee, and then I wanted to check in on Anna and Win. God only knows what had transpired between the two. Then I would see what the natives were up to in Taliferro's suite.

There were a few people still lingering in the reception room. I stayed as well, needing a few minutes to myself to construct my mental notes.

"Excuse me, do you have a light?"

I turned. It was the buzz blonde. I remembered her from earlier. She had been seated at the bar when Magdalena and Volaré were standing there. I opened my purse, pulled out a lighter, and flicked it. She leaned over and lightly steadied my hand with hers, a gesture that indicated that my hand was shaking, which it wasn't. Or that she was interested in making some sort of physical contact, which didn't interest me. But then I recalled, since I'd been up at the bar, that various men, white and black, had been trying to pick her up. That could still be a bad sign for me if she was cruising, but sometimes a woman merely wants to sit at a bar by herself and be left alone. I know I did, particularly at that moment.

Pretty, she was about the same age as I. She thanked me for the light and went back to her business, which was a stool away. From time to time, I caught a glimpse of her in the mirror behind the bar. There was something familiar about this woman. For a few seconds I tried to picture where I might have known her: school, the district attorney's office, the last few years being an investigator . . . ? I, like most people, have met thousands. Also, she could be wearing her hair differently from when we last met, if I knew her at all.

I was about to shrug the whole thing off when I noticed that she had a heart-shaped tattoo on her left arm that read, "*Andre and Alison forever.*" I looked at her and she smiled at me, and she had a nice one: full lips.

You've always had a very nice smile.

I recalled Win's compliment about my smile and saw that hers was actually quite similar. I was becoming distracted. There was something about this woman. I looked at my watch and it read nine-ten. I had to get back to my room soon and meet Zee. I collected my things and slid off the stool.

"You know, Nina, everybody has one," said the woman with the buzz.

Uh-oh. She had called me by my real name. I had to play dummy. "Excuse me, were you talking to me? My name is Alexis," I said, peering at her over my wire-rims.

Rising from her stool and placing herself in front of me, she announced herself. "My name is Nadia. Nadia Gordon." She offered her hand and we shook, but it was a strange feeling, as if I was shaking hands with myself. She kept her blues eyes on me.

"Who're Andre and Alison?" I asked, looking at her tattoo and then back at her face.

"My children," she answered.

That unsettled me. She had a familiar vibe. Too familiar. I started to back away from her, but she handed me a card and then walked off.

NADIA GORDON
PRIVATE INVESTIGATOR
800-347-1818

I flipped the card over and noticed that she had also scribbled her room number. When I left the bar I glanced down both directions of the hall, but she had vanished. Poof!

I had an uneasy feeling. This woman knew who I was, and she was an investigator. As I returned to my room on the twentieth floor, I could hear the *thumpa-thumping* sound of loud music. The hotel had made its top floors available to the conferees and there seemed to be all sorts of activities going on: people laughing, doors opening and shutting, men and women shuttling back and forth between rooms in various stages of dress or undress. My nostrils caught the unmistakable smell of my favorite controlled substance. Well, we had been wrong about the dampening party mood of some of the attendees.

I slid my card key into the electrolock and entered our room. I should have been thinking about what had transpired at the dinner and some of the night's activities, but that woman, Nadia Gordon, was still distracting me. I went into the bathroom, splashed some water on my face, and looked at myself in the mirror. Eerily, I began to recognize her. There was a major difference in appearance: She was white and had blond hair and blue eyes. But the shape of our faces was the same, the same mouth, almost the same nose and eyebrows. It was as if I had run into a pale version of myself. She even had short hair.

I went into the living room and got her card from her my purse. I thought for a moment: What was I doing? Why was I calling her? I felt myself both drawn to her and repelled. Simultaneously, she appeared to be dangerous and nonthreatening. I felt as if I were confronting some secret persona that I had revealed only to myself, yet now it had taken on a life of its own.

When I dialed the number and she answered, I only said one thing: "Who are you?"

She paused before her reply: "Why don't you come down and find out . . . Nina." She hung up. I left Zee a note to hold the fort and let her know I'd be back in half an hour, around ten o'clock. I opened one of my cases, retrieved a gun that I had packed earlier, and wrapped a holster around the inside of my thigh. I went back into the bedroom and looked in the full-length mirror to see if it was too conspicuous. It passed the eyeball test.

Nadia Gordon was down on a lower floor where the tourists were. When I got off the elevator I made a left turn toward the odd numbers and proceeded toward her room, 1105. Heading my way was that little elfin man, Mr. Ibn, strolling down the hallway, cane in one hand, a cigarette holder between his teeth. Bobbing along with his signature fez, he recognized me as one of his tablemates at the dinner, bowed his head, and continued on his way. I thought that was odd. Mr. Ibn down here with the peasants? He had a suite upstairs and would probably be holding court with the likes of Fergus and the real movers and shakers.

I heard the distinct sound of live guitar strumming as I approached her room. When I knocked on the door the music stopped, confirming that indeed it wasn't a radio or a CD. Nadia Gordon opened the door and I was convinced that I was looking at myself *sans noir*. She stood aside and let me into her economy-class room. It didn't have the magnificent accoutrements of the upstairs suite, but it was more intimate. She asked if I wanted a drink and I told her that I just wanted to know who she was.

"You want the 411?" she asked. She was still wearing the dress I had seen her in earlier, what I would call a "fuck-me" dress, the kind that followed every curve of the body. It had a dramatically low neckline that rested just off the shoulders. It also had tulip-shaped side shirrings that flattered her torso. With a dress like that, accented by smoky stockings and black heels, she was advertising something, and it wasn't unreasonable that some men wanted to find out what. Her buzz cut was incongruous, a punk coif that gave her a slightly androgynous look, but then, when it comes to men, as Glen reminded me, a stiff dick . . .

"Yeah," I finally replied. "The 411. Who are you and what do you want?"

She said nothing for a few seconds. She just stared, admiring me or, rather, gazing at her "black" self. "Can't you feel it?" she said. "The vibe."

Unmistakably, there was something going on between us—and with the Pasha. He smoked a clove-scented brand of cigarettes and the room still had its lingering smell despite an open window. She was waiting for me to catch up with her vibe, but I was a busy woman: I had rumors to verify and a man I wanted to make love to. I turned to leave. "I'm not in the mood for this."

"No, wait," she said.

"Then tell me, Ms. Gordon, what this is about." I snapped. "I'm a busy woman!"

Gordon walked over to where I stood. "I'm sorry. I should have been more professional about this, but how do you tell someone that you're her double?"

"Double?" I said.

She nodded, slowly. "Don't you feel it, Nina?"

Perhaps that was the problem: I *was* feeling it. It was beginning to be too much for this kid. I was having an out-of-body experience with someone else's body. I can be as intuitive as the next person and even more analytical, but this was a sensory overload for me. I could feel it. This woman was my double, a doppelgänger. I turned, making a slight motion that indicated I might leave, but she grabbed me with both hands. I tried to resist, but her grip was firm and comforting, like a mother holding onto a frightened child. My first instinct was to protect myself, but she was not really a threat to me. It was as if I was telling myself to get a grip and doing it at once.

"I'm not going to hurt you," she said. "And I'm not trying to fuck with your mind."

I attempted to get away from her, but she held on and kept telling me that she just wanted to talk. I could have tried to punch her out, but it would have been like trying to knock myself out—but then, she wasn't me.

"Just answer me this," I said, fully breaking free of her once I had calmed down. "That tattoo? Is it really about your children?"

"Yes," she sighed.

"Are they . . . dead?"

"No. My ex-husband has them," said the strange woman. "I'm forbidden to see them for a while. Bad divorce."

I breathed my own sigh of relief, but felt bad about her maternal circumstances.

"Want to hear the whole story?"

"Only if you tell me about the Pasha," I replied.

"I'll tell you more than just about the Pasha," she said. She went over to the coffee table and reached for a cigarette.

"I don't want to know any more than—"

"Even if it's about Valerie Gordon?" She exhaled and a stream of smoke rolled out of her nostrils. "My sister?"

That perked up my ears. After her admission, she showed me her license, which *looked* legit. (After all, I was running with a purse fun of bogus IDs!) But I decided to do something risky: I decided to trust her, trust my instincts.

Nadia Gordon was a Californian. A former employee of the Los Angeles Police Department, she had been an exemplary officer who had made it to sergeant but had committed a major mistake. She was caught in a romantic relationship with a fellow officer, a Chicano, while married to Leigh Merriweather, an aspiring Republican attorney. It was bad enough that the affair was discovered by a Democractic opponent who used it to undermine her husband's claim about "family values," but her lover, Miguel, was then shot and killed by another police officer. That colleague was a white male who had the hots for Sgt. Nadia Gordon and felt insulted that she preferred a Mexican-American over him. The enraged cop was the one who had tipped off her husband's Democratic opponent. The divorce was nasty. Worse, she had suffered a nervous breakdown, getting clobbered all at once.

She was declared an unfit mother because of her adultery, depression, and the fact that she had a drinking problem—not unusual for police officers. It didn't help that she had gotten into a physical altercation with her former husband. Trying to start her life over again, Nadia moved to San Francisco and established herself as a private investigator.

I learned that we had both been born on the same day and year, and both had mothers who were teachers. Her father had been a career cop who had worked his way up in the police officers' union, while my father was a musician/machinist who had also made "the transfer" to a union office position. Both of our tragedies happened at about the same time: the murder of my husband, Lee, a professor, and my children; and the death of her lover, Miguel, who was studying to complete his doctorate in Mexican and Mexican-American history. Her divorce and loss of visitation rights to her children had occurred at about the same time that Anna discovered I was suppressing evidence in a high-profile case, thus forcing me to quit. Both of our mothers had passed away in the same year, leaving our fathers widowers. Spooky.

"And what about Valerie?" I asked her. We were sitting on the couch in her room. "How did she wind up dead with SugarDick?"

"She was in love with him," said Nadia, "as well as working with him on recruiting hip-hoppers into the American Writers Union."

"Did she know the rumors about him?" I asked. "What about his bitch-bashing lyrics?"

"About him being gay?" Nadia shrugged her shoulders. "Valerie didn't care about that. She saw it all as an act, the macho shit. Besides, what we might consider gay, others might consider bi. The kids today are more comfortable with the interdeterminacy and ambiguity of sexuality than we are. She found him to be the best lover she ever had. Go figure. Also, she had a political commitment to music."

"You mean the union organizing?"

"Yes," sighed Nadia. She reached over to the table and pulled another cigarette out of her packet. She was a smoke queen. I told her that rock musicians are too individualistic and stupid for that kind of organizing.

"To see the benefits of collective action?" she replied, lighting her cigarette and blowing the smoke away from me. "I agree with you, but my sister had a vision and it started with rappers."

"Who are even more stupid," I said. I thought of Mbooma and the idiocy I'd heard in my classroom days ago. "They all want to be big moneymakers, but they can barely read their contracts!"

Valerie had met SugarDick at a few parties and rap/rock collaborations. Glen had said SugarDick was trying to change his gangsta image and get with a new program and label, and Nadia now verified it.

"That's when the trouble began," she continued, "when he decided that he wasn't going to renew his contract with Big Poppa Insane—or if he did, it was going to be under a whole new set of circumstances."

"Who do you think killed them?"

"Keepie Kwazinela," she replied.

"South African?"

Nadia puffed on her cigarette and nodded. "Fergus's private liquidator. He's a former ANC turncoat who was captured by South African intelligence. He flipped and was trained to infiltrate the ANC. He performed assassinations for them and has worked for Fergus for years. You know about Fergus?"

"You mean him being in the South African intelligence service? Yes."

"He also has CIA contacts," said Nadia. "Kwazinela is assisting the thug department of Nigga Lovin' Records and Black Death."

"Just killing people?"

"That too, but also using intelligence techniques such as identifying potential dissenters, people who may have a predisposition to join the union or balk at signing onerous contracts. The first thing they have been doing is pinpointing the hip-hoppers who have a political consciousness and getting rid of them. He made sure that the upper echelon of the black labels understood the program while also making sure that the street-level hip-hoppers who are politicized knock each other off. Plays right into the so-called East/West feud. There's no feud."

Just egos with Glocks. "Okay," I nodded, "what about the Pasha? What's the deal between you two?"

"Valerie was in contact with the Pasha," she said.

"About what?"

"Valerie was thinking big . . ."

"Well, that can get a woman killed," I acknowledged. "About what?"

Nadia stubbed out her cigarette. "Valerie was pushing for a coalition. She wanted to get a big player behind her for a racketeering and influence-peddling charge against the majors, especially InfoNews."

She was moving a little too slow for me. I snapped my fingers. "The Pasha, Nadia, the Pasha."

"I'm coming to it, Nina," she replied. "You know about RICO?"

"Nadia," I said measuredly, "if you feel we have a vibe and that I'm your double, then you know I was a former prosecutor and that I would know about RICO. Right?"

"Oh, yeah . . ." Nadia said, thinking it over. She was quiet for a second. "You know, you're kind of responsible for me becoming a private investigator."

Impatiently, I slammed the space between us on the couch and rose from my seat. "Come on, Gordon, out with the story. I got people to kill and a man I want between my legs. A working woman ain't got all night!"

"I'm sorry," she said. "You were such an inspiration after what happened to you and your family. I read about you out west and how you—"

"Kept on keepin' on," I replied mockingly. "Yeah, I know. I'm a tireless upholder of the black tradition. We shall overcome and all that. Look, Nadia, I got the NYPD chasing me. My apartment was bombed yesterday . . ."

"Was that your place I read about in the newspaper?"

"To top it off, my husband has dragged me into this case and all I wanted to do was get laid, have a kid, and get on with the rest of my life!" I hissed between my teeth. "So I'm a bit on edge."

"I can see that," she replied, watching me carefully. "You do have a reputation for being tough."

"You want me to walk, Sergeant Gordon? Huh?"

"No," she said. "I just admire how you kept it all together."

I threw up my hands at that. "You, too, for $15.95, can purchase the Nina Halligan Spiritual Improvement Guide for Emotionally Crippled Wenches. Complete with empowerment affirmations for 365 days of the year!" I snapped my fingers. "Move this story or I'm out of here!"

The Pasha, she told me, was having trouble. With the increasing monopolization of the music business, his distribution outlets were being taken over by others and he was being pressured to sell. Those outlets that weren't bought were being sabotaged, trucking firms bombed, owners intimidated. Increasingly, it pointed to Fergus's operation, HØT MUZIK. And—surprise, surprise—Reggie Baxter was the person who had approached the Pasha, on Fergus's behalf, and told him to get with the program. The Pasha, God bless him, threw Baxter out of his office.

"I came east to take my sister's body home," she said, "and while I was cleaning up her place I saw the stuff she was working on and what she had been documenting. She had the Pasha's name in some of her material and I called him and told him who I was."

"He was willing to work with you?"

"Yeah," she nodded. "You see, some of Fergus's new playmates threatened him at the music award show in Atlanta."

"So you were the one who rattled Fergus's balls, huh?"

She smiled. "Yeah." Then the smile quickly disappeared. "It was nothing compared to what happened to my sister. The back of her head was blown out."

"I'm sorry." I'd seen what punctured and bullet-riddled bodies looked like. I kept thinking that I could get away from that world, but here I was talking to some strange woman who was claiming to be my double—and what was even weirder was me believing her. I casually looked around and saw a lone guitar propped up in the corner. Immediately I thought of my first husband, who'd played guitar. Lee loved classical, blues, bluegrass, folk, rock, and anything else that could be transcribed to six strings. I also realized that since we had been on the run, Glen had not played any music and that it must be slowly killing him. I thought about Nadia being in this hotel with just her guitar and figured it was good cover. No one would think that she was a PI—if indeed she was one.

"Listen, I have to go back upstairs and poke my nose into other people's business. You want to come and hang out with me and meet the family?"

"You mean business, right?"

"Business *and* pleasure," I corrected. "I got a date for later."

"Lucky you." She smiled.

Nadia said she would be up to my place in ten minutes. I left her room, returned to my suite, and found Zee. Ibrahim had gone home. I told her that we were going to head to La Bomba's party first to see what was cooking there and then cruise up to Taliferro's. I also told her about Nadia. I left out the salt-and-pepper aspect.

As I was throwing water on my face in the bathroom, Zee knocked on the door. She had a very strange look on her face.

"Zee, what's wrong?"

"Nadia Gordon is here," she replied. "She looks awfully familiar. I just can't place her face."

I smiled and told her it would come to her.

TRACK 19

A GRRRL PARTY

When we arrived at La Bomba's party it was in full force and for ladies only. Some water buffalo of a woman was providing security and she let us in. La Bomba had deemed the evening wear to be lingerie *only*. So it was somewhat of a shock to step into a room full of women in just their undies. The three of us stood there watching scantily clad women dancing, sitting around talking, laughing, eating (food, mind you) in the near nude. A handful of women were standing about nonchalantly in their birthday suits and high heels.

Zee shrugged her shoulders and began disrobing. I forgot that being an army officer she was used to mass female nudity. The only thing she was worried about was her pistol clashing with her teddy. I told her to wrap the holster up with her jacket but put the gun in her purse. That worked. We hung our clothes up and joined the rest.

"All right, girls," I said underneath my breath, "the first bitch who pinches you, clock her." Suddenly the Police's "Don't Stand So Close to Me" began playing in my head, competing with the Me'shell Ndegeocello that was funking up the room.

We moved through the crowd and got appreciative looks. I couldn't figure out if they were appraising the wrapping or the contents. Zee figured both. Nadia didn't think everyone was cruising. I had to admit there was a lightness and sense of felicity that one would not have found if menfolk were present. This confirmed that women were the more sociable creatures, exuding a sexuality but still communicating, emotionally and intellectually seeking to connect with each other. Of course, there was a certain kind of connection some of the women were inclined to make. Sisterhood is sexy.

The hostess of the party waltzed up in an open leopard-print rayon robe over a leopard-print stretch satin bodysuit. She held a fan in her hand.

"*¡Hola! Amigas!*" Magdalena had a fat cigar in her mouth, as did some of the other women in the room. "Glad you got here, Alexis. Zee." When Magdalena was introduced to Nadia she did a double take, but she didn't say anything. "Ladies," she said to Zee and Nadia, "fix yourselves a drink while I speak to Alexis here!"

Magdalena took me over to a corner while the girls got their refreshments.

"Where's Volaré?" I asked.

"She's talking to that woman in the silk chemise."

I glanced over to the couch and spotted the red-haired Volaré, wearing an ivory, button-front camisole, engaged in an animated conversation with another woman who was of ample girth but not fat.

"Well?"

"You have to be kidding," said La Bomba. "This is going to take some time, doña. One has to . . . ah . . . cultivate these things. And it may not happen overnight . . ."

Volaré seemed to be vibing on the other woman. "You sure that you and the babe are scheduled?"

La Bomba stepped back and suddenly produced a fan and flicked it open with gusto. "Doña, very few women or men can resist me—only you puritans! This is a done deal. She shall be *fucked*, and lovingly. Don't worry. Have I ever failed you?"

"No, you haven't, but there's . . ."

"You doubt the power of this body coupled with such a mind?" She placed the fan underneath my chin. "Child, I'll see you tomorrow morning."

"Right. Ten A.M. The sauna."

"Now that's settled," she said. "What's going on with Anna? Our friend is disappointing me."

"Huh?" I feigned.

"Don't dummy up on me, *puta*," said La Bomba in fluent Americanese. She flicked open the fan again and brought it up to our faces, covering them both. "I saw her in a dark corner of the hallway all over some man."

I shrugged my shoulders and sighed. "La Bomba, you know these modern women. They want it every way past Sunday. If I see her, I'll tell her you did voice some concern about her, uh, public activities. *Ciao*." I kissed her on each side of her face and turned. Before I made it over to Nadia and Zee, I felt a sharp sting on my rear. I knew where it came from but kept moving.

"Okay, girls, I gotta find my husband," I told them. "Y'all can stay if you like." Zee said that she would leave as well since she was also a married woman. Nadia said that she had met a guy downstairs who might be at Taliferro's. We grabbed our clothes and got out of there. The fact that Anna was doing "bad" things with Win meant that good things *might* be happening. One never knows with us modern women.

A few floors down we headed to Taliferro's funk emporium and the place was rocking. You could hear the rolling thunder as we stepped off the elevator. "Okay, girls, every woman for herself and God against all," I said as we entered the devil's rec room. There was a thick cloud, a slight marijuana haze mixed with the pungent smell of human bodies in close quarters. Someone knew about mood control. Unlike upstairs where the gals wanted to see each other's pores, someone knew about lighting down here. Things couldn't be too brightly lit. That would have spoiled the fun. The element of controlled dusk had to be invoked. Bodies were dancing, some standing like interior lampposts in corners and in front of tables and bookcases, watching, sizing up ambulating opportunities, male and female.

This was the professional Negro set that felt under the cover of subdued light it could act and do the forbidden, namely be niggacool™. This had more to do with class than essence. It was a warped cultural exchange: Many middle-class blacks conformed to the prescribed norms of acting "white," and many whites loved to act "black" when they wanted to relax from the strains of civilization. And usually music provided the salve or the release. Black music, with its association of unremitting carnality, passion, ecstasy, and emotionalism, allowed them to connect with the greatest fear of some whites: their *inner* nigga. That's why educated blacks are always a threat. They are not striking the correct nigga chords within the white psyche. Whites have their own idea as to how a certain class of blacks should keep it real.

But for the Afro nouveau riches, what was slightly disconcerting was the new jack syndrome that had come into play—the Taliferros and, God forbid, the Big Poppa Insanes and Icy Ds. Unquestionable blots on black achievements, they had more wealth than those with educational credentials and corporate status.

And it was the bad niggas who knew how to throw the parties—and brought the bitchez. Such was the cynicism of the times. The bougies hated the image of rap and its associations, but bucked their asses to the illicit and nignorant observations of a Baby Cakes, who vulgarly sang of the joys of getting over—and bending over:

Yeah, motherfucker, rub it slick,
You better give me a Lexus before I suck that dick,
Think I'm a scuz? You got that right,
Story is I'm a smart bitch who be more than bright.

Fuck me to death
Suck me to death
Rub me to death
Fuck me to death

"Did I hear that right?" said Zee, whose face showed no appreciation for the artistry that was assaulting her ears and sensibilities. "Is this what the kids are listening to? What's the name of that song?"

"'Fuck Me to Death,'" replied Nadia. "Very subtle, huh?"

"Oh, I wonder how I missed that," said Zee. "Sounds like a Sick Daddy Inane production."

"It does have its liberatory elements, mind you," said Nadia.

"Zee, I told you it was the end of black civilization," I chimed in as we squeezed our way through the gyrating crowd. "And that's merely the radio airplay version."

"That's not the whole picture, Zee," said Nadia. "That's the shit you'll hear on the boom boxes on the street."

"Yeah, where it can cause much more damage to innocent three-, five-, and ten-year-olds," I replied, getting rear-ended by some dude who looked as if he was going up for the downstroke. "But who can argue with success? Rap makes over a billion dollars a year and is known all over the world. Black folks just don't control it." I found myself sounding like Glen, wanting to protect the music.

"Is that the only important thing?" challenged Nadia. "You think it would be any different if blacks did?"

I shrugged my shoulders. I'd had this discussion with Glen days before. "Blacks, in my opinion, are just glorified employees."

Nadia was about to respond, but I saw a familiar sight in a dark corner, drinking a bottle of Red Stripe. Glen was by himself, standing alone and staring across the room.

"Eduardo!" I shouted as I walked over to him.

It took him a flat second to recognize me in the semidarkness. He smiled and put his arm around me, pulled me into the corner, and whispered in my ear, "Be cool, I think the nigga sitting across from Taliferro and China is *the* motherfucker." I slowly pulled away and took the bottle from him and sipped on it, turning in the direction that he had been scoping. Across the room there was a small cluster of people among whom Taliferro and China were sitting.

"Yeah, see the guy in the dark suit and banded collar?" said Glen.

I spied a man dressed as Glen had described, sitting with the kings of korruption—Insane, Icy, and Taliferro. Also in the cluster were the Pasha and my cousin Maxine Devereaux, the CEO of Groove Records, one of the very few black female executives in the industry. Our elusive "Scarface" was a thickset man who seemed to enjoy being in the middle of things, the big moneymakers, fine women, and the excitement of just hanging. Interestingly, Keepie and Poppa shared a resemblance—a set of matching bookends.

"That's the man I saw coming from Sugar's room," Glen said, eyes focused on him. "That's the motherfucker who killed Sugar . . . scar and all."

Nadia also spotted him. "Yeah . . . that's Keepie Kwazinela."

Glen squinted at her. He locked in on our facial resemblance and then turned to me.

"Yeah, I know," I said. "She's Valerie Gordon's sister."

A boisterous roar of laughter cut through the cigar smoke and all the men except the Pasha were guffawing over some idiocy that was probably a "bitch story." China didn't look too interested in the company that she was keeping. I felt that she had been tortured long enough. Disgusted, she suddenly rose, but Taliferro tried to stop her. She protested and continued to move away. Maxine took that as a signal and was about to leave as well.

"OH, LET THAT STINKY BITCH GO," said Insane to Taliferro. "I'VE TRIED TO FUCK HER, BUT SHE BE INTO HER BITCHES' BUTTS . . ."

"Okay, that's enough for tonight!" snapped the Pasha, incensed that Insane would speak to a major artist that way. "Big Poppa, you're a disgusting lowlife! You and your fellow hoodlums have debased music. It's nothing more than a front for your thuggish, antisocial behavior!"

Insane snapped his fingers and pointed to Mr. Ibn. One of his goons grabbed the elderly gentleman from behind, pinning him against the armchair he sat in. Insane rose and planted a solid punch into the elder man's chest. It sounded as if a rib cracked. Insane pulled his arms back to deliver a second, but my arm was quicker. I had pulled off one of the metal stars and flung it, hitting him midarm. Another went into the upper arm of the goon that held the Pasha.

"BITCH!" screamed Big Poppa, holding onto his arm, eyes blazing at me. "I'M GONNA FUCK YOU UP! BITCH!" He moved his big-ass self in my direction but suddenly stopped.

Zee had pulled out her pistol and trained it on them. She understood too that Keepie was a liquidator and may be armed. She knew how to watch all but concentrate on one.

"No one moves!" I shouted over the music that kept most of the dancers ignorant of this little sideshow. "China! Max! Pasha! Over here! Pronto! The rest of you fatherfuckers, don't move!" I pointed to Insane's goon who stood behind Ibn. "Back off!"

"You got it, baby!" he said, wincing. "You got it! Shit! Just don't throw another one of them stars! You be a motherfuckah! Goddamn . . ."

"Nina . . . ?" said a surprised Maxine, who was edging her way over to me and the others. The last time we had seen each other was days ago at my place. I looked different then.

"Move it, Max! My arm is getting tired!" I had my arm up, cocked to throw another star. Keepie was cool. He just sat there watching the show. A sly grin appeared on his face. He enjoyed watching fellow professionals in action.

When we had collected Maxine, China, and the Pasha, I told Glen to lead the way. Zee and I kept our eyes on the rest as we backed out of there, with Zee bringing up the rear. When we got to the hallway we ran to an elevator. The party was over for us. Insane and his goons would undoubtedly try to make a retaliatory hit. Or, if they were smart, they'd call the police, people we really didn't want to deal with. Glen took Maxine and China down to the lobby and ushered them out of the hotel and into a cab. Zee and I checked the Pasha in my suite to make sure that he was all right.

"I'm fine," he slowly breathed. "I'm fine. All this convinces me that what Whyte said was true about them! They are criminals hooked up with an even bigger one! Fergus!"

"Whyte *who?* Bobby Whyte?" I asked. I briskly walked around the room and began gathering everything that was ours. Zee was also collecting things. Nadia was standing by the door with one of my guns. "You know him?"

The Pasha nodded. "He told me that a killing had taken place at his home in Bronxville. And that Fergus had known about it . . ."

"Where is he?" I asked, stopping and looking around the room. "Where is Whyte?"

"At my home," he said, "in Paris. Do *you* know him?"

"About him, sir." I decided it was time to announce my true identity. "I'm Nina Halligan . . . I'm . . . uh . . . a semiretired private investigator. The man I'm with is my husband, Glen Sierra, and we're investigating the death of SugarDick."

"Ah, Nina Halligan? That explains it! You women were magnificent!" he exclaimed. "Amazons, true Amazons. Your reputation precedes you, my good woman."

"She's the best, Mr. Ibn," said Nadia.

I would have stopped to bow, but I had things on my mind like getting the hell out of the hotel. If Insane and his posse didn't come looking for us, the police might.

The old man nodded in agreement. "So you know things, my dear."

"Some things, Mr. Ibn," I replied. "What is Whyte doing in Paris?"

"Hiding out from those criminals and Fergus," replied the old man. "The man is scared. He's not used to these hip-hop criminals! He knows things about Fergus and others."

I looked at Nadia. "You know anything about this, girlfriend?"

"No," she said. "Not about Whyte."

"I didn't tell her, Ms. Halligan," said the Pasha. "I promised Bobby that I wouldn't. I came here to see things for myself and find out if what he was telling me is true."

"What did he tell you?"

"The killings and the deaths. Something is going on."

"That we know. The question is what exactly. Did you know that one of the men sitting near you was SugarDick and Nadia's sister's killer?"

"No," said the man, shocked. "Who was that?"

I described Keepie to him.

"That's Fergus's bodyguard," said Mr. lbn.

"Taking a break from murder and mayhem," added Zee. "Nina, we have everything."

All of our luggage had been collected. I nodded. Zee was now going around the room wiping off everything that could have been touched by one of us or our guests. "Pasha, I need to speak to him."

The door opened and Glen walked in. "I got China into a cab and called Bass and told him to be on the lookout. Now, who is this 'him'?"

Glen was informed about the missing Bobby Whyte. "Where is he?"

"France," I said, then looked at the Pasha. "Mr. Ibn, I really need to speak to him. We have to bust this thing, whatever is going on."

"I can tell you partly what's going on," he said dramatically. "It's the end of a certain era of the music business! The gangsters have taken over!"

"Pasha, the music industry has always had its share of scoundrels," said Glen. "The government doesn't care about what's happening in music unless there's a major scandal. They won't regulate it. They are only interested when they hear of a payola scandal or some corn-fed kid blows his brains out over alleged satanic rock. Now, we have cartels developing."

"Yes! I'd be the first to admit that, but this is different. Now it is out in the open and there is no sense in trying to elevate the music, clean up the past performances. No sense of reform or professionalism. It's just about getting paid!" The Pasha stood and looked at me. "I'm an old man and I can see that my time has passed. But what about Groove Music?"

"What *about* Groove Music?" He was getting close to home.

"Fergus is trying to squeeze me out. I'm thinking about aligning myself with the Groove, trying to keep one black company independent. The Devereaux are not criminals."

"I should say not," I answered.

"You know them, dear lady?"

"Maxine is my cousin, on my mother's side," I informed him.

"Then you *must* come to Paris with me, young lady, and Bobby will talk."

I looked at Glen, who nodded his head in agreement. "Go, Nina.We'll hold down the fort."

"But stay out of sight," I said, as I went over and clasped his hands. "We're still wanted."

It was agreed that I would go to Paris and talk to Bobby Whyte. Glen, Zee, and Nadia would continue our investigation stateside. The Pasha offered to make his town house available. That gave us a base of operations other than China's. We left the hotel—without checking out. I got into a limo with the Pasha and would soon board an unexpected flight to the land of *parlez-vous*. I had to make a special request of Zee and Anna. I was trusting them with the life of my husband and I wanted to find him alive when I got back. They would protect the one I loved.

TRACK 20
IL DUCE

When Bobby Whyte learned that Shawn Butterfield had been dispatched in his house and that they expected to hide the body on his property, he panicked. When told that Fergus's bodyguard had killed the young man, he knew it was only a matter of time before he would have to bite the bullet. Initially, Fergus knew that Whyte understood and would keep his mouth shut because he had a million-dollar investment in his firms. But Fergus also suggested that he could make it look like Butterfield had been Whyte's lover and that another lover of his had taken out Butterfield.

The whole thing had a bitter ironic twist given that the dead young man had been caught shtupping Baby Cakes and was unquestionably straight. But being a former intelligence agent, Fergus could give it a nice homoerotic slant, especially for today's prurient media. America had whetted its appetite on Gianni Versace's murder and his alleged HIV-driven gay killer. The public would be ready for a nice all-American-homo-prep-boy–b-boy story.

Days later Whyte boarded a plane, flew to Paris, and went directly to his good friend, Pia Ibn, the Pasha's wife and a fellow designer. The poor man was frightened out of his wits. He cursed the day that he met Andre Taliferro and had listened to the marketer's advice about clothing some hip-hoppers and using them on a runway. "Of course it made me money," he said, "but I didn't think I was getting into Murder, Inc., *noir*. It was a Faustian bargain and now Shylock has come to collect."

"I think you're mixing your literary allusions," I said, as we sat in the Ibns's book-lined library in their spacious Parisian apartment. I hadn't had much sleep and wanted to find out what I needed to know and get back home. I knew I was going to be a wreck because of the time change, crossing back and forth in twenty hours and then some.

Bobby Whyte was slightly put out by the fact that Mr. Ibn had brought me. He wanted to keep the thing hush-hush, and didn't understand that the quieter he kept it, the more likely he would be dead-dead. No. He, being a businessman, a relatively wealthy young man, wanted to keep the whole thing out of the press so it would not sully the name of Bobby Whyte, Inc.

"Look, Miss Nina . . ." said the sandy-haired former athlete. He had the kind of WASP image that graced magazines and any mother hungry for a son-in-law would swoon over. Yet the little girls and the fathers knew differently.

"Don't call me that." I felt there was a condescending gay guy–straight girl thing about to start and I wanted to nip it in the bud. He could save that shit for a TV sitcom. "Call me Nina or Ms. Halligan."

"Whatever," he said, in a mildly petulant tone. "I have an investment. Bobby Whyte is a publicly traded company. I already put a lot on the line when I became involved with those who were, ah, melanin-inclined."

"Robert," said the Pasha, setting down his coffee cup, "let's not go that way."

"What way, Mohammad?" asked Whyte, not too innocently.

"The signifying," he said. "That isn't necessary. Ms. Halligan is a former prosecutor, an investigator, and a teacher. She saved my life and deserves respect. She doesn't *run* when trouble occurs."

Mr. Whyte didn't have much to tell me other than what he had mentioned earlier. His friends, Andre Taliferro and Rolf Fergus, had convinced him to host a party meeting for some of the high muck-a-mucks of the recording industry. The usual suspects had shown up, the same people who attended InfoGlobal: the crew that Nadia had denounced as sellouts and bootlickers. However, I surmised, that was more of Mr. Ibn's moral position than Nadia's. She just wanted her sister's killer.

Something must have happened to make Fergus want two people dead. Baby Cakes and Shawn must have inadvertently heard something they weren't supposed to. I wanted to know what.

"What went on? Were you there?"

"I was there as the host, but there were meetings with all the record people who gathered."

"And they talked about what?"

Whyte looked at me as if I was a fool. "Records! Music! Business! What else do people talk about at such a thing?"

I thought for a second and looked at Mr. Ibn. "You weren't there, Pasha. Why not?"

The old man sighed. "I guess I hadn't signed on with the program. Neither had Groove Music, mind you."

"Was there anything suspicious that was said that you might have caught a snippet of, Mr. Whyte? I know you were not part of the meetings, but . . ."

He couldn't think of anything, or at least he wouldn't say. Needing a break, I stood up and went to the French windows and looked out over the activities of the *arrondissement* where the Ibns lived. I'd been to Paris twice and was always struck by the similarity of the Haussmann-styled buildings. There was a uniformity to them that confused me. I could not easily pick a noted landmark among the buildings when I lost my sense of direction. Time stood still in Paris, unlike in New York, where you could never quite remember where one building had stood before they had torn it down and built up another, usually more hideous or bland than the preceding one.

But Paris was a beautiful city that was as diverse as New York, with its Africans, Asians, and Algerians (different from their sub-Saharan co-continentals). I liked the city and thought about living there for a couple of years. Maybe if I decided to write a serious book, the unfinished manuscript that my first husband started about the political demobilization of black America. Now I was learning about it the hard way. I could do it in Paris. Bring a child here. Such dreams . . . But that had to wait like everything else that was good in life.

"Nina?" said Whyte. "I don't know if this means anything . . ."

I turned from the sunlight that was bathing my face. "Yes?"

"I got the impression that something was going on between Rolf Fergus and Poppa. There was a lot of tension between them. Fergus acted as if Poppa intimidated him."

"Fergus scared of Poppa?" I stared at the Pasha.

"Well," said the Pasha, "I've seen him throw his weight around with Fergus. People do clear a path when he's around. Even Fergus himself has said, 'That man is dangerous.'"

"Big Poppa?"

Mr. Ibn quietly nodded his head. "Fergus left the party at my house early," continued Whyte. "Later, I heard Poppa mention the name of a person who hadn't been there."

"And who was that?"
"Radeem."

"*Radeem?*" said Glen over the phone. "I don't think he's a music executive. I never heard of him. The games? Everybody talks about *playing the game* or being *true to the game.*"

"Yeah, that's what Whyte said. It seems that Fergus and Poppa had a falling-out. I think that Baby Cakes mentioned that also," I said, trying to get comfortable on the Pasha's plane back to New York. The dear man remained in Paris and I decided to head back with what I knew. I told Glen to tell Zee about the name and to feed it to the computers in the Womb.

"What about the games?" said Glen.

"Well, let's work on Radeem first. He may have a connection to the *games*, whatever that is."

"When will you be home, love?"

I looked at my watch. "A couple of hours, baby. Miss me?"

"You know I do, my tigress," he said. "I must say, I was impressed by the way you handled the situation at the hotel."

"Well, that's why you married me. So I could protect your ass when you get into trouble."

"Hmmm. I thought it was the other way around."

"Glenito," I purred, "you know that behind every brother's back is a good sister. So, you gonna rock 'n' roll me to death when I get home, as my reward?"

He began saying the most salacious and lascivious things over the phone to me, fifty thousand feet up. Doing it in my eardrums. Promising what he would do, making love to my mind.

"What the—*uffh!*"

"Glen?"

I heard the phone fall to the floor, then what sounded like scuffling, furniture being knocked over, objects crashing.

"Glen! Glen!" I shouted. "What's going on?"

The noise ended and the phone went dead. I repeatedly pressed redial but no one answered. It was three o'clock in the morning and I was still over the Atlantic. It would be a couple of hours before I landed at JFK. I began dialing again and reached a sleepy Zee.

"Zee," I said breathlessly into the phone, "you have to go over to the Pasha's town house! Something happened to Glen. It sounded as if he was being attacked! I'm still flying . . . Please!"

"Don't worry, Nina," she replied, sounding alert and ready for an action that I couldn't handle. "I'm on my way!"

My mind raced back and forth after I clicked off the phone. We had been extremely careful about not being followed to the Pasha's east side town house, but obviously someone had entered and . . . I didn't even want to think about that, about becoming a three-time man-loser. Yet I'd heard no gunfire. That was good, but that could have meant a knife was . . . The possibilities weren't encouraging. Either way, something had happened and there was nothing I could do about it.

I picked up my cell phone and called Anna to relay the news.

"Oh my God," she said, her voice still thick with sleep. "What do you think happened?"

"I don't know, Annie. I'm just praying to the Guy Above that whatever, he's okay. I have to believe that. Either it was a robbery or a move by Big Poppa Insane. From what I learned in Paris, it seems that Fergus is scared to death of him."

"Of Big Poppa? Why?"

"I don't know, but it seems we underestimated mouth o'mighty. He wants to be a serious player in the industry. Even Glen had heard rumors that BPI was the power behind Fergus's musical throne, but had discounted it."

"And you didn't endear yourself to him when you punctured one of his arteries," she proudly teased. Anna was the one who had given me my first set of kung-fu stars.

"I was going to let him beat down an old man like the Pasha? That would have been like watching my own grandfather being assaulted on a street corner and not do anything."

I had heard the stories of Big Poppa Insane's legendary beat-downs and shuddered at the thought that that could be my man's fate. Big Poppa had walked into editorial offices and balled up many a scribe. He busted them up and tossed them into wastepaper baskets. If the writers were women, he would humiliate them by making them disrobe at gunpoint. He would never exchange bodily fluid or do anything else in those sessions. No, he was into the mind-fuck of humiliation.

"What's happening with you and Winston?" I asked, needing to change the subject.

"Oh," she said, yawning, "he loves me to death. He's out of town this weekend."

"And?"

"I still miss her, Nina," said Anna in her small, little-girl voice. "I miss her very much."

"Esperanza?" I replied. "Of course you do. I still miss Lee and Luc . . . But remember this, Anna.

She left *you*. By dint of fate, Win showed up. The guy cares about and loves you. Just remember that when you get all hot and bothered over Ranza."

"I'm relieved I don't have to make that decision," she sighed. "I'm also relieved that someone really wants me."

"Come on, Anna. You're a Miss Chinatown winner. Everybody wants to get down with a Lucy Liu or Ming-Na nowadays."

"Yeah, and that's what has made me vain," she confessed. "Remember, Esperanza was the second woman who dumped me. First, there was Shinyun. Three, if I count you."

Three, I thought. That's what I feared becoming, a three-time man-loser. I'd dreaded this case and had wanted to get out and go about our business. Glen, however, pushed this issue with gleeful abandonment. The music . . . stupid, goddamn music. He just didn't know when to quit and now it seemed as if somebody was going to make him—us!—pay.

TRACK 21

THE TEN PERCENT SOLUTION

An hour later, Zee told me the good news and the bad news: Glen had not been found at the Pasha's apartment.

"That's good news?" I exclaimed as the jet approached the United States. "That he's missing? Come on, girl, help me out!"

"Good compared to what I did find there," she answered. "Nadia is dead."

I was stunned, not merely by the news of her death but by the fact that I'd completely forgotten that she had retreated to the Pasha's place with Glen when I left. Now she was gone.

"Strangled," said Zee. Zee and Mustapha had entered the town house and methodically searched the place from top to bottom. They couldn't detect any visible signs of a break-in. Upstairs they discovered Nadia propped up in a chair, arms tied behind her back, her face bruised. Her shirt had been pulled back and the killer had written with lipstick on her breasts the words, "*John 10:34*."

Glen hadn't been found, meaning that he might have been kidnapped in exchange for something. Or that he had been taken somewhere else to be subjected to some sick and twisted torture.

When we ended the conversation, Zee and her father removed the body from the Pasha's and took it to the Situation Room—sometimes called "the Womb"—below her father's electronics store on

Canal Street. Anna met me at the airport and told me not to lose faith. We drove straight from the airport to Kincaid Electronics in Manhattan.

Thirty minutes later I found myself looking down at Nadia's bruised face. She lay on a metal table in a room that had been used for medical emergencies on some of my assignments. Sometimes I didn't want to deal with doctors, who had to report gunshot wounds or any other deadly assaults to the police. The room, attended by off-the-book doctors, made things discreet and affordable.

"Zee?" I looked at the words that had been written on her chest, above her breasts. "What is this referring to?"

"It's an obscure remark by Jesus . . ." began Zee, looking at the Bible.

"Zee, nothing said by Jesus is *ever* obscure," I said, disgusted and exasperated at the prospect of having to deal with religious fanatics in the mix. Zee stopped and peered at me. "Okay . . . I'm sorry," I added. Both Anna and Zee were aware that I hadn't slept much since hearing of Glen's disappearance. I had kept myself awake by literally pacing over the Atlantic in Mr. Ibn's jet.

Zee explained that the inscription referred to a passage in the New Testament, the Gospel of Saint John. Jesus was replying to his fellow Jews who had been critical of a previous remark he had made. They accused him of being blasphemous. Charged with comparing himself to God, he replied, "*Is it not written in your law, 'I said, you are gods'?*"

"Okay, girls, let's wrap this up," I said. "This isn't telling me much of anything." I looked down at Nadia and pulled up the white sheet, but Zee caught my arm. "What?"

"When we saw her like this at the house we thought so, too, until we got her down here and stripped her." Zee guided my arm downward, pulling the sheet back to reveal an area below Nadia's navel. She had been branded with a sign, a circle with a five-pointed star. Each point, clockwise, had a letter: *K*, *S*, *P*, *W*, *S*. In the middle of the star was the Roman numeral *V*.

"What do the letters mean," asked Anna, who had walked in while Zee was reading from the Bible, "besides being the work of a kink freak?" She handed me a cup of coffee.

"Knowledge, Science, Purpose, Wisdom, and Strength." Zee laid the Bible on a small table in the examination room and fully covered Nadia's lifeless body. "The Five Points—an offshoot of the Original Kingdom of Afrika, second generation—third, in some opinions—of Ten Percenter theology, cosmology."

"What?" asked Anna. "You mean this stuff has something to do with Dr. Isiah Afrika?"

I sighed. "This is that run-amok, original–black man bullshit masquerading as Islam, that has warped an entire generation of knucklehead nationalists!"

"Amplified by hip-hop," Zee added. "Ten Percenter cosmology permeates some nation-conscious rap, and a very influential group was the Five Points. It consisted of Big Poppa Insane, Icy D, Mbooma, SugarDick, and Radeem. Some people have argued that the Ten Percenters are a perversion of Du Bois's notion of the talented tenth. And Terrell X from Chicago was known as Terrell Miller—he and Jonny Coke, the singer, used to belong to a Chicago gang called the Annihilators."

I raised my hand. "Whoa, girl. Are we talking about *the* Jonny Coke?"

Zee nodded. "Yes, the lead vocalist for the Sanctifiers."

Jonny Coke had caused quite a stir in gospel circles during the fifties when he left the Sanctifiers and recorded what some called the "devil's music," rhythm & blues. After a few pit stops at other record companies, he signed a contract with Groove Records and became one of the major stars of soul music until his untimely and controversial death.

"Jonny Coke," continued Zee, "is considered a spiritual uncle of the Ten Percenters because he knew Mallory Rex, and was supposedly influenced by the Original Kingdom of Afrika's philosophy of black empowerment and black control over black music."

"These guys were basically sold a refried version of Christianity via Islam, with aspects of Yoruba culture tossed in," I opined. "It gives it just a dash of Africano."

"*Izlam*," Zee corrected me. "They call it Izlam."

"See, they even fucked that up. Islam means submission to God. What is Izlam? Willful nignorance?"

"Wait. Wait," interjected Anna. "Are you saying this"—she pointed to the body—"was done by the Five Points?"

"Or somebody influenced by their philosophy," Zee replied. "Like I said, Big Poppa Insane was a Five Pointer. Old Five-P."

"Ladies," said Anna, casting a wary eye on the body before us, "let's get out of here." Anna was never very good at morbidity reviews when we were prosecutors. Dead bodies gave her the creeps. To be honest, they never did anything for my complexion.

We locked the door and returned to the Situation Room. On a white board Zee wrote the names of the members of the Five Points: Big Poppa Insane, Mbooma, Icy D, SugarDick, and Radeem. Of the five, two were dead. BPI was the prime suspect. Icy D was a runner-up. Radeem? No one had heard of him.

They had initially started off as poor but enlightened teachers who knew the way of the TRUE ORIGINAL BLACK MAN, as their writing and obnoxiously loud voices proclaimed from their street-corner assemblies in New York. They preached to the WALKING DEAD NIGGROS and collectively pooled their money and spread the word by means of hip-hop. Each had a specialty: Poppa, SugarDick, and Mbooma were the microphone fiends, the emcees who castigated whites as devil and faggots, exhorting the BLACK MAN (and ladies who weren't "evil cooze bitches") to be GODS and EARTHS. Icy D ran the turntable, and Radeem played instruments: keyboards, saxophone, guitar, and percussion.

"You know, I ran across them years ago," recalled Anna. "A rookie officer tried to make a case against them and I had to let them go."

"Why?"

"First Amendment," she replied. "Freedom of speech. I couldn't hold them for being obnoxious. Maybe disorderly conduct, but they had protective speech coverage." Anna vaguely remembered them, or others like them, who dressed in neo-Islamic and African garb—turbans, kufis, colorful tunics, baggy pants, vests over magnificently buffed torsos—and dark shades and beards. They preached from the Koran, the Bible, and from the teachings of Dr. Isiah Afrika and Terrell X, the founder of the Ten Percenters.

I listened, but I had to know a few other things. "Okay, let's say they nabbed Glen and killed Nadia. Why?"

"They want something from you, Nina," said Zee. "Nadia? She's a blond, blue-eyed devil in their eyes, and deserved to die."

"Duh?" I responded. "What?"

"You are onto something and they want to stop it. Your investigation."

I put up my finger. "It's not my investigation," I counterpointed. "It was Glen who—"

"True," answered Zee, "but you may be getting too close to finding out what's going on."

"Why not Fergus?" I asked. "Couldn't he be behind this?"

"Nina, you said that people think that Fergus is just a straw man, a paper tiger, if you will," argued Anna. "Is he? Keepie is the gunsel who fired a grenade into your apartment. He works for Fergus. Isn't Fergus the one who's controlling the mayor?"

"Maybe he wants us to think he's pussy-whipped," I said. "Wouldn't Big Poppa Insane be a good front?"

"Well, as Sun-Tzu stated in *In the Art of War*," Zee reflected, "'*While strong in reality, appear to be weak; while brave in reality, appear to be cowardly.*'"

"But which one, Zee? Fergus or Poppa Insane?"

The kidnapping had happened hours ago, but no one had contacted me as of yet, nor had there been a note left behind. It was still early in the morning and the city would begin to awaken. The behemoth called New York would start all over again. The rhythm of the city would soon kick in. We were operating on the assumption that the kidnapping was a way to get my attention. Nadia's death was their way of letting me know that they meant business. While pacing I noticed several items on a desk in a semi-lit corner.

"Those are Glen's and Nadia's belongings," Zee informed me. "We made sure there was no trace of them in the Pasha's apartment."

"Thanks," I said. I opened a suitcase that belonged to Glen and found his shaving kit and clothes. I wanted to pick up a gray shirt of his and search for his scent but felt that was a bit desperate. Maybe later, but not now. Nadia's belongings, however, already had the stench of death on them. Her guitar stood in the corner. I then realized that something of Glen's was missing. His . . . My phone began vibrating. I reached into my shirt pocket and flipped it open. "Hello?"

"Nina?" It was Mr. Ibn.

I sighed, and before I could speak he let me know that he had heard from Big Poppa.

"My daughter," he said, "I heard what's happened. Glen is alive, but Big Poppa told me to tell you to go to the twenty-fifth floor of a building at 100 Livingston Street in Brooklyn, room 2501, at one P.M. He will give you instructions about the situation, his demands."

I looked at my watch and at Zee's and Anna's expectant faces.

"Who's that?" Anna quietly asked. I placed my hand over the mouthpiece and said, "The Pasha."

"That cur Big Poppa is going to try and make you his plaything. Please be careful, dear woman. I will pray for you and your husband."

"Thank you, Mr. Ibn." I folded my unit and placed it back in my shirt. "The Pasha said Big Poppa called him. It's official: Poppa has Glen. I have to go to Brooklyn for a meeting."

"Well, at least we know he's alive," Anna reasoned. "Poppa wants to talk to you?"

I nodded my head. The stress of being on the run, the Atlantic crisscrossing, and Glen's kidnapping were wearing me down, working my last good nerve. I had caught very little sleep on the way over and even less on the way back. I told the girls where I had to be at one P.M. Zee insisted on going over there first to check the place out and act as backup. I wasn't going to refuse her offer.

I felt incredibly drowsy. My eyelids began fluttering, laden with fatigue. I was about to experience a supreme narcoleptic slowdown. It was sleepy-time and the sandman was dropping big grains on me. I moved back to a corner of the Situation Room that had been set up as a lounge area with old furniture from my former house in Brooklyn. I had four hours of sleep coming to me before I met the man who would be king. I told Anna and Zee that someone should wake me at noon. I laid myself down on the couch, closed my eyes, and tried not to think of what was going to happen next.

Hours later, I stood outside the R train station at the Canal Street entrance, listening to Zee on my phone. She had gone over to the building in downtown Brooklyn, around the corner from the MTA headquarters and New York City's Board of Education. As expected, the door to the office was locked. She knocked, but no one answered. Was it a trap?

"Well," I said, as I descended the stairs to catch the train, "we'll soon find out." In less than thirty minutes I was leaving the Court Street exit to Borough Hall. My rendezvous with Zee was at one of those ubiquitous Starbucks. There, she wired me as I sat and drank my coffee. Sitting in the back of the faux café, she handed me a brown earpiece.

"If I say, 'I have to leave now,' that means I need help." Zee was going to follow me up to the twenty-fifth floor, hole up in the women's bathroom, and monitor me. For a few minutes we quietly sat and watched downtown Brooklyn's lunchtime crowd. Years ago I would have been one of the anonymous many walking the Court Street corridor, looking for somewhere decent to get a bite. The better restaurants were blocks over in Brooklyn Heights, but such places were reserved for after work. Brooklyn was experiencing a renaissance. Increasingly it was the place to be. Property values were going up and there were a wide variety of new places to eat.

"Nina, are you okay?"

I shook my head. "No, Zee . . . not really. This madness never ends. I'm really sick of this life. I just want a little bit of happiness with someone, but there's always another cavalry charge. What for? Just so somebody else can call you a hero or live vicariously through you? This isn't how I thought I'd be spending my life, living out an existence that I wouldn't even want to read about in a fucking detective novel!"

"You're really angry, Nina," my friend replied soothingly, like a therapist, telling me the obvious. "But you ought to direct your anger at the people who are doing this. Focus on them!"

"But I'm just as angry with Glen!" I snapped. "He dragged us into this! I'm sick of this stupid hip-hop shit! A bunch of knuckleheads are either running around talking about it being revolutionary, or are so stupid or depraved that it gives credence to *The Bell Curve*!"

Zee's eyes shifted quickly from my face, looking to something or someone beyond my shoulder. I turned my head and saw others peering at us. I hadn't realized the depth of my anger until I noticed people staring at us. I'd been speaking too loudly, violating the first rule of doing this kind of work by drawing attention to myself. I looked at Zee.

"I'm sorry, Zimbabwe. I really feel bad about dragging you into this. A couple of days ago you told me about becoming a mother, and now you have to watch my back."

"We're friends, Nina," she replied, shrugging her shoulders. Her eyes were trying to read me, to determine if I was ready to saddle up and go ahead. "I know we don't have the same kind of history as you and Anna, but I would like to think that you consider me a friend and sister."

"Who else can I talk to about the trajectory of a 9mm bullet or the idiocy of today's black orthodoxy? . . . Just one thing."

"Yes?"

"Don't name your child after me. I'm honored that you want to, but no child should come into the world trailing after my bad luck." I finished the last of my coffee, feeling the caffeine revving me. I stood up and was ready to walk, but Zee grabbed my jacket sleeve.

"Nina, you're forgetting something." She handed me a folded *New York Press*. The weight told me all I needed to know. I smiled. "How could I have forgotten this? Silly me."

I entered 100 Livingston Street and walked past a nearly somnolent receptionist at the front desk. Despite it being lunchtime, I was the only person in the elevator going up, and that gave me an opportunity to slip the pistol from the newspaper and place it in my jacket pocket. The door opened and I entered the twenty-fifth floor and ventured to suite 2501. Another elevator arrived and Zee stepped out and went into the ladies' room. I pressed the buzzer and then turned the door handle. It was unlocked. I went in, mumbling to Zee via my wire, "I'm entering the office."

The suite was completely emptied, but what caught my eye was a sweeping view of Brooklyn. I realized that I'd never been this high up in the borough. I could see the trees of Prospect Park, but much of the landscape consisted of two- or three-story tenements or multi-unit buildings that weren't very tall or imposing.

I moved slowly through the office, carefully peeking around corners. I pulled out the gun and told

Zee that I was advancing through the empty office. Soon I came across a path of white sheets of paper with arrows leading to a room. I stopped at a door with a sign that read *ENTER*. I slowly opened the door and found myself facing a large curved silver screen placed before a desk. Above the screen were several digital cameras aimed at a chair. On the desk was a headset and laptop computer. A note addressed to me instructed that I put the headset on and enter a series of numbers into the laptop. I recognized the apparatus as a three-dimensional tele-immersion unit. 3-D T/I was a new telecommunications medium in the making and combined aspects of virtual reality with videoconferencing. What made it unique was that it allowed for a more detailed appreciation of nonverbal communication, of eye contact. I followed the instructions and a rough approximation of Big Poppa Insane materialized before my eyes.

"How do you like this shit?" he asked, flicking a cigar into an ashtray. He smiled broadly, showing off a gauche set of gold-capped teeth.

"Send me one for my birthday," I replied. "Let's get down to cases."

"Baby, I like your style. We can do business. Nina Halligan. Yeah, I heard about you, a red-hot mama from Louisiana."

His pixelated image wasn't as fine as that of television or film, but more akin to what one saw via a slow-moving modem—not fully detailed but enough to get the basic idea of the face and form. "I want to see my husband."

Poppa pulled his cigar from his mouth and slowly blew out smoke. "Why doesn't that surprise me? Roll that nigga over here."

Poppa turned and looked off-camera. I heard something being wheeled in, and Glen appeared on the screen. His eyes were covered, and although his image was as rough as Poppa's, I could make out that he had been beaten. His arms were pinned behind his chair.

"Glen?"

"Nina?" His head moved in the direction of my voice. "Where are you?"

"I'm on a screen in front of you," I said. "Are you okay?"

"Yeah . . ." He nodded. "They jumped me while I was speaking to—"

"The brother bumped into a few things," interjected Big Poppa. "That's all. We're taking good care of him. Now let us get down to business."

Glen remained on the screen. Poppa wanted him as a reminder of who was in control.

"I want you to tell those pimps Ibn and Fergus that they are to sign over to me seventy-five percent of their black music assets. Naturally, they can keep some control. Like most capitalists, I know they need an incentive to work."

"What makes you think that they are just going to sign over their assets to you?"

"One, Ibn is an old man and ain't got no heart. If I kill this nigga next to me, I know he'll feel bad. He wants out and I'm gonna give him an exit. Second, by the time you speak to Ibn, Fergie is going to have an even greater incentive to make me happy. He'll see that I'm a serious motherfuckah and he ain't!"

A plume of smoke rose from the image's cigar. Poppa was a disturbing example of what had become truly dangerous: a headmoe who had evolved from believing in a whacked-out quasireligion into an outright criminal propensity to get over by any means necessary, mostly by violence. It fit the whole masculine fantasy of the original black man being kept down but released by action. Poppa was Capone, Scarface, Don Vito Corleone—but not Tony Soprano. He was the noble warrior prince coming back to engage in divine retribution, and it didn't matter how many black people he murdered. To him, they were the living dead if they didn't accept his leadership. It was the American Way, the way of the gun.

"You know, this may not even be real." I said to his smug image. Poppa was the original mouth o'mighty, but maybe he was finally in control, the proverbial cool, calm, and collected—he was winning and no longer had to shout.

"Open up the top drawer, bitch."

I did as told and found a red envelope. I tore it open and emptied its contents on the desk. It was a wedding band, Glen's. I was convinced.

"Let's get this straight: If I don't hear from both of those bloodsuckers of black music, this nigga of yours is dead! At nine P.M. tonight, be at the Maltese Falcon. 'Tell me something good' is the password!"

"Nina?" Glen's voice trembled. It had a fearful edge that clearly made Poppa feel supreme.

"That's right, nigga, beg your woman to save your fuckin' ass," Poppa sneered. For good measure, he slapped Glen upside the back of his head. "Punk!"

"Gl—" was all I could muster before the screen went blank.

I removed the headset and walked around the screen. A bank of processors with a monitor sat on a case of metal shelves behind the screen. I followed a cable from a processor to a telephone closet a couple of feet away in the next room.

"Zee, come in and follow the signs." Zee entered with her gun drawn, but holstered it when she saw that we were alone.

"Where's Poppa?" Zee furtively looked around. "Is he gone?"

"He was never physically here," I told her. I nodded toward the screen. "I had a charming conversation with him via this, a three-dimensional tele-immersion device."

She looked at the 3-D T/I unit. "I read about this in an issue of *Scientific American.* What about Glen?"

"Toast, if Mr. Ibn and the Beast don't sign over some of their assets to him."

"They're supposed to just open up their wallets, huh?"

"Something like that," I said, as I motioned her to follow me behind the screen. "But Big Pop predicted that by the time I talk to Ibn, Fergus will be cooperative."

I showed Zee the stack of processors that powered the 3-D T/I. We disconnected the cables and searched the processors until we found what I was hoping for, a serial number and identification tag. Somebody was sloppy.

TRACK 22

SOLID CITIZEN BUT WANTED BY THE HAGUE

Zee drove us back across the Brooklyn Bridge in her black VW Beetle. By the time we arrived at the Situation Room, Big Poppa Insane had pulled off his version of the Saint Valentine's Day Massacre. He had wiped out a brother Five Pointer, Icy D, along with his minions.

Anna was watching the news on television when we entered the room. "Poppa has struck again." The killing happened at a party in a hotel, after Icy D had been found innocent on murder and gun-possession charges. Icy and an entourage of fellow thugz and thrill-seeking cuties had rented a room to celebrate. But what gave the incident a particular psychosexual bent was that one of the alleged gunmen was, in fact, a white woman.

As sketchy as the initial reports were, it seemed that a woman had been picked up at the hotel and was taken to the room of Icy's wild afternoon party. This woman, according to one of the surviving female participants, had been enjoying herself like everyone else.

". . . and then she pulled out a gun and killed the guy she was—[bleep]!" cried the woman before the cameras. "And then . . . and then she shot another guy and we all started screaming and tryin' to get away from that crazy—[bleep]—white—[bleep]! Then that—[bleep]—kept firing and then Icy D got his piece. He shot at the—[bleep]—but then she fired and killed him! He saved us! He saved us all—"

According to the woman, a group of black men had stood by and watched as the woman shot and stabbed others. As she did so, they rapped a tune called "Force Ten from Allah." The woman was described as a blonde, and she sang the praises of Euro-Afrika.

That stopped us cold in our tracks, for we all knew of only one source for that lunacy, Eve Shandlin. She had perished in a blaze of glory several years back when the government overran her estate and engaged in a firefight that led to the demise of her Republic of Malik.

"Nooo," I cried. I could not deal with that, if it were true. I had enough on my plate trying to get Glen back. "Please don't do this to me, God."

Zee looked at me. "Hmm. The Ten Percenters are a nationalist group and it would be out of the ordinary for them to have a white woman in their midst."

"You're assuming that they are Ten Percenters," I argued. "Anyone can claim to be that and rap some incoherent rhymes about TOBM and—"

"TOBM?" asked Anna.

"The Original Black Man!" both Zee and I shouted at her.

"You haven't been studying your blaxology notes," I chided. Looking at the board with the names of the original Five Points, I crossed off Icy D's. Now there were only Poppa and Radeem. I looked at the board again.

"Girls, something funny is going on."

"My dear, I think that has been well established," said Anna. She used a remote to mute the sound of the television.

"We know all the Five Points—Mbooma, Big Poppa, Icy, SugarDick—except for Radeem, but who has heard of him?"

"What do you mean, Nina?" asked Zee.

"I mean, all these guys had a career after the Five Points except him! Who the fuck was he? Where is he?"

"It may not mean anything, Nina," said Zee. "Most rappers don't have a long shelf life. Very few make it to a second or third album."

"True, but all these guys had some careers beyond their group recording."

"Does it matter, Nina?" Anna countered. "Don't we know who's behind the killing of SugarDick, Big Time, and Matucci? We thought it was Fergus, and now it seems it was Fergus acting under the orders of Big Poppa Insane."

"If so, why is he pulling the beard off of Fergus? Why not allow himself to remain in the shadows?"

"I think I know what happened," offered Zee. "I think Big Poppa Insane felt dissed when Nadia called him out at that dinner gathering. It was okay for Fergus to take a hit, but now he has to let people know that he's the king. He's a real Big Willie. His prestige has been tarnished. This may not fully be about rational calculations. He believes that he's the Lucky Luciano and Meyer Lansky of black music. He's even renamed his company the Music Syndicate. There's a strong emotional core for some brothers to prove that they are in control, men of action. That's why Saddiq Farouk was able to pull off the Brother Man Assembly in Washington. Black men have been so demonized that the vast majority of them weren't going to question the motives of Saddiq Farouk's self-coronation as the new HNIC."

"Sister, you've earned every bit of your Ph.D., but what about this gray-girl factor?" I threw out. "What aspect of Ten Percent philosophy is that?"

Zee shook her head. "I don't know, Nina. Adaptability?"

Zee was trying to put all the pieces together, but I was not convinced that they fit. However, what she laid out did convince me that there was a certain criminal element that had emerged from the black underground that had once been kept in check. Years ago, Lee and I had argued over the reasons why the post–civil rights middle class found rap objectionable. It reminded them of their desire to always suppress what they perceived as too black and raw, that which was projected as the "nigger" by whites and internalized as such by some blacks. They walked away from the Bantustans, and the Bantustans had come back with some bold, black noise. Big Poppa was that "niggaish" element, the unalloyed "African" souped up with a turbo-charged capitalism that knocks anything out of its way, even what it's trying to preserve.

What troubled me now was the posssible return of Euro-Afrika lunacy, and the remaining two points of the Izlamix star, Big Poppa and Radeem. The last thing I needed to worry about was some crazy white bimbo—doped up on niggratude and trying to prove her bona fides—running around the city shooting hip-hoppers. That had the makings of a race war.

"Anna, I need to know everything about the Five Points, especially about Mr. Radeem."

"Gotcha," said Anna, heading off to the Situation Room. "The riddle of Radeem."

Turning back to the board, I stared at Radeem's name. He was an X factor. I had a sneaking suspicion that he was lurking about and pissing on me every chance he got. I turned to Zee, who was searching through a file.

"Let's get some lunch." I sighed. "I'm starving."

Zee agreed. We stopped by the Situation Room, got Anna's order (also dropped off the serial number we found in Brooklyn), and continued upstairs, passing through the stockroom and the retail section of the electronics store and onto the street. We had crossed Canal Street and were walking south in Chinatown when I felt my phone vibrating. It was Mr. Ibn. He was back in New York and urgently needed to see me. We were to meet at his office on West Fifty-seventh Street.

"Zimbabwe, you are going to love this," I told her. "We have to meet the Pasha, and he has a guest: Fergus."

After I called Anna and told her that she had to get her own lunch and why, we hailed a cab instead of taking Zee's car. I didn't want to spend the afternoon looking for a parking space. When we arrived at Fez Records, Mr. Ibn met us in his secretary's office. He looked grim despite the jaunty blue blazer he was wearing.

"This is really bad, ladies," he said. "Fergus called me and told me that his daughter Heather has been kidnapped by Big Poppa!"

Zee and I looked at each other. "I met him an hour or so ago and he alluded that he was going to take some sort of action. Have you heard about Icy D?"

Mr. Ibn shook his head. "No. What?"

I told him that Icy had just been killed at a hotel "celebration."

"Gangsters . . ." muttered the old man. "Bloody gangsters." He lowered his head and led us toward his office. "Your people have my deepest sympathies."

"Uh . . . thanks, Mr. Ibn. I'll relay your condolences to the Negro High Command." I looked at Zee, who rolled her eyes. He opened the door to his office and we followed him.

His office was an audiophile's delight: The Pasha had nearly three walls of neatly lined and categorized albums and CDs rising to the room's ceiling. Behind his desk was a window that looked down on West Fifty-seventh Street. Gazing out the window, his back to us, stood Rolf Fergus. The Beast turned and faced us when he heard the door close. He was holding a cigarette in his right hand.

"Rolf, this is the young lady I mentioned," said the Pasha. "Ms. Nina Halligan."

Fergus looked at me. "I know you. I believe I met you a few days ago at the hotel."

"Yes, I was there with my husband. We were investigating the murder of SugarDick and a few rappers who were signed to Big Poppa Insane's label, and your music company has an interest in his label."

"That bloody kaffir!" swore Fergus, using the South African equivalent of the N-word. "I curse the day I ever met him!" Fergus took a pull of his cigarette and exhaled. His loose, leathery skin, with folds and creases, was a sure sign of a longtime smoker.

"Rolf, I told Ms. Halligan that Heather has been kidnapped by Big Poppa."

"Is that correct, Mr. Fergus?"

"Yes." His left hand went inside his pocket and withdrew another red envelope, which he handed to me. I opened it and then showed it to Zee. It was a card with the Five Points emblem.

"I was waiting for my daughter at the Copenhagen Restaurant when that card arrived instead of her. As you can well imagine, I thought it was some kind of mistake, a joke. Then I was asked to take a call, and it was Big Poppa, laughing, telling me that he had my 'little girl' and that someone would be delivering me a message. He then hung up."

"Have you contacted the police?" Zee asked.

"Are you daft? That bloody kaffir has her! God knows what he's capable of."

"No, Rolf, we *do* know what he's capable of," replied Mr. Ibn. "He's also kidnapped Ms. Halligan's husband!"

"Let's not lay all the blame on him," I countered. "What about Keepie Kwazinela?" I looked at Fergus. "You farmed him out to Big Poppa."

"Mr. Kwazinela is no longer in my employ," he replied coolly. "He expressed a desire to go on to other things and I did not stand in his way."

"But first he was knocking off rappers who wouldn't get with *your* program, right? Poppa was convenient then, but his appetite was for something that you didn't find palatable. What was it?"

"Drugs," replied Fergus. "Big Poppa Insane is a major narcotrafficker. He picked up the pieces from the Colombian cartels and he wants to use HØT MUZIK as a means to launder his drug profits. I can't allow that."

"Oh no, you're a *legitimate* businessman who enjoys using blacks as ashtrays."

Fergus puffed on his cigarette and slowly walked over to me. "I don't apologize for defending my country and my way of life, Ms. Halligan. I am an American citizen now, and while I question this country's obsession with diversity and other quota schemes, I do think you'll find that I treat my Negroes well."

"That's cute coming from a war criminal." I turned to the Pasha. "Poppa told me to tell you and *this* model citizen that you're both to turn over seventy-five percent of your black music assets to him. I'm to deliver your response to him by nine P.M. tonight." Turning back to Fergus: "I can't tell you what to do in regard to your daughter and your company, but if my husband dies I'm going to find *you* after I get Poppa."

I turned on my heels and walked away. The Pasha simultaneously called after me and berated Fergus for his insolence. "You fool! We need her! Ms. Halligan? Please! Rolf, apologize. Ms. Halligan!"

Going down in the elevator I fussed and fumed over Fergus. "I've never come across a more arrogant and obnoxious son of a dick," I said to Zee. I was almost glad that his precious little girl had been kidnapped. I recalled reading the dossier on Fergus. He had engaged in what some called "extreme interrogation"—rape. "Now his precious little white daughter has been kidnapped by a drug trafficker. Fuck him. Goddamn Boer fatherfucker."

We left the building and headed for the subway. My rage subsided when I saw a policeman walking nearby. I was still wanted for questioning by the police and still had no intention of turning myself in. I couldn't now. I had to worry about Glen.

Neither Zee nor I fully believed Fergus's story about Poppa. It would not have surprised me if Poppa were pushing drugs. After all, if the founder of the Ten Percenters, Terrell X, could rationalize playing craps and base it on numerology, any twisted idea was possible. And Poppa had been a Ten Percenter. Selling drugs to the "living dead," five percent of the black population, would be permissible in order to help the righteous ten percent save the eighty-five percent who were considered merely deaf, dumb, and blind. No, there was something else going on. Something that Fergus didn't want people to know.

We had walked into Zee's father's store and made our way downstairs when Mr. Ibn called and told me of their decision to comply with Big Poppa's demands. But even more surprising were the contents of an envelope that had been delivered to the store addressed to my attention.

"WHOOOA!" cried Anna when she saw what La Bomba had sent.

"Jeeesus." I couldn't believe my eyes.

"By the beard of the prophet," Zee remarked. "Damn."

"*Diapers,*" wrote La Bomba in a note. "*The man likes intimate moments in baby apparel.*"

The three of us stared at a photograph of Mayor Kevin "Il Duce" Carlucci in Pooper Scooper–brand diapers.

"So this is what Fergus has on him," said Anna. "Gee, he looks cute with his thumb in his mouth.

Another photograph showed the mayor sucking on some woman's big toe, presumably Babe Volaré's.

"Too bad it doesn't stay there when he gives a press conference," I snorted, and shook my head.

"Yeah, well, this is the sort of thing that would allow Fergus to compromise Il Duce's police department—and him. Shit, he can almost order the mayor to do anything with this over his head."

I thought about Matucci, a good cop dead because of bullshit like this. Then something occurred to me. "If Fergus has this on the mayor, he wouldn't have to have Matucci whacked. He could just give an order to the mayor for him to stand down."

"Yeah, but suppose he did," argued Anna, "and Big Poppa decided he wanted something more drastic. Maybe that's why Fergus doesn't want to be bothered with Big Poppa. He's too much of a wild card. If Zee's analysis is correct, Big Poppa considers himself more of a warrior than a businessman. Businessmen are pragmatic and make deals. Warriors impose themselves on others and take command."

I looked at my watch. "Hey, I betcha I can get the mayor to hold a press conference and have his dogs called off me.'"

"How?" Zee asked.

I picked up the phone and called Charles Warren, my brother's boss and a bona fide Republican.

Normally, whenever the police made an important announcement, Mayor Kevin J. Carlucci was there. Commissioner Ronald Blinkon was merely a figurehead; everyone knew that the police department was commanded by City Hall, not police headquarters.

So it was and wasn't surprising when the commissioner stood before the television cameras and announced that neither Glen nor I was wanted for questioning in regard to the bombing of my apartment. We were free to go home and pick up the tattered pieces of our lives. The commissioner explained in officialese that upon further investigation, blah, blah, blah.

"Lies, lies, lies," I said, as we watched the retreat of the mayor via his police commissioner. A sterling citizen, Mr. Charles Warren, had approached the mayor. It was a delicate mission that required a delicate hand, and Mr. Warren had offered to serve as emissary. I had informed Mr. Warren of Il Duce's fondness for intimate baby apparel. If the mayor called our bluff, we were going to hire the most beautiful array of women to march around City Hall with diapers as banners.

Mr. Warren, who had some experience with extortion, had delivered the message beautifully. He was considered a plum Negro and had initially endorsed and campaigned for the mayor, but he had become unhappy with some of the mayor's policies in regard to minorities, especially when it came to education.

We weren't threatening to be crude and go to the media with this. Instead, we had thought of something far subtler and dearer to an ever-aspiring politician: potential donors. Flash around the sight of Il Duce voraciously licking Volaré's toes like a suckling babe nursing at a mother's nipple, dressed in a broadsheet diaper, to a group of wealthy conservative Republican donors, and Il Duce would have become the subject of a hit on himself. That would surely take the kink out of his diaper.

Hence, the mayor's absence at the press conference was understandable. We had simply told the mayor to back off and leave us alone. Nothing more, nothing less. Now, the bully had to worry about a new factor: us. It was bad enough that he was in the grip of Rolf Fergus, but now there was someone else who could cause him damage. He had no choice. We were the new wild card. Fergus wanted Carlucci around. We wanted him off our backs.

Anna, who had made it back to the room just in time for the press conference, blew a sigh of relief. "One less thing to worry about. Now we don't have to look over our shoulder every time a white-and-blue cruiser zooms by."

"Lucky me." I picked up the remote and turned off the television set. I was now free to run the streets again in order to hunt down the man who had my husband. I had a few hours to myself before I was to go to the Maltese Falcon, located on the Upper West Side. I decided to relax on the couch and sleep. Kicking off my shoes, I was about to recline when my eyes caught sight of Glen's belongings on the nearby desk. I went over to the box and, once again, an uncertain feeling pricked me, a feeling that something obvious was missing from what had been saved.

TRACK 23

TELL ME SOMETHING GOOD

How does it feel to be able to have a drink without the police breathing down your neck?" Anna asked me through my earpiece. Seated at a bar inside the Maltese Falcon, I was sipping a glass of red wine.

"I'll feel better when I can get laid by my husband," I informed her, speaking into my glass. I didn't want to draw too much suspicion by looking as if I was having a lively conversation with myself. However, if I looked crazy enough, that would definitely free me of any unwarranted male eyeballing, and there were a lot of sperm-laden barracudas swimming about.

"Zee, are you still there?" I asked. The microphone in my lapel pin was transmitting my voice to both her and Anna.

"Standing by, skipper," she replied. Anna was waiting for me in a café across the street and Zee was parked in her Beetle. Once I identified the person who was fronting for the BPI, Zee would follow him. I looked at my watch and it read nine P.M.

"Show time." I sipped my wine and scoped out the environment. The place was chock-full of third-leggers and smoothies. It had a bump-and-grind vibe and a spacious dance floor. Uptown ghetto glamour mixed in with gangthumpers.

"Well," said Anna, returning to my earlier theme, "Win's open to threesomes."

"Humph. Why doesn't that surprise me?" I replied. With my elbows on the bar and my hands cupped over my mouth in a prayerlike manner, I merely looked as if I was watching one of the bar's two televisions.

"We're also open to foursomes, Nina," Anna added. "Winston's got a yang about black women."

"And it's my yin that he wants, right?"

"Does that include me?" Zee asked. She had been silent during the initial check-in.

"You girls are a bit randy for expectant mothers," I remarked.

"Say what, miss?" The bartender turned his eyes to me.

"Uh," I smiled at him. "Another, please."

"Let me get that," called a voice from behind me. China Mercury lowered her posterior onto a bar stool next to me.

"Sounds like we have activity," said Zee. "I'm off my mike; standing by for monitoring."

"Ditto," said Anna.

"Hi, China," I said. "What brings you here?"

"I happened to stroll in and saw you at the bar, Nina." She gave the bartender an order when he returned with mine. "So, uh, tell me something good."

So this slut, I thought, was now in cahoots with the BPI. Can't trust anybody. "How did he get to you, China? I'm sure it wasn't his suave and debonair manner."

"Well . . . you . . . know," she said, fumbling. The bartender arrived with her vodka and tonic, and she sipped it. "Look, Nina, I don't like this any more than you do . . ."

"Have you heard what happened to Glen?"

China sighed, scratched her head, twisted one of the many gaudy rings she wore on her fingers, and displayed every other tic that a nervous or compromised person engages in when being confronted with a straight question. "I'm just an errand girl, Nina. You got something for that motherfuckah or not?"

"Yeah, I got something for him," I told her. "Fez Records and HØT MUZIK will accede to his demands."

"Good" was her only reply. She stared ahead, not wanting to look at me. Funny how things change. Days ago I had come over to her place and done security for her. Had to step in when Big Poppa was getting ugly with her, dissing her in public. Now this.

"Look, Nina, I don't have anything to do with what happened, the thing that happened to Glen."

"You know, China, I have a hard time believing that when you're sitting here and fronting for that maniac."

"Nina, you don't understand. This is about business."

Business? I thought. I was getting murderous hot flashes but chose to hold onto a civil reality.

"China, you seem to be in denial about what's going on." I quickly looked over at the bartender who was taking care of another customer at the other end of the stretch. "People like Glen normally don't come out well at the end of such, uh, *business* transactions. More to the point, they usually wind up dead, as in not living to be a witness."

"That's not going to happen, Nina," she said somewhat coolly, "unless you and the others do something that Poppa doesn't like, something stupid. He told me that this is a period of consolidation. Nation-building is sometimes messy."

"This isn't about nation-building, China! This is kidnapping, murder, extortion, and all the bad motherfucking things in life our mamas told us to stay away from!" I tried to keep my voice down, but hearing her use a fifteen-cent euphemism for criminal activity was too much. It never ceases to amaze me how glib and casual humans can be when their asses aren't being poked and skewered by the vicissitudes of life.

China quickly finished her drink and put a twenty-dollar bill on the bar. "I have to go. Nothing is going to happen to Glen."

"You believe that," I pressed, "knowing what you do about Poppa?"

"Poppa will be in touch with you or the Pasha," she answered, ignoring my question.

"When will we hear from him?"

"Tomorrow. Have a nice night." She pushed off from the stool, gave me a saucy wink, and moved on.

"Zee," I called in, "it's China Mercury."

"I heard, Nina. I won't be buying any of her records anymore. Over and out."

I described what she was wearing. Zee confirmed her sighting and was in surveillance pursuit.

I left the bar and walked across the street into the café where Anna was waiting for me.

"I'm proud of you," she said tightly. "The moment she said it was business I had a vision of you decking her, the way you popped Donna a few years back."

"That scumbag hussy deserved it more than Donna," I said, slowly sitting down. "Business. Nation-building, or as Glen said, 'Dying for the rhythm.'"

"Well, we do have other business to attend to."

"What?"

"I got a call from La Bomba and she wants to talk to us. It seems that Babe Volaré has taken off."

"Where are we meeting Bomba?"

"The same place this whole misadventure of yours began."

La Bomba met us in the sauna room at her hotel. The steam felt good. I could feel each rivulet of perspiration streaming down my face as I sat there. My pores were opening and the toxins sluicing out. My body felt whacked. This was the only way I could relax myself in preparation for some sleep.

"Where's Volaré?" asked Anna, as she wiped her brow with a forearm.

"Protective custody," La Bomba replied. "She needed to get away. After the death of her brother and this whole thing with these hoodlums, she was becoming unhinged."

"Where is she?" I asked.

"Misericordia," replied the ambassador, using the former name of her country.

"What are you talking about, Magdalena?" I asked. "What's the story with her brother?"

"Babe had a brother who was arrested for drug trafficking," she explained, "and was incarcerated in a Texas prison as a death row inmate. She met someone who said he could get her brother out if she was willing to do something for him."

"That being?"

"Big Poppa Insane."

Anna and I looked at each other. Zee was right: The BPI had been making a power play. Poppa wanted the impending investigation regarding SugarDick's death quashed. The whole thing came about, said Magdalena, due to Poppa getting Keepie to silence troublesome rappers. Fergus didn't care about rappers getting whacked but drew the line at a cop getting the same treatment. Babe appeared at NYPD headquarters and said that City Hall wanted X, Y, and Z to happen. No one would ask questions if Volaré said so—except for one cop, John Matucci. When he started to balk he had to go, according to BPI's twisted scheme of things.

Poppa's southwestern drug connection set up an early-release program for Babe's brother, which, in turn, led to the biggest manhunt in Texas history. It was a spectacular prison break made possible by lax security at a commercially operated facility. Ten men had escaped. Low wages had made it possible for guards to look the other way when seduced by drug money.

"He was the guy who blew his head off in that pickup truck rather than being taken back," said Magdalena. "The news of his death hit Babe hard."

"What did she expect?" I remembered reading the news. The tabloids had recklessly hinted that some of the escaped men may have made it to New York.

"Look, Nina, it's easy for you to play the big-city persecutor," argued Bomba, getting a bit huffy and defensive.

"That's *prosecutor*," Anna and I both corrected.

"And I don't apologize for the work I did," I announced. "I've also busted my share of thug cops."

"Bruce Springsteen ought to do a song about us," chimed Anna.

"Word up, Sistah Anna," I lazily exclaimed from my laid-back, cornerpocket position against the sauna's moist walls.

"She was desperate! Her brother was on death row in Texas!" exclaimed Magdalena. "Her brother didn't have the kind of profile of Omal Abdul Salim. He wasn't a black celebrity cop killer, lionized by the glitterati. Her brother stood a good chance of being executed."

"Particularly in the home-fryin' state of Texas," added Anna. Her eyes were closed as she sat in a corner with her head against the wall. "I've done pro bono death penalty work down there and it is a disgrace how the criminal justice system works. They really like killing people . . . Excuse me, ladies, but it's about that time."

Anna opened up her towel and let it fall to the side. We shrugged our shoulders and did likewise.

Up to a point, La Bomba was right. Death row inmate Omal Abdul Salim, certified as a cop killer by a court, had become a celebrity. The whole spectacle had offended some of his earlier supporters, including my late husband. The man had become a pop star, a cult. As a matter of fact, the greater the cult, the more likely he was seen as guilty by some.

No matter the outcome, what we all thought had happened—Fergus ordering the killings—wasn't the case. Big Poppa was the man, and it seemed that Keepie wanted to pick up some pocket money by freelancing.

"Bomba, what's going on with you and Babe?" I inquired. "You two getting biblical?"

"Well, since this *puta* dumped me," she nodded in Anna's direction, "I have to get my needs met somehow, don't I?"

Anna sheepishly sat in the corner, her legs drawn up to her chin. "Look, I'm becoming a mother and I need someone I can depend on. Magdalena, I just can't imagine you changing diapers!"

"All you counterfeit dykes are alike," Bomba teased, then turned to me and said, "They all want that authentic experience with another woman, but when they get, uh . . ."

"Knocked up?" I added.

"NINA?!" exclaimed Anna. "Knocked up?"

"*Sí*, knocked up," Magdalena agreed. Bomba flipped the bird and jerked her finger upward. "They become sanctified. Holy. Desexualized. A bunch of screaming Marys. Birthing is sexual for some women. They become more vital as they look like they're going to explode."

"Since we're traveling in that territory, I was knocked up by your sister countrywoman, Esperanza," Anna threw back at the ambassador. "Talk about acting like a common dick! She ran out on me! Right, Nina?"

"Girls, I don't have a dog in this fight," I replied. "I have my own problems."

La Bomba looked at me. "Doña, how is it? I mean, will Glen be all right?"

"I hope so, Magdalena," I said wearily. "I hope so. Right now, everything is out of my control. Someone else is calling the shots."

I was enjoying a guilty pleasure being with them. For a moment I wished Zee were here more so than even Glen. Glen had become another *problem* to solve, something to be dealt with. I loved him, cared about him, but wished that the whole problem would go away without any assistance or recognition on my part. I was tired of being a superwoman, or being mistaken for one. I wanted a life that had nothing to do with gunplay or solving crimes. I wanted to be left alone, but felt disloyal about taking a break while Glen was suffering as a captive. I knew the chances of him surviving were grim given that he had been kidnapped by Poppa, a man who did not always view the taking of life as a strategic necessity. He was like so many modern sociopaths nowadays: He enjoyed hurting people.

It was the same way with Nate Ford, who took the lives of my family. He liked fucking and killing women, choking them to death, because it provided him the pleasure of power. Maybe that's why Poppa and Fergus got along. Fergus and Kissinger could walk the streets as unrepentant and untried war criminals, and they had even more blood on their hands than Poppa. They, however, committed their activities in the interest of the "state," national security. Milosevic, on the other hand, was a loser and had to go to jail. Poppa was merely a thug and had been icing primarily blacks.

As soon as Poppa got what he wanted, Glen could easily wind up dead. In Poppa's eyes, he would be another useless nigga. "*DIE, NIGGA DIE,*" I could hear Poppa scream, imagining him pumping Glen with endless slugs, mindlessly munching on something, like James Cagney in *White Heat*.

Cagney, while eating a hot dog, shot into the trunk of a car that held a body. A classic cinematic killer.

"Doña, where are you staying now?" Magdalena asked me.

"Huh?" I heard Bomba's question, but my mind had drifted off, focusing on Poppa. It was something about Poppa's tone of voice at the "meeting" in Brooklyn. Maybe it was because it was being transmitted through a new communication device, but his voice had seemed to lack something, or was I imagining it?

"Where are you staying?" La Bomba asked me again.

I didn't really focus on Bomba's question until I felt her hand on my shoulder, though I was already being spoken for.

"She's staying with me," announced Anna. "Right?" Anna had a serious don't-fuck-with-me glint in her cocked eye.

I looked at Anna and then at Bomba, and thought about the couch in Mustapha's basement. Staying with La Bomba would be sinning in a lap of luxury. Her hotel would cater to my every need, but I would probably have to fight her off. La Bomba wanted to fuck me, and badly. Anna and I were sisters, and even though she was still carrying a torch for me, we had already resolved the issue. This was an Anna-and-Nina thing that could not be breached.

I kissed La Bomba on the cheek. "Thanks, but I'm PJing with Anna."

La Bomba ostentatiously rolled her eyes. "Okay, but if this situation continues, I'm going to expect bivouac privileges at my hacienda. *¿Tu comprendes*?"

"*Sí*," I nodded. We languidly strolled from the steam into the cooler air of the locker room.

Being naughty, we gathered up our clothes and made our way down a flight of stairs to Bomba's floor wearing only our towels. Bomba started something by trying to pull the towels off Anna and me. We laughed and giggled as we tried to pull off each others' towels. Anna lost hers and Bomba snatched it up and chased her down the hall, popping her little ass.

When we got back to Magdalena's apartment, Anna and I dressed and had one for the road with Bomba.

"Just remember, doña," she said to me as we headed out the door after good-bye kisses, "if you need someone killed, I'm at our service. You are my sister and a heroine of the Misericordian revolution."

I thanked her, more for her explicit enthusiasm than for her contractual offer. (Besides, I can always do my own dirty work.) In the elevator, I turned to Anna. "How come you never want to kill anybody for me?"

"Maybe, sweetie," Anna replied as she pressed the button to the lobby floor. "I know it's illegal—and something a mother-to-be shouldn't be doing."

TRACK 24
A WALK BY THE RIVER

I was going to sleep on the couch, but Anna insisted that she would do so. I didn't want to put her out, so we both slept in her bed. Well, she slept; I tossed and turned, thinking about Glen and everything that had befallen me. I decided that I needed either a stiff drink, some killer weed, or a good fuck. I rose from the bed with Anna sleeping soundly and walked over to her bureau. I'd been over to her place so many times in the past, I knew where she kept her stash, but since she had just moved back into her apartment after it had been a mini–art gallery, things had changed. I couldn't find it.

Frustrated, I decided to get a drink in the kitchen. Walking in the dark, I stubbed my toe and yelped loudly, waking up Anna.

"Wha . . . ?" Anna raised her head from a drool-stained pillow. "Nina?"

"Go back to sleep," I told her, and sat down on the edge of the bed, holding my injured toe.

"What are you doing?"

"I got up to look for some weed. I didn't find any and thought I'd fix myself a drink, but stubbed my toe. Ouch."

She yawned. "Can't sleep, huh?"

"I'm kind of wound up."

"Don't worry, sweetie," she said, turning over and switching on the light. "I've got something for that." Anna reached over and opened the drawer to the nightstand on her side of the bed. She pulled out a pipe and a little vial of a black, thick-looking substance.

"Opium?"

"Uh-huh," she said, as she worked it into a pipe and handed it to me. "The stuff that made China the sick man of Asia." She then mumbled something in Chinese about the British being hypocritical scumbags and drug dealers.

I lit the pipe and inhaled. "Now this is nice, but illegal." I lay back and let the drug do its work.

"Yes. Don't try this at home, boys and girls." Anna took a puff, put away the pipe, and turned off the light. We sat in silence for a while until she broached the subject of whether to carry the child to term.

"You don't think it's going to work out with Winston?" I asked. "I worked so hard on this."

"It's not that, Nina," she said. "I had a major epiphany."

"About what?"

"Don't laugh."

I told her that I wouldn't. "What?"

"The world is corrupt."

I tumbled out of bed so hard and fast you would have thought I'd been given a royal shtupping or something. "Gee, Anna, didn't your years as a prosecutor hip you to that? Duh? What brought that on?"

"I was watching television and I saw an ad that used Dr. King's 'I Have a Dream' speech for some telecommunications company. I was shocked—shocked!—that his family would allow him to be used for commercial purposes!"

I looked at her. "Either give me the pipe or wrap this up quickly."

"That's one of the greatest speeches ever made, Nina," she said, "and that commercial drove home the point that everything, *everything*, is for sale in this country. We don't stand for anything!"

I could not see her face clearly, but there was an unmistakable emotional undertone in her voice.

"For his family to have licensed that is unconscionable. That's their legacy. Their family's name and honor."

"They want to make money," I sighed. "Somebody else would be doing it if not them."

"That's my point, Nina. No one ought to be doing it. This constant money-go-round for the almighty dollar without any consideration for other values is making this country increasingly hollow! It really hit home when I saw that ad. We are a commercial society that values nothing, and then we wonder why you have people like Big Poppa Insane. If King's family can be all about the Benjamins, why not he? Why should any gangthumper pay attention to Reggie Baxter?"

"Poppa's killing people," I reminded her. "There is a big difference."

"Pardon my metaphor, but isn't King's family killing his dream; compromising his legacy for commercial purposes? For money? This was a great man whose integrity has been purchased. I was thoroughly *disgusted*."

"Okay, but what has this to do with you?"

Anna was silent for a second. I could hear a nearby clock ticking away in the wee hours on her night table.

"I don't know if I can really be an effective parent in a society that mocks every decent value or sentiment that isn't about mere money grubbing. Nothing fucking *matters* anymore. Nothing matters in this world. I don't know if I have the strength or the moral fortitude to offer my child something better than the prevailing values he or she might face in this country."

Anna was confronting that age-old question of the modern world: Is it irresponsible to bring a new and innocent life into a corrupt, violent, and increasingly overpopulated world?

"Free will," I said. "Anna, you have the power to raise an ethical and morally responsible child, but at some point free will takes over and the child makes her own decisions."

Maybe that was what truly troubled her. She had exercised her free will and paid a price for it: Anna's family had disowned her. I told her that she was reading too much into the King family project, but on a certain level Anna was right. Big Poppa Insane's machinations underscored the essential ethos of the postintegration period: It was all about getting paid, the Benjamins. Everyone pimped off King's legacy, so why not his family? That's why La Bomba was so refreshing. She was honestly corrupt and knew it. But here in America everybody is frontin'. The country is a nation of grifters and wannabe grifters.

"Anna, listen, maybe you have other issues going on," I yawned, "but it seems to me that if you are at least trying to connect the dots—the King ad and how that kind of huckstering breeds people like Poppa—maybe you do have what it takes to be a good parent. I mean, you have to explain the world to children as it is and as it could be. And believe me, most parents don't talk to their children. When

I was clocking hours on the Nate Ford case I barely had time for mine."

"But they had Lee," she interjected. She breathed slowly and I could hear her head rustling against the pillowcase. "I don't know, Nina . . . I feel . . ."

My phone chirped. It was two-forty-four in the morning. I reached over to the night table on my side of Anna's bed and flipped open the cover of the phone.

"Halligan," I answered. "What? Okay. Uh-huh. Right. Okay. Keep us posted. We'll be right down. Over and out."

"Zee?" asked Anna.

I nodded yes. "Come on, we gotta roll." I stood up and began searching for my clothes.

"What happened?"

"Zee tailed China to her house and staked it out. About fifteen minutes ago she saw two men leave the place with a rolled-up carpet."

"Huh?"

I snapped my fingers. "Annie, who takes out a rolled-up carpet this early in the goddamn morning?"

"Someone with a body to hide," she answered. Then something suddenly dawned on her. "Oh my God! Glen?"

I pulled up my jeans and fastened them. "Let's not go there until we get there. Okay?"

We hailed a taxi and zoomed down the West Side Highway and were dropped off a block or so from the Hudson River. Zee had phoned in another report: The two men had taken the carpet to the river and dumped it. Zee had then called in for a Kincaid Electronics van outfitted with diving equipment. We made our way over to the vehicle and knocked on the back door. Zee opened it and jumped out. Suited up in diving gear, she showed us where the body had been dumped.

"Don't you just love Zee?" I said to Anna. "She can do anything."

"Our hero," Anna chimed in. Despite the situation we were still high from the opium.

"Oh, be quiet," Zee said, "and help me with the tank."

With the tank of oxygen on her back, a flashlight in hand, along with a tug line and hauling rope, Zee was miked for communication. She swung her legs over the railing, jumped into the river, and began her descent. Anna and I stood by the railing, watching the bubbles.

"Zee? You find anything?" I asked, speaking into a walkie-talkie.

"Skipper, I just jumped into the river," she answered back. "I'm not Supergirl. Give me a few minutes."

"Oh, yeah, right. Sorry."

The late-spring night air made this salvage operation somewhat "pleasant." Across the river we could see the lights of New Jersey, the other side of America. Anna stepped away and went into the van and retrieved a thermos full of coffee. As we waited for Zee, we were entertained by the sounds of passing cars on the highway. I sipped my coffee and looked at my watch. It was three-twenty A.M.

"Nina!" transmitted Zee. "I found it! Lower the bag."

Anna and I attached a black nylon bag to the tug line and it disappeared into the water. The bag's contents consisted of ropes and clamps that would be used to secure the carpet and enable us to hoist it out of the Hudson. While Zee did her work underwater, Anna and I clamped a pulley to the metal railing and stood by to receive instructions. Everything was going fine until we saw approaching headlights and realized it was a police cruiser.

"Christ Almighty," said Anna. "Don't they have anything better to do this time of night?"

"What's wrong?" asked Zee.

"Stand by. Static inference," I told her.

"The police?" asked Zee from below.

"Yep. Stand by." I slipped the walkie-talkie into the pocket of my jacket.

Anna and I casually turned toward each other, dropped the end of the rope to the side, and blocked the approaching police from seeing the pulley. "Just act casual. Act as if we're two girlfriends enjoying the night air."

I put my arm around Anna and pulled her closer to me. I heard a door open and saw an approaching figure from the corner of my eye. I was hoping this cop was a certain social type, one who'd be offended by what he would see next, namely two women kissing.

"Let's make this look good," I muttered to Anna before I placed my lips on hers.

"Give it to me, baby," she said. "Mmmm."

I was purring and moaning to put on a show. Anna, however, was taking advantage of the situation. I was receiving more tongue than I thought the situation warranted. The whole thing was an exhilarating release of pent-up sexuality and exhibitionism, along with the danger of being caught—and getting over on the police. What more could two hussies ask for? When the beam from the patrolman's flashlight hit our faces, we cued ourselves to stop and feign lovers' surprise at being caught in the innocent act of dyke smooching.

"Excuse me, ladies," said the officer, slightly smirking, "but you should be careful. There have been reported assaults on same-sex couples."

"Oh," said Anna, looking flustered, "thank you. Maybe we should go home, huh, sugar?"

I said nothing but nodded. I was embarrassed. I was getting hot and becoming moist. The officer turned off his flashlight, returned to his car, and drove off.

"That was close," I said, feeling weak after the ruse. I held onto the rail, breaking out in a cold sweat, and pulled out the walkie-talkie.

"Good thinking," said Anna. She patted me on the back. "I remember you being a good kisser."

"Will somebody tell me what's going on?" It was Zee.

"Nothing, Zee," I said. "The cops are gone."

"How did you get rid of them?"

"Never mind."

"It was delicious, Zee," teased Anna. "Good to the last drop."

Minutes later, the tug line became taut and Zee gave us the signal. Donning gloves, Anna and I heaved and hoed for about ten minutes under the moonlight. The waterlogged and body-laden carpet broke the surface of the river, but became heavier as we tried to get it onto dry land. Zee scrambled out of the water, took off her tank, and helped haul the carpet over the railing and down to the ground.

As we let the water drain from the carpet I went inside the van and retrieved a large, dark tarpaulin. The three of us rolled the carpet onto it and secured the ends.

"Goddamn, this *fucking* thing weighs a *fucking* ton," Anna muttered as we lifted it into the van.

Soon, I was saying the same thing as we got the thing down into the basement and into the examination room. Not having enough room to unroll the carpet, Zee produced a set of industrial shears that could cut through anything, metal or bone, and handed them to me. Soaked, the carpet made my work easier. I cut my way up lengthwise, layer by layer; peeling it back to get to the last stretch that covered the body.

"Please, God, don't let it be Glen," prayed Anna. Though not a Catholic, she made the sign of the cross.

Sweating, I began hacking at the last layer of carpet. Working upward, we discovered a pair of feet attached to legs, which led up to a waist and torso. The last cutting revealed the entire body.

"What the fuck?" Anna's statement summed up our collective surprise at finding Big Poppa Insane peeled from the sheared carpet.

I praised the Lord that it wasn't Glen, but now knew even less about what was going on. "Ladies, I don't like the looks of this."

The top of Poppa's bald head had an exit wound. Zee helped me pull the body onto its side and we discovered an entry wound at the base of his skull. There were two other wounds in his torso.

"Well, girls, got any theories about this new revelation?" I asked. I threw down the shears and looked at the deposed king of noise. He was useless. It was four-thirty in the morning (or damn near it) and I was ready for a drink.

TRACK 25
LOVECHILD

A dead Big Poppa Insane proved my theory that while he may have been criminal-minded enough to instigate a takeover of the black music scene, he wasn't cunning enough to survive a hit. The bullet in the back of his head suggested someone who had access to him, a close personal friend or colleague.

"Someone with smooth legs," suggested Anna.

"Why not Radeem?" I said, drawing a line through Big Poppa Insane's name on the chart of the Five Points.

"Could be, but we don't know who he is," answered Zee. "Or where he is."

"Well, we do know that the late Poppa's body was found coming out of China's house."

"See, I said someone with smooth legs," added Anna. "They kissed and sort of made up after that row at the hotel—with China, or associates of China, putting a bullet in him."

"So, is it China? Is she making all the moves?" I asked.

"No one would suspect her," said Zee. "China was trying to get out of a Poppa contract earlier. She decided to stay around and help get rid of Poppa."

"Someone must have offered her something really big to risk heaven and earth to get rid of him,"

I intoned, pacing in front of the white board.

"Nina, I think this may be a third heist," added Anna. "I've got this feeling. This thing has the zigs and zags of a third heist."

"What's a *third heist?*" queried Zee. "Something that's been boosted three times?"

Anna wobbled her hand as if to say kinda, sorta. "It's when two parties are fighting over something and a third party casually swoops in and takes it all. First, you have Fergus trying to take over black music and then BPI tries to muscle him out. He winds up dead and now someone else is playing Don Godfather."

"Another question is, how long has Poppa been dead?" I said. "If he was killed prior to my seeing him, then someone else was impersonating . . . Wait a minute . . ."

"What, Nina?" asked Zee.

"Keepie!" I said. "Damn! He and Poppa resemble each other. Remember at the party? The two sitting together as if they were kings. They both shared the same big frame, complexion, and phenotype. Coming over that 3-D T/I, who would notice the difference? I knew there was something odd about him. Big Poppa is loud and wrong."

"*Was*," Anna corrected.

"And the stand-in for Poppa talked at a normal volume," I continued. "It sounded like Poppa but lacked something, his normally loud and obnoxious behavior. Also, whoever it is doesn't know that we have the body. They think it's still in the river."

"Keepie?" asked Zee. "Is he running the game?"

I didn't think so, and said likewise. Keepie was a button man. He'd been flipped. China had been flipped. The flipper? Fergus? Radeem? This was all being organized by someone who wanted to control the record companies from the shadows. It was known that Big Poppa was becoming a recluse, holing up in his various houses, importing cuties for booty parties. Keepie playing Big Poppa could keep up the appearance, while control was held by someone who really understood the music business and had an agenda.

"Our best bet is to find Radeem," said Anna.

"Duh?" I remarked. "Is this the best you can do? Tell me shit I already know?" I looked at my watch: nine-thirty in the morning. "Did we ever find out who that serial number belonged to?"

Anna said that her contacts at the police department hadn't gotten back to her. I told her to step on the gas. I needed to know who bought that equipment. Whoever was handling that 3-D setup might lead us to the faux Poppa, and to Glen. I told them I was going to get breakfast and left the room to quest for an Egg McMuffin or a reasonable approximation.

Standing in line I was saved from slow death at the local Micky D—where the concept of fast food had become an oxymoron—by a desperate phone call. Salud Fergus, the Beast's wife, had obtained my number from Mr. Ibn. The woman sounded hysterical and I could well understand that, but her speech was also slurred. I wasn't in the mood to deal with an early-morning drunk, but she expressed concern that "black fascists" may have kidnapped her daughter. Given what was going on I told her that I'd meet her at her apartment. I called the girls and told them they would have to fend for themselves and let them know where I was heading.

I arrived at Trump Tower and announced myself to the concierge, who told me to go to the fortieth floor. Arriving at said floor, I found myself looking at apartment doors that had no numbers. The concierge had told me the first door on the right; I hesitated but soon pressed a buzzer. The rich always like their anonymity. Anna once told me a relevant Chinese proverb: *Great wealth is guided by stealth.*

The door opened and Mrs. Fergus ushered me in. She looked as if she hadn't yet gotten ready for the day, quite evident by the drink in her hand. She looked about fifty, or "fifty rich," meaning that she—rather, her husband—had the wherewithal to keep a body smooth and taut. Salud Fergus looked like a spa babe. Heather vaguely resembled her.

"Thank you for coming, Ms. Halligan," she said as she led me into the living room. The most outstanding thing in the room wasn't its furnishings, but the pedestrian view of New York. It was basically a view of all the other cold, gray, and unattractive buildings that surrounded Trump Tower that high in the sky.

"Can I get you anything?" she asked. I said no. I had a cup of coffee on the subway ride up.

She gestured for me to sit in an armchair. When I asked her about the statement regarding her daughter being kidnapped by "black fascists," that cued her to reach for a decanter atop a smoke-colored glass coffee table. She poured three fingers and got herself together by downing it in one swallow. I had thought about doing that hours ago, but upon seeing its effects on this woman, I was glad I decided otherwise.

"My husband isn't telling you the whole story, Ms. Halligan," she said, catching her breath. If she had sounded hysterical before I arrived, the juice was calming her down. "I'm concerned that the people who kidnapped my daughter may want to do her harm for ideological reasons."

"Ideological reasons? I don't understand?"

Mrs. Fergus stared at me, trying to size me up. "How much do you know about my husband?"

I did the whole recitation of the life and times of Rolf Fergus—including his career as an intelligence officer in the South African army. "He has that special character trait of all sociopaths," I informed her. "He enjoys hurting people."

"You have strong feelings about my husband?"

"Let's say I think that he should spend some time in prison for the things he did."

"He wasn't always like that," she defended. "The situation in South Africa made him that way."

"Sociopaths are usually made, not born," I countered. I checked my watch. This woman gave me the impression that she was like so many of her ilk: too much time on her hands and nothing better to do with it. She wanted someone to talk to.

"Things were different for us after we got Heather," she said wistfully. Her gaze veered to the window. "I admit that he had quite a reputation for being aggressive during the state of emergency."

"Mrs. Fergus, your husband is a known rapist," I argued. "There are some women who will never forgive him."

"I know, Ms. Halligan," she sighed. "One of them is Zizzie Mantwila."

It had been rumored that the South African security force had raped the wives and daughters of some of the leaders of the anti-apartheid movement. Called "extreme interrogation," rape was used as a psychological weapon of terror: It drove home the point that the men were emasculated and could do nothing to protect their women. It also made the women look as if they had collaborated with the Boers.

"I'm not proud of what my husband did. He was full of rage driven by his impotency. For years we tried to conceive, but we were told we couldn't because he had contracted paramyxovirus."

"The mumps?"

She nodded and said that her husband's testes had been afflicted. "He was shocked when Zizzie Mantwila gave birth to a boy. He had been her main interrogator and, well . . . Anyway, he had always wanted a son, and the two of us wanted a family. I didn't care how it came about. God gave us a son!"

The child's birth was interpreted as a sign from above. The Lord gave Rolf the power to sire. But there was a BIG problem: The baby was black and they were white. The baby didn't remotely look of mixed race. Given the conventions of the time, adopting him was prohibited. However, being in the intelligence service had advantages other than disposing of bodies. One could also *get* bodies, especially those of children.

"What do you mean?"

"Well, Rolf had heard of this situation in America," Heather's mom explained, "about an American Negro leader who had a child by a white woman."

Zizzie's boy-child was exchanged for an apparently white child, a girl. Years later they went on to have two sons of their own.

I looked at Mrs. Fergus and I could see that she was telling the truth, or what she believed to be true. "Who was the father of the American child?"

She reached for the decanter on the glass coffee table, but I stopped her. "Mrs. Fergus, I would be more inclined to believe what you tell me if it isn't under the influence of alcohol."

"Yes, of course." The woman reluctantly saw my point and reclined back onto the sofa. "Dr. Isiah Afrika."

"THE MESSENGER?" I blurted out. Believe me, if there was one man who let you know about his position on "those white devils," it was Dr. Isiah Afrika.

Salud Fergus calmly nodded and reached for the decanter. "There had always been rumors about him having children out of wedlock. I think he called it his 'divine seed program.' Anyway, Heather is his thirteenth and *last* child."

Heather, according to her adopted mother, was the lovechild of the most hated black man in America in the mid-sixties. The mother of Dr. Afrika's thirteenth and last child was Edith Bovene, a nurse. Nurse Bovene assisted the "doctor of hate" at a Sante Fe sanitarium where he was convalescing. Nurse Bovene was what some called a "feverish" believer, particularly when it came to Negroes. While not expounding a philosophy of "Euro-Africaneity" like Eve Shandlin, she could be depended on to go places prohibited to Negroes before the mid-sixties and act on their behalf.

The rumors about this special relationship between the leader of the Original Kingdom of Afrika and the white nurse led the doctor's most trusted assistant, Mallory Rex, to leave the Kingdom of Afrika. Mr. Rex was subsequently assassinated after alluding to "internal and moral corruption" in the Kingdom. Followers of Brother Rex left the Kingdom, including Terrell X, the founder of the Ten Percenters, the spiritual father of the Five Points.

"They kidnapped Heather," said Mrs. Fergus. "They may not be interested in money, but merely want her dead."

"Why kill her?"

"She's the living embodiment of how the 'white devil bitch' has tricked another great black leader," she answered. "This is what these people think, Ms. Halligan."

"What happened to Zizzie Mantwila's baby?"

"He was given to a family, but not in the States or in Africa. He was taken somewhere in South America or the Caribbean."

"Mrs. Fergus, I find this hard to believe," I replied. "I need proof."

Upon hearing that, she rose, left the room, and returned with a folder of documents that attested to Heather's birth by Edith Bovene and Isiah Ridley, Dr. Afrika's "slave-name." There were also Heather's adoption papers, signed by Rolf and Salud. I still didn't want to believe it: Heather, the lovechild of Dr. Isiah Afrika and some white nurse? Anna was right: The world is corrupt.

"Want further proof?" she asked me.

"Yes, I'm a lawyer by training. These documents could be forged. I need an unimpeachable source."

Mrs. Fergus reached for a pen, wrote down a number, and told me to call it. It was the number of former Ambassador Leon Devereaux, chairman emeritus of Groove Records, and my uncle. She told me to have him explain his signature on a State Department document concerning the baby formerly called "Child Carol."

TRACK 26

RADEEM [DYIN' FOR DA RIDDIM]

Ambassador Leon Devereaux was the go-between for Dr. Isiah Afrika and Rolf Fergus. The ambassador owed Dr. Afrika a favor: He had assisted in one of the record industry's most important secrets—namely, securing the release of Sophie Devereaux, Leon's sister. The doctor had helped the Devereaux family get their daughter back from mobsters who had kidnapped Leon's only sister and wanted a piece of Groove Records. Lorenzo, Leon's half-brother, had contacted the doctor. The Messenger's Afrika organization was the only operation that had the discipline and the audacity to go up against organized crime. The doctor put his most trusted man on the job, the flamboyant Mallory Rex, a.k.a., Brother Rex, an ex-marine who understood the "ways of the devils."

Mallory and select members of the Shield of Afrika, the security arm of the Kingdom, disguised themselves as musicians and abducted "Fat Charlie" Marzolo's daughter Kitty at a jazz club. Everybody knew that Kitty had a taste for *moulianis*. With Brother Rex acting as the middle man, the Devereaux only wanted their daughter back, and the whole thing would be forgotten. The two sides returned each other's young lady, called it an "unfortunate misunderstanding," and, most important, promised that it would never happen again. And it didn't. Groove Records was left alone.

Years later, when the Messenger found himself in a delicate situation, he called upon Ambassador Devereaux—appointed by President Nixon and stationed in Nigeria—to arrange an exchange, a switch, in the night. As an envoy to Africa, he was one of very few blacks to have the ear of the American government. When word filtered over from the South African government to Washington, Devereaux was the man chosen because of his special relationship with Dr. Isiah Afrika, who had mellowed by the seventies. The doctor was too stupendously rich to keep denouncing "AmeriKKKa." No, he had even helped the government monitor other groups who were more nationalistic than the Kingdom and more inclined to act.

After speaking to my uncle on the phone I was in a state of shock and information overload. I didn't know where all this was leading. However, I was able to prune away at the leaves of this overgrowth and come upon one possible bit of fruit. What Big Poppa had over Fergus was the knowledge of Fergus having raped Zizzie Mantwila, a popular South African activist and the former wife of that country's first black president. Fergus could not hold onto any black record companies with that sort of pedigree, and I was quite sure that Keepie had supplied Poppa with that knowledge. I was less sure of who was now the master behind the throne. My focus shifted back to Fergus: He had the motive and an instrument called Keepie. Then there was Radeem, though I still had no clue about him—until the elevator opened on the thirtieth floor, as I was going down. In stepped Delores Sierra-Vargas Estaban, Glen's overripe mother and my father's sweet meat.

"Nina!" she exclaimed, delighted to see me. She began smothering me with kisses, motor-mouthing to me in Spanish.

I began hyperventilating. "Hello . . . Delores."

"When did you get back from Europe?" she asked me. The door to the elevator closed and continued its descent.

"Yesterday," I answered. "How did you know that I was in Europe?"

"Glen told me," she said. Apparently they had talked the day before his kidnapping, while I was still across the Atlantic.

"You haven't heard from him since then?" I asked, knowing full well that she hadn't.

"No," she smiled, "but listen, we have to have a woman-to-woman talk."

"Talk? Not a chat?"

"A talk," she confirmed.

"About what?" I asked. I was in a bit of a quandary. It seemed that Delores didn't know about

Glen's disappearance but that she should be told. However, I didn't want to broach the subject until I heard from whomever was holding him. "Glen?"

"No, your father." She smiled. "Glen can take of himself. He has you, right?"

"Heh-heh." I felt warm and claustrophobic. "What about Daddy . . . I mean my father?"

"*Daddy.* I like the way you said that," she replied, smiling. "Daddy. *Popi. Mi popi.*"

The elevator door opened and, as we stepped out, she told me that she was in love with my father. We marched out of Trump Tower with her arm around my shoulders. We looked for a restaurant or a coffee shop and found one on Madison Avenue. Delores sat me down at a window table and told me all sorts of things about herself and my father, especially their plans to marry. I had bumped into her because she was visiting a wedding planner who lived at Trump Tower.

"I know that it would seem odd, given that you are married to Glen," Delores explained, "but I don't think it would be incestuous, do you?"

"It's more like the timing, Delores," I said. If my father and this woman were talking about getting hitched, there was no way I could not tell her about Glen. "Have you spoken to Glen?"

"Yes, and he's very supportive," she gushed. "That son of mine surprises me. He was the one who suggested that we all fly out to New Mexico and celebrate."

"Huh?" I asked. "*¿Como?*"

"Glen said that he would suggest to you that we all go out to my place in Santa Fe and spend some time together. The time at your brother's house doesn't count." She laughed. "I'm so embarrassed."

"That must have been before he was kid—"

"The boys are already out there," she said, as she handed me a cup of coffee that a waitron brought over to us.

"The boys *what*?" I asked, not sure to whom she was referring. "Out where?"

"Glen and Earl," she said. "They flew out to New Mexico. I only stayed in New York to take care of some business and plan the wedding. Glen said that you would join us later. We can fly out together, hmmm?"

"Glen and my father flew out to Santa Fe already?" I stared at her, trying to get clear about what she was saying.

"*Sí*," she answered. "It was Glen's idea. He said it would be a great way to get to know Earl. Spend some guy-time together. He was intrigued that your father was formerly a musician."

Ding-dong. The bell of recognition sounded. I could not figure out what had been missing from

Glen's things when they were returned from the Pasha's house, but now I knew: his saxophone. A kidnapper would not have taken it. *But an amateur like Glen would have brought it along to New Mexico if he were trying to provide cover for a kidnapping.* Then a second bell struck: my father. Not only had I come to the sudden and horrifying conclusion that Glen was behind this third heist, but he also had my father. Maybe he wasn't such an amateur after all.

Delores kept jabbering about the problem with men, being a successful woman, and romance, while I tried to figure out her role in all this. Given how Glen had talked about her and responded to her, I assumed that she wasn't in on it. She told me how glad she was that Glen was beginning to take an interest in her communications company. She might, I thought, even be the next target of the encroaching music syndicate. Taking over black music and *then* Latin music would be a master stroke.

"It's all going to be his someday," she said. "I guess you may have picked up on the fact that Glen and I have our difficulties."

"Parent-child conflict is one the pillars of family life." I shrugged my shoulders. "He alluded to things, but never said anything specifically."

"We used to be close," she confided. "Things changed when he discovered that I wasn't his real mother."

"Oh?"

Glen's discovery, according to Delores, led to an estrangement. He had been adopted and brought into an Hispanic household, and was raised to be the son of a Puerto Rican father and Dominican mother who wanted to be Cuban, pre-revolution of course. Instead of embracing his Hispanic and African heritage, he opted for an African-American identity. He used the name Glen Sanderson. He met a band of brothers who took him in when they discovered him holding street-corner symphonies with his saxophone. The knowledge they imparted to him made him see that he had the discipline to develop the science within to deliver the WORD.

"Everything was *black this* and *black that*," Delores remembered. "You know how some black people are about that. I could never be black enough for him. He accused me of stealing his heritage from him! I saved his ass!"

"What were the circumstances of Glen's birth?"

"I can't say," she responded, and her smile suddenly vanished. "Glen ought to tell you that, but let's say no child should have to come into the world like that."

I looked at my watch and told her that I had some errands to run and that I'd call her later that evening about going out to New Mexico. We parted as family members-to-be, but I knew that one of us was soon going to be missing an important man in her life.

TRACK 27

THE LAST DAYS OF NOIR SOUL [NINA'S THEME]

Oooh, baby watcha do to me,
Groove me like the essence of noir soul,
You got the power to use me, abuse me,
Do it to me like noir soul,
Just remember what the wise heads once said,
"We got the soul but they have the gold."
Uh-huh, that's the story of our people: noir soul
—"The Last Days of Noir Soul [Nina's Theme]"

"Are you sure, Nina?" asked Anna as she watched me pace, slowly burning a hole in the rug with my constant back-and-forth in her living room. "Glen?"

"It's there, Annie. It's all there! I *heard* him being kidnapped; I didn't see it," I said. "I saw him with somebody looking like Poppa, but that was over a digital communication setup. Perfect for giving the illusion of a kidnapping. There's been no real verification of Glen's abduction. His own mother said that he had flown out to Santa Fe the day before I came back from France."

"I don't know, Nina," she said skeptically. "Think about what you're saying."

"Well, *you* said that he was sick!" I tossed back at her.

"No, I said his constantly yammering about music and having you sleep with his saxophone was kind of weird. Anything beyond that was sick."

"Well, now we know what a warped mind can come up with!" I stopped and looked at her. "Anna, if he hurts my father . . ."

"Okay, we know that Poppa is dead," she said. "That's the only thing we know for sure."

"We also know that China is in on this," added Zee, "and she was brought in by Glen."

"And he had Heather kidnapped," said Anna.

"Or she walked in," I interposed. I'd begun to see the outline of a convergence of mutual interests.

"You think she's a part of this?" asked Anna. She handed me a bourbon while she and Zee sipped decaffeinated green tea.

"Glen's a musician and a journalist. He would know all this shit. Also, his mother has a communications company and is willing to let him run it. She mentioned his 'lost years' with a rap group, and it sounded like the Five Points. She said the Six Stars! Second, China and Glen were planning to go into business before this shit broke. Periodicals like *Billboard* and *Vibe* said she was thinking about setting up her own label. A few years ago she was going to produce a TV cable show with Lee, *¡Niggerama!*, before he was killed. She wants to do something. Third, Glen mentioned that Heather wasn't going to be allowed to take over the helm of the Fergus empire. Now we know why."

"Heather Fergus is the thirteenth daughter of Dr. Isiah Afrika," offered Zee. She shook her head. "This is the end of black nationalism as my family has known it."

"The last of his line," I added. "Wait a minute." I thought for a second. "Glen's record company, KS&P StudioWorks."

"What about it?" asked Anna.

"The Five Points motto is . . ."

"Knowledge, Science, Purpose, Strength, and Wisdom," answered Zee. "Coincidence?"

"Stupid me. It was under my nose," I said. Murch thought I'd let Glen's loving cloud my faculties and he was right. Glen's treachery was staring me in the face every time I looked in the corner and saw his belongings. The only thing missing was the tip-off, his saxophone. It was so obvious that I had to deny recognizing its very absence. To have done so would have meant facing the obvious: My marriage to Glen was a sham. I'd been played a fool.

"Earth to Nina." Anna was trying to reel me in. "Are you okay, sweetie?"

"Not really. I'm trying to digest all of this," I told her. "I'm going to have a real hard time trusting any man after this. Fuck me. Damn it!" I turned to Zee. "You get me that number yet, captain?"

Zee tapped the keyboard. "In a few seconds."

I had to find out about that serial number I picked off the 3-D equipment in Brooklyn. It was the only thing I had in order to find out who else was working with Glen. "You know, I betcha Heather is the other dame in this game."

"What?" asked Anna. "Did somebody say something about sex?"

"*Cherchez la femme*." Zee smiled and clicked her teeth.

I told them how Glen had been previously involved with China but said he had lost out to another, a woman.

"Oooh," said Anna. "In the immortal words of Kid Creole, 'Hold it! Hold it!'" She got up and ran over to a stack of magazines, pulled one out, and began rifling through it. "I read something like that in *Out Front* magazine."

Anna found it: a tidbit about China Mercury and her new "secret love." Tantalizing, a woman executive with a powerful father figure was CM's latest heartthrob. Rumors abounded but no sightings. Tip: She's a blonde.

"Got it," said Zee. "The equipment is registered with TNT Communications."

"What's that?"

Zee read the computer screen and a devilish smile appeared on her dark face. "That's the office of one of our distinguished brother gentlemen, Andre Taliferro."

By tonight I was going to be on an airplane to New Mexico. Zee said that she would handle backup. Anna wanted to go, but I needed someone here. I told her to get tickets to Albuquerque and ask Mustapha if we had any contacts in New Mexico for hardware. This trip was going to be made possible by Mr. Niggacool.

Hours later, Zee and I sat in her VW Beetle and waited for Taliferro to leave his quaint office building off University Place. We spotted him as he walked out. He caught a cab and headed over to a restaurant and grill in Chelsea called YG&B, a place for those who were young, gifted, and black.

"What are we going to do, Nina?" Zee asked. We watched the customers passing back and forth through the restaurant's door.

"I guess we'll wait, follow him home, and grab him."

Zee didn't like that. It would mean kidnapping, perhaps in front of witnesses. If we didn't do it right, and he escaped, then he could inform Glen.

"You have a better idea, Captain Kincaid?"

"Go into the bar and do a pickup, and then bring the bait home."

"Zee, I'm not in a flirtatious mood," I told her. "That requires more energy than I can muster."

"I'll do it," she said.

I looked at her. Zee is a lovely woman, but I never saw her as having "pull-man" qualities, meaning an ability to get a man hot and bothered and pull him into a lair. I have it. Anna has it with both sexes. Ditto for Esperanza. And I'm quite sure that Bomba has it with anything that moves. Zee? She was such a good and studiously proper person that I didn't see it, and she must have read the skepticism on my face. I guess I had always viewed her as a sort of nice-looking but asexual woman.

"You don't think that I can walk into a place that's nigga-thick and pull a guy out, do you?"

"Not just any man, Zee, but the right one." I wasn't sure where this was going, but I knew I didn't want to even begin it.

"Look, I know you don't have the energy to do this, skipper. First we thought it was Glen who was in trouble and now he appears to be in on it," she reasoned, keeping her eye on the door of YG&B. "I can handle this. I'll go in and get this dawg."

"You sure about this?"

Zee winked and converted her voice into a seductive Senegalese French accent with traces of Wolof. "*Oui*. For you see, man has but one weakness." She sprayed herself with a scent. "Woman. *Moi*."

She turned the rearview mirror her way and applied gloss to her lips; untied her hair and let the braids fall to her shoulders. Zee then undid the top three buttons of her blouse, creating a universal cleavage effect. She had made herself look busty and come-hithery.

Captain Zimbabwe Kincaid, United States Army Reserve, got out of her car and put a rhythmic swish in her hips that I know every drill instructor would have commended *after* formation.

Zee pointed at her ear. "*Écoute*."

I was to listen, and I did.

". . . Oh, yeah, I likes you French girls, even the white ones," said Taliferro. "You be some freaky motherfuckers . . . Y'all like sex . . ."

"... Free-kay?" asked Zee, in her accent. "What is this free-kay?"

"... Like this, baby ..."

"... Oh, you naughty boy," said Zee. "You better stop, *monsieur! Arrête! Arrête!* Why don't we play with these, *mon doux ami*?"

This was taking longer than I had imagined. Zee had gone into the bar and pulled him out in thirty or so minutes, with a two-drink minimum. They hailed a cab and I followed them up to his place in New Harlem. I watched and listened as she got him upstairs. He was now humming in anticipation with a third drink, stripped down to his shorts. Zee must have disrobed as well.

"Damn, sistah," he said. "You got a mean little machine of a body ... You work out, gal? Good. 'Cuz I'm gonna work your ass out! Oooh la-la!"

Where have I heard that hollow claim of admiration, I thought. These guys really do know how to work us.

I'd picked the lock open when I heard the handcuffs clicking into place. I entered the bedroom, and Zee, clothed in bra, stockings, panties, and heels, was standing over him and relieving herself.

"Zee?" I was stunned. Zee let loose a mild rain of reserved water onto Taliferro. He treated it as if it were the nectar of the gods, moving his head back and forth like he was underneath a shower. This guy was a great big freak.

Mr. Niggacool looked up from the floor when he heard my presence. His eyes expressed shock at seeing another person—another woman—and he shook his head, his voice muffled by a ball gag. Zee had cuffed him through one of the stainless steel railings on his high-tech version of a bedroom classic, the brass bed.

"He likes this sort of stuff," Zee said. "Degenerate niggro." She smacked his ass with the palm of her hand. "He likes it rough and nasty."

Zee stepped off the bed and bent over the trussed subject, loosening the ball gag. "He's got a whole collection of nasty toys."

"Whoooee!" He looked at me. "You another freak? Her playmate?"

Zee told him who I was, and when he no longer detected her sweet accent, Andre's tumescent twelve o'clock high became a six-thirty low.

"I don't know anything," he said. He remembered what I had done to Poppa and his flunky at the hotel when defending the Pasha.

Zee told him that we had traced a serial number to his company, TNT Communications. That we knew his office had set up the 3-D T/I. We also knew about China being in league with Glen as Radeem. And then she pointed to a tattoo on his arm, the emblem of the Five Points. He denied it all and began calling us bitches.

I told Zee to go into the living room and turn up the volume on the Cool One's stereo, and she pumped up Mystikal's "Shake Your Ass." Uh-huh. While she was still out of the bedroom, I pulled a pistol from my back and attached a silencer to it. He started to yell, but that only got him a rap across his mouth. When Zee reentered the room she discovered that his blood had sprinkled the sheets.

"Can't take you anywhere," she said to me.

"Okay, this is how it's going to be," I explained to our captive. "You lie, you die. First, you'll get shot, but eventually you'll bleed to death."

Zee had found his stash of Cohiba cigars. She pulled up a chair, straddled it, and lit one up. Zee tossed me a black leather dog collar and I secured it around his neck. Zee unlocked the cuffs from around the bed's railing and I immediately pulled him headfirst into the bed. I placed the barrel of the gun just behind his right ear. Zee grabbed his arms and locked the cuffs behind his back. I yanked him over to a chic soft metal chair and fastened his arms to it.

"Three questions," said Zee. "Answer correctly and we'll be out of your life. *Tout de suite*. Wrong answers, no answer?" She shrugged her shoulders. "But we don't want to think about that. Hmmm? We could get this all out of the way and do something else, something nice and nasty. Right, Nina?"

"Yeah," I replied, standing in front of him with a loaded gun. "My Tourette's been acting up and I could use some cheap sexual healing—after business. Yeah, mutt, you might do." I let him see the nervous twitch in my gun hand.

"You hear that, dawg?" Zee cooed. "Mama bitch is gonna let you satisfy her twitch. Sistah bitch gonna suck your . . ." Zee double-rolled Taliferro with her stockinged feet. Zee had insinuated her left foot into his crotch, playing with his balls, while stroking his hard-on between the first two toes of her right foot. She was working Taliferro into a busy fever. The most audible sound in the room was his heavy nasal breathing, interrupted only by Zee's voice. After a while I could see that she was controlling Taliferro's breathing by her ministration.

"Woof-woof," she pouted, keeping eye-to-eye contact with him. "You like that, don't you, dawg?"

Taliferro's head rolled in blissful captivity. But that wasn't the proper response. I slapped him to let him know this wasn't about his pleasure.

"Pay attention!" I snapped. "Answer your bitchress, mutt."

The man nodded affirmatively and tried to get a reckoning on my position. But I told him to heed Zee, his mistress of the moment.

"Who is Radeem?" I pulled the gag from his mouth. He gulped for air but didn't attend to the question at hand. I looked over at Zee. She removed her right foot from his lap and returned it to the floor. She wiggled it for a moment and returned it to his crotch with her black pump's five-inch heel. Zee's right foot pushed the high heel deep into his groin.

"He . . . will . . . kill . . . me," Taliferro grimaced.

My hand tightly gripped the collar around his neck, twisting it.

"He may do that tomorrow if he catches you," I said, informing him of his real problem. "But you have two gals on your ass who may not allow you to wake up tomorrow morning. Getting to the next day ought to be your first priority. My friend can say *nasty* in enough languages to make this last all night!"

Later that day, as we flew to New Mexico, Zee and I both knew that we had crossed a line earlier. The man listened to reason but better understood Zee's heel digging into his jewels. He was bound and gagged. He wasn't beaten, but slapped. It was coercion.

"Does this mean we're now like all those other scummers we complained about as human rights violators?" posed Zee.

"Only if we continue doing it," I answered. I adjusted my pillow and tried to find a good sleeping position on the airplane seat. "I'm not making a career out of it. Besides, boyfriend looked as if he'd been meting out the treatment to others. If something can bring you pleasure it can also bring you pain."

"I guess you could say that he was merely getting some extreme attention," said Zee. She switched off the lights above us.

"Exactly," I affirmed.

I was willing to tolerate the gray world of right and wrong. In that world, the law was an irritating nuisance. There was something liberating about being a certain type of outlaw, not merely a criminal-minded thug, and living up to your own code. You had to be constantly on the alert, thinking for yourself, and not let others prescribe nonsense. Yet you also had to be honest enough not to fool yourself, and that was the most difficult task of all. Everyone is a damn fool at least five minutes of the day; wisdom entailed not exceeding the limit.

We landed in Albuquerque and drove straight to Santa Fe after picking up some hardware. Delores had said that we were all to stay at her hacienda, but I didn't think that my father would be housed there. Taliferro told us about a place that Big Poppa had gotten for himself in the Santa Fe area. It was a few miles outside of the city, secluded. Just the sort of place for wild parties and drug deals. It seemed that Fergus was right. The BPI was into drugs, and New Mexico was a good place to keep track of what was coming into the U.S.A. from Mexico.

Up on a hill we could see that the *new* Big Poppa Insane was having a high old time. A party was going on in the patio near the pool of an adobe mansion built into the side of a rising mountain. Women in bathing suits were abundant, as well as men walking around with guns. China stepped out from the back of the house onto the patio and dived into the pool. So did Heather and the man of my dreams, the elusive Radeem, a.k.a., Glen Sierra. A crew of players seemed to be gathering. It looked as if a good time was being had by all. I wasn't interested in the world conquest of the music industry. I just wanted to find my father and leave.

Observing them from the hill, we mulled over a course of action. Zee and I argued back and forth about making plans on the little bit of information we had. We would have to spend time researching the joint. We noticed that there were several smaller adobes to the side of the grand hacienda. Near one stood a couple of men who looked armed, or at least on duty.

I was ready to move; Zee didn't think we had enough to go on. But she also knew that we were under a time constraint.

"Have any idea about what you might say to Glen if you see him?"

"Not really." I continued looking down at the compound through binoculars. "Maybe, 'Die baby, die.'"

Zee nudged me. "Well, maybe you ought to start thinking about it."

"Why?" I turned around to see what she was looking at. Three men were standing near our car with automatic weapons aimed at us.

One man took a yellow lollipop out of his mouth. "The boss is expecting you. Come on. The party is getting started."

Hands behind our heads, we were marched down the hill and across a red rock–strewn ravine to where the hacienda stood. Security was taking us down the back way. One guard, Mr. Lollipop, marched in front of us and the other two were behind Zee.

I noticed we were approaching what looked like an old corral with a wooden archway. Since it had no gate, I gathered that it no longer served as a means to hold horses. I decided it was time to improvise, and feigned twisting my ankle. When Zee knelt down to help me up, I told her my idea.

We resumed walking, with me hobbling, toward the archway. Zee was several paces behind me, but I was within striking distance of the guard who led us. Since our hands were resting on our heads, that made it easier for Zee to grab hold of the horizontal post of the archway. She flipped herself over and feet-first into the backs of the guards.

I couldn't see it, but from the sound of the wind being knocked out of them I could tell that Zee had been successful. Mr. Lollipop also heard it and turned around, only to find my fist in his face and a foot in his solar plexus. He was a toughie. Stunned, he hadn't relinquished his rifle. I grabbed it from him and smacked the butt of it into his jawline, and down he went. Cute guy, I thought, as I dragged him behind a boulder.

I looked around our immediate area and then at Zee. She was pulling our gear bags off the two guys she has downed. The boys were such gentlemen. They had searched our car and brought along our gear for us. We dragged their bodies behind the same boulder and then cuffed and gagged them. We moved up toward some other rocks and checked out the establishment.

"You know, Nina," she marveled, "I didn't think that would work."

"Yeah, I was also surprised. I guess the marines are right. The more you sweat in peace, the less you'll bleed in war."

Mr. Lollipop was right. There was a party going on and we—along with the New Mexico State Police—were going to crash it. The deal was that we would be allowed to go in and get my father, and the police could have the collar.

As we changed our pants and shirts for party dresses, heels, and kung-fu stars masquerading as jewelry, I called in our situation to Lieutenant Alvarez. I told him that we had entered the zone and were proceeding. He gave us fifteen minutes to locate my father and get our asses out of there before he and the troopers stormed the place.

Zee and I hid our bags and made our way down from the rocks decked out in satin and silk dresses and sandal high heels. I was wearing a blond wig, doing my best to look like some Lil' Kim wannabe. Zee went for a raven tress look. We carried our hardware in our purses.

The closer we got to the hacienda proper, the louder the music became. We wended our way through the place. We wanted to get to where the smaller units were and had to walk through a crowd of what looked to be local Santa Fe dwellers and imported talent, people who appeared a bit too fresh to be mistaken for windblown, sun-baked yokels. People were drinking and snorting, diving into the pool. Dancers were doing nudie twists and turns to some wicked DJ. He was grooving the crowd with Steel Pulse's "Blues Dance Raid."

"I like the music better here," said Zee.

"You don't think this is as decadent as that soirée in New York?" I asked, looking around.

Zee's large eyes took in the scene; she shook her head. "No. Maybe it has something to do with this being outdoors."

We made our way out of the main courtyard and headed down a gravel path that led to several small adobes. From some we could hear the sounds of smaller, more intimate partying. The house farthest back seemed to have something special going on. Two bruisers dressed in black pants and white T-shirts with Five Points emblems stood before it. As we approached the adobe, the guards began to stir. We got up close enough for a handshake or a kiss.

"Can we help you ladies?" one of them asked.

"We heard that there was another party back here," I answered. "Know anything about that, sugar?"

"Nah, sistah," he replied, looking over the wares, "not back here." He glanced at his watch. "Come back in an hour and I'll show you something to party with, though."

"Dawg," I replied and winked.

"Woof!" he affirmed. "I'm off in an hour."

We were about to turn, but the door to the adobe opened and out stepped Big Earl, my father, apparently annoyed.

"Look, you guys ought to keep me fresh with some ice cubes if you want me to be a cooperative prisoner!" He rattled an ice bucket. The dude I'd conversed with turned around and glared at him.

"Get back in the house, old man!" he said.

Daddy didn't jump.

"DO IT!" replied the other FPer when my father didn't move fast enough.

"Games!" spat my father. "All you Ten Percenters are just bullshit!"

That stirred their ire and they rumbled toward the door. What stopped them were the butts of ours pistols against the backs of their heads. They crumpled forward and kissed the red dirt.

"What the hell . . . ?" My father had seen two hip-hop floozies pistol-whipping a couple of hard legs and wanted to know if he was next. "Get back inside the house, Daddy," I said. I pulled out another set of plastic cuffs and yanked one guard's arm around to his back.

"Nina?" he asked.

"Inside, Dad! Now!" I shouted. He closed the door and Zee and I dragged our "dates" behind some trees. We entered the house, looking behind our backs.

"What did you do to that husband of yours?" he demanded as soon as I stepped into the adobe. Zee went to the back of the house to check the rear.

"I didn't do anything," I said. I looked through the window of the house, checking to see if others were coming.

"Well, you must have done something," Big Earl said. "His mother and I were talking about one thing and the next thing I know he's got me locked up in here! You must have done something, or haven't been doing enough of something for him to want to take it out on his father-in-law!"

"I didn't do anything, Daddy," I repeated. "This isn't about what you think it is!"

"Look, that husband of yours ain't wrapped too tight," he continued. "He keeps talking about all this Five Points, Ten Percent nonsense. About him being the son of one of Africa's greatest daughters, Zizzie Mantwila! Is this what you do to men? Drive them crazy?"

"Daddy, Glen is Zizzie Mantwila's prison baby!"

"You didn't tell me that," said Zee when she came back from the rear.

"Yes, I did. I told Anna."

"Nina, do I look like Anna?" questioned Zee.

"It's true, then?" my father interrupted.

"What? You know about this?" I asked.

"We heard about things over there. You know, movement gossip is international." Daddy stood digesting the information. "A lot of people would pay good money to know that."

"And kill over it," I added. I told him about Fergus and how Big Poppa Insane used the information against him, and how Glen killed or had someone kill Big Poppa Insane. "Now Glen is running the show."

"What show?"

"The music industry, or parts of it."

"Jesus! All you young people think about is music! At least in my day it was about getting laid!" he complained. "And another thing: Your husband calls himself Radeem! Now how many psychoses does this boy have? I'm not in the mood for this shit, baby girl. I came out here to get married and now I find you pistol-whipping knuckleheads—"

"—To get your ass out of here, Daddy." I peered at Zee and we looked at our watches. "We better move, Zee."

Zee concurred and we were about to go for the door but heard gunfire. We ducked. I went to the window and peeked out. Standing as bold as daylight was a group of armed Ten Percenters with Heather Fergus, front and center. She held a knife against a black woman's throat. Another woman, white, was sprawled at Heather's feet, with a bleeding wound to her neck.

"I'm going to give this one a break and count to three!" she shouted. "One . . ."

"Now that's a sick bitch," my father grunted. "She claims to be the daughter of Dr. Afrika!"

"Two . . ."

I looked at Zee. "This is how we earn our notices for redemption," I told her.

I speed-dialed Lieutenant Alvarez and told him that we were having a slight problem. He gave us ten more minutes. That provided us time to stall by surrendering.

"Three!"

Zee, my father, and I were marched up to the grand adobe and taken to the living room, which offered a spectacular vista of the area, with New Mexico's blue sky, white clouds, and red earth stretching ad infinitum. Glen Radeem, dressed in a brightly colored African robe, was spinning vinyl for his guests outside in the courtyard. When he saw us he slipped a cassette tape into the stereo. I guess he had other things to deal with now.

"Look, this is not personal," he assured me, as we sat on a couch with a beautiful New Mexican Indian blanket. We were told to keep our hands on our knees. Keepie and Heather needed to see them at all times.

"An opportunity came my way and I decided to take it!"

Radeem saw his mission. It came to him in a divine moment when he was furiously shtupping Nadia behind my back while I was in Europe. *He could save black music*. Everything was in play: Big Poppa was consolidating black music into a music syndicate. He was moving in on Fergus and pressuring Ibn. The BPI was using extramarket forces to discipline rappers who hadn't gotten with the program. But Poppa himself had become a liability. The Poppa had to go.

"It was a universal hit," Glen Radeem informed us. "China got him over to her house and into bed. She fired the first shot and I stepped out of the back room and did the second."

"And I delivered the *coup de grâce*," said Heather proudly. "I finished him off."

One big happy family, I thought.

"What about him?" I said, looking at Keepie.

"Keepie?" said Radeem. He went over to the African and wrapped his arms around him. "I made him an offer he could not refuse. I made him the Vice President in charge of World Music!"

"No, Glen," I said. "He tried to kill you! Us!"

"Oh, that's when he was working for Poppa's internal liquidation program," Radeem explained. "When I decided to take over this thing, I got Heather to contact him and made him an offer. He was the guy who initially told Poppa about Fergus."

"That dog!" snarled Heather. "Raping us African women with impunity!"

Zee and I exchanged glances. Heather had to be watched. She had that compensation-syndrome glint in her eye. She would be the most zealous in killing people to prove her "blackness" and her bona fides as the daughter of the Messenger. I noticed the way she kept staring at Zee. She was probably jealous of Zimbabwe's exquisitely dark complexion. If you're claiming to be the daughter of the man who invented blackness, being melanin deficient would be a credibility problem when dealing with the black masses.

"We got to talking and Keepie told me about Fergus's son, meaning me, but I hadn't connected the dots," continued Radeem. "And I remembered Delores telling me some vague details of my birth. I called her one night while you where away and . . ."

"So you're the long-lost son of Zizzie Mantwila?" I said. "Here to reclaim the Fez?"

"Of sorts." Radeem bowed his head.

"Glen, why? Why are you doing this?" I asked.

"Somebody had to step in and clean up the mess, Nina. This is just like in the days of the Five Points! We had a program and things got messed up because too many niggros could not keep their minds on the purpose of God. I was tossed out of the Five Points because I wanted to do away with the drug dealing! My brothers set me up! Big Poppa! Icy D! Mbooma! SugarDick! The original FPs set me up! I was about to go down for a drug bust I didn't have anything to do with!"

Glen's playing with SugarDick on *ZDO* had been a reconciliation of convenience, he told us. SugarDick and Big Time wanted to reorient the noise away from the violence and male braggadocio, but something else happened. Keepie got there first. Poppa used him to silence recalcitrant rappers who didn't want to get with the new game plan. Yet people were talking—SugarDick, Big Time, and others—about rappers keeping their own points by acting in unison on certain key issues, by embracing digital music technologies like MP3 and Napster. The two rappers were going to create a new group, Black Jihad, and spread the word of Poppa's wickedness, but Keepie got there first. Mbooma had the word and wanted to reunite, but then the police offed him.

"Poppa became drunk with power," continued Radeem. "He crossed the Rubicon when he tried to interfere with SugarDick's investigation. You yourself said that the cops would probably write off his death as something beneficial to the community and move on."

"Normally, that is how it would have happened," I said.

"But I knew something else was going on," he marveled. "Divine intervention."

"What?"

"The explosion at the apartment was God interceding for me—us."

"No, Radeem," I said. "You were right the first time: you."

Glen Radeem interpreted our surviving the bomb blast as God stepping in and plucking him (and me, but mostly him) from the wicked machinations of his enemies. Our subsequent flight paralleled that of the Prophet's and the Messenger's. Glen Ra would fight the profanicators and defilers of black music. If both SugarDick's and Mbooma's deaths were beneficial to the community, what about Big Poppa Insane's?

He called Insane out whenever he played at my uncle's club. The word went forth that there was a cat who sounded like the FP's Radeem, Glen Sierra. Glen's idea, his plan of action, was the result of both introspection and a self-loathing over sexing a blonde who looked like me. Nadia died the night that Radeem the Redeemer was born. Had I not gone to France, his lust would not have overcome him. Things would have been different.

As he rattled on, I counted Glen's charges. He murdered Nadia and then Big Poppa Insane. Add to that taking over Poppa's drug trade. He also planned Icy D's death and then kidnapped my father. I then added possible RICO charges. He was going down, but not on me.

"But then there's you, Nina," he said. "I realized that you were a problem."

"Me? I was never interested in this case! This was your doing. I'm ready to get out of this with no questions asked. Just give me back my father and let us go."

I was doing all that I could to throttle a surging murderous rage in me. If I had a hatchet, Glen's head would have been a prime resting post for it. I cursed myself. How could I have been so utterly blind? Like I said earlier, the signs had been there but I didn't want to read them and, because I didn't, my father's life was now in jeopardy.

"But you are also connected to Groove Records. And that would mean a problem," he said. "I'm going to have to take over the Groove, and Maxine is as intrepid as you."

"It runs in the family," announced Big Earl. "The distaff side. The womenfolk be mighty independent!"

"That's right, Daddy, give him one more reason to ice us."

"You're too organized, Nina," continued my estranged husband. "When I saw how organized you and your folks were, I knew I needed a team like that."

"Why didn't you come to me?" I asked. "We could have worked something out, Glen. You didn't have to do it this way. Glen, don't you see that all you have done is replicated the same thing? It's all based on violence and coercion. Worse still, you won't be around to guide it through."

"Why not?"

"Do you really think your partners share your views? This whole Capone-Corleone-Soprano madness is built on the fantasy of strong black leadership, but you guys keep bumping each other off! Did the Messenger leave behind a coherent and orderly institution? Any means of a democratic succession to power?"

"Don't besmirch the name of the Messenger," warned Heather.

"No," I continued, ignoring her. "Saddiq Farouk is now looking over his shoulder because the Kingdom has been built on nothing but charisma and violence. It's the same thing with Poppa and the others. Look who's gone: Tupac, Mbooma, Biggie, Big Time, SugarDick, Jam Master Jay. Why do you think 50 Cent is walking around with flak jackets and guards? Hip-hop has now made it so that the only way for a brother to be taken serious is to be dead! And you know what? You're the only rapper among your partners. Think about that, original black man. You still rap, don't you?"

"I bust a rhyme from time to time," he answered. But he didn't deliver it with any flavah.

"There you go," I said. "You're the next dead nigga, Radeem. And you believe this wild bunch—Heather, China, Taliferro, and Keepie—is watching your back?"

"Yes!" shot Heather, who purposefully strutted over to us three captives on the couch. "And that's the way we like it, uh-huh, uh-huh. And we have to do something about you three. Radeem?"

"Heather," he said, moving over to the bar, "I'll handle this."

Meanwhile, Lieutenant Alvarez's men were recording the dialogue and entering it into the various annals of jurisdiction that would prosecute this if enough of us came out alive. Through my undetected earpiece, he also took the time to inform me that in five minutes SWAT teams would be crashing through the hacienda. Five minutes. I peered at Zee and gave her a certain look; she knew that all hell was about to break loose.

Still dressed in a swimsuit, China entered the room drying her hair. She looked at us sitting on the couch, unsmiling, our hands placed on our knees.

"Oh, I don't like the looks of this," she said grimly, and turned to Glen. "Look, you said Poppa would be the only one. I'm not going to kill her and her friends. She's the widow of one of my best friends."

"You don't have to," said Heather. "Radeem and Keepie will see to that."

"This is not how we talked about saving black music!" China exclaimed. "This is the same old method! All this big-dick shit is just killing people! What was I thinking when I let you talk me into this?"

"Well, China, where did you think this was going to go?" I said to her. I looked at Glen. "This isn't going to last, Glen."

"I'm sorry," responded Glen. "But this is part of the deal." He came from behind the bar with a pistol.

"What deal?" I asked, feeling the tension mounting in the room. I glanced down at my watch.

"I would have to kill you if I wanted Heather in on the scheme."

"Why?"

"Like I said, you would be an impediment to us taking over Groove Records, and you're just a little too organized for my taste. A little too intense. It was the bomb fucking you, but this is business. Besides, I can always get another wife. Another record company? I don't think so. In Izlam, a man can have as many wives . . ."

"Get it over with, Radeem," Heather snarled.

"I can't believe that the great Radeem is going to kill a black woman at the orders of some yakub!" said Zee. "You're a disgrace to black men!"

Heather withdrew her knife and walked toward Zee. But I caught her eye by standing up with my hands raised. She stopped.

"Heather, I don't know what your problem is," I began, "but you're not going to get any leadership position with black folks by claiming to be the daughter of Dr. Afrika! You're not black! You don't look black! And no one will accept you as such! Fergus doesn't even want you in charge of his company because you're not white. Blacks won't accept you because you aren't one of them!"

"My daughter's right! You look too much like the kind of devil your father preached about to be accepted by colored folks, be they black, Negro, nigga, or African! And you're the *thirteenth* child!" my father informed Heather in one fell swoop.

Dr. Afrika's lovechild was so taken with Big Earl's gutbucket analysis that she wanted to kill him. I could tell by the way her eyes lit up and the vicious scowl that appeared on her face. She didn't say a word, but her blazing eyes spoke volumes: *Nigga, I'll kill you*.

"You see! You see!" she said, turning to Radeem. "That's why she has to go! She knows too much and can influence others! I can't have my position of leadership with that kind of living-dead mentality around!"

"Look, this is all getting out of hand," cried China. "We're acting like Big Poppa! Talking about killing people over music? This isn't why I became a pop star! It used to be about the music!"

"IT WAS ALWAYS ABOUT THE MONEY!" shouted my father. "It was always about the money! You're all criminals! This generation, this so-called hip-hop generation, made it possible for dead men with phat catalogues to have more influence than those who are living! Imagine that!"

"Radeem, this empire of yours is built on a throne of blood!" I shouted. "This isn't going to last! You may be the next one!"

Radeem looked at his partners. Keepie was a killer with no allegiance to anyone. China was merely a pop star gone astray and trailing after Heather. Heather, the most unstable, was acting out her Negrotopian fantasy. The smart money was on Keepie, who, true to form, wasn't saying anything. He understood the principles of a third heist: When your enemy is destroying himself, do nothing.

Glen shrugged his shoulders. "Well, as Himmler once said, 'It is the curse of greatness that one must step over dead bodies to create new life.'"

"Enough philosophy!" Heather shouted in Radeem's face. "I want to see some *real* black-man action! KILL THEM!"

Tired of her Daughter of the Messenger act, Glen popped her a black-man special across her mouth. "Stop acting like some fuckin' stupid white bitch!"

Not having time to acclimate to the quaint and affectionate terms of endearment that some brothers have for sisters, Heather took Radeem's words to heart. She returned the sentiment by plunging her knife into his chest. Her venomous act was swift.

"Don't *bitch* me!" she screamed. She backed away from Glen, leaving the blade in his chest.

"GLEN!" screamed China. "Oh my God!"

Just as Glen Ra dropped to the floor, the New Mexico State Police announced their presence outside the building and went into raid mode. They came on hard and strong. I could hear the pandemonium outside, women screaming, gunfire, and helicopters.

I pushed my father down to the floor, tore off a metal star, and hurled it at Heather. She clutched her throat and stumbled back onto Keepie, who was going for his gun. China began screaming Heather's name. Zee reached over and grabbed a stone ashtray and launched it at Keepie's head. He ducked but didn't have time to line up a shot before Zee dove onto him, knocking his gun to the floor. Keepie energetically shoved Zee off and scrambled for the gun, but she pounced on him again and pinned his hands to the floor with stiletto-like hairpins she had tucked away in her thick braids.

The cavalry burst into the room. Lieutenant Alvarez and his men swept the house and arrested everyone there. Handcuffed, China kept sobbing over Heather while Glen, bleeding profusely, cried out my name. I was more concerned about my father.

"Daddy, are you okay?" I asked, helping him to his feet.

"I guess so," he answered heavily. "Now, I guess I have to call his mother and tell her this thing is off and her boy is . . ." He looked down at Glen, who was making feeble attempts at calling out to me. "Is he . . . ?"

I made a gesture that said I didn't know—or care. I left him for the EMT as I ushered my father out of the room.

We got Big Earl into the courtyard. The police had gathered in full force and so had the news reporters. The partygoers were being rounded up and processed on-site and loaded into wagons. DEA agents wheelbarrowed and hand-trucked contraband that looked like cocaine. I had a medical assistant look over my father and he was taken down to a medical van. Zee and I stayed on the porch to be available for the police to take our initial statements.

Behind me I heard Glen's voice calling me. Zee looked back at the opened door.

"Nina," she said, "he's dying. Don't leave him like this."

"I don't care, Zee," I told her. "He betrayed me. He murdered people. Kidnapped my father. There's nothing back there. *Nada*."

Zee could never understand how I had loved him and wanted to be loved by him. I now understood that music was his mistress, his first love. I never wanted this case; he did, and he got it. I was to be his soul sacrifice, an offering to that other troublesome bitch, *music*. I was expendable. It was obvious how he felt about me: He had allied himself with a psychotic lovechild reject, Heather

Fergus. He could always get another wife. Well, now he was a modern black classic: another phat death. His name will be up there with the other martyrs who died for the rhythm: Tupac, Mbooma, SugarD, Biggie, Baby Cakes. But he was also something else—a womanless man, unloved and dying alone.

"You have to go back," Zee reminded me.

"Why?"

"He's your husband, for better and for worse. This is the worse, Nina. You must forgive him. He is your husband and it's his last request. You have certain duties as a wife, Nina. He's still your husband."

I turned and looked at the open door. I could hear Glen's last breath oozing through him, mixed with blood. He coughed and gurgled, softly crying my name. *nina . . . nina . . . ninaaaahh*. Silence.

"*Was*, Zee," I told her as I stepped down from the porch. "*Was* my husband." I pulled my wedding band off my finger and dropped it along with the other remains of the day.

Also from **AKASHIC BOOKS**

THE BIG MANGO by Norman Kelley

The second installment in the Nina Halligan mystery series.

270 pages, a trade paperback original, $14.95, ISBN: 1-888451-10-6

"Want a scathing social and political satire? Look no further than Norman Kelley's second effort featuring 'bad girl' African-American PI and part-time intellectual Nina Halligan—it's X-rated, but a romp of a read . . . Nina's acid takes on recognizable public figures and institutions both amuse and offend . . . Kelley spares no one, blacks and whites alike, and this provocative novel is sure to attract attention . . ." —*Publishers Weekly* (starred review)

R&B (RHYTHM & BUSINESS): THE POLITICAL ECONOMY OF BLACK MUSIC, edited by Norman Kelley

338 pages, hardcover, $24.95, ISBN: 1-888451-26-2

"Seminal rapper Chuck D of Public Enemy once asked the musical question, 'Who stole the soul?' In this anthology, perhaps the first to deal solely with the business of black music, Chuck D, editor Kelley, and other name contributors (including Courtney Love) attempt to come up with some answers. The history of the modern recording industry is dissected in several eyeopening contributions that should be required reading for anyone interested in popular music." —*Library Journal*

ADIOS MUCHACHOS by Daniel Chavarría

Winner of a 2001 Edgar Award.

245 pages, a trade paperback original, $13.95, ISBN: 1-888451-16-5

"Celebrated in Latin America for his noir detective fiction, Chavarría makes his English-language debut with this fast-paced novel. *Adios Muchachos* spins the tale of a caper gone awry, where no one is particularly bad and everyone is on the take. Castro's Havana has not appeared this sunny in many years, nor have its crooks been this good-natured. Mixed together, the ingredients make a zesty Cuban paella of a novel that's impossible to put down. This is a great read." —*Library Journal*

"Daniel Chavarría has long been recognized as one of Latin America's finest writers. Now he again proves why with *Adios Muchachos*, a comic mystery peopled by a delightfully mad band of miscreants, all of them led by a woman you will not soon forget—Alicia, the loveliest bicycle whore in all Havana." —Edgar Award-winning author William Heffernan

SOUTHLAND by Nina Revoyr

348 pages, a trade paperback original, $15.95, ISBN: 1-888451-41-6

A Book Sense 76 Pick; nominated for the *Los Angeles Times* Book Prize; a selection of the InsightOut Book Club.

"Revoyr gives us her Los Angeles, a loved version of that often fabled landscape. She sifts stories out of the dust of neighborhoods, police reports, and family legend. The stories—black, white, Asian, and multi-racial—intertwine in unexpected and deeply satisfying ways. Read this book and tell me you don't want to read more. I know I do."
—Dorothy Allison, author of *Bastard Out of Carolina*

HIGH LIFE by Matthew Stokoe

326 pages, a trade paperback original, $16.95, ISBN: 1-888451-32-7

A selection of the **Little House on the Bowery** series

"Stokoe's in-your-face prose and raw, unnerving scenes give way to a skillfully plotted tale that will keep readers glued to the page . . . Stokoe's protagonist is as gritty and brutal as they come, which will frighten away the chaste crowd, but the author's target Bret Easton Ellis audience could turn this one into a word-of-mouth success."
—*Publishers Weekly*

SEED by Mustafa Mutabaruka

*Selected for the *Washington Post's* Best Novels of 2002 list.*

*Selected for *Library Journal's* Best First Novels of Spring/Summer 2002 list.*

178 pages, trade paperback, $14.95, ISBN: 1-888451-31-9

"Mutabaruka's deft maneuvering between past and present, Morocco and the United States, blurs distinctions and creates a mystical and frightening story . . . [P]lain prose and interesting characters keep this novel on its feet and make it dance."
—*Library Journal*

These books are available at local bookstores. They can also be purchased with a credit card online through www.akashicbooks.com. To order by mail send a check or money order to:

AKASHIC BOOKS

PO Box 1456, New York, NY 10009

www.akashicbooks.com, Akashic7@aol.com

(Prices include shipping. Outside the U.S., add $8 to each book ordered.)

PHOTO BY MARCIA WILSON

The author of two previous mystery novels featuring Nina Halligan, *Black Heat* and *The Big Mango*, **Norman Kelley** also edited and contributed to *Rhythm & Business: The Political Economy of Black Music.* He resides in Brooklyn, New York.